Generations' Curse

*****

Generations' Curse

Drake H Grayson

Blue M Publishing—Chicago

Library of Congress Cataloging-in-publication data
Name: Grayson, Drake H
Title: *Generations' Curse* Description: First edition | Blue M Publishing (Paperback), Chicago, IL
[2021] | Contents: Summary: A series of gruesome serial killings lead a detective to uncover
chilling similarities to recurring murders that seem to happen with every new generation. |
Audience Note: Recommended for readers seventeen and over

Subjects: LCSH: sh85062076/2084/2085 fiction, horror tales/American, sh98006096 fiction,
murder mystery | BISAC: FIC015000 FICTION/Horror, FIC022000 FICTION/Mystery &
Detective, FIC024000 FICTION/Occult & Supernatural, FIC031010 FICTION/Thrillers/Crime,
FIC031070 FICTION/Thrillers Supernatural | GSAFD: 00000cz a2200037n 45 0-455 Fiction
Horror/ -555 Occult Fiction | Classification: LCC PS370-380/PZ (1)-(4) | DDC 813.161
Detective Crime/ -311 Horror/ 412 Mystery/ --dc23

Grayson, Drake H. *Generations' Curse*

ISBN 978-1-945385-26-1 (Paperback)

Printed in the United States of America
www.blueMpublishing.com
Book Design by Allendorf—Vignere

Blue **M** Publishing
Chicago, IL 60521

Rating: R* Readers 17 and over

**Rating is provided by the author as a parental guide and is not based on any established rating
systems. Contains extremely graphic violence, obscene language, and sexual assault.*

Contents

Contents v

Generations' Curse ix

Book Summary..ix

Introduction xi

GENERATIONS' CURSE 13

Part I 13

CH 1 – The First...13

CH 2 – Sara 20

CH 3 – Dumitra 25

CH 4 – The Horned Goat 29

CH 5 – Dark Intruder 34

CH 6 – Rosco Arthur 36

CH 7 – Twilight Zone..38

CH 8 – In Critical Care 47

CH 9 – Mother & Son..51

CH 10 – The Third...60

CH 11 – A New Partner 62

CH 12 – End Around...70

CH 13 – Road trip 75

CH 14 – Psychic to the Rescue 84

CH 15 – Mitzie's Call..94

CH 16 – The Attic-Part I...104

CH 17 – The Attic-Part 2...108

Part II 111

CH 18 – Psychic Visions 111

CH 19 –Visiting Claire 120

CH 20 – LJ's Boyfriend 123

CH 21 – The Business Card 127

CH 22 – Down in Records 130

CH 23 – Mark of the Beast 139

CH 24 – A Young Reporter 142

CH 25 – An Invitation 147

CH 26 – Digging Deeper 151

CH 27 – Another One Dead 155

CH 28 – Deep Dive 158

CH 29 – Lunch with Mitzie 165

CH 30 – In Too Deep 173

CH 31 – A Horned Image 177

CH 32 – The Attic – Part 3 181

CH 33 – Reassigned 185

Part III 192

CH 34 – Bad Juju 192

CH 35 – Visiting the Priest 197

CH 36 – Questions for Mitzie 201

CH 37 – Interrogation 208

CH 38 – Lenny and His Bat 213

CH 39 – Father Jose 217

CH 40 – Up the Ass 220

CH 41 – Missing 222

CH 42 – Hogan's Heroes 225

CH 43 – A Talk with Bessie-Part 1 229

CH 44 – Slow Progress 238

CH 45 – Diary Entries 241

CH 46 – Another Disappears 243

CH 47 – The DA Gets Tough 246

CH 48 – Mitzie's Warning..252

CH 49 – A Talk with Bessie-Part 2..265

Part IV 271

CH 50 – A Secret Affair 271

CH 51 – No Free Ride 273

CH 52 – A Second Affair 276

CH 53 – Dag and the Cult..278

CH 54 – Morrie Investigates 282

CH 55 – In Handcuffs...286

CH 56 – Charred Remains 288

CH 57 – About Demons 290

CH 58 – A Talk with Bessie-Part 3..300

CH 59 – Legal Defense 310

CH 60 – Visit to the Prison..314

CH 61 – Driver's Interrogation 320

CH 62 – "I'm Afraid Not"...334

CH 63 – Ghost...337

CH 64 – Sschooled by the DA...343

CH 65 – "Come forth, My Child"..346

CH 66 – The Trial...350

CH 67 – Some Advice 354

CH 68 – Cases of Robbery 360

CH 69 – Daughters 365

CH 70 – Surprise Witness 368

Part V 377

CH 71 – Coming Clean...377

CH 72 – DA's Anxiety...383

CH 73 – Sacrificial Lamb 390

CH 74 – Jerel 393

CH 75 – A Jeweled Clue 396

CH 76 – Wedding Time.. 398

CH 77 – Caught 402

CH 78 – Expert Witness 404

CH 79 – Late Night Visitor 411

CH 80 – Cult Meeting.. 414

CH 81 – Revenge 422

CH 82 – Terror in the Cell 425

CH 83 – Outcome 427

CH 84 – The Grand Grimoire 430

Part VI.. 432

CH 85 – On the Run... 432

CH 86 – Final Vengeance 443

CH 87 – Twilight Zone Nightmare... 447

CH 88 – Fire and Brimstone.. 455

CH 89 – One More Soul.. 457

CH 90 – Final Report 461

CH 91 – Cases Closed 463

CH 92 – Dinner for Three 466

Epilogue... 471

Appendix A 475

About the Author:... 478

Generations' Curse

Book Summary

When a detective finds a decapitated, mangled corpse but the head doesn't match the body, his work only begins to get interesting.

The story of deceit and betrayal spans over seventy-five years, as Detective Dag Gallagher investigates the horrific murders occurring in Boston. Things become even stranger when a pair of local psychics get involved in solving the crimes. Are they helping the police or are they part of the complex murder scheme that seems to be the curse of generation after generation? Slowly, the picture becomes clearer as their families find out the shocking truth and cause of their misery.

*****

Introduction

This book took countless iterations to create a cohesive narrative and plot line. References to years, families, case numbers, locations and other details required a great deal cross-referencing and clarification. Tying together the many facets of the storyline to ensure the reader could easily follow them was a primary focus.

If one enjoys complicated plots, one will enjoy the many elements of this novel. Events unfold during multiple eras within multiple generations and their inter-related characters. Flashbacks are used regularly, which tie together the multi-generational plotline. Dates for each chapter are provided as subtitles to aid the reader in keeping the sequence of events during each era straight.

Although most of the events occur in 2020, there are three other main periods: 1945, 1970, and 1995. Small details have significance and contribute to the ultimate resolution of the mystery. In addition, Appendix A is provided as an helpful tool; it lists characters, their eras, and their relationships with others in the story.

The author hopes you enjoy it and the many surprises to follow.

*****

GENERATIONS' CURSE

Part 1

CH 1 – The First

1945

Detective Gallagher of the Boston Police Department came out to view the gruesome scene in the middle of a torrential downpour—the remnants of a nor'easter that had just struck the upper East Coast. It had also been a year during which the town had been lambasted by epic snowstorms—the worst that part of the country had seen in decades. It was not the kind of day the detective would have picked to conduct a murder investigation—especially something as heinous as this one.

The detective's birthname was Taggert Arthur Gallagher, but he was known throughout the force as *Tag*. He was a stocky, hard-nosed detective who had grown up in the West Roxbury neighborhood in south Boston. He was only half Irish; yet most people thought he was one hundred percent through and through. The Irish half came from a long lineage of Irishmen that was of hardy stock and carried a rough, unpolished demeanor. However, those who really knew him saw a softer man, more jovial and quick-humored than quick-tempered. He could drink with the best of them, but he also knew when to stop. After only four years on the force, he could sense when things at the bar were likely to get out of hand and was not hesitant to hail a cab and go home.

Indeed, he was a newly minted detective. His father, Michael Arthur Gallagher—who went by *Mag*—was a long-time veteran in the police force. In fact, he had been the first in the family to become police chief. Tag, on the other hand, had started as a beat cop right out of high school. Then a few years later, Uncle Sam had called him up for service after the attack on Pearl Harbor in 1941. Having served his country honorably, Tag was discharged and went back onto the force, being allowed to take the detective's exam right away and passing it on his first attempt.

But on this rainy day, there was nothing left to a sixth sense, even for an experienced detective. The crime spoke for itself. It was bloody, horrific, heinous, and a whole host of other such synonyms. But figuring out the who, what, why, and how, was another matter, and that responsibility had now fallen to Tag, whether he wanted it or not.

Inside the apartment lay the remains of Janice Prodescu. The body was badly decomposed. There were few facial features that were still recognizable as the skin hung off the body in gray and mottled folds, like bad curtains on a broken rod. The detective estimated her age at between twenty-five and thirty, but it was hard to tell much else. What was particularly unusual was that the victim had only been dead a few days even though it looked like it had been there, rotting and being eaten by the household cats, for months. The cats in the house had been gnawing away at some of her soft tissue for a while, having gone unfed since her death.

Wearing a white handkerchief over his mouth to lessen the stench, Tag continued through the rest of the cramped apartment, trying to keep his breathing as shallow as he could to avoid getting sick. The foul odor wafted through the corridors of the building too as the door to the violated apartment remained open while investigators processed the scene. Most of the apartment residents on the floor—and some on other floors—had towels stuffed into their thresholds to do what they could to keep out the foul odor.

The first call about the incident had been phoned into the precinct from a neighbor who had reported the bad smell coming out of the apartment next door. He hadn't seen Miss Prodescu for several days and worried that something was wrong. She was active and sociable—normally out and about, coming and going like most women in their twenties. Between her job and her social connections, she had kept a busy lifestyle—perhaps too busy, some thought.

When the police arrived, they used the supervisor's key to unlock her apartment. It was then that the odor overwhelmed them, causing two of the officers to gag immediately and leave the room, vomiting in the hallway outside. Backup was called, and the detective and someone from the coroner's office showed up shortly thereafter.

From the position and condition of the body, there was no doubt it had been a homicide. The corpse was a disturbing sight, twisted in a way that was completely unnatural. The scene was right out of a horror film with Miss Prodescu lying on the sofa, her arms and legs pointing outward toward the large, refrigerator-sized, radio set that had been pushed up against the wall at one end of the room. But her head and the front of her torso faced the seat cushions behind her. Her milky eyes were open—frozen in time as if she had been glued to her seat listening to one of the late-night radio programs like *Fibber McGee and Molly* or the *Lucky Strike Jack Benny Program*. At the same time, her eyebrows were raised and taut, as if stitched in place, and her mouth was agape, trying to shout or scream, but incapable of either.

Just above the body, written in streaks of blood on the dull, white wall, were the chilling words: *Hello Plottar*. They were smeared to the point of being almost undecipherable, and there were no traces of individual fingers that may have been used. Instead, the letters were grooved—carved into the plaster—as if sharp claws had dug them.

When the coroner arrived, he shuffled to the backroom where the corpse was discovered. Malcom "Mack" Kelly was an older gentleman, having retired as an emergency room doctor at Boston's Carney Hospital ten years earlier. This was his last year in the coroner's office, having served since being elected Chief Medical Examiner and County Coroner for Suffolk County for the first time in 1927.

The coroner came up behind the detective and stopped in his tracks once his eyes fell upon the victim. Shaking his head, he said, "Boy, I don't know about this one. In all my years as the county coroner and as a doctor, I've never seen anything like this."

Moving toward the body, Kelly looked it over to get a visual understanding of what had taken place. The police photographer also arrived and began taking pictures with his office-issued, Kodak Vigilant Six-20 camera—one of only eight in use on the force. It would be several days before the photo lab at the department would be able to process the film and generate good pictures for study and future reference at a trial. Technology was improving, albeit slowly. Yet, as far as forensic evidence was concerned, fingerprinting was still the most critical piece of the investigation, and great care was taken not to contaminate the crime scene.

"What happened, Mack?" asked Tag, talking through his neatly folded handkerchief.

"Beat's me," said the coroner. "It had to take a huge amount of force to do this. I don't know how anyone could have torqued her legs and torso around like that to make them point the other way. The head and arms are one thing, but the torso. Boy, I just ... I just don't know."

"What about that smell, Mack?"

"What?"

"The stench—it's really bad for something like this, isn't it?"

"Yeah, maybe a little, but after so many years of doing this, I guess you eventually lose that sense—probably intentionally. It doesn't smell worse than any other five-day-old body in ninety-degree heat. I don't have any clues for you on that, Tag. I don't think that has anything to do with the murders."

"Well, for now, Mack, let's keep this one close to the vest. I don't want any details leaked to the newspapers. There's too much about this case that worries me. I haven't worked that many of these as a detective, but you don't have to be an expert to see that this one is really bizarre. We'll collect what evidence we can from the apartment, but I'm really interested in what you learn from the autopsy. Call me when you have something."

"Will do Tag—as soon as I finish it."

Tag turned to one of the other officers who was assisting at the scene.

"We need next of kin and any other information we can get on the vic. Let me know when you finish here. I'm going to talk to the neighbors to find out what they heard, saw, or didn't. Maybe we can get something from that."

The medical assistants from the coroner's office were placing the corpse on a stretcher and covering it over with a sheet when Tag noticed something in the victim's right hand. He tried to open it, but it was frozen shut from the *rigor mortis*.

"Mack, let me know what that is too ..." Tag said, pointing at the victim's hand, "... you know, after you finish the autopsy."

Mack smirked at him and nodded. "When I'm finished."

The coroner's attendants made sure every part of the body was shrouded by the sheet before carrying it down the stairs and out the back door of the apartment. But although there was a large crowd forming around the front of the apartment, there were still several reporters who had snuck around to the back alley, having had success in scooping stories from there in the past. Tag had given orders for officers to be stationed around the entire perimeter of the building to ensure no one got inside and contaminated the scene. Yet, reporters were clever in finding ways to get into position for their "money shot." Once the ambulance drove around the backside of the building, there was a sudden rush to get to the alley. But the attendants were already outside with the body and quickly loaded it into the stubby-looking black-and-white ambulance which whisked it away as photographers snapped pictures. The reporters pummeled Mack with questions as he left the scene; however, true to his word, he merely raised his hand and shook his head. "No comment," he answered, while climbing into his 1941 Buick Super. But after they blocked his way, he finally shouted out, "We don't know anything of substance at this point. Now, clear the way. I have an autopsy to perform."

Inside the apartment, Tag finished talking to the residents but didn't find much to go on. So, he returned to the apartment to scour the place on his own. He took out his flashlight, scanning underneath the furniture for anything that may have been left behind by the killer or killers. It was a clean apartment with almost nothing out of place, and that made it easier for him to see anything that was askew. He was, at least, happy for that.

In the bedroom, a jewelry box lid was opened and most of the jewelry was missing. Oddly, the only thing inside was a red, Zippo, cigarette lighter. The box looked musical, but it wasn't wound and remained eerily silent—telling no tales—as Tag used his handkerchief to handle it and look it over.

Even with the other foul smells in the apartment, he noticed the scent of something else—of apples. Raising the box closer to his face, he noticed the distinct aroma of apples as if they were still hanging on the trees. As odd as that was, it was stranger that nothing else seemed to be—odd that is. The drawers to the dresser were neatly closed, and her robe was folded and lying perfectly in alignment at the foot of the bed.

The closet door was open, and he saw that her clothes were separated on the closet bar to reveal a small, olive-colored safe that was screwed tightly into the floorboard. The door to the safe was open, but there was no indication of it being forced open—no scratches, dents, or other marks. Nevertheless, the safe was empty inside.

Combing the apartment for other signs, Tag noticed that the front door had been locked from the inside—double-bolted in fact. More perplexing was the fact there was no indication of forced entry anywhere around the apartment, except in the spare bedroom where the latch on the window facing the alley was broken. Outside the window was a rusted, iron, fire escape ladder that connected to a series of platforms that made-up the building's fire escape route—all of which led down into the dark and narrow alleyway below.

Tag went to the window, and using his handkerchief, he moved the broken panel in and out to see why it was ajar. He soon saw that the latch on the side was sheared off, keeping it from shutting all the way and allowing a faint, cool breeze to seep in through the slit. Along with the broken latch were fragments of molding, suggesting the window had been forced up. Yet, Tag wondered how an intruder could have gotten in through the tiny opening, broken out the molding and not alerted the victim to his presence.

Maybe Miss Prodescu just fell asleep and didn't hear anything. Maybe she was heavy sleeper or, he thought, *maybe she was drunk.*

"Is there any alcohol in the place?" Tag bellowed to the officers in other parts of the apartment. "Was she drinking?"

"No, sir. Not that we can find. There was no glass or bottle anywhere near her, and we certainly didn't find any booze stored anyplace suggesting that she drank," said one of the officers, looking through the cabinets.

Tag nodded. He hadn't thought so—it wasn't something he would expect based on the neatness of the apartment and the way it she seemed to live her life.

Here was a woman who was meticulous in her housekeeping, and as far as he could figure, her everyday life. He hadn't found any liquor in the place. He hadn't even found a stray hair on the sofa, except those left by the cats. However, she had sat on the couch listening intently to the radio while someone had burglarized the place and then murdered her. She had either gotten up and confronted the

18

killer, only having her body put back on the sofa and posed in the most grotesque way after the murder took place, or her life had been taken as she sat on the sofa—her body parts rearranged as she sat there with a vacant stare. It made no sense.

Of course, the pink elephant in the room was the last piece. *How could the intruder have killed her in the way he did? It would have taken tremendous force to twist her head and body like that—just as Mack had said.* At this point, Tag had no answers or at least none that were any good.

He finished his work, packed up his things and headed home. His wife, Iris, understood what his work meant to him, and she tolerated his obsessive behavior when it came to solving murder cases. Yet, he would work on this case for weeks and still make little progress. Those weeks then turned into months, and the months into years. Ultimately, it would leave an emptiness within him that would never be filled. Like similar murders that would follow, this one would be haunting—not only to Tag but to future generations of detectives in his family.

News of the murder reached the police chief's desk within hours, but it would reach that of the distract attorney for another day. Then, still, it would take another day to be picked up by the mayor. By that point, it had been leaked out of the precinct and was in the papers and front-page news. Everyone on the street was talking about it, hearing rumors of how horrendous the killing had been. Theories began sprouting up everywhere suggesting everything from a serial killer to aliens from another star system.

They would have no idea about the full nature and extent of the horror actually responsible, and that was probably just as well.

*****

CH 2 - Sara

2020

Only five feet tall, Sara McLaughlin was petite but perky. At forty years old, she had been married to Vince for twenty years. They had just one child, a daughter named Lucy Jean, or LJ as they called her, who was a teenager and growing up quickly.

As for Sara, she had the same energy level as her teen-aged daughter and then some. That too had been a hereditary trait within the family. Everyone on her mother's side had been extremely driven— always working on something, always planning something, always talking to someone, and rarely taking time off to kick-back and relax. So, keeping up the house, being involved in the school's PTA, growing her business, volunteering at the food pantry, and many more things at the same time were all in a day's work.

She was fifteen when her mother, Abagail, or Abby as she was known, suddenly disappeared, leaving her to be brought up by her Aunt Mary. Unfortunately, tragedy had become part of the family heritage by then. Sara's grandmother, Cora Rae, and her great grandmother, Janice, had both died suddenly— viciously murdered in their apartments in town. What had happened to her mother, Abby, had never been learned, as her body or whereabouts had never been located. Her mother and grandmother had lived in Roxbury, Mass., just as Janice had before them.

Sara's aunt told her that her mother had been a quiet person who had counted only a small few as her group of friends. Abby had gotten pregnant out of wedlock but had married her boyfriend later. She had given birth to Sara in her house instead of going to the hospital, as her new husband had abandoned them soon after the wedding. Abby had done the best she could trying to raise her daughter on her own, but soon the hereditary traits on her mother's side of the family began to close in on her. Her friends became worried as she plunged into deep fits of brooding and depression. Often, they would come by and find the young girl, Sara, playing by herself downstairs while her mother was locked away in her bedroom upstairs.

When Abby didn't show up for work one day, a missing person's report was issued; yet she never returned and was never found. As for Sara, she had been lucky to land with her aunt when her mother went missing instead of being shuttled off to a foster home. So, it was her Aunt Mary who had raised her and done the best she could with the girl of special talents.

However, life with her aunt and uncle had been good. Sara had enjoyed her aunt's kindness and her uncle's good sense of humor. They lived in a house not far from where Sara had been born, and she was able to play with other cousins who lived in the Boston area. But, during her younger years, Sara also claimed that she played with mysterious friends who, she said, lived in the attic. Her aunt eventually grew worried about her, repeating over and over that her niece was just fantasizing about her playmates. Eventually, Sara stopped telling her aunt about them and kept the whole thing bottled-up inside. By the time she started grade school, Sara's aunt and uncle thought she had grown out of it—or at least she never mentioned it to them again.

It was during her teen years that Sara discovered she had a special gift. Like her mysterious attic friends, Sara kept her talents secret from her family and especially from her aunt and uncle who, she knew, frowned on such blasphemous ways. Sara didn't understand her skills fully either until she did some digging into her past. From letters written between family members, journals and other scraps she found, she pieced together that her mother, her grandmother, and her great grandmother had all experienced similar things: the ability to talk to the dead.

At the age of eighteen, she held her first séance—mostly as a joke and as something to do with some friends during a party. However, the group had been terrified when the only locked window in the room blew open in the middle of Sara's trance, extinguishing the candle and knocking a picture and a ceramic cup off the fireplace mantel. Some also swore they heard willowy, wispy voices echoing in the room.

Although Sara had tried to push aside the visions and suppress the voices in her head, they were relentless. Soon, she could do nothing but confront an irrefutable fact: she was a medium. Not only was she clairvoyant; she was also clairaudient—hearing as well as seeing spirits.

Over the years, Sara had channeled those energies for the good of others, contacting departed loved ones in hope of healing broken hearts and troubled minds. She had become a widely-sought-after medium as word spread of her abilities. Yet, deep down, she worried. Her daughter, LJ, was now at the age when she had first noticed and begun to understand her talents. Although she had hoped her daughter would not inherit the "medium" gene, she feared she had.

However, on the surface, Sara, Vince and LJ tried to live a normal life. Sara and Vince had married and moved into the small Cape Cod house her Aunt Mary had left to her niece after she had died. It was in Roxbury, in the South End of Boston. Her uncle had passed years earlier, and when her aunt died, Sara inherited the house with the stipulation that she and Vince work hard to renovate it and make it their own.

Vince's family was also from Boston, although from the western suburbs. His father was a sixth-generation American—his ancestors having come over from Ireland during the potato famine of 1845. Vince's mother had been a strict disciplinarian, while his father had stood in the background, directing his attention toward his business, a small machine shop that had employed half a dozen machinists. The home had been his mom's job; the machine shop, his dad's.

At night, Vince would come home from work at the machine shop, which he had taken over after his dad had retired. He would stretch out in his favorite, chocolate brown recliner, ready to relax and finish reading the paper, the *Boston Globe,* just like his father when he was a young man. While Sara got dinner ready, Vince would pick up the sports section and, sipping from a freshly popped beer can, would check on the latest Red Sox baseball news and statistics. Whether intentional or not, he paid little attention to the endless quarreling between his wife and his daughter. These arguments had only gotten worse as LJ had entered high school and entered the "my parents are stupid" phase of adolescence. As a teen, LJ had become rebellious and defiant of her parents. They tried everything to get to the source of her impudence, and it was only by chance that they discovered that she was caught up in a strange cult at school.

"LJ. What is going on with you?" her mother had demanded. "What's with this cult thing you're involved in?"

Vince heard the tone of Sara's voice and knew it wouldn't take long to trigger his daughter. He pulled the paper up a little higher as if that would block out more of the raucous that was the coming storm.

"I don't know what you're talking about," said LJ, munching on an apple before going upstairs.

"The cult! That's what Maggie's mom told me. That you and some others were going out into the woods after school and practicing black magic."

LJ looked up at her mother. "And you believe her?"

Sara stared at her daughter. She could read her like a book. "Yes. I think I do."

"Well, you're all crazy," said LJ, finishing her apple and wiping her face with a napkin. She got up to go upstairs to her room.

"Wait, LJ. We're not done here."

"What?"

"I asked you a question, young lady. Are you part of a black magic cult at school? Tell me the truth because I know other moms I can call."

LJ looked down. "Yes," she answered, "but so what."

"Why on earth would you do something so stupid?"

"Because it's cool, okay!"

"It's not cool! You should know! I can tell you ..."

"Mom, I don't want to hear about it."

"I don't care, LJ. I know what the dark side is all about. You don't screw around with it. It's not something to be messed with. I've told you that before!"

"It's not going to hurt anybody. It's only for fun. It's nothing serious," said LJ.

"There is nothing fun about conjuring up evil. There is nothing fun about getting involved in satanic rituals. There is nothing fun about putting yourself and your soul at risk."

"Lighten up, Mom. It's nothing like that," said LJ. 'You're all so serious about everything."

Sara went over to her daughter and took her firmly by the shoulders.

"No, I'm afraid you don't understand, LJ. I've *seen* it. I've *felt* it. I know what it can do. I've seen how the darkness slowly creeps into your mind—into your world—when you don't realize what it's doing. It deceives you. It makes you think it's on your side—that it can and will only help you in your life. You have struggles, like everyone else, LJ, but it will not fix anything. Before you realize it, that evil will trap you inside a prison you can't escape from. Then, it's too late. When you wake up and realize it's happened, there won't be anything you or anyone else can do about it. You'll be lost forever."

Her voice trailed off, and she looked away.

"You're so melodramatic, Mom."

Sara swung her gaze around to confront her daughter once again.

"LJ, I'm your mother. This is something beyond being a good parent. I forbid you from doing this anymore! For your sake and for that of your soul. You must—you *will*—stop!"

LJ growled at her mother and stormed up the stairs, slamming the door behind her.

They forbade her from associating with others in the cult and carefully watched her comings and goings after school and on weekends. Still, LJ found ways to sneak around them, meeting-up with her friends to go out into the woods near the school and perform dark rituals they had found on the Internet.

Sara and Vince began working with a social worker and then a psychologist, but nothing seemed to work. LJ was a straight-A student, but they were still worried. In the end, they hoped it was just a phase—something she would grow out of. At least that's what Vince thought. Sara, on the other hand, could only hope—no pray—that he was right.

*****

Janice Prodescu was born to Dumitra Nicolescu Prodescu and her husband, Nicholai Prodescu. However, the marriage hadn't lasted, and Dumitra had gotten a divorce. The fact that both women were murdered in such grotesque ways and so closely together suggested an obvious link to someone. However, there were still no leads as to who might have committed the crimes or why.

Weeks later, Tag went back to his friend in the coroner's office.

"We've got nothing, Mack," said Tag, clearly discouraged. "How is that possible? We've got a mother and daughter murdered in the same year and both killed with the same MO. Not only the same MO, but one that would be hard to replicate by another killer. This makes no sense!"

"I hear you, Tag. These killings truly are baffling," said Mack listening as Tag vented. Mack had hoped the Janice case would be his last, and he could retire in peace. But he'd been wrong. Now, he worried that he'd be asked to stay on for several more months until more evidence was gathered on the two twisted murder cases.

"Any thoughts?" Tag asked. "I couldn't find the man with the *S* on his chest."

"Yeah," said Mack, "let me retire. Call me when you've solved them."

Tag smiled. "I know, Mack. It's come at a bad time, but as you say, this is where we are."

"Well, then I'd say it's got to be someone they both knew—a relative or friend of the family. Maybe it was a handyman who worked for both of them. I just don't see any other possibility. These weren't random murders, Tag."

"We've checked out all the family and friends. There were no handymen employed by either of them. We've talked to neighbors of both and still nothing. Everyone has an alibi."

"Could a family member have hired someone to kill both of them?" asked Mack.

"Someone in the *family*?"

"Yeah, the family or a friend."

"There's no motive—none that we can find." Then, Tag asked, "Say, what was it that you found in that Janice girl's palm? Was it anything important?"

27

"No, just a Zip lighter—a red lighter. You'll get it with the rest of the evidence."

"I don't think she smoked," Tag answered.

"But you don't know?" asked Mack.

"No, but there weren't any cigarettes at the apartment."

"Doesn't mean she didn't smoke occasionally."

"We'll look into it," said Tag, making a note. "There wasn't anything different about it—the lighter?"

"No. Simple lighter. That's it."

"Crap. I was hoping for something more," said Tag.

"Well, there's got to be something you're missing. You just have to dig deeper. If not, then you'll have to go to Plan B."

"Plan B?" asked Tag.

"Looking into the supernatural."

Tag laughed. "You've got to be kidding, Mack. You of all people? I thought you were out there with Superman, but now monsters and demons? You don't believe in that stuff, do you?"

"I never used to—not until these two cases, anyway. I guess I'm gettin' old. I've seen a lot of things in my day, but nothin' like this."

"Well, let me know when the Devil is back in town carrying his bag of black magic," said Tag. "You'll recognize him, Mack—he's the one with red, scaly skin, horns and a long tail. Tell him I'd like to talk to him about this and a few other things."

*****

CH 4 - The Horned Goat

2020

The phone call was not unusual. It was the type she had received many times before. However, this time it was from a woman named Claire who had just lost the love of her life. They had been seeing each other for years. Both were middle-aged, and she had been trying to convince him to leave his wife and marry her. However, his life had been cut short—killed while serving the community he loved. Now, she was alone with only her two dogs, Bullet and Mug. Without her man and a future with him, she felt abandoned and adrift.

Sara drove to the high-rent suburb of Brookline. Claire's address showed a multi-level apartment complex that was meticulously cared for, allowed pets, and had security and a concierge on staff in the lobby. It was convenient for Claire because there was a doggy park nearby where Bullet and Mug could exercise and a neighborhood grocery and laundromat where she or the concierge could easily and quickly take care of weekly chores. Claire's apartment was up two floors and at the far end of the hallway—number twenty-five.

Marvin Fletcher, Sara's bodyguard and driver, always went with her to her meetings with new clients. She never knew what she might confront either before, during, or after a session. Marvin was licensed to carry a firearm, but Sara forbade it, saying that it interfered with the energy fields in the room. However, she did allow him to carry mace and a nightstick, just in case.

Ding-dong.

The doorbell rang inside the apartment, and as the door opened, an attractive woman with shoulder-length, reddish-blonde hair appeared.

"Hi," she said with a smile. "I'm Claire, and you must be Sara. Please come in."

Sara walked in with Marvin following close behind her. She put down her oversized, faux-alligator purse and took a spot on the love seat that was buffered on each end by side tables and matching pewter lamps. As Sara could tell, there was a keen sense of symmetry in the room and in all the details. Bullet and Mug came trotting into the room to see their visitors. Both were short-haired, Irish terriers, and both the same shade of gray. Wagging their tails furiously, they hoped for a pat on the head or rub on the belly. When they received neither, they jogged back to the kitchen and lay down on the white, marble floor to take a nap or wait for their owner to take them to the doggy park.

"Claire, I just need to go over how I work," Sara began. "It will take me a few minutes to feel the energy here. Once I do, then I'll channel anything I hear or see and communicate it directly to you. When I connect, I don't like to be interrupted. I will convey to you what I sense. but, most importantly, I will tell you things you want to hear and things you probably don't. I'm not the one who should decide that. If Spirit tells me something is important to tell you, then I will. That's just the way it is. I don't control things—they do."

"I understand," Claire said nervously.

Sara closed her eyes and took a deep breath while she pressed the fingers of both hands together. Surprisingly, it didn't take her long before her breathing slowed, and she became quiet and still. It was a bit unnerving to Claire, as she watched the psychic's eyes roll back and forth under her closed lids as if she were in a deep REM sleep.

"There's a young man who is with us," said Sara, opening her eyes and looking not at Claire, but just behind her. Still in a trance, the medium sat, unblinking, as she continued the session. "He has short, black hair and is wagging his finger at you. He looks either angry or disapprovingly. Does that mean anything?"

"A young man? Is he tall and broad shouldered?" asked Claire.

"No. He's rather short and stout."

"What is he wearing?"

"He's wearing work clothes, I think—likely from the mid-twentieth century if I was guessing," answered Sara.

"I don't know who that could be. My grandfather, maybe?

"He's pointing to your ring finger," said Sara, interrupting but frozen in her gaze. "He says something about your getting involved where you shouldn't have?"

"I don't know what he's talking about."

Sara then said, "There's another person here with us now. He is older and says he misses you, but that he's all right. He wishes things had turned out differently between the two of you, but there was a higher power that determines those things."

"What does he look like?" Claire asked.

"He is tall, short brown hair and broad shouldered—like the person you described before. It looks like he's wearing a uniform of some kind. Is that someone you were close to?"

Claire began to choke up. "That's my guy ... that's my boyfriend," she said. "He was killed downtown—beaten up by some thugs. It was awful, terrible."

"I can see the love in his eyes. He still loves you; you know. He says he's your guardian angel now and will look after you." Sara became quiet but furrowed her brow. "He says that it was destined that you not marry. It was better for you that way."

"No! That can't be!" Claire exclaimed.

"He says he was never faithful to anyone but his job. He regrets any hurt he caused in your life." Sara stopped and closed her eyes again. "He is telling me that you should be careful and warns there is evil that lurks nearby. He says you should protect yourself, but he will be there with you should something happen."

"What's going to happen?"

Sara shook her head. "I don't know. This is most peculiar. I've never had a spirit say anything like this to me before. All I can do is tell you what I'm hearing and sensing, Claire. I can't tell you anything more than that."

"What's he doing now?"

"He's stepped behind you and ..."

It was then Sara smelled it ... apples. She smelled apples.

"I smelled something," she said.

"What?"

"I smelled, uh, ..." Sara stopped. It was hard to explain; no, it was impossible to explain why she would suddenly smell apples. "I felt something ... a warmth, right here," she said instead, putting her hand on her own shoulder. "That's where he touched you. He said he'd be there for you."

"I think I felt it," said Claire smiling. It was unusual for a client to feel the presence of a spirit too, but sometimes the connections between them were so deep that the energy passed through.

But as Sara watched, the phantom image of the man in a uniform transformed. Like a chameleon, it changed into a black, smokey cloud. Deep inside the mist, she saw another image emerge—that of a goat with a boney face and long horns. Instantly, she recoiled. For her, it was the sign of only one thing—that of pure evil.

"Uh!" stuttered Sara, trying to catch her breath.

"What's wrong?" Claire asked.

"I'm afraid that's all I have for you today," said Sara shaking. Her face was pallid; her eyes wide with terror.

"That's all? My boyfriend didn't say anything else?"

It was an image and a feeling that had become increasingly present during her client sessions—the image of a goat and a clammy death-like sensation that entered her body and wrapped its frightful, cold fingers around her heart. She felt as if it had squeezed it to the point of bursting, making it stop completely for a second or two or three. She shivered uncontrollably.

"Uh, no. He didn't. I'm sorry," said Sara, abruptly getting up. "I felt a draft. That's all—probably when he opened a portal to return back into his realm."

Sara got up and called out for Marvin, who had gone into the kitchen to help himself to a cold soda from the refrigerator. "Marvin, it's time to go," she said, picking up her bag. She managed a feeble smile and extended her hand. "Claire, I hope that helped. You know where to reach me if you want another session."

Sara couldn't get out of the apartment quickly enough. Something had touched her too—something that was most unwelcome: an uninvited spirit that was surely dark and malevolent.

"What's wrong?" Marvin asked, opening the door to her car once they were in the parking garage outside. "You weren't in that session very long."

"I don't know, Marvin. There was something else there with us— something threatening and sinister. Whatever it is, it's getting stronger. That's the third time in the last few weeks that I've felt that sensation. It's not normal, and, well, it's upsetting," she answered. "I just have to get things under control, that's all. Perhaps I should take a few days off and come back to this after a short break. You can take the time off. I'll call you next week about my next appointments."

On the drive back to the house, Sara tried to suppress her anxiety. The feelings were more intense than she'd ever had before. It was also the first time she had doubted her own ability to keep the two worlds separated—to control the darkness that also lurked in the spirit world and keep it from getting into her body and soul that existed in this one. She feared she was losing those battles, and if she lost enough of them, she would lose the entire war.

*****

CH 5 - Dark Intruder

2020

Claire was in a deep sleep. It was nearly two in the morning when she rolled over in her bed, pushing her face deeper into the soft, down pillow, unaware of everything else around her. She sighed and folded her leg, bringing it up to knee level with the other in a fetal position.

The windows in the bedroom were sealed shut—a precaution of most apartment building owners to keep out burglars and vandals, especially on the first two floors. Yet, the sheer, white drapes on both sides of the window began to billow into the room like ghastly specters as if the window had mysteriously dissolved on its own accord.

Then, the front door of the apartment opened and closed quietly. Moments later, there were noises as if someone were pulling out drawers and rummaging through her effects. It only took a few minutes, and then there was a faint creaking sound as the front door opened once again and shut with a simple *click*.

Claire turned onto her side, pulling the covers up tighter. With her eyes still closed, she was unaware that the door to her apartment had been opened. Yet, the danger was far from over.

Now, her bedroom door cracked opened slowly before stopping. Then, it moved a few more inches before stopping again. But suddenly, things changed.

Bang!

The door swung open, flying wildly into the wall and crashing against it, rupturing a deep, wide hole in the drywall.

Claire jolted upright in bed, startled. She had been deep in a dream and now struggled to wake up. And although she didn't notice the crack in the bedroom door, she did watch as her closet door began to open on its own. Emerging from the blackness was a dark, shadowy figure which floated hauntingly across the floor to the far wall of the bedroom next to the window. It watched the bed from a distance—staring at Claire with its black, lifeless eyes.

Claire gasped—terrified at what she saw. Her mind was paralyzed with fear, and she couldn't get out a sound to scream.

The phantasm floated toward her and the foot of the bed, standing motionless and looking directly down at her. Claire shook her head, pulling the covers up higher as if it would shield her from the demon.

Creeeeeak! The door to the bedroom began to close. Then, picking up speed, it slammed shut.

Bang!

"Ahhh!" she shouted, finally able to find her voice. She looked back at the foot of the bed. The phantom had dissipated, but although she couldn't see it, she could feel it. It was still in the room.

From the nightstand, she grabbed the Glock 19 her dead boyfriend had bought her and loaded the magazine, chambering a round. She then got out of bed and went to the door that had shut. But as soon as her hand touched the knob, the door flew open once again, knocking her onto the floor. Claire fired three rounds through the door opening into the darkness of her living room, shattering an old, wooden floor mirror just outside in the hallway. The glass shards blew back into the bedroom slicing her hand and arms as she tried to cover her face. Then, something grabbed her legs and began dragging her out of the room. She started to scream.

***

It was nearly 3:30 AM, when Sara—in another part of the city—sat straight up in her bed too. She had awakened suddenly, confused and disoriented. Something was wrong. There was nothing strange lurking or hovering in her room. Her husband Vince was sleeping soundly beside her, and the house was quiet and seemingly at peace. But her dream had been upsetting.

She could remember it vividly, and she couldn't shake the horrible feeling. She had been lying in bed but could see doors opening and closing all around her. Then, there was a black shadow that had come out of the closet and seized her by the ankles, dragging her out of bed. She had screamed, but Vince hadn't heard her. The wraith had violently pulled her out of the room over the hardwood floor, and she had heard the shattering of glass and felt the pain as the shards sliced her skin.

The next thing she knew, she was awake and shaking with fear.

Generations' Curse

*****

CH 6 - Rosco Arthur

1938

The Medford High School class of 1938 had been special. During the previous four years, the school had won more state athletic championships than during any other time in its long history. Among the graduates were Bessie Belzikov and Janice Prodescu—two very good friends who led a tight-knit group of girls that some considered a clique. However, there were a few boys who hung out with them as well.

Rosco Arthur was one of those boys. No one even knew his last name—he always went by Rosco Arthur as a nickname of sorts. Rosco was from a well-respected family that lived in Medford, and although he occasionally got into trouble, it was usually nothing serious.

He was handsome and had a lot of energy. Although not the captain of any of his sports teams, he did play varsity football and baseball. He was too short and stout for the basketball team, but he was built sturdy and rugged with a broad chest and wide shoulders. He had short, dark hair, strong facial features, and a pleasant, captivating smile. His only distinguished feature was a birthmark on his neck. But that never made him feel self-conscious, and few noticed it after they had known him awhile.

"Rosco Arthur? What are you doing Friday night?" It was Bessie Belzikov. "Me and some of the girls are going to Thompson's. You're welcome to meet us there if you and the boys are up for it." Bessie smiled coyly at Rosco and cocked her head to get his attention. It was no secret that Bessie had a special crush on him.

"Thanks, Bessie," Rosco said casually, trying to be cool. "I'll think about it. Maybe we will."

That night, the boys found the girls all gathered around the soda bar, having strawberry colas and giggling over the latest gossip they were spreading. Rosco had his friends too. There was Bill Fortano, Bobby Prescott, and Taggert Gallagher, who they all called Tag. All the boys were on the football team, and some played with Rosco on the baseball roster.

"Well, look at what we found here, boys," said Rosco, always the extravert. He was what the boys called a "closer"—not only in baseball as a relief pitcher, but also with the girls. He could get just about any he wanted, when he wanted.

"Oh, Rosco, stop!" said Bessie, smiling. "We're just minding our own business, and here you show up." She was, of course, flirting with him. "Nobody invited you."

"Yeah, right. Just mindin' your business talkin' about people—telling stories about 'em. I know how you-all work." Rosco too was flirting. With a toothpick in his mouth, he gave a head nod to the soda jerk to fetch them some colas. "What are you sayin' about me?" he asked, adjusting the straw on the drink he was given.

"There's too much to say, Rosco Arthur. Way too much," Bessie said giggling.

"And what about me?" asked Tag. "My ears have been burnin' lately."

This time Janice spoke up.

"Tag, dear," she said, giving him a subtle grin, "it only took us ten seconds to talk about you."

"Ouch!" said Rosco, lightly punching his friend in the arm. "She got you bad, then. Real bad!"

However, the night went along as it usually did. The girls would eventually breakoff with a boy and find the backseat of a car to make-out. Sometimes, it was more than that, but no one ever told.

But after high school graduation, the boys went their separate ways. The war kicked in within four years, and all were drafted. Bill Fortano was killed in Belgium by a mortar shell, and Bobby Prescott died when his B-17 bomber was shot down over Germany. Tag had enlisted in the navy and found himself on the destroyer *USS Kidd* in the South Pacific. Rosco had been deferred due to an injury he had suffered in high school. He held regrets about that as he watched his friends go off to war.

It had been a difficult time during the war—both overseas and at home. The young women of Medford High School waited at home for word of those they knew in school. There were many tears for those who perished, but there were also many shouts of joy for those who returned. Rosco and Tag were two of the lucky ones.

*****

CH 3 – Twilight Zone

2020

It was again supper time, and Vince was in his favorite chair reading the sports section. Meanwhile, Sara and LJ were in the kitchen competing in a sport of their own—sparing over LJ's friends and their bad influence on her.

The match pitted two head-strong women who looked a lot alike. As tall as her mother and equally small-framed and skinny, LJ had gotten most of her physical attributes from her mother's side of the family. Her short brown hair had a deep, silky sheen that looked almost wet to the touch. Girlfriends thought she should try-out for a hair product commercial, but she would only laugh at the prospect. Like her mom, she had small, thin fingers, an oval face with high cheekbones, deep-set brown eyes, and a soft, milky complexion. Her lips were full, and her teeth nearly perfect, except for the small chip on the front lower one that she'd gotten at age eight when she accidently knocked her face against the edge of a chair.

Fortunately, this night the bickering was minimal, and Sara finished putting the food into the serving bowls before calling Vince to the dinner table. It rarely happened that he reacted instantaneously, and this time was no different. On the second request, she said it a little louder to get him moving in her direction. As Vince approached the table, Sara asked LJ to get some napkins while she finished the place settings.

"Vince, before I forget," said Sara, "I've got another appointment tomorrow morning, so you'll need to get LJ's lunch ready."

"Why can't she make her own lunch? She's old enough," he mumbled.

"Come on, Vince. Can't you help me out, just once? I've got a very early meeting. It would really be great if you could ..."

"Fine," he said, sitting down, pouting. "I just need to know what I should make."

"The same thing I *always* make for her," said Sara.

Vince rolled his eyes. "But I don't know what that is. I wouldn't have asked if I'd known what that was, now would I? I'm not clairvoyant, like you." His tone was one of agitation.

"She takes an apple, Frito chips, and a PB&J sandwich on whole wheat cut down the center with the crust cut off. You got that?"

LJ interrupted. "No, Mom. I don't want those chips anymore. I want the Wheat Wafers; you know, the ones you bought the last time."

"Sorry," said Sara, only half-heartedly, "then use the Wheat Wafers. okay?"

"Of course, dear. I'll handle it with LJ in the morning," he said shortly. It was his way of saying *I'll deal with it later.* Then, a startled look came over his face. "Wait," he answered. "I thought you gave up sessions for a while? That's what you told me after the last one?"

Sara sighed. "I will ... after this one."

"You know, I've got a tee time in the morning," said Vince. "Can't you reschedule your meeting for later?"

"Look, I always have to rearrange my meetings around your stupid golf game on Friday mornings. LJ has to be driven to school, so someone has to rearrange something. Why don't you do it this time?"

"I can't. I already promised my boss I'd play in his foursome."

Sara sighed. She felt she always had to give in, and she thought it was always unfair.

"Fine. I'll reschedule. But you'd better be home by noon. I'm going to change my meeting to one o'clock. LJ has a doctor's appointment at one-thirty, so don't be late."

They finished dinner, and Vince cleaned up. At least he was good about doing that. He couldn't cook to save his life, but he could get things tidied-up so that the kitchen always looked spotless.

Sara yanked the white, plastic garbage liner from the pull-out drawer and tied the red, wire band around the top to keep things from spilling out. After replacing the liner, she carried the bag outside so Vince could take it down to the curb for the weekly pickup.

Meanwhile, Vince picked up the TV remote rather than engaging with his daughter. He flipped some channels until he got to the local news, hoping for sports to be the next in line for broadcasting.

"Late today, Police Chief Malloy gave an update on the attack and murder of former Chief Zag Gallagher. Gallagher's death came as a shock earlier this year when he was beaten to death in a downtown alley. Malloy said his department has been working tirelessly trying to track down his killer or killers. However, to date, they have yet to identify any suspects. Chief Malloy is asking for the public's help in the case. So, if you have any information you think may be relevant to the case, please contact the Boston Police Department at 555-231-9001.

"Now, in other news ..." said the anchor, moving on to the next story.

Sara came back into the house after having taken the garbage out from the kitchen.

"Anything on the news tonight?" she asked, glancing at the wide, thin TV hanging on the wall across the room. She walked to the end of the sofa and sat down, watching as LJ gathered her backpack of schoolbooks to go study.

"No," said Vince, "just the usual—murders, accidents, deaths, accidental deaths, accidental accidents ... you know. About the only thing missing so far are the accidental murders."

"Oh, okay," Sara answered, really paying little attention to what he was saying.

But after hearing the last news story, Vince shook his head. "It's really tragic what happened to the chief of police a few months ago."

"Yeah, why? Did they find someone?" asked Sara.

"No, the chief just said they have no leads," he answered.

"I don't understand how that's possible. You would think they would pull out all the stops when their police chief gets killed. It's been months and still don't have anything?"

But by then the news had switched to sports, and Vince was riveted to the ERA statistics of that night's starting pitcher for the Red Sox.

41

LJ approached the brown, corduroy sofa where her mother sat. "I've finished my homework. Can I watch *the Twilight Zone*, Mom?" she asked, smiling coyly.

"What? Of course not! That show is too scary!"

"Oh, Mom! They're old! They aren't scary anymore—not like things are now. They're only reruns!" pleaded her daughter. When she got no reaction from Sara, she turned to her other parent. "Dad?" she asked, hoping for a different answer.

But Vince was absorbed in the evening sports segment that had just come on, so he didn't really hear her. "LJ just do as your mother asks, okay?" he answered.

"Are you sure your homework is done?" questioned her mother.

"Yes! It's done, Mom! Just an hour of the show. Please!"

"An hour. No more," said Sara, giving in.

LJ ran to the top of the stairwell and made a b-line to the guest bedroom, where an old, portable TV was sitting on top of the dresser. She made sure the volume on the set was turned down, barely audible and sat on the bed waiting for her show to come on. She already planned to be there for longer than an hour—much longer.

Yet, before the show started, LJ jumped up and hurried down the hall to the bathroom to grab a towel. Taking it back to the room, she shoved it into the gap between the threshold and the door to keep the eerie glow from flickering into the hallway outside and betraying her late-night horror fest.

"Good evening," came the deep voice from the television speaker. *"This is Rod Serling. This highway leads to the shadowy tip of reality. You're on a through route to the land of the different, the bizarre, the unexplainable. Go as far as you like on this road. Its limits are only those of the mind itself.*

"Ladies and Gentlemen, you're entering the wondrous dimension of imagination. The next stop—The Twilight Zone."

LJ curled up on the bed. The show always scared her, but there was something about it that kept drawing her back. Although the black-and-white TV show was old, it was still good and easy for LJ to sneak in late at night whether her mom approved or not. For LJ, it was

42

hypnotic—putting her into a trance as she watched and not letting her go until it was over.

"This evening we are going into another dimension, but we are only getting there through a strange and sinister portal—an opening created by man but used by creatures on the other side to haunt those in our world, on this side. We call this episode the 'Demon's Doorway'."

The flickering image changed, revealing a typical home of the 1960s with the short-cut, square lawn in front, the yellow-bricked, one-story home in back, and the cement driveway with a red 1963 Ford Fairlane parked outside.

The story started out as they usually did with a typical family in a typical situation where the viewer would become comfortable. However, for those veterans who knew how the show unraveled, suspense would build quickly. Something unexpected—and bizarre—would happen. It always did.

As the episode got creepy, LJ sank deeper under the covers and snuggled closer to her chestnut-brown Teddy bear.

"LJ?" came her mother's voice in the middle of the show. "It's bedtime. In fact, it's after your bedtime, young lady! Is your light off?"

"Just another minute, Mom!" she shouted back, her knuckles white with tension.

As she watched the flat screen, a black, bumpy, grotesque hand appeared, pushing open the closet door in a child's bedroom. Then, the viewpoint changed to the eye of the creature coming out of the closet. Whatever was in the closet was watching a little boy who was playing with square, wooden blocks in his room, stacking them neatly.

Suddenly, the lights in the boy's room flickered briefly but stayed on. However, the youngster seemed not to notice. He giggled as one of the block towers collapsed spilling the squares across the floor, some landing close to the closet door.

"No, don't!" LJ said with a strained voice, as the boy inched closer to the closet door to pick up his blocks. "Don't!"

Then, just as the boy reached the last block, the hand grabbed him by the arm.

"No!" LJ shouted.

"LJ! You're supposed to be in bed!" cried her mother from downstairs. But LJ didn't notice. She was too absorbed with the monster in the bedroom.

The creature dragged the little boy, as he screamed, into the closet before the door slammed closed. Both disappeared into the nothingness of the room, as if neither had ever existed.

"Oh, my God! Oh, my God!" squeaked LJ as quietly as she could, her breathing shallow and fast.

Sara stomped up the staircase, noticing the lights were off in LJ's room, but the door was open. LJ had forgotten to close her door, so her mom knew instantly where she was. Forcing open the door to the guest room, Sara flipped on the light.

"LJ! I thought I said one hour! It's been ... well ... almost two and a half. I want you in bed, little lady."

"Oh, Mom! It's almost over. Can't I see the very ending?"

"No! Now go to your room!"

LJ threw off the quilt and stormed down the hall to her room. After brushing her teeth and setting her alarm, she again pulled the covers up to her chin and rested her head on her pillow. But her eyes wouldn't close. She kept thinking about that hand—that creepy, hideous hand—that had grabbed that little boy. He had screamed, but no one had heard him. No one knew he was gone. He just vanished.

She glanced around her room, watching the faint beam from the streetlight outside filter in through the window and its six glass panes. The shadows the light made on the far bedroom wall were haunting, and as the wind blew, the jagged, spindly tree limbs just outside her window made frightening silhouettes on the walls. They looked like spidery arms that were coming for her as she lay helpless in bed.

Her eyes darted from the reflection on her wall to the closet door. It was closed, but she felt it would open at any moment. She watched and waited, fearing a terrible hand would suddenly fling open the door and come out to grab her. Seconds passed slowly—then minutes. She waited. *She would be ready,* she thought. *She would fight anything that came out of her closet!* But soon, her eyelids drooped and then closed—she could resist no more. If something came out, it would have an easy time taking her back into the closet and down into the depths from which it had come.

***

It was late. Everyone had gone to bed, but Sara couldn't sleep. One o'clock ... two o'clock ... then three o'clock ... they all came up on her digital clock that night—albeit painfully slowly. She tried everything, but she couldn't get her eyelids to close and stay closed. Twisting and turning in bed, she fought the anxiety that had been building inside her for weeks, if not months.

It was hard for her to describe. She felt a burning sensation inside her--something that wanted out. Yet, equally troubling was she also felt like there was something on the outside that wanted in. The one outside her worried her more. It was something she never wanted to let in, as her aunt had always warned her. *There were good spirits and bad ones,* she had said. *The good ones are there to help; the bad ones are there to harm.* Sara did all she could to keep the bad ones as far away from her and her family as possible. But these burning forces were like raging fires trying to consume her. She had felt these even as a child. Yet now, they were burning hotter than ever before, and the whole thing scared her.

She fidgeted, flipping her pillow several times and pulling her covers on and off before finally giving up. She looked over only to find Vince sound asleep as he always was. Nothing seemed to bother him. *He is lucky*, she thought.

Getting out of bed, she reached for her robe. She was wide awake, and there seemed to be nothing that was going to change that.

The nightlight was on in the outside hallway, and she navigated around the pair of flats left there by her daughter after she'd come home from school. Trudging, heavy-footed, down the stairs, she turned on the kitchen light and opened the refrigerator door. The small, incandescent bulb inside was dim, but she could still see well enough inside to find something to munch on. The only thing she spotted on the shelves was a green, plastic container with a matching lid—something that held the remains of a baked potato from a dinner two nights earlier.

Sara put the round container on the black-granite countertop and turned to open the utensil drawer to get a knife and fork. Then, she swiveled back to put the potato in the microwave to heat it up.

45

What? she thought. The plastic container was gone.

She looked around the ends of the kitchen island in case it had slid off, but there was no sign of it. *Must have been Enzo*, she thought, believing the family Labradoodle was to blame.

"Enzo? Where are you? Come back here," she said. But she didn't hear the pitter-patter of his paws on the wood floors.

She didn't have the energy to go to the basement to see if he'd gone down there. That's where the dog usually went after he had absconded with something he shouldn't have from the kitchen. So, she shrugged it off and traipsed back upstairs to try once more to get some sleep. It was now 3:35 AM when she climbed back onto her side of the bed. She curled up and tried again to fall asleep. Soon, she did.

But what she hadn't noticed was Enzo; he was sound asleep at the foot of her bed; he hadn't moved all night.

Downstairs, the refrigerator door swung slowly open, and the light inside flickered on and then off again. And as the refrigerator door closed, *all* the doors to the cabinets opened at the same time, creaking from the lack of oil. Sara's eyelids fluttered at the noise and then closed, going back to sleep.

Just as the last door in the kitchen opened, they all abruptly slammed shut.

Bang!

Sarah awoke; her heart was racing. She had heard something. She knew it for certain. It hadn't been a dream. It hadn't been something in her head. She had heard something downstairs in the kitchen.

She waited, holding her breath, to see if she would hear it again. Vince was still sleeping next to her, his mouth open but not yet snoring. After a few minutes of eerie silence, she lay her head back on the pillow. She didn't want to go downstairs. This time her eyes stayed open. This time, she was afraid.

Downstairs, two candles on the dining room table sparked on, letting puffs of gray smoke float upwards toward the ceiling. Then, they too suddenly went out.

***

The next morning Sara put on her robe and slippers and let her hand slide down the banister as she descended the stairs. Yawning and rubbing her eyes, she hurried through the dining room and into the kitchen to see if anything was amiss.

The kitchen appeared in order. All the cupboard doors were closed; however, there was one thing that was different. The refrigerator door was open.

Did I forget to close the refrigerator door? she thought, seeing it was open. She grabbed the milk, but it was warm. Dumping it into the sink, she washed out the carton and tossed it into recycling. Then, after checking if anything else had gone bad inside the frig, she shut the door, giving up on her breakfast.

Starting to walk toward the stairs, she stopped again feeling something else was wrong. *That's funny*, she thought. *I don't remember having used those candles before.* She went over to the two rose-colored wax sticks that had been on the dining room table for years unused. She looked at each noticing they had been lighted with hardened dribbles of wax flowing down the side of each. *How could that be?* she thought. *Perhaps they had been lit by someone at some time, and she hadn't noticed. Yeah, that was probably it.*

She shrugged, going back upstairs to prepare for the day. *Everything seemed in order,* she thought, trying to rationalize it all. *At least there were no goat's heads or things dangling from the chandelier, anyway.*

This was true—at least not yet anyway.

*****

CH 8 – In Critical Care

2020

Claire Horvath awoke. She was lying in a hospital bed, her right leg in a cast and her ribs wrapped so tightly she could hardly breathe. However, there wasn't much pain; the IV drip next to her made sure of that. Her eyesight was blurred, and she felt a slight bruise on the back of her head. There was no one in the room with her, but she could certainly tell that she wasn't at home anymore.

She reached down and pushed the red button next to her bed. In less than a minute a nurse came in.

"Good!" said the nurse warmly, giving Claire a big smile. "I'm glad to see you're finally awake. Do you know where you are?"

"No, but I guess I'm in a hospital."

"Yeah, you had a wild night last night. We still don't know how it happened, but perhaps you can tell the police when you're feeling up to it."

"Police?" asked Claire, with alarm. "Why the police?"

"Well, honey," the nurse said fluffing her pillow, "you were outside, crumpled up in the alleyway, until one of your neighbors spotted you when they came home late from their shift. They said you must have jumped from your second-floor apartment window. It's a good thing you didn't live on the thirtieth floor. That would have been a lot messier for us to clean up." The nurse laughed, but Claire was still too groggy to see the humor.

"I just don't remember," Claire answered, her mind racing to recall what had happened.

"That's okay. You need to rest right now. Your body went through a lot last night. I'm surprised you're not more traumatized by it all. Your blood work came back, and you weren't doing anything illegal. Still, something happened that pushed you out of the window or made you jump. Like I said, nobody quite understands it. They'll probably order a psych evaluation to see if there's something there."

"A psych evaluation? But I'm not crazy!"

The nurse laughed. "Maybe or maybe not. I don't know, and it's not up to me to figure out. You'll need to talk to the doctor on staff, but also with the police." The nurse tucked the thin, gray hospital blanket in under her chin. "By the way, I'm Anne. If you need anything, just ring me like you did before. I'll come by to take care of it for you."

The nurse got halfway through the door but then suddenly stopped. "Ha! Well, speak of a devil. There's a police officer coming down the hallway now. Let me see what he needs."

She shut the door, but moments later it opened again.

"The officer says he needs to talk to you," said Anne. "Are you up to it?"

"Now?"

"He talked to me earlier today and asked me to let him know when you regained consciousness. He's the one who got the call and brought you in. He was asking about drug/alcohol tests, but we can't release those to him without a court order. He said he'd be back, and, well, he's outside now." She paused and added, "If I were you, I'd just get it over with."

There was dread in Anne's voice, as if she had personally dealt with the officer on another case that she would have preferred forgetting.

The officer came into the room dressed in his official blue uniform—his gold badge glittering under the florescent lights overhead. He approached the bed and pulled out his tablet and e-pen to take notes.

"Sorry miss, I'm Sergeant Costas, from Boston PD," he said, not very warmly.

He was an older cop who'd been on the force for many years. Not yet balding, he had spots of gray that spoiled the pure black canvas of the rest of his hairline. He had a heavy girth—big and barrel chested—with rounded shoulders and thick arms. With his heavy, East Coast accent, he was Bostonian through and through. For him, it was just a job, and it was likely he knew to the day, hour and almost minute, the time left before his retirement.

"I've gotta' ask ya' a couple things if you don't mind," he began.

Claire only nodded. She knew she had little choice.

"What were ya' doin' in the alleyway beside yawr apaahtment at three in the mornin'?"

"I ... I really don't know, officer. All I remember is being in bed when someone came into my room."

"Someone came inta' your room? Did ya' see who it was or what they looked like?"

"No. The last thing I remember is being dragged out of my bedroom and into my living room. Then, I guess I blacked out," she said, still in a fog.

"Yawr neighbo's heard gun shots—do ya' own a gun, Miss Horwaaath?" he asked with his drawl.

"Yes. It's a Glock."

"Do ya' have a permit, Miss Horwaaath?"

"Yes."

"And you bought the gun legally?"

"Uh, well, I don't remember exactly how I ..." she began to explain.

"That might be a problem, seein' as ya' put three holes in the wall between you and yawr neighbo's apaaatment. Good thing no one was in the room next doa' to ya'. I'm afraid, I'm goin' to have to arrest ya' for illegal ownership of a fire-aaam and use of a fire-aaam, miss."

"Come on, officer," Clair answered, mildly protesting. "All I was trying to do was protect myself. Really. There was someone in my apartment. He or it attacked me! I was just defending myself!"

"We didn't see any evidence of someone breakin' into yawr apaaatment. So, yawr alibi is a bit flimsy. It's gonna' be up to a couwrt to decide," he replied, smugly. "But we'll wait 'til yu've recovered enough to stand trial. Good day, Miss, Horwaaath."

Claire watched in disgust as the officer started to leave her room.

"Excuse me, officer. If it wasn't someone who broke into my apartment, do you know how I got down in the alleyway?" she yelled at him as he left. "I don't remember, but surely you or one of your officers do."

"Don't know nothin' ma'am," he said curtly. "Perhaps you're mental?" He slammed the door shut behind him.

Now the pain seemed to grow worse, but she wasn't sure whether it was due to the police officer or the pain medication wearing off. She pushed the button on the drug-dispensing pad next to her and waited as the morphine flowed into her veins. Relief came quickly, effortlessly. But all the same, there she lay in a hospital room, wrapped up like Tutankhamen's mummy, not knowing what had happened to her and being interrogated by a could-care-less cop.

It's been a great couple of days, she thought.

*****

CH 9 - Mother & Son

2020

The detective on duty was Douglas Arthur Gallagher, or "Dag" for a nickname. As with his father and three generations before him, his name had been shortened to just three letters. His family had been in the police business for as long as anyone could remember. His great, great grandfather, Mag, had been at the precinct from 1913 to 1948 and police chief from 1933 to his retirement. His grandfather, Tag, had been a detective in the same precinct from 1939, just before WWII, to 1969—some thirty years—and had walked the same beat as Dag when he had first come to the force. Their family legacy was something of which they were very proud and something they would do just about anything to protect.

Like his paternal ancestors, Dag had coarse black hair, wiry and cut short. Under his bushy eyebrows were dark, chestnut-brown eyes, set close together, which made his oblong face look that much narrower. Yet, his smile was broad and welcoming when he was able to muster one.

Never having smoked a day in his life, his teeth were pearly white and even. He might have been mistaken for a movie star if he hadn't been so short and stocky. The other mark against stardom was his penchant for a Guinness draft which made his belly a bit more rotund than that of the average Beverly Hills VIP. In the same family mold, Dag was a rough-and-tumble New Englander with a face cracked from the cold Boston winters and hands like sandpaper— scratchy and raw as if he'd been a lobster trawler's son instead of a police brat.

Just as Tag had followed in his father, Mag's, footsteps, Tag's son Jag had come behind him, joining the force in 1961 during the Vietnam Conflict. The next in line, Zag, had entered the police force in 1983 in quick succession while his father was still active on the squad. Dag had continued the tradition of the family, graduating from the police academy in 2005 during the post-911 terrorist period. Policing had become more difficult after that, having to protect the citizenry against foreign agents as well as neighborhood thugs.

The blue blood of the family ran deep with respect to the chief of police position as well. Every Gallagher except Dag had held the position for some period of time. Zag's career and term as police chief had been cut short in early 2020 when he was found dead in a dark alleyway. He had pulled his service revolver but hadn't fired a shot during the attack. He was badly beaten—so badly, that he couldn't be immediately identified. It was only when they pulled his badge that they realized it was the police chief.

Dag had taken the death hard, as had the rest of his family. Zag had been a role model for him his entire life, and he had wanted to grow up just like him. Now, he would have to continue on, hoping he could live up to the high standards and, perhaps, one day becoming the police chief himself.

But to date, that standard had been something hard for Dag to live up to. His Grandfather Jag had been a real hero among the Boston elite and the political class. He had saved many lives in his day—political lives that is—and that's what had mattered most. He had been shrewd and politically savvy, which had enabled him to rise through the ranks and gain favor amongst those seated in the city's highest positions of power.

However, Dag hadn't been like his father, grandfather, great grandfather, or even his great, great grandfather in that respect. He had been more black-and-white; there had been little gray in his way of thinking. He stuck to principles—always doing what was right, even if it meant running afoul of those in power. Although he knew his family had used the system to get where it was, that position was something he refused to cow to. He was unlikely to cut a corner here or there to curry favor with anyone with money or prestige. As a result, the only reason he made it to the level of detective was because of his family name. In some ways, this made him bitter. In other ways, he was grateful. At least, he thought, his family could thank him for setting the right example and teaching them the value of honor and integrity.

At the same time, Dag was highly respected by the rank and file within the force, particularly by the beat cops in his own unit. He was known as the unwavering voice of rules and regulations. He was the conscience of the department. Sometimes annoying others who had their own agendas, he would persist with his point and opinion until he was heard. He just wanted his voice of reason to have its day—whether or not it was ever heeded.

53

As far as marriage went, Dag had tried and failed. He had a son, William Arthur, and a daughter, Theresa Maye, by his first wife. They had separated and then divorced when his career had taken precedent over everything else. His job consumed him, and his wife, while tolerant, finally gave up trying to compete. She had given him plenty of ultimatums, and he had promised to do better. However, he either wouldn't or couldn't, and time had run out on them. At last, Dag came home one morning after spending another night at the precinct and found his belongings out by the curb; his keys no longer fit inside the lock of the front door. For him, it was as if a sign in the front window had been posted in red neon: "No Vacancies."

***

Dag jogged up the stairs to the crime scene and ducked under the yellow tape. There were several cops just outside the entrance, and Dag recognized them immediately.

"Hey Al ... Manuel. What do ya' have for me?" Dag asked.

"It's ugly, boss," said Manuel. "I'm not sure you should be on this case, though."

"Why not?" Dag asked, chewing on a cherry-flavored succor.

"The bodies are mangled."

"Okay ..."

"You know. I just thought with your dad and all, ya' might not want to ..." began Manuel.

Dag nodded. "I appreciate the thought sergeant, but I'll be fine. It's my job, right? I have to deal with it, sooner or later, and it just happens to be sooner. That's all."

Dag went inside and looked at one of the bodies. It was sitting up in bed, two pillows stacked behind the head with the covers pulled up to its neck. The vic's eyes were wide open as was his mouth. It looked like he had seen something so terrifying it had stopped his heart. Dag later would have a term for it; he would call it *The Medusa Effect* after the mythological Gorgon monster with a hideous face and hair of snakes that Perseus killed for Athena. Just as Medusa's face turned men to stone, so too was the look on the victim's face— as if he had been petrified, turning to stone by looking at the same beast. Partially hidden behind the head—again the same phrase: *Hello Plottar.*

This was a strange homicide for Dag; sure, there was his dad's untimely death, but there were many homicides in the city of Boston and surrounding suburbs—more than thirty already that year. Usually, they were the result of a familial dispute, a store robbery, a drug deal gone bad or gang violence. However, these murders were committed inside a single home, in a good neighborhood, at night, and with no apparent motive. Worse yet was the state of the bodies.

"Other than the expression on his face, it doesn't look that bad," said Dag jokingly.

Al pulled back the bedcover.

"Whoa. How in the hell?" Dag began.

The policeman looked at him blankly and then shook his head in disbelief. "I don't know either," he answered.

"How could anyone do something like *this*?" asked Dag, pointing to the lower part of the bed.

The body below the victim's chest was gone. It had been severed cleanly and cauterized by something that had kept the body from bleeding-out. There was no sign of blood anywhere on the bed, around the bed, or under the bed—not a drop. Yet, the boy had died anyway.

"Where's the rest of the body?" asked Dag.

The policeman shrugged. "I don't see it anywhere, do you?

"Did you look under the bed?" Dag asked, although he wasn't being serious.

"Nope, not here," Manuel answered. "We actually looked. And we've looked everywhere else in the apartment."

"What about the other vic?" asked Dag, motioning toward the other bedroom.

"That body is about the same, I'm afraid—well, kind of," said Manuel.

"Huh? What do you mean, kind of?"

"You have to see it, detective. That's all I can tell you."

Dag followed Manuel into the second bedroom just down the hall. He walked in and this time saw a middle-aged woman sitting up in bed, just as her son had been.

"I don't see any difference," said Dag. "I assume her lower half is gone too?"

"Uh, yes and no," said Manuel.

Dag looked oddly at the sergeant and grabbed the covers as he had in the other room. As he turned back the sheets, he saw the lower half of the body, but it was on the other side of the bed. Like her son, she had been sawed cleanly in half, and again, there was no blood.

"Same Medusa look," said Dag. "Something scared the crap out of her. Probably the same thing that did it to the boy in the other room."

"What do you think, detective?"

"I think it's probably a mother and son," answered Dag. "That would account for the ages. Where's the father?"

"We don't know," said Al. "It doesn't look like he lives here. Perhaps they're divorced or separated or something."

"Okay, I need that information right away."

"He must have been a body builder or somethin' to do this," Manuel said, shaking his head.

"Even for someone like that ... I just don't know how they could do this. It's a question I have no answer for. But if you think of something else, let me know," Dag said. "Oh, you called-the coroner's office, right?"

"Yeah, they'll be here any minute."

"I want a full report on both bodies as soon as possible," said Dag. "Have the coroner call me when he's finished."

"Will do," said Manuel.

Dag put on his latex gloves and began examining the crime scene. He looked for anything amiss, anything that shouldn't be where it was and anything that wasn't where it should have been. It was far from an easy job, and it took someone with a keen eye to spot those things that would yield fruitful evidence.

Eventually, he got to the third bedroom, which was being used as a storage area. It was small, but had a simple, Mission-style desk; a tan, three-drawer filing cabinet, some wooden, Do-it-yourself bookshelves full of books, and a black, swivel chair made of vinyl. In between were still-sealed boxes stacked high and deep with stuff that appeared not to have been used for a while. The thick layer of dust on top was also a testament to that.

"Detective!" came a voice from one of the other officers down the hallway. "There's something here you may want to see."

Dag didn't recognize the voice but followed it back to the boy's bedroom. Lying in the corner, near the bed, was a metal trunk. It had curved aluminum plates across it and was graffitied to make it look old and weathered. The lock was broken, and the lid opened. The young officer kneeled beside it and pointed inside.

"I think it's stuff for Voodoo, sir," said the officer.

Dag looked inside and began pulling out a few things. There were long, black candles, a Ouija board, incense of various kinds, pentagrams of different shapes and sizes, and knives—many knives.

"*Hmm*," said Dag, examining the contents. "I don't see any dolls or pins like you'd see with Voodoo, but it does look like stuff they use in black magic. We'll have it boxed up and taken down to the precinct to get an expert opinion on it."

"Do you think this has anything to do with the murders?"

"I've seen a lot in my time on the force," said Dag, "so nothing would surprise me. However, if I were a betting man, I'd say no. I don't believe in that sort of stuff. It's just around to keep people occupied doing things they shouldn't be doing and giving them an excuse to do them."

Dag turned to the young man and extended his hand. "I don't think we've met. What's your name, officer?" asked Dag, impressed with the young man.

"Tommy. Tommy Walcott, sir."

"Good work, Tommy. I'm sure I'll be seeing more of you."

Dag walked down the stairs to his car, and after pulling together his thoughts, he called the office.

"Just finished at Brookline," he said. "I'm on my way back. Get me Chief Malloy …"

A few seconds later another voice answered. "This is Malloy," came the familiar greeting to which Dag was accustomed.

"Chief, it's Dag. I'd like to go over with you the homicide at Brookline. It just came in, and it's something that, well, it's something that you and the DA should know about right away."

"What's wrong?" asked the chief.

"Honestly, there's nothing *right* about it. But as for what's wrong— everything and nothing. We'll have to wait for the coroner's report for more answers, but right now it's something well above my pay grade."

"Stop in, and we'll chat. I've already gotten a quick briefing from Thompson who was first on the scene," said Malloy. "I'm more concerned about controlling the story than anything else right now. The last thing the mayor needs is for this to leak out."

Dag wrapped things up and went back to the police station where he found the stairs to the basement. Both the Evidence Room and Central Files & Storage were located there, and it was a familiar place for Dag. The two basement departments were separate, but both were managed by Nathan Ritter, a long-time employee of the city. He was responsible for checking things in and out and keeping the meticulous records necessary to ensure there were no mistakes that might screw-up a prosecutor's case in the courtroom.

"How ya' doin' Dag?" said Ritter, the keeper of the keys.

"It's been another one of those days, Ritter," said Dag. "Just when you think you've seen it all, something new pops up."

"Yeah? Well, I've been doin' this a lot longer than you have. I think I *have* seen just about everything, Dag. Some days I just want to retire and write my memoirs on all of it. Sad thing is ... nobody would believe me."

"You sound like Mack."

Ritter laughed. "Yeah, he and I talk often about how many hours we have left."

"Well, you certainly wouldn't believe what we saw today, I'm afraid."

"Try me," said Ritter.

"You'll see the file soon enough," Dag answered. "I wouldn't want to spoil it for you."

"Which file should I look for?"

"It'll be the Jenkins file."

"All right then. So, what are *you* lookin' for today?" Ritter asked.

"Didn't we have a case several years ago that involved twisted or dismembered bodies. I distinctly recall seeing pictures," asked Dag.

"Uh, yeah. It was the Roxbury case a few years back," said Ritter. "Is that what the Jenkins case is like?"

"Yeah."

"The Roxbury case was in 1995 or '96. I think. I seem to remember the name Jose Mercato?"

"The Mercato case. That's it," exclaimed Dag, the light bulb going off in his head. "Yeah, I knew you'd remember it. You know what I'm talkin' about now."

"Everyone knows that case, Dag. Are they still out at the Jenkins' crime scene?"

"They should be. You'll see everything when the file comes your way."

Ritter retrieved the Mercato case file and handed it to Dag after the proper paperwork was signed off. "But I think there were other ones too. I'd have to look," said Ritter.

"Would you do that?"

"Sure," said Ritter smiling, "and good luck with it. Let me know if you get anymore good ones. I'll need them for my autobiography."

The Mercato case of 1995 was still unsolved. It was old but not that old. Still, it had stymied the Boston police for decades. A particularly nasty murder, it had generated few leads and even fewer witnesses. What was most baffling was why anyone would kill a priest?

Jose Mercato had been a priest at the Holy Family Catholic Church in town. Extremely well-liked, he had been young and energetic, spreading joy and goodwill everywhere he went. However, he had met tragedy in his apartment, choosing to live outside the church grounds and the rectory. No one could understand what anger could have led someone to the violence that took place that night. The gruesomeness of the scene turned many stomachs, and since that day, no one had been able to solve it.

Dag leaned back in his swivel chair, bending it as far as he could without tipping over. He read the file front to back without a break. *How could this have been done?* he asked himself, taking out the photos from the old case. *It was bizarre how the body had been twisted like a pretzel.* It was haunting—and almost taunting—the way the body had been left.

What kind of force did it take to do that? he wondered. He was also having a hard time figuring out how it could have been done. *Someone with tremendous strength,* he thought. Both questions needed answers and were things he would have to follow-up on. He wrote himself a yellow, sticky note and put it on his computer monitor which read: Follow up with someone at MIT, referring to the elite technology college of the Massachusetts Institute of Technology where many of the finest brains went to school.

That night, Dag spent a few hours combing the Internet for something, anything, that might help him solve the two unusual crime scenes. *There were definite similarities, but how could they be linked to the same killer since they were committed more than twenty-five years apart?* he thought. *Who or whatever it was could cut or mangle a body in unspeakable ways using brute force and without the loss of blood? Who or whatever it was could do that over a span of twenty-five years and not lose their strength?* It was baffling.

Dag looked at dozens of websites, but nothing resembled what he'd seen at the crime scenes—nothing that could justify or explain how murders like those could be committed.

By now, it was late. He sighed and closed the browser. It would have to wait for another night when his eyelids weren't so heavy. He just hoped the next few days wouldn't bring a repeat performance by someone or something.

*****

CH 10 - The Third

1945

It wasn't long after the deaths of Janice and Dumitra Prodescu that another body was discovered. It too was badly disfigured, and pieces were twisted into a knot the likes of Gordian.

"Three in a matter of months," said Tag, shaking his head in disbelief. "Who's the vic this time?"

"They say his name is Rosco," said Mack, the coroner.

"Rosco Arthur?"

"I dunno. I don't have the complete name yet. Maybe. Why?"

Tag stood silent. He was in shock.

"Detective? Are you all right?"

Tag shook his head. "*Shit!*" he said finally. "I went to high school with 'im. He was a good guy ... came from a good family."

Tag had to kneel. He was feeling light-headed.

"Are you sure you're all right?" Mack asked, putting his hand on his shoulder.

Tag nodded, but he was far from all right. Rosco Arthur had been his best friend in high school, and the news was shocking.

"I'm not going to be able to work on this one. Chief will have to assign someone else. He'll understand."

"Do you want me to tell him, then?" asked the officer.

"No. I'd better do it," said Tag. "Dad will want to be involved in the case regardless of who it's reassigned to. He knows Rosco's mom and dad personally."

When Chief Gallagher, Mag, heard the news, he was devastated. He dreaded breaking it to the young man's parents, but he did so with as much compassion and empathy as possible.

True to the Tag's prediction, his dad wanted to be apprised of the investigation at every step. Unfortunately, like the other horrific murders, this one also came to a dead end. Stymied and frustrated, the Boston PD were soon out of answers. There were no motives, no methods, and no suspects. It didn't get much worse than that.

*****

CH 11 – A New Partner

2020

Dag sat at his desk reviewing the thick stack of police reports filed on murder cases in Boston during the previous twenty-five years. Ritter found several he thought might be of interest, but he didn't look farther back than 1995. There had been two cases that year although the body count had been three. Besides Mercato, there had been another that had matched the same MO. It had resulted in a double homicide.

Dag slid the thumb drive into his computer and loaded the pictures. They were graphic, and the photographer on the scene had taken more than three hundred of them. The pictures, the scene and all the evidence were baffling. In front of him lay photos of a victim, whose face showed signs of trauma from seeing something horrible: most likely his attacker. He had been alone in his apartment. His partner had been scheduled to go out of town on business for the weekend but had been forced to move the trip out one day. There had been fingerprints at the scene that hadn't matched those of the young man, his partner or any relative they'd been able to find. However, checking the prints against those of neighbors and friends hadn't resulted in a match either.

As Dag's mind drifted, and as he thought about the case, the phone rang.

"Yeah?" Dag answered. He listened momentarily and then said, "Send it over. I want to take a look myself."

A half-hour later, the courier arrived with a package. Usually, reports were emailed from office to office, but this source had insisted on hand-delivery of the package to the detective to get a physical signature rather than an electronic one.

After signing for it, Dag sliced open the tan envelope and let the contents fall onto his desk. Among the items was a blue folder with a tab marked *Case DOR89002-95*. He set aside the four other files and singled this one out to open.

"Coroner's Report" read the heading. The report was dated a week after the time they had discovered the bodies in Apartment 306. The

report continued, and Dag read through it all before coming to the summary findings.

Final Findings: *First victim is a middle-aged, Caucasian man. The body is found to have no signs of external wounds, cuts or lacerations. The left and right femoral heads and ischiofemoral tendons and cartilage are fractured, caused by severe force, as is the intervertebral disc between the 4th and 5th lumbar vertebrae—L4 and L5. The latter is totally fractured and fragmented, having been twisted 180 degrees or more from center.*

At the neck, the discs between the cervical vertebrae—C2 and C3—are both crushed as well. Both show the result of a tremendous torque force that separated the disc from the bone.

These ruptures were caused by the twisting of the torso along the vertical lines of the spine as well as the frontal chest being rotated to face the posterior of the body.

Rupture of the left pelvic vein caused massive hemorrhaging in the ...

The report continued, describing not just the first victim but also the second. The summary concluded that both had died when their spinal cords snapped and they bled-out internally. Had Dag not seen the pictures and witnessed the crime scene he was now charged with solving, he would not have believed it possible that someone could have put so much force on a body to sever bone, rip arteries, and all but tear the head from the neck.

Dag looked over the rest of the police file. There was no forced entry that they could find, and nothing seemed out of place with the apartment. Cited as unusual in the report was that there were two bodies, and that it appeared the two men were living together. Although much more acceptable by 2020, homosexuality was much less accepted when the murders took place in 1995. Especially in Boston, the old guard frowned upon it while the college youth didn't find much wrong with the lifestyle.

Dag combed through what evidence was in the file. He was persistent, and the fact it was a cold case like the others made it all the more important to him to find an answer. It was clear there was more to the murders than what met the eye. It was like a horror story torn from some old TV creep show. He half-expected Rod

Serling to walk into his office, telling him the plotline the show's writers had come up with for this episode of his life.

"Hey Dag!" It was Tommy, the officer he had met at the Jenkins' murder scene. "What are you doin'?"

Tommy was known for his laid-back style, wise-cracks and smart-ass attitude. He had no reverence for anyone and treated them as if they were all fresh out of the police academy, whether they were captains or rookies. Yet, there was a fun side to him as well. He had a quirky personality that people grew to love or to hate—there was no in-between. Unfortunately for Tommy, his last partner had learned to hate it. On the squad for twenty-six years, Sergeant Brady had finally had enough of Tommy and been glad to see him switched to someone else.

Still in his mid-twenties, Tommy was brash and thought he knew it all. Arrogance and narcissism were two quick traits that came to mind when describing him. He was handsome with dark wavy hair, a high forehead and square chin. Most striking were his large and brilliant blue eyes. He was also slim and muscular, addicted to his daily workouts in the gym and lifting weights. So, it was not surprising that he never had a problem getting dates whenever he wanted one. He thought of himself as *the* catch in Boston. Life was his oyster, and he was enjoying every minute of it.

"What am I doin'?" Dag repeated, not bothering to look up when Tommy came in. "I'm just—oh—workin'. What do you expect me to be doing? It's two in the afternoon, after all. Why aren't *you* working? You should be out on patrol?"

"Oh, you didn't hear?"

"Hear what?" Dag asked, finally raising his head.

"I'm your new partner. I passed my detective's exam."

"Hah! That's a good one. No really."

"No, really!" said Tommy, "I've been assigned to help you on the Jenkins case. They were a bit worried about you, given what happened to your dad and all earlier this year."

"I don't need a partner," said Dag.

"Well, you got one now."

Dag grimaced. "There must be some mistake."

"Nope. I'm your guy."

Dag picked up the phone on his desk.

"Hey, Chief, this is Dag. What's going on with the ..." Dag stopped and listened. "But Chief, I really don't need anyone helping me. I've got this." Dag kept quiet for another minute before finally saying. "I understand. Yes, boss. Okay."

Dag hung up.

"Well? Aren't you going to welcome me to your team?" Tommy asked, beaming.

"I ain't got a team," said Dag. "You can keep the passenger seat warm in the car and do some grunt work for me. These are *my* cases, and I call the shots on them. Do you understand?"

Dag was visibly angry. Finding out he had a partner from this newbie rather than through the chief was upsetting and demeaning. He felt he deserved better.

"Sure. Whatever you say," Tommy answered, shrugging and starting to walk away.

"Well, since you're now my assistant, you'll have to kick it into high gear. In detective work, you clock in for eight hours and work twenty-four—day-in and day-out. Are you up for that? Are you up for *real* work?"

"*Ewww!* That many hours?"

Ignoring the reaction, Dag said, "I want you to go down to the evidence room and talk to Ritter. There's a section of cold files down there. He's given me some that I need but see what else you can find on cases similar to the Jenkins one. You were at the scene; you know what to look for."

"Yeah, I just have to look for mangled bodies, right?"

"Pretty much," said Dag, thinking that was about the best he was going to get. "But talk to Ritter. He can help you." As Tommy walked away, Dag called to him. "Oh, and Tommy?"

"Yeah?"

"Look for cases that go back a long time too—say sixty or seventy years. But they all should be in the Boston area or near suburbs.

We'll start there. If we don't find anything, we'll expand the search to other cities. Got that?"

"Got any cases in mind?" Tommy asked.

"That's for you to figure out. You should come across them if you do a good enough case search."

Tommy gave a wink and pointed his finger like a gun at Dag. "Yep. I'm on it," he said, before disappearing out of the office.

It was the end of the day when Tommy returned carrying three files in his hands.

"This is what I came up with so far," he said, giving the thick folders to Dag. "The one on top is from 1948. Ritter said it was strange because it involved a murder out in a rural part of Boston at the time. They found the victim in a field, stripped to his undershorts but with burn marks all over his body. He'd been strangled. Nearby, there were remnants of a campfire. They thought it might be some ritual cult thing, but they never figured it out."

Dag took the file, looked at it and tossed to the side of his desk. "Next," he said flatly.

"The next one was from 1958," Tommy said, continuing. "That one was a double homicide in the basement of an apartment building. The door to the basement was locked from the inside, and the victims died from drinking muriatic acid—one used for cleaning stone. Suicide was ruled out after an investigation into their lives and talking to families and friends. All said they were doing well with no indication of any personal troubles. They also had no reason to have access to that kind of acid."

"Nope," said Dag, putting it in the same pile. "Next."

"And, finally, I have this one," said Tommy, handing over the last file. "This one is from Roxbury—from 1945. It involved a mangled body."

"Give me the Roxbury case. The others you can take back to cold storage."

"Why?"

"Were the other bodies mangled?"

"No, but ..."

"Didn't we agree on that?"

"Yes, but ..."

"Get me more like the Roxbury one," said Dag, turning away. He immediately opened the 1945 case file: ROX80982-45.

"Janice Prodescu," Dag began, reviewing the cover sheet. "Caucasian female aged twenty-five. Died in an apartment in Roxbury, Mass, June 3, 1945." Dag looked up. "You say the body was mangled?"

"Yeah, it goes on to say that Prodescu's body was found sitting on her sofa. Her head and the front of her torso were twisted one hundred eighty degrees from her legs. Her eyes and mouth were open as if she'd seen something that had frightened her." Then Tommy added, "Does that sound familiar?"

Dag thumped the eraser end of his pencil on the desk as if he had a nervous tick. "How could someone get in, kill her, and get out without any witnesses, and what kind of person has that kind of strength to twist a body?"

"Nobody I know," said Tommy. "Even the monsters at my gym who bench over three hundred couldn't do that. I'm sure of it."

Then Dag saw something else. "Here it says she was clutching a red lighter in her palm."

"That's it?"

"It says there may have been jewelry stolen too—a necklace, in particular."

"What did it look like?" asked Tommy.

"It says relatives claimed it was a short silver chain with rhinestones and a blue zircon. The zircon was at the center of a ... oh!"

"Oh what?"

"... the center of a pentacle. Isn't that like a pentagram? That's a pentagram encircled by a ring," said Dag.

"So, maybe the whole thing was a burglary to get that weird necklace. It sounds pretty expensive."

Dag looked at the young man in disbelief. "Expensive? Rhinestones and zircons are *not* expensive," he said.

"Oh. How am I supposed to know that!"

Dag thought for a moment. "You know. Let's check the evidence room and see if they ever found it."

"A pentagram ... then it was a cult thing," asked Tommy.

"Maybe. Go ask Ritter and see if he can find it. We need to take a look."

Dag glanced at the list of people who'd given testimony in the case all those years ago. It gave their names, addresses, phone numbers and the relationship they had with the victim. There were a couple of names he would have wanted to re-interview, but it had been so long he wasn't sure they would still be at the same address or phone number—or even alive. So, he picked up his cell phone and dialed the first one. Quickly, someone on the other end picked up.

"Hello?" a woman answered, her voice thin and raspy.

"Yes, Ms. Turner? Beatrice Turner?"

"No, that's my mother," said the woman. "Who is this?"

"This is Detective Gallagher from the Boston Police Department."

"Oh my!" exclaimed Terri. "Is there something wrong, officer?"

"No, no, ma'am. I'm just calling to see if I could ask her a few questions. It's about a case that happened a long time ago. It was a homicide in Roxbury—nearly seventy-five years ago, back in 1945. Do you ..."

"I'm Terri Campbell. I'm her daughter. That incident you're referring to—we don't speak about that in our family anymore. I'm sorry," said the woman abruptly. Her tone had instantly changed to one colder and more distant.

"Ma'am, I'm sure the memories are painful, but I'm tasked with looking into this cold case file."

"We've been through all this before. It's been a long time. I was young then; now, I just want to be left alone."

"I understand, but your mother was questioned in the case, wasn't she?"

There was quiet on the other end of the line.

"Terri?"

"Yes, I'm still here," she answered.

"Well? Can you help me?"

"It's been a long time since the murder. It was traumatic then and is still painful today."

"Then, will you talk to me about it?"

"If you want to talk to me about it, you'll have to come out and do it in person. I won't talk about it over the phone. They tell us older folks not to talk about money or things like this with strangers."

"I understand, and I will—come out, that is. I just need to go over a few things I spotted in the file—nothing that you should be worried about. They're just things I think would help us with solving the case." From the address, Dag knew it would be a lengthy drive. "Are you still at 182 Broad Street in Newcomb, New York?"

"Yes, I'm nearly eighty-one, and I've been here for forty-three years. I'm not movin' tomorrow, if that's what you're worried about."

"Okay, then. I'll stop by tomorrow at two o'clock. Would that be okay?" said Dag.

"I'll give you an hour," Terri said curtly, "but no more. It's been a long time, you know. You're not going to find out anything more than they did all those years ago. It's a waste of time."

"So, you'll see me tomorrow?"

"Two o'clock." Then, she hung up.

Dag shut the file and got out his keys. It would be a long, five-hour trip to Upstate New York. He just hoped it *would* be worth his time.

*****

CH 12 - End Around

2020

Tommy Walcott was bored. He'd been sitting in the cold case room for three days, going over more files. Yet, he hadn't found another one similar to the cases Dag and he were working. One case involved a dismembered body in Roxbury in 1920. The police had found pieces of arms and legs in several old, rusted drums out on a pier. Each had one part of the body; except the head, hands and feet were never found, so there was nothing to identify the person who'd been killed. There were scores of missing persons, but none could be matched to the physical attributes of the body parts.

Another case in 1945 told of a crazy sister who was accused of killing her brother in a fit of rage. The brother's body—at least the upper torso—was found in a pond some twenty miles from his apartment. However, there was never enough evidence to convict the woman who later died in a car accident thought to have been a suicide.

"Tommy, what have you found out?" asked Dag, stopping in to see what progress his new partner was making before he left for his Upstate New York meeting.

"Sorry. I ain't got nothin'. I've been in this stinkin' room for three days, and all I've found are a bunch of weird-ass cases to be sure—but none with mangled bodies."

"So, you don't have *anything*? Nothing at all? Nothing more than the one you gave me earlier?"

"Well, I just read about a case. It was in 1920, in Madison, I think. The murder was never solved."

"Madison?" Dag asked. "There are a lot of Madisons in the country."

"Wisconsin, Dag. Madison, Wisconsin. And there was another in Dade County in 1945. That's in Florida."

"I do know that," said Dag, defensively.

"Okay, but what I'm sayin' is none of them are in Boston."

"What are the case names?"

"I don't remember."

71

"Well, you need to get that information. It may be important. That's why we pay you the bucks, son! I want them on my desk when I get back later tonight."

"But you said just Boston."

"Changed my mind. Just get the information—call me when you have it," said Dag, leaving Tommy to fend for himself.

Tommy went to the basement to talk to Ritter again. He needed his help—especially now that he was supposed to find cases inside *and* outside of Boston and during such a long period of time. It seemed to be an Augean task.

Of medium build and dark complexion, Ritter had always kept a wad of chew tucked into his lower lip and a diet root beer can nearby to spit out his tobacco. His head was full of short, curly gray hair, and his forehead was just as full of many finely-etched creases—a sign of the stress he'd dealt with during his long career in the precinct.

"You say *what?*" Ritter asked as Tommy handed him a long list of case files he wanted pulled. "I don't have access to *all* these files! You'll have to contact Madison and Dade for ones from those municipalities. How the hell do you expect *me* to have 'em?"

Ritter could be cranky at times, and although he usually meant well, his recalcitrance sometimes got the better of him. He was only a few years from retirement, and he hoped to follow his father in retiring from the force after a long and rewarding period of service.

"All I know is that they're cold case files—*really* cold," said Tommy. "They were bizarre murders, though, and that's why Dag wants me to look them up—to see if there's any connection with the ones on the south side. Can't you just pull them up on your computer?"

"Do I look like a magician to you?"

"Come on, Ritter. Help me out here."

"All right," said Ritter, calming down. "Did you get the ones in Dorchester and Medford?" asked Ritter.

"Yeah," said Tommy, "the ones in 1995?"

"No, not those. The ones in *1945!*"

"1945? Oh, you mean the Roxbury case—Prodescu. Dag's got that one already."

"No, everyone knows about the '45 Roxbury case around here," said Ritter. "but I'm talkin' about the *other* two that were just like it." Then he added, "The ones in Dorchester and Medford were never solved either, you know—a mystery to this day." Shaking his head, he added, "In fact, I never thought I'd see the day when there'd be other ones like 'em 'till now. Those and maybe the ones my father handled and told me about."

"Other ones?"

"Yeah, I've been trying to find them. I don't remember the dates or names."

"So, you think all these murders are by the same killer?"

"The ones in 1945? Hell yes."

"The Jenkins case can't be connected to the ones in 1945. That's impossible. They're seventy-five years apart!"

"Seventy-five?"

"Yeah, from 1945 to 2020. That's seventy-five years," explained Tommy.

"Well, like I said, there were the ones in 1995 and then some others too," said Ritter.

"When did Dag start on the force? Wouldn't he know about those in '95 already?"

"Dag didn't start until ... well, I'd say it was about 2005. I came in 1980, and that was when Jag was our chief. Zag didn't join until about three years later, in 1983, I think."

"Why didn't I find those other cases when I was going through all the cold files down here?"

"I dunno," said Ritter. "It ain't because I can't file right, that's for sure. I *always* file right. It's the guys here that don't always bring stuff back when they should. They lose stuff."

"Maybe somebody doesn't *want* us to find them," said Tommy.

"What? I don't follow."

"Doesn't it seem strange that all the really weird cases—ones that haven't yet been solved—are missing from the evidence room?"

"Are you sayin' something? Are you accusing me of ...?"

73

"No! No! I'm not accusing anybody of anything ... yet," said Tommy.

Ritter crossed his arms, staring at the young, newly minted detective.

Seeing he was upset, Tommy backed off. "Okay, okay. I'm not accusing you either. I'm just trying to find the files."

"Not all the files are missing," said Ritter. "Just some of 'em."

"How can I find out who worked the cases?" asked Tommy.

"I can show you that," said Ritter, grudgingly.

He got up and flipped on his computer, entering his ID and password, and gaining direct access to the Records Department files. He clicked a few buttons here and there until he reached another level of security. After five quick keystrokes, he pressed the *Enter* key. The screen went black for a moment, and then came back with the picture of a manila folder and the words *COLD CASE FILES. X1B* was written on it in big, block letters. Ritter then entered more words into the search box and waited until six items popped up on a list.

Case No. ROX98331-95

Case No. DOR89002-95

Case No. DUD44902-95

Case No. WES89002-70

Case No. ROX20934-70

Case No. MIS85593-70

Ritter clicked on the first one, and more information came up immediately.

Summary: Case No. ROX98331-95

Incident: Homicide

Location: 3388 Crawford St., Roxbury, Mass.

Reporting Officer: Gallagher

Date/Time: June 11, 1995/0300

"This was Dag's case?" Tommy asked, confused.

"No, son. It was Z. A. Gallagher—Zag. That was his father."

"What about this one?" Tommy pointed to one in 1970.

Ritter clicked on it and up popped that data.

Summary: Case No. WES89002-70

Incident: Homicide

Location: 197 White Street, Brookline, Mass.

Reporting Officer: J.A. Gallagher

Date/Time: July 17, 1970/0310

A cold shiver went up Tommy's back, as if a demon had passed through his body. "And JA?" he asked, already knowing the answer.

"JA is Dag's grandfather. As I told you, they were all on the force at one time or another."

Tommy pulled out his cell phone and dialed. The number he punched-in rang five times, but no one seemed to answer.

"Pickup," he murmured. Getting no answer, he disconnected the call. "Damn it!"

"Who were you callin'?" asked Ritter.

"He wasn't there," Tommy answered, obliquely. "I'll have to call my backup."

"Who's that," asked Ritter.

"The Chief."

"The Chief? *Our* chief?"

"Well, he sure as hell ain't the head of the Apaches," Tommy said sarcastically.

*****

CH 13 - Road Trip

2020

The town was small, a population of just sixteen hundred. But it was a bucolic area, thick with pine trees, red fox and white-tail deer. The old, downtown area was just off the main, state highway and had a small, white sign that read simply: *Newcomb*.

Dag's GPS hadn't been updated in a few years, but it wouldn't have mattered; the county's Middlesex hadn't seen any significant changes in a couple hundred years except for the stringing of electrical wires and the paving of the main roads—formerly gravel—through town.

Once off the highway, he found the county road he needed and drove down the narrow, two lanes until his car caught a dip in the asphalt. Instantly, he heard the rough, grinding noise of the pavement against the undercarriage. Getting out of the car, he checked to be sure he hadn't ripped the muffler from its strapping. Seeing it was still intact, he drove another mile or so before spotting the Belzikov property—a two-story, farmhouse with white clapboard siding. The house was simple with moss-green shingles and a sky-blue front porch no more than three-by-four feet in area. The windows were old-fashioned double-hungs, and each held a yellowed and furled parchment shade with a small, white ring dangling from a cord in the center. It instantly reminded Dag of his grandfather Jag's house which had the same style of windows and blinds.

Dag pulled off the road and onto a long, white gravel drive that wound through some scrub trees and up to the residence. There were no other trees around—just farmland on both sides. That time of year, the oats should have been at least knee high, but the lack of rain had stunted their growth. Next to the house was a barn that had once been painted white but now revealed mostly what was left of the original gray primer. Standing tall, yet not-so-proudly, beside it, was a rusted windmill that had served a purpose long since abandoned or forgotten.

As soon as Dag stopped and got out of his car, a big, pointy-eared—and slightly overweight—German shepherd rounded the corner of the house, alternating between barking and panting. It was a hot day, and clouds of gnats darkened small patches of blue sky behind it.

Seeing the dog, Dag's first instinct was to reach for his nightstick, but he could tell the pet was more likely to beat him to death with his tail then sink his teeth into him. The black and gold animal trotted over, wagging his backside and waiting for the stranger to rub his head or his belly. Dag obliged, scratching him behind the ears and then smoothing the coarse hairs along his back. The dog just continued to swish his tail in total and utter bliss.

Going to the front door, Dag rang the lighted doorbell and waited. It wasn't long before a middle-aged woman came to the window next to the door and peered out, pulling back a small shade to see who was coming to visit. Moments later, she left the window and opened the door.

"Hello? May I help you?" she asked.

Her face was distinguished by her broad, appealing smile and perfectly white teeth. The woman's short, dark hair had whiffs of highlights and bangs that partly covered her olive-shaped, blue-green eyes. There was a unique sparkle about those eyes that Dag had never quite seen before—something enticing and alluring. He figured she looked like she was in her mid-to-late forties, but something told him she was a bit older.

"Hi, I'm Detective Gallagher with the Boston Police Department," he began, showing her his detective's badge. "I spoke with probably your mother or ..." He hesitated—a bit unsure how to address the apparent age difference. Then he just said, "I spoke with someone on the phone. I'm here to ask her a few questions about an incident that happened many years ago. Is it all right if I come in?"

"You say your name is what?" the woman asked, amiably, but a bit perplexed.

"Gallagher. Detective Gallagher. I'm sorry," said Dag. "I'm looking for Terri. Is she home?"

"Gallagher?" she answered, her eyes shining even more brightly. "Huh, well then. You'd be here to see my mother. She's the one who lives here. I'm just visiting her for the week. Why don't you come in?"

The woman held the door open for him. "Please have a seat. She'll be right with you." She then left through a narrow, arched doorway leading to the back of the house. "Mother! There's someone here to see you!" she yelled. "He says he's from Boston. He's a detective. His name's Gallagher, and he wants to talk to you."

At that moment, Dag heard the back, screened door creak open and then slam shut, bouncing twice before becoming silent. An older woman in her late seventies or eighties, came into the room, wiping her hands on a red-and-white checkered towel before running it across her sweaty forehead.

"I was just out back working the garden," she said, neither smiling nor frowning.

Dag grinned. "You must be Terri. Thank you for seeing me, ma'am," he said politely. "I won't take too much of your time." He pulled out his computer pad and used an electronic pen to scribble the date, time and place at the top, noting his interviewee's name in the upper left-hand corner.

The younger woman who was standing next to Terri looked very much like her. Both were small and thin-framed; each had broad smiles and white, pearly teeth—something God had given them as a hereditary gift. But instead of dark hair, Terri's was silver—short, but nicely quaffed into an elegant flip to the side of her head.

"Well, as I said on the phone, I only have an hour. So, please have a seat," Terri said with business-like efficiency. "It's about Aunt Janice, isn't it?"

Dag was stumped for a moment; he hadn't been aware of any family tie between them. Oddly, there had been nothing in the file about that.

"Uh, yes, it's about Janice Prodescu. I'm working the cold case," he said. "So, you're her niece?"

"No, not really, but my mother always called Janice her sister. She and my mother were very close friends. They were almost like sisters, you know. We all grew up in Boston, the same suburb anyway and the same neighborhood. But I've lived here for over forty-three years now. I had enough of the big city and moved with my husband after we got married."

"What can you tell me about your aunt?" Dag asked, scratching a few more notes on the page.

"Well, she died in 1945, but you already know that. It's been a long time. I don't remember everything like I used to—my memory just isn't that good these days, I'm afraid. I was about five at the time of her murder."

"I understand. It *has* been a long time, but I'm afraid it's important."

Dag started again, "To the best you can remember, what were the circumstances of her death? I'm sure your mother and others talked about it."

"I was told that I was with her the day she died. Mother and I went over there to see her and drop off some things—things mother had of hers since they'd been in high school together. Mother said Aunt Janice was in a good mood that day—that's what she said. They talked and laughed most of the time, I guess, telling stories of things that had happened to them when they were in school—that sort of thing."

Dag could tell there was a gradual thawing of her tone as she went on to describe the relationship they had with Janice. It was clear there was a closeness with the woman—one justifying why they called her "aunt."

It was then that the middle-aged woman came back into the room bringing a tray of white, porcelain cups with a matching teapot and a small, metal box of different flavored teabags.

"Care for tea?" she asked.

"No, I'm fine, thank you," said Dag politely.

"You've met my daughter Patti, I guess," said Terri as she took a cup for herself and tied a teabag to the handle.

"Hi! I'm Patti," the woman repeated. "Sorry, I didn't introduce myself earlier."

Terri lifted her cup, and her daughter filled it with hot, steamy water from the teapot.

Dag nodded and smiled at Terri before returning to the questioning. "So, you were saying, Ms. Campbell?" Dag prompted.

As Terri continued, telling the detective what she recalled of those days leading up to and following the murder, she unwound the dip string and began gently dunking the double-bag up and down inside the cup, letting the brown liquid swirl around inside. Her daughter took a cup too, and after getting her tea, walked to the arched doorway some distance from Dag. She stood pensively, sipping on her drink and listening to the two as they talked.

"I see," said Dag. "So, it came as a shock then, when you learned of Ms. Prodescu's death?"

"Oh, yes! It stunned us all—particularly my mother. She was devastated."

It was then that Patti stepped forward from the archway. She had a puzzled look on her face and asked, "Excuse me, but did you know a Zag Gallagher?"

"Why yes. He was my father."

Patti smiled.

"Did you know him?" Dag asked.

"I don't recall. We met at a party, I believe, but it was quite a while ago. I heard about him. I'm sorry for your loss," she said.

"Thanks," said Dag.

"But as far as Aunt Janice is concerned," said Terri, continuing, "she was living life to its fullest, and it was tragically cut short."

"I take it from the records that she was unmarried," said Dag.

Terri looked at Patti before saying, "As far as we know."

"As far as you know? I didn't see in the file that she had a husband."

"That's true, but she did have a daughter," said Terri.

"Oh, really? From a previous marriage, then?"

"No. Out of wedlock. As you can imagine, it was not something condoned or accepted back then," said Terri. "She was not held in high esteem in the community after that. She lost most of her friends and quickly became isolated from most."

"Yes, I can understand that. So, what happened to the daughter?"

"I wouldn't know," said Terri, quickly.

Dag glanced over at the wall where a pale blue sideboard sat as the center piece of the room. Hung in a neat row above it were different shapes of crosses—from the Greek and Latin versions to the Gothic, Byzantine, and Celtic styles.

"I can't help noticing your collection," Dag said looking at the wall. "You've got some unique pieces there."

"Yes, I collect them," said Terri. "I've got all sorts of crosses that I've accumulated over the years."

"She's one of those religious fanatics," said her daughter, interjecting. It was hard to tell whether she was joking or not, but that became clear an instant later.

"I am not!" said Terri emphatically, suddenly aroused to anger. "I *do* go to church though, unlike *others* in this family."

"Yeah, church, Bible study, retreats, you name it, and you go to it."

"There's nothing wrong with that," said Terri. "The good Lord has provided well for us, and it's okay to give Him thanks once in a while."

"Whatever," said Patti, rolling her eyes.

"Can you tell? She's my only daughter. I've got one son too. They're both married. They still live in the big city, like I used to. She's certainly never been a country girl and certainly not religious—as you can tell."

"*Hell* no!" said Patti, smiling mischievously. "Life's what it is—nothing more and nothing less. You can pray all you want, Mother. There's no God to hear you."

"I just wish you'd change your mind like I did," said Terri, getting more annoyed. "It's as if you deliberately go out of your way to irritate me."

"God damned, right. I do."

"That's blasphemy, dear. Pure blasphemy," said her mother, shaking her head and sighing.

"It's called being modern, Mother. Being 'with it.' I choose to live in the present, not the past or the future. I don't want to live my life chained to the ancient ways of your generation. I'm going to embrace those of this one."

"Whatever," retorted Terri, rolling her eyes. "But there is still something of mine you do love that goes back generations ..."

"What's that?" asked Patti.

"You still love my vanilla custard," said Terri with a wink. "You drive me nuts most of the time, but I still love ya'."

It was an odd relationship, thought Dag, *One minute stormy, the next minute loving?*

Then, something connected with Dag. "That one cross on your wall—third one from the left—is very much like the one noted in the case file for ..."

"Yes," said Terri, cutting him off. "It *was* like my Aunt Janice's. She really liked it. The two found them in Peabody's Jewelers in town and got them at the same time."

"I've not seen a cross with a pentacle in the middle of it before," said Dag.

The cross was very unusual in that it mixed Christianity with mysticism and Judaism. Dag remembered the notation in the case file that Janice had one her family thought had been stolen the night of her death. Nothing had been mentioned about the cross design, but it was Celtic with very short points extending from the center. Dag also noticed something else: that although Terri had a traditional gold, cross necklace around her neck, Patti was wearing one with only the pentagram.

"I see that you wear something different from your mother's," Dag said to Patti.

"That's her pagan symbol," said Terri, with some disgust. "This is mine."

"Yet the one like Ms. Prodescue's had both," added Dag.

"Yeah," said Patti, "So, it's just like yours, Mother."

"No, it's not! Not at all!" Terri answered.

"You have a pentagram in the middle of yours just like I do," said Patti.

"Mine's a Celtic cross. It's a *cross.* Yours ... yours is a pentagram—pure and simple. There's no cross—there's no Christ—there's no ..."

"There's no bullshit," said Patti, finishing the sentence on her own terms. "I don't need your faith's bullshit, mother. No one does."

Patti pulled out the black-corded necklace from under her crew-neck top. The necklace was a single string with a silver pendant at the bottom. It was small, but recognizable—a pentagram.

"It was Grandma Bessie's," said Patti. "She gave it to me."

Dag didn't say a word, fearing he would only cause more unrest than he already had. Instead, he pressed on with his questions for Terri.

"Would you say your aunt was religious?" Dag asked Terri.

"Yes, quite. She always went to church and to confessional."

"Yeah, but she only did that because she felt guilty," said Patti, interrupting.

"What do you mean?" asked Dag.

"She was well known as a psychic—you know, she communicated with the dead," said Terri.

"Yeah, that and other things," said Patti laughing. "She had a lot of *skeletons* in her closet, you might say." She was very amused with her own play on words.

"Patti!"

"Yes, she was, mother! You've never wanted to admit it, but it's true. You know it's true!"

"She was a Christian woman! She was a believer!"

"Well, she was also a medium, like grandma, and a tramp. She'd do anything to make a buck and to get what she wanted."

"She quit doing that after she got religion," Terri said emotionally.

"Yeah, and after she had the kid," said Patti.

"The police report didn't say anything about a child," Dag said again.

Patti shrugged. "Makes no difference," she said, "whether she did or didn't. It all gets 'cleansed' in the end."

Dag wasn't sure what she meant by that but wanted to get back to his questioning.

"Do you know if your mother talked about any séance customers she had problems with? Any that would have wanted to do her harm?"

"It was so long ago, I don't remember, detective," said Terri. She looked tired, and Dag knew the session was exhausting her.

"Okay. Well, I think I have all I need right now, Ms. Campbell" said Dag. He pulled out two cards and handed one to each of the ladies. "If either of you think of anything, please give me a call."

"I changed my name back to my maiden name after my divorce," said Terri. "It's been Belzikov for a long time now."

Dag started to leave, when he turned back toward Terri.

"I'm sorry, one more thing I forgot to ask. I was wondering when your mother passed. Bessie? She was the other witness with you who saw Janice that day."

"Passed?" asked Terri. "What do you mean?"

"Well, she would have been in her twenties or thirties at the time of the murder. That was seventy-five years ago, so I just ..."

"Mom is in a nursing home in Boston. We were just there yesterday visiting with her," said Terri. "She'll be one hundred and one next month. Still as sharp as a tack, she is."

"I'm sorry. I just assumed. That's great—wonderful that she's lived such a long life." Dag was stumbling all over himself trying to make amends for his *faux pas* but only making things worse.

He left the house with more questions than answers. The only thing he knew for sure was that he had to look more closely at Janice's psychic business and any clients she had who may have wanted her dead. That was about the only lead he'd gotten, and he had many hours to think about it as he drove back to Boston.

*****

CH 14 - Psychic to the Rescue

2020

Mitzie Wilkins read the paper. It was her favorite pastime. Typically, she would go straight to the obituaries, or *obits* as she called them, and work her way toward the pages that held the crime stories. She relished the time when she could read about someone's untimely death, especially if it were bizarre and gruesome. Best of all were those with close, but older, relatives. To her, these family members often provided entertaining insights into the lives and livelihoods of the ones who had died.

The last few months had been a bonanza for Mitzie. She had seen stories about strange, macabre deaths and had been particularly taken by the murders in Dorchester. The news articles about the crimes hadn't contained much detail, but they had been enough to spark her interest. One piece merely stated that the deaths were "abnormal," citing that the bodies were found in positions that "contradicted the natural state of a human being." Other sources described the bodies as contorted and twisted, while still others mentioned that the coroner's office was baffled by it all. As time went on, the murders disappeared from the headlines. It seemed that the police had nothing to go on, and they were becoming desperate.

But the unusual events hadn't ended there. The papers also reported a woman who was found in an alley after having been thrown out her second-floor window. The story claimed she fired her gun at some phantom intruder but hit nothing. She didn't remember much and certainly didn't recall how she had gotten thrown out the window. This one, like the others, the paper said, remained unsolved, and no suspects were in custody.

Born with the name Maria, Mitzie had a colorful and storied past herself. She had been in prison for a short time, swindling people out of their money while running a psychic and fortune telling business illegally out of her home. It was a small establishment with a blue neon sign out front that read *Fortunes and Readings by Madam Mitzie*. She was arrested after one of her patrons turned her in, having spent over ten thousand dollars on private sessions. The gig was blown when one of her fog machines in the back room malfunctioned sending real smoke into the séance room and forcing everyone out of the building. However, at that time she had only been charged with running a business without a license. It was later that she spent twelve months in jail for defrauding her clients. She also had to repay them the money she'd taken.

Ironically, Mitzie claimed the arrest and jail time had changed her life, vowing to work with police to find and expose the charlatans of her industry. She swore not to let anyone else get swindled as she had done to others. She had "gotten religion" turning into a self-prescribed "Born-Yet-Again-Christian."

"I'm here to see Sergeant Peterson," Mitzie said approaching the bullet-proof reception area at Police Station No. 583 on the south side of Boston.

Overweight with a double-chin and other rolls of fat around her neck and ears, the uniformed-officer was not happy with being assigned the menial job of the front desk. Yet somehow she managed the exhaustive feat of raising her listless eyes to meet those of the visitor. "Yes?" she said flatly, her mouth downturned and sulky.

"I said, I'm here to see Sergeant Peterson," Mitzie said again, this time a little louder. She controlled her impatience by smiling as though she had all the time in the world.

The police officer looked at her roster and glanced back at the woman. "He's not in," she said gruffly, going back to her magazine.

"When do you expect him?" Mitzie asked.

"Dunno. Could be ten minutes; could be midnight. Could even be next month. Dunno."

Mitzie sighed, knowing better than to get into an argument with a police officer.

"Well, would you give him a message that Mitzie Wilkins stopped by. I have some information on the murders that happened last month—you know, the ones in Dorchester."

Dag was passing by the front desk when he overheard the visitor's message. He stopped and peered over the desk officer's shoulder. Seeing the odd-looking woman standing in front of the bulletproof window, he smiled. It was a face he recognized, and one that he often saw come into the station to meet with officer Peterson.

"Yeah, yeah, fine," said the front desk officer. "I'll give him the message." But she didn't move finger to write anything down, only dismissing the woman out-of-hand.

Dag leaned over the officer and interjected, speaking directly into the microphone that bridged the protective divider. "Excuse me for interrupting, but who are you looking for?"

"Sergeant Peterson. I have information on the murders of the woman and young man that happened in Dorchester about three months ago."

"Yes, yes," said Dag, his interest piqued. "Why don't you come in and talk with me. I'm the detective on the case."

The desk officer shook her head and leaned toward the detective, putting her hand to the side of her mouth so the woman outside couldn't hear.

"She's loony, detective. She comes in every once in a while telling us that she has some critical piece of information that will solve one of our cases. She says she's a psychic or something. I wouldn't waste your time."

"Maybe she just wants to help us out," said Dag, giving the benefit of the doubt.

"She's a nut case if you ask me," answered the woman police officer. "She's a fraud."

"Let me talk to her just for a minute. What you say might be true, but it won't take me long to figure that out."

"Okay. It's your time, not mine," said the officer.

The officer buzzed Mitzie through the front door, where Dag motioned for her to come back with him to an interview room. He grinned as she entered and pulled out a chair for her. After she sat, he took an opposing chair at the opposite end of the short, rectangular table.

Mitzie was very short, not over four feet eleven, even though she always claimed she was five feet two inches tall which was probably true too as she wore three-inch heels. This day, she fashioned a long, colorful gown that fell below her knees. It resembled a *salwar kameez* from India and was gayly decorated, rich in hues of tangerine orange, sky blue and various shades of yellow. However, she was not Indian; rather, she was light-complexioned with dark brown hair and eyes, a long, narrow nose, and makeup that was slightly overdone for the time of day. Although about forty, she looked younger—possibly even in her early thirties—with high energy and a youthful exuberance. Dynamic and garrulous, she projected her charisma easily—just as she had when captivating her clients in her fortune-telling parlor those years earlier.

"So, what do you know about the case?" Dag asked her, placing his arms on the table and folding his hands. He looked at her sternly, hoping that would break through any pretenses and make her nervous enough to make contradicting statements and reveal any intended deception. He had been admonished already but now wanted to find out for himself whether to spend much, if any, time on this person. He was, as the papers stated, desperate for a lead.

"How long do you have?" she began.

"Five minutes—that's it," Dag said curtly. "So, we need to be quick about this. It may be your only chance to convince us that you have something of value to offer."

"That's a bit harsh," she said, taken aback by his brashness.

"Listen, ma'am. We get people in here every day who say they know things about this or that, and they don't. They're just bored with their lives and want to fill in the day. If we spent an hour of our time with each of them, we wouldn't have time left to solve a single case. So, if you don't mind, tell me what you think you know, or we'll just have to move you along. Okay?"

Mitzie scowled at Dag. "I'm not one of *them!*" she exclaimed.

"We'll then you'll have to prove that to me, and you've got about four and a half minutes left to do that," said Dag looking at his watch.

"Fine. Then this is what I know. You be the judge of whether it's worth anything to you."

Dag stared at the woman and looked at his watch again.

"Okay, okay," she sputtered. "I have dreams about cases—murders. Sometimes I can't connect them to anything in the papers; sometimes I can. This one I had was particularly creepy. In it, there was a figure standing over a woman's body holding a rope. I guess he used that to kill her."

"Ma' am, we have about ten murder investigations right now involving strangulation. Is there anything new that you'd like to share with me?"

"Well, the figure really isn't a person, you see."

"What is it, then?"

"I'm not sure."

Dag laughed and started to get up. "Okay, I think your time is up."

"No, listen to me," said Mitzie. "I think it's an energy or something. It's a black force of some kind. The phantom that killed that mother and her son also tried to kill the woman that got thrown out of her window—the one they found in the alley."

"You're telling me it's a phantom—a ghost—that killed these two people?"

Mitzie leaned forward, rolling her eyes in an unsettling way. "I think it's the work of a psychic, serial killer."

"A psychic, serial killer, ma'am?"

"Yes, that's what I said—a psychic, serial killer, detective."

"Have you been watching a lot of horror movies lately? There have been a rash of serial killer movies on late-night TV during the past few weeks."

"*No!* These were strange, bizarre killings, weren't they?" she continued.

"You tell me. It was your dream."

"Okay, then in my dream, the phantom had a dagger. It looked like one of those ancient, Persian sabre swords. It gleamed, wet with blood dripping from its blade."

"Okay, I think I've heard enough," said Dag, finally getting up and going to the door. "It was nice to chat with you, miss. I think we can handle things from here."

Once she mentioned the blood-drenched knife, Dag knew she was what the front desk officer had described—your typical loon. There hadn't been any blood at the scene of the double murder. In fact, that was what was so odd about it.

"But I can tell you who did it. I'm sure I can!" she said defensively.

"Okay, then. Who did it? Was it Colonel Mustard in the kitchen with the knife or was it Mrs. Peacock in the ballroom with the candlestick?" asked Dag, calling her bluff.

Mitzie smiled slightly. "You'll just have to trust me to get you the information you want. But how can I be sure that I can trust you?"

Her affect was unsettling. She seemed unhinged, but there was something else there Dag couldn't put his finger on. He wondered if it were even safe for her to be out on the streets. Yet, at that point, the only thing he was sure of and could do something about was ending the session and escorting her out the front door.

"Listen, lady. You're the one who came in here telling us you solved the case—that you know who the murderer is. However, you're not willing to—or can't—give me anything to go on. I'm afraid there's nothing more I can do."

Mitzie got up and walked to the door.

"Just in case something else comes up or you change your mind and want to talk," she said, handing Dag a white card. "I know I'll continue to have these visions, but it's up to you to contact me about them. I won't bother you again."

Mitzie let herself out, asking the front desk attendant to buzz her through. She was overtly upset and much put-out by Dag's treatment.

Dag looked down at the card,

Mitzie Wilkins

Psychic

"My Mission is Only to Help Others

555-904-8093

That's got to be the strangest meeting I've ever had, he thought. *I'll let Peterson handle her going forward.*

Dag stuffed the card into his front pocket, determined to throw it away later when he had the chance. Right now, he had more important work to do, and it involved the very same case—the double homicide in Dorchester.

***

It was late morning when Tommy Walcott opened the door to Dag's office.

"Hey, Dag. Any progress on that Dorchester case? Word has it that you had a visitor this morning who had all the answers for us." Tommy was grinning, already knowing the answer.

"Very funny. Actually, no," Dag replied. "How many cases have you cracked today?"

"I'm not a seasoned detective, detective. If I were, I'd have your job," answered Tommy unabashedly. "But I do have a message for you. Chief wants you in his office—says it's important."

"What's it about?" Dag asked, raising his eyebrows.

"How should I know. You think he tells me everything?" Tommy shot back. "But maybe once I'm at your pay-grade, I'll understand those kinds of high-level things." He laughed.

The demeanor on Dag's face changed quickly as his eyes peered beyond Tommy. He cleared his throat and grinned. "And you were saying what about the chief, Tommy?" said Dag.

"Uh, as I said ...," Tommy said again before stopping, "... oh, why? Is he right behind me?"

Tommy turned around. Sure enough, the chief was standing behind him, and Tommy was just in time to see his mock-scowl of a face.

Dag sat laughing, and the chief chuckled too.

"As you were, Tommy," said Chief Malloy. "I just need a moment with the detective here."

Tommy left, allowing the chief to come in and close the door behind him. Generally, the chief left Dag alone with his casework. Although sometimes overzealous, Dag was about as good as they got when it came to investigative work, and the chief relied on him a lot. He didn't need prompting or direction; he just got the job done. So, it was unusual when the chief came calling.

"Dag, we need to talk." The chief was stern and direct.

Walking to the inside window of the office, the chief twisted the cord on the blinds, closing off all contact with the outside world before taking a seat on the opposite side of the desk.

"What is it chief? You look serious."

"I am, Dag. The DA is all over my ass about the murders in Dorchester. He's afraid more of the facts may get out, making the department look bad. He thinks it's going to be a hard case to crack, and based on what I've seen, I agree with him. Boston has seen gruesome murders like this before, and he's concerned that you don't ... well ..."

"Just say it, boss."

"He doesn't think you're the man for the job, Dag. I think he's wrong—no, I *know* he's wrong. I've known you a long time. He hasn't. He's new to his job—what can I say."

"He's just got a problem with us Gallaghers, is that it?"

"No, I don't think that's it at all. He read through the crime reports and is worried."

"About what, the mayor's re-election?"

The chief frowned. "Let's just say the chief is concerned about how it might look out in the public eye. You know how the media twists things. It wouldn't look good for any of us if we can't get it solved quickly."

"Have I ever let you down before, chief?"

"No, Dag. But I do agree with the mayor on one thing—these are very strange cases. If the details ever get out into the public, there may be hysteria. So, let's be proactive and get ahead of the ax instead of waiting for it to fall on our heads. Shall we?"

"Is that it?"

The chief sat back in his chair. "Dag, I'm worried about you too. Your father just died a few months ago and we all know how you looked up to him. It had to have come as a shock, and I'm not sure you're over it."

"I'm fine," said Dag.

"Maybe. But I think you're just trying to hide your feelings." The chief shifted in his chair. "That's why I'm concerned about you on these cases. I think they're too much like what happened to your father, and I'm not sure you can see them clearly."

"I can, chief. I can do my job. I'll solve these murders."

"Well, the DA and I will be keeping a close eye on what's going on. Don't be upset if I check in regularly to see the progress."

"My work isn't suffering. I assure you," said Dag.

"I don't know if it is or not. That's why these cases need to get solved quickly. Personally, I think you should have taken more time off after your father's passing."

"I couldn't. There were too many cases to ..."

"Dag, there will always be cases to solve. You and I both know that. That will never change, unfortunately."

Dag sat solemnly. He knew the chief was right.

"Okay, chief. I'll work a little harder."

"You've got Tommy to help you now. He can do some of the low-level work to ease the burden a little." The chief leaned in and put his folded hands on Dag's desk. "I don't want you working harder, Dag. I just want you to realize when you're overwhelmed and seek help."

"Thanks," said Dag, less than enthusiastically.

"Speaking of Tommy, he mentioned a few things."

"Like what?"

"Like the fact that you have a streak in your family when it comes to strange murder cases."

"What do you mean, chief?" asked Dag.

"He showed me the list of notorious murders in Boston over the last century. Your family's name comes up pretty often in the investigations."

"Of course," Dag answered. "Our family has been a big part of this department for nearly a century. Are you saying that somehow we've been involved in these murders?"

Dag was noticeably upset by the insinuation and even more so that his partner had gone around him and directly to the chief about it.

"He only showed me there was a connection, that's all. Don't take it out on the kid. He's young. He's learning."

"Yeah, it sounds like he's learning a few other things too—a little too quickly, if you ask me," said Dag.

"Well, use him. He'll be a good resource to help you get this solved fast." The chief got up to leave. "You should start using the CSI team too. The one here in Boston—CS-1—is about as good as it gets. But whatever you do, get this thing solved!"

CS-1 was one of the forensics teams with the Massachusetts state police and the one dedicated to the Boston area. The CSI teams had special funding and used highly technical laboratories—the most sophisticated of which was in Boston. There were several teams, but CS-1 was the best. It was usually assigned to cold case files and other extremely hard-to-solve cases. That part was good news. What concerned Dag was the part Tommy had played in all of it. The last thing he needed now was an overly ambitious, young man who had a reputation of throwing his partners under the bus. Even though Dag appreciated his intelligence and his insights, his partner was obviously a smartass at best or an obsessive self-promoter at worst.

"Yes, sir," Dag said, as the chief left, closing the door behind him. *Crap!* he thought. *Now what the hell am I supposed to do?*

Dag hurried down the hall, hoping to avoid getting questioned about why the chief was in his office. Usually, someone coming out of the chief's office or the chief coming out of their office got cornered and interrogated by other detectives at the precinct. Everyone wanted to "be in the know."

But Dag wasn't in a sharing mood and he picked up his pace. He rounded the corner by the coffee station and started to push on the men's room door when he heard, "Hey, Dag. How did it go in there?"

Dag stopped. He was cornered. He twisted his head and smiled disingenuously. "What?" he answered.

"How did it go in there ... with the chief?" It was Tommy who had obviously been waiting to ambush him. Even with the earnest look on his face, Dag could tell he was being fake.

"Fine. No problems," Dag answered. "But it sounds like the chief may have some news for *you*. You should stop by his office."

Earnestness changed to puzzlement as Tommy took in what Dag had said. "Right now?" he responded.

"Why not? Now is as good of time as any."

Dag knew the chief didn't have anything to tell Tommy, and he smiled, knowing he'd given Tommy the same dose of *agita* he'd given him.

*****

CH 15 – Mitzie's Call

2020

It was early in the morning when Sara sat down to her plain bagel, lightly toasted with strawberry cream cheese. The coffee was only instant, but it was black and hot—as good as she could manage after helping her daughter off to high school and her husband off to work. Finally, she had a few hours to herself before her first appointment. Although she had sworn off any more meetings—especially after the last one—Marvin had convinced her to continue on. *What's life without a few challenges?* Marvin had told her.

Sitting at the kitchen table, Sara closed her eyes, letting her mind drift. She relished the quiet time so she could relax and recharge her batteries. Then, after fifteen minutes or so, she forced herself to get up, thinking of all the things she needed to do that day. *"Time's a wastin'"* her mother had always told her. It was something that had stuck.

She sat up and pulled out her tablet computer, calling up her favorite news site to see what was happening in town and around the world. She glanced at the middle section, just above an advertisement for a new Taurus at Blossum's Ford in town, and there an article caught her attention:

Woman Lives After Falling from Third Floor Apartment

At first, it seemed like the same old news story just repackaged to seem fresh and relevant, as if everyone knew someone who jumped out a window. However, this one was different.

.... and the Boston police department is assisting with the case because of its unusual nature. The department spokesperson said that the victim, a fifty-three-year-old woman who lives at the Wayside Apartment Complex in Brookline was found in an alley just outside her apartment building very early this morning.

Sara's heart rate jumped, and she pressed on to read more.

The victim apparently jumped from her apartment window at approximately 3 AM, falling two floors to the alleyway below. She suffered some broken bones and is being treated at Faulkner Hospital.

> *What is unusual about the case is the victim claims she has no recollection of how it happened. Police don't believe there was foul play involved and attribute her memory loss to the fall. Someone close to the investigation said there were shots fired inside the apartment, but the police would not comment further. No charges have been filed at this time.*

Sara picked up her cell phone and dialed Claire's number, but she got no answer. Then, she looked up the number for the hospital. Just as the line started to ring, her phone vibrated, telling her someone was trying to reach her at the same time.

"Hello?" she answered.

"Yes, Miss Prodescu?"

"Uh, no. This is Sara McLaughlin. Who is this?"

"This is Mitzie Wilkins. You don't know me, but I was wondering if we could meet?"

"I'm sorry, but I really don't know who I'm speaking to. What is the purpose of your call?"

Sara was direct and firm. She was impatient with solicitation callers and usually just hung up on them within a few seconds.

"Well, as it turns out, your great grandmother and mine were close friends. In fact, they went to the same high school together here in Boston. They both graduated in 1937. I believe they were only two of twenty-five in their graduating class."

Sara recalled her grandmother talking about how small her mother's class was, but she didn't think the dates quite matched.

"I'm afraid I'm really booked up today ... this week. Perhaps some other time," Sara said dismissively.

"But it's important that we meet," said the voice, now more urgently. "I have other information you might find interesting," said Mitzie.

"Why should any information about my great grandmother be of interest?"

"I just thought your family and its history would mean something to you. Typically, people like to know more about their heritage and where they came from."

"I'm sorry, I'm not one of them," said Sara.

"All right, but I'm afraid later in life you will wish you had met with me."

"Which high school did they both attend?" asked Sara, challenging the caller.

"They went to Boston English High School. I'm pretty sure," said Mitzie.

Sara paused. "Well, my great grandma did go to that high school, but she didn't graduate in 1937. She graduated in 1938."

"Oh, you're right. I guess I'm remembering it wrong. My great grandmother's name was Beatrice Belzikov, but they all called her Bessie."

That name was familiar to Sara too. Her mother had even mentioned it once or twice, although usually not in a favorable way.

"Yes, Bessie. I do remember something about that," said Sara. "They *were* high school friends, now that you mention it. That was a long time ago. My great grandma's been dead for, well, about seventy-five years. Is your great grandmother still living?"

"Heck yes. Bessie's still alive. She'll be a hundred soon," proclaimed Mitzie.

"No! Really! That's amazing! I can't imagine ..."

"Yep. Great grandmother is still kickin'. Her memory is as sharp as ever too even though her body is starting to give out. She's at a nursing home here in Boston. I go see her once a week or so."

"Well, it's been nice talking to you. And your name again was?"

"Mitzie. Mitzie Wilkins."

"Of course," Sara answered.

"But, since we have a common bond of our great grandmothers, I thought we could at least meet each other. What's the harm in that, right?"

"Fine, I can do it in ... let's see ... two weeks. I have the twenty-fifth open."

"I'd really like to meet before then. I'm going out of the country on business and won't be back for a few months."

"Perhaps we should get together when you get back, then," said Sara, still trying to get out of the meeting.

"What about next week? Anytime. I'll open my schedule. You name the time and place," said Mitzie.

Sara groaned. She knew this woman would not go away easily, and it was probably better just to get it over with.

"Well, I may be able to reschedule something on the seventeenth. I can meet you at two thirty. I'll call you or send you a message about the place. I'm not sure where I'm going to be that afternoon."

"Tell you what," said Mitzie. "Let's make it twelve thirty, and I'll buy lunch. That's the least I can do." But before Sara could reply, Mitzie added abruptly, "Oh, I've got another call coming in. I'll see you at twelve thirty on the seventeenth. Thanks again," and she hung up.

That was strange, thought Sara. *Someone calls me like that and then expects me to drop everything to meet with her? We'll see. Maybe if I just let this go, she'll forget.* Then she thought again. *She's a determined one, who usually gets her way. So, that probably won't work either.*

Nonetheless, Sara decided she would wait and see, hoping the whole matter would just go away.

Unfortunately, it did not.

***

Mitzie hung up the phone and dialed another number.

"Hello, yes, this is Mitzie Horwath, Claire Horwath's sister," she said, lying. "Is she still in intensive care? ... Oh, yes, I see. Well, I'd like to come down and see her this afternoon ... Uh, huh, so visiting hours are from two to four thirty. That would be great. Thank you so much."

Mitzie hopped in her car and drove to the hospital. After signing in at the front desk as Mitzie Horwath, she was directed to the third floor where non-critical patients were convalescing and awaiting discharge orders from their doctors.

"Excuse me. Could you tell me where Claire Horwath's room is?" Mitzie asked a nurse at the central station on the floor.

"Oh, she's in Room 3112," answered a nurse, not needing to look up the number. "Just down the hall and to your left."

99

"Thank you so much," Mitzie answered as sweetly as she could feign.

Once she found the room, the door opened on its own, and she entered carrying a plastic-wrapped bouquet of fresh yellow tulips that she'd picked up on the way to the hospital.

"Claire. How are you?" she asked, moving toward the bed. "I'm Mitzie Wilkins, I'm a friend of the family, and I heard that you were injured last night."

"I'm afraid I don't know any Mitzie Wilkins," Claire answered, sitting up straighter in her bed. "How did you get in the room?"

Mitzie smiled and then found a spare plastic pitcher. She stripped the plastic wrap from the flowers and stuffed them inside after pouring some fresh water for them. Then, she casually plopped them on the windowsill, not bothering to tidy-up their haphazard arrangement.

"The nurse said it was okay to come in and see you. How are you feeling?" Mitzie asked.

"I'm ... well ... as good as can be expected," Claire said, taking a sip from a clear straw that was sticking out of her blue water cup.

"I'm glad. So, tell me. What happened to you?"

Even though confused, Claire continued, seeing no harm in talking to the woman.

"I'm not sure, really. It was the middle of the night, and I heard a noise. I woke up thinking it was someone in the other room of the apartment, but for some reason, I couldn't stay awake and fell back asleep."

"Maybe you were dreaming."

"Yeah, that's what I thought too, but then I woke up again—later. This time, I saw that the door to my bedroom was open and felt like someone or something was in the room with me. I wanted to scream, but nothing came out. It was like I was paralyzed."

"That must have been frightening."

"I was petrified!" said Claire.

"What else happened?" said Mitzie.

Claire stopped and thought. "Well, it was cold—like the room had dropped about twenty degrees from the time I went to bed. I swear I could see my breath in the air. And that same chill ran down my spine when I saw my closet door open. It was the scariest thing I've ever felt in my life."

Mitzie shook her head empathetically.

"That's when I lost it. That thing came out of my closet."

"Thing?"

"Yeah, that ... that black shadow. I'll never forget it as long as I live."

"What did it look like?" asked Mitzie.

"It looked like a ... well ... not like anything I can describe. It was like a black cloud with the outlines of a head, arms and a body." said Claire.

"And this shadow moved on its own—like it was alive?"

"Yeah."

"I heard you took out your gun and shot at it?"

"Yeah. I didn't know what else to do. It grabbed me and started pulling me off the bed and out of the room!"

"You didn't hit whatever it was, so how did you get outside in the alley?"

"Like I told the officer, I don't know. All I remember was firing my gun. I don't know how I didn't hit anything; it was right there pulling on me. After that, my mind went blank. I must have knocked my head on the floor, because, like I said, I don't remember. They tell me that my apartment window was shattered. I have a few cuts on my stomach from the shards in the windowpane. It must have thrown me out the window."

"Whatever it was? You don't think it was a person, then?"

"I've been going over that in my mind—over and over. I'm not sure what it was," said Claire.

"A ghost, maybe?"

"A what?"

"Well, a ghost. I know that sounds crazy, but that's what it sounds like to me. My question is what *kind* of ghost?"

"I don't know. Are there different kinds?"

"Yes. There are human spirits who didn't leave the earth plane after they died. I think of them as ghosts. There are good ones and bad ones. Then there are all kinds of demons that were never human but can come through a portal to terrorize people. They're much harder to deal with. This one sounds like a demon to me," said Mitzie.

"You believe in 'em—demons, that is?"

"Yes," said Mitzie, without hesitation.

"I do think there are spirits out there," said Claire. "I know people who can see them and talk to them."

"Really?" asked Mitzie. "Who?"

"No one you'd know," said Claire not wishing to bring up that she'd met with a psychic earlier that day. "I always imagined spirits to be good, not bad."

"No, that's not always true. There are a lot of malevolent ghosts out there and even worse demons."

"How do you know so much about them?" Claire asked.

"I'm a psychic. I have experience in these sorts of things."

"Oh, so you do believe me!" Claire's tone became higher pitched; she was now much more animated and engaged. "And you think it may have been an evil spirit?"

"Demons can take on any number of forms. What did you tell the police?"

"I certainly didn't say it was an evil spirit. They don't believe in that stuff. And since they already don't like the fact that I fired off my gun, I don't want to make things worse. They have a lot of reasons to be suspicious of what I'm telling them."

There was a knock at the door as someone else came to visit.

"Hello, Ms. Horwath?" asked the man, opening the door slightly. "You don't know me, but..."

"Well, hello detective," Mitzie said from across the room.

Dag was surprised to see Mitzie there. He hadn't recognized her at first, but his face quickly turned from an expression of surprise to that of concern.

"What are you doing here, Ms. Wilkins?" Dag asked.

"Just showing concern, detective. "

"Do you know each other?" asked Claire, now more confused.

"Yes," said Mitzie, almost immediately.

"No," countered Dag, distancing himself from the odd woman standing nearby.

"Come on, detective! I spoke with you just a few days ago at the precinct. We had a nice talk. You remember that, surely."

"Mitzie, you didn't answer my question. Why are you here?" Dag asked again.

"I'm a psychic, detective. I see things. I know things. I told you that when we spoke."

"Did you see who or what did this to me, then?" Claire asked Mitzie, sitting up in bed.

"Ms. Horwath, I would advise caution if you are listening to this woman. I don't believe she is here for your benefit. Anyway, I'm here on official police business. We need to talk about a few things," Dag said, showing his badge. "I'm Detective Gallagher with the BPD. I just have a few questions to ask you about the other night."

Dag looked at Mitzie, expecting her to leave, but she didn't move. He then cleared his throat, but Mitzie ignored him, smiling back as if daring him to do anything about it.

"Ms. Horwath, I assume you don't want this woman here while I discuss what happened to you last night, right?"

Claire looked at Mitzie, feeling an odd connection to her, just as she had with Sara only a day earlier.

"No, it's okay. I don't think it will do any harm."

At that, Mitzie broadened her smile and took a seat in the only chair in the room. Dag groaned as he pulled out his computer note pad and began scribbling.

"But detective," said Claire, "I've already talked to one of your officers; he was going over everything with me. I answered all his questions. What else is there to talk about?"

"I can appreciate that, but there are some things he might not have asked you. Now, about last night."

"I was just explaining that to Mitzie, here. I'm just not sure, but this is what I remember."

Claire told her story—the same one she'd told Mitzie moments earlier. Of course, she intentionally left out any suggestion that it had been a ghost or demon that had been in her room.

"So, you say that someone or something ... you don't know exactly which ... dragged you out of bed and then, after you were knocked unconscious, threw you out your window?" asked Dag, somewhat puzzled. "So, who or what was it?"

"I already told you I don't know," Claire repeated.

"You claim you can't describe the man who ..."

"I didn't say it was a man," said Claire.

"A woman?" asked Dag.

Claire glanced over at Mitzie who was ever so subtly shaking her head.

"Well, what was it?" Dag asked, trying to understand.

"... uh ..., it was dark. I just don't know," Claire said, defensively.

Now it was Dag's turn to shake his head. "You're not giving me anything to go on. You have no idea what the person looked like or what they did to you. All you know is that you ended up in the alley two floors below your apartment."

"I'm afraid that's it, detective."

At that moment, the nurse came into the room. "I think it's time Ms. Horwath got some rest. All this talking has taken it out of her. Now, if you both will leave; I believe visiting hours are over."

Dag put away his notepad and started to leave the room. But before he got outside in the hallway, he turned and pushed the door open again.

"Ms. Horwath, if there is anything you remember or wish to discuss with me, I left my card on the nightstand next to your bed. Call me any time."

"Detective?" said Claire.

"Yes," he answered.

"The officer in here earlier said that you would be filing charges against me for not having a valid gun permit. Is that right?"

Dag scratched his head. "I tell you what. If you cooperate with me and give me some information, we might be able to help you out with that little problem. But you have to work with me. Do you understand?"

Claire nodded. After the detective left, the nurse stared at Mitzie long enough to make her point, and this time, she rose reluctantly from her chair.

"Well, I guess I should go too," Mitzie said. "I've got a lot of things to do before the day's out."

After her visitors left, Claire sank into her lumpy, hospital pillow. *What option do I really have but to tell the detective what I really think happened?*

She picked the detective's card off the nightstand but put it back down, only pushing it closer to the phone.

I'll do that after I take a nap, she thought, settling back and closing her eyes. It didn't take long, and she was fast asleep.

*****

CH 16 – The Attic–Part 1

2020

Boxed away for years in the attic were old yearbooks and pictures of Sara's mother, grandmother and her great grandmother together with their families. In the early days, the yearbooks were little more than a year-end diary of stories and well wishes from classmates who would try to stay in touch but inevitably would go their separate ways. In rare cases they stayed friends for life.

In the bottom of one of the boxes, Sara found her great grandmother's senior class yearbook. It was dated 1938. There weren't many in her class, so there were fewer than thirty pages bound within the lemon-yellow paperback. Stuck between a few pages were sepia photos which had faded over the years despite being stuffed where sunlight couldn't betray them.

"Dear Janice," began one entry, "You are a wonderful friend, and someone with whom I shall stay in regular contact. Yours, Cecilia."

Another read, "Dear Janice, although you were always an unusual sort, I liked you very much anyway. Fred."

But it was awkward in every high school, Sara thought as she read the notes. *My yearbook probably had strange quotes in it too. Things really haven't changed that much, except for the formality of the language.*

Inside the yearbook were two other photographs. One was torn—ripped in two right down the middle with her great grandmother as a young girl on the right side, and another young girl on her left. Both girls were smiling and had their arms around each other. Sara flipped both over, finding something written on the reverse side. After she pushed the pieces back together, she was able to read the entire script.

> *To my best friend ever. You are a rare find—someone else who knows what it feels like to be different. I can only hope that we stay in each other's lives forever. Love always, Bessie.*

The other photo was of a group of girls—six in all—sitting in a row, smiling with their arms around each other. The picture looked like it was taken in front of some wooden bleachers in a gym. The caption read: *Mystics Club*. It was evident that this was more than just a club photo from school. These girls were likely best friends at the time and believed they would remain so the rest of their lives. But two of the girls in the picture were the same ones in the ripped photo. Clearly, the friendship had not lasted as long as they had expected for whatever reason.

Inside the box was another journal too. This one had a faded, pink cover and doodles in black ink all over the front. The markings were mainly pentagrams and triangles—each with a circle around it. The word *THAUMATURGICAL* with a question mark after it was written in big, block letters at the bottom of the page. Above it in the center was a drawing of a goat's head and several *X*s marked through it.

Sara cracked the cover and flipped through the pages. This was a personal journal with each page dated at the top. Some had written the name of an event with a place, person and time. Others were only comments on what happened during the day—whether pedestrian or "earth shaking" for an eighteen-year-old, high school girl.

The journal not only covered her great grandmother's days in high school, but they continued for a few years thereafter. This was her personal diary detailing everything from the normal days of talking about who was dating whom during lunch hour and what Mrs. Clark gave as a homework assignment in Chemistry to the "wee-bit" unusual. Yet, even Sara found that these "wee-bit" unusual incidents were often much more than *a wee bit.*

Sara read page by page as her great grandmother's strange and sometimes haunting words leaped from the journal. The handwriting was clean and perfect, as if she were practicing her letters in third grade.

March 28, 1939

Place – Melissa's house

Who was there – Judy, Melissa, Julie, Tammy, Bessie, and me

11:00 PM

We all got together to have a session. My friends thought it would be fun to do a séance as a group. They know I have the ability to contact the other side.

Those last few words piqued Sara's interest.

After we lit the candles, we sat in a circle and held hands. We closed our eyes, and I started to relax, feeling my body float and my brain drift. Almost immediately, I felt others in the room with us. These were people I didn't know, but I felt that someone in the room did.

I opened my eyes and started describing whom I saw.

First was an old man—short, frail, with skinny fingers and arms. His face was drawn and gaunt, and his eyes dark and spiritless. He smiled at me and whispered, "Tell Julie that her grandfather is taking care of her father. We're both just fine, and we'll be looking after her."

Julie asked what he looked like, and I described him as having a chipped front tooth, down-turned mouth, and rather large ears. Her eyes grew wide as I talked about him, and she squeezed my hand very hard.

"What else did he say?" Julie asked, but I told her that someone else wanted my attention.

I turned to Tammy. I wasn't sure how to phrase it, but I just told her that her father was there with us too. She said she didn't know him very well as he died when she was very young. The man's image before me was good-looking, but he was quiet. He didn't say anything, only nodding his approval of what I assumed was how well his daughter was doing.

But, in an instant that image vanished – replaced by a sudden and violent feeling of cold and fear. I struggled for breath. Bessie asked what was wrong, and I opened my eyes, shaking. She pressed me on what I had seen, but I didn't answer her. I broke up the séance, saying that I was tired, and it was late.

But that wasn't the real reason. It was what I'd seen that had made me tremble.

Sara took a gulp of air as if it were a glass of spoiled milk. She paused before she read any further. Throwing her head back, she was afraid to continue, but curiosity got the better of her. Like a mosquito drawn to the glow-of a bright lantern, she read on.

I really hate to record here what I saw because I'm afraid it will remain forever on this page—even if the journal is ravaged by fire or destroyed by water. I fear it will leave an indelible stain that will always be attached to me somehow—like an evil possession.

However, something else pushes me forward, and my words follow unabated. So, here I go ...

After the last encounter with Tammy's father, I felt a chill that cut me to the bone. It was so dark and terrifying that I had to close my eyes to block it from my thoughts and my memory. However, when I opened them, I saw *It!* Something that will remain with me forever.

*****

CH 19 – The Attic–Part 2

2020

Sara continued reading in her great grandmother's journal; her heart was pounding.

> *Standing right next to Bessie, in fact right behind her, was the most hideous demon I could ever imagine. Horned, black, and scabby, with short, yellow, jagged teeth and pus oozing from the pores of its face. There were black sockets where eyes were supposed to be, and the foulness of its breath made me want to vomit. I knew it was looking right at me or through me, and I instantly knew how powerless I was against its pure evil.*
>
> *When Bessie asked me what was wrong, I was frozen with fear. I couldn't utter a sound—not a peep. Certainly, I couldn't tell her. I only hoped that the creature would leave and never come into my thoughts or my life again.*

Sara sat just as petrified as her great grandmother had been when she'd seen the monster. Her heart raced, and beads of water formed on her forehead and around her neck, eventually dripping down her back and chest. She had felt the same things at various times in her life, especially during readings with certain clients. The coldness, the hopelessness, the emptiness that she felt had been as real to her as they had been to her great grandmother. Sara's haunting visions were becoming more frequent every day, and the struggle to fight against them was getting harder. Deep down, she knew the same monster was waiting there for her. She had felt it. She had sensed it. It was only a matter of time.

Maybe it was caused by being overly tired, Sara thought. *Her Grandma Janice had said that in her journal—writing that she was tired that night. Maybe that's why she saw such a strange thing; it was just something her mind created on its own. There was nothing to worry about—nothing to fear.* She kept telling herself that, hoping it was true.

Sara had read about dark forces that can cast a pall over someone, gradually sucking away the positive energy that motivates them to push on with life. Scientists and doctors claimed it was something caused by chemical imbalances in the brain. Those in the psychic world believed it was caused by dark spirits feeding on the energies of the unwitting and vulnerable.

Which is it? she asked herself. *Maybe both?*

For Sara, her sense of fear and gloom was deep inside her. It bore into her heart, into every breath, and into her very existence. Its very presence sometimes froze her mind. It was a numbness that paralyzed her and left her unable to find lightness, hope and goodness. This thing—this feeling—was more than just clinical depression, she thought; this feeling was evil. This cold cloud smothered all warmth, all love and all happiness. This dark spirit was wicked, as pure of evil as any fundamental Aristotelian element of air, earth, fire or water. But perhaps this came from his fifth element: aether.

Sara recoiled again, but this time it was from the smell—of apples. That scent had come with every feeling of demonic presence she'd had—both before and after the incident. *What was the connection? Why the smell of apples?* she had always wondered. She had questions, but fewer and fewer answers.

The smell seemed to be coming from a picnic basket that had been shoved into one corner of the attic. There was a musty smell too, but the overpowering odor was that of apples. And that is what drew her closer.

Sara lifted one end of the hinged lid and looked inside. Oddly, there were no apples inside, but there were several odd things. The first was an antique doll. Very plain and unremarkable, it nevertheless looked like a middle-aged woman rather than a baby. By the look of the dress it was wearing, Sara thought it was very old—perhaps dating to the late nineteenth century. Its hair was done in a style of that era, but it was the face that surprised her. Rather than a happy, smiling face for a child to play with, it held a stern, austere look, like a mother scolding her children. Next to the doll was a book—*The Garden of Eden*, by Ernest Hemmingway. Written in 1946, it wasn't published until 1986, long after his death. *It couldn't have been Grandmother Janice's or Grandmother Cora Rae's,* Sara thought. *It must have been Mom's.* Abby had been Sara's mother—the one who had abandoned her as a child. The whereabouts of Abagail Knight Prodescu had remained a mystery to that day.

However, there was a third item in the basket. This was a wooden, antique jewelry box. It looked musical, with a tiny crank on the side.

It was cordated, that is, shaped like a heart, but there was a deep crack down the center which nearly split the top in two. To Sara, it looked like something from the mid-to-late nineteenth century— something well before the time of her Grandmother Janice.

Sara tried to turn the crank, but it was broken. Opening it, she found a red cigarette lighter and a thin, brass ring. The ring was like a signet ring and had the symbol of a five-sided star on it, albeit, turned upside down. Beside it were many old, polaroid pictures. Faded and hazy, the photos showed people with burn marks on their arms and legs. None showed heads or faces, so it was impossible to know who they were. Frighteningly, she also couldn't tell if the bodies were alive or dead. As Sara looked closer at them, she gasped: the marks were of a five-sided star—just like the signet ring.

A chill blew through the room, and she shivered. She could feel the presence of something nearby and again smelled the strong aroma of apples.

I have to get out of here, she thought panicking.

Sara left everything and hurried down the attic ladder, folding it up and slamming it tight against the ceiling. She shuddered, afraid for herself and her family. Knowing that a demon had revealed itself to her great grandmother—like the one that haunted her—only reinforced her worst fears. Then, there was that smell. *Did the apple scent mean it was hiding, living up in her attic?* She couldn't bear the thought.

She decided she would need to clean out the attic, throwing away all the things linking her to her past, to her family, to her great grandmother. She was scared—scared that she might be possessed by the same ghoulish monster her great grandmother had seen. If that happened, she wasn't sure of the outcome—that of her family or her soul.

*****

Part II

CH 18 - Psychic Visions

1970

Cora Rae checked her appointment book. She had only two meetings scheduled for the day. Her business was doing okay, but not great. It seemed like the use of psychics had waned over the years—either from a growing disbelief in the practice or from the downturn in the economy.

She pushed back her wavy, brown hair and asked her driver to pull over to the side of the road. She had gotten a sudden chill and felt sick and nauseous. This happened from time to time and would be followed by random images or sounds flooding her mind and overloading her senses. All of it ended up making her sick. If she shut her eyes and let things settle—taking deep breaths and calming herself—she would usually return to normal. But this time, she felt herself being sucked into an ethereal trance against her will by something over which she had no control.

Racing through her mind were images of a woman in bed watching late-night television. All seemed normal until flashes of panic crossed the woman's face. Cora Rae couldn't hear what was happening, but she could only see a vapory, misty cloud in her vision. As the mist faded, she saw the twisted, contorted body of the same woman, her eyes staring blindly—not at the television but at the ceiling. Her head was cocked at an inhuman angle, and her mouth was open trying to scream but with no life left inside to utter a sound. It was a scene right from the pages of a Stephen King or H.P. Lovecraft novel.

Cora Rae shook head, trying to break the stranglehold on her mind and took several deep breaths as the image began to fade. The episode didn't last long, but it was becoming more frequent and more graphic. She was increasingly worried about them, as her ability to control such thoughts was becoming weaker every day.

Cora Rae opened her eyes, forcing herself back into the present moment.

"Are you all right?" asked Moseby, her driver, watching her in his rearview mirror. Cora Rae was hyperventilating, and her eyes were glazed. "Slow down, Miss Cora. Slow down. You're breathing too fast. You're going to make yourself pass out."

She put her head between her knees and slowed her breathing like the doctor told her to do. Eventually, she felt better—the blood coming back to her head and her mind clearing.

As a medium, she was aware of what could happen if she let spirits run rampant through her mind and her body. It was dangerous enough letting them inside to talk to them for a short time. There were rules in her business: how to allow them to enter, but not to stay. She was to tell the spirit world before every session with a client that she would only communicate with good spirits—ones that meant her no harm. She would also state that they would only be allowed to visit as long as she wanted them there—not as long as they wished. But there were some spirits that wouldn't listen no matter how strongly she set down the rules. These were ones that were stronger than she was and didn't have to obey her.

"Okay, Moseby, I think I'm fine. Let's get going. I don't want to be late," she said.

Moseby was not only her driver, but he acted as her bodyguard as well. This came after a few scary client meetings and the insistence of her husband.

Cora Rae had never wanted anyone to accompany her until a scare three months earlier had changed all that. That was when Cora Rae had received a call from a person asking for her help in contacting a familial spirit. The person seemed nice and cooperative, and Cora Rae had little reason to think anything might be amiss.

She had arrived at the client's house and been greeted at the door by a young man—not the older gentleman with whom she had talked on the phone. The young man was handsome and well dressed. He told her that his father, who had called her, had stepped out to get some cigarettes at the local *7-11* down the street. He asked her to come in and take a seat at the kitchen table. However, after she sat down, she heard the front deadbolt click shut. The young man came into the small, cramped kitchen with a new smile—one that was ugly and disturbing.

She managed to smile back, but knew his intentions were not good. Thinking quickly, she began coughing, clutching her throat and acting as if she were choking. She murmured in a thin, raspy voice that she needed some water and waved her arms erratically to get his attention. Instantly, he reacted, going to the sink and filling a glass with water. When she got it, she threw the water in his face and smashed the glass over his head before running for the door. He had chased after her, but she had managed to unlock it and bolt for her car before he could get there. She drove off, vowing never to find herself in that position again.

This appointment was in Brookline, northwest of Roxbury on the west side of Boston. The client lived in a small apartment building— only four floors high as were most in the area—and likely built sometime during the early part of the century. It was not in an unsafe neighborhood, yet Cora Rae still held apprehensions.

"Do you want me to come in with you?" Moseby asked politely, opening the car door for her.

She hadn't known Moseby long, but he had been recommended by a friend and been very reliable. During his short employment, he had never called off when she had needed him—even with last-minute appointments. When she asked him to pick her up at 9:00 AM, he was there at 8:55. Always pleasant, he seemed quiet and shy—more than willing to help-out when needed.

"No, I think it will be fine. If I need you, I'll press my emergency button, so you'll hear the beep on your receiver," she said confidently.

Cora Rae got out of the car and walked to the front of the house.

"Twenty-three-oh-nine," she said to herself verifying the number on the outside of the building.

The sun was out, and it was a warm, clear day in Boston. The temperature was balmy for May—in the mid-70s. *A perfect day for a reading,* she thought.

She pushed the egg-yolk-colored button that marked the doorbell for Apartment 306 and waited for some sign of life within.

"Yes?"

It was a young man's voice, not that of a middle-aged woman she had expected. She pulled out her emergency button to summon Mosely but decided she might be overreacting and let it slide back into her purse.

"Uh, I'm Cora Rae," she said, taken aback by his gruffness. "A Virginia Carter called me. Is she home?"

"Mom!" yelled the man, "you've got company!"

Suddenly, there was a buzzing noise at the door signifying that she was allowed to come in.

Nervously, she climbed the two flights of stairs to the third floor and made a left at the top, going down the dark, narrow hallway until she reached 306. There, she knocked on the door. The door opened promptly, and a young man showed his face. He looked haggard—his hair uncombed, his beard unshaven, and his eyes bloodshot.

"You're here for Mom?" he growled.

Without saying another word, he turned and abandoned his post, leaving Cora Rae at the doorway wondering what would come next. Again, she thought about pushing the emergency button for Moseby, but when she saw a woman in her late-forties or early fifties come to the door, she relaxed.

The woman's hair was dyed black but with roots that were silvery white. She was slender and had long, thin arms and bony fingers. Her face was pale and drawn as if she had endured hard times recently. It was a weariness that projected outward and all around her, like a sickly aura crying out for help. Dressed in a simple, cotton dress imprinted with pink and purple flowers, the woman smiled faintly as she greeted her visitor.

"Hello," said the woman, pushing open the door. Strangely, her demeanor changed instantly when she remembered her visitor, and there was a sudden burst of energy—a focused radiancy of warmth and kindness. "Oh, you must be Cora Rae. How good of you to come on such short notice. I apologize for the inconvenience, but things have gotten to the point that I just had to see you."

"No problem, Virginia. I usually don't do last-minute meetings like this. But I did have an opening in my schedule, and I was able to fit you in. What's going on?"

The woman shut the door behind her and motioned for Cora Rae to come in. "Please," she said, gesturing with her hand. "And please call me Jenny."

As Cora Rae entered the small apartment, her nose was struck by a pungent odor that shot up through her nasal passages as if she'd bitten into a jalapeño pepper. It was a musty and stale smell—like that of an old nursing home or funeral parlor. The windows were covered with heavy, thick drapes, and there was little natural light coming into the place even though it was a beautiful day outside.

"Sit, my dear," said Jenny. "Can I get you something?"

"Oh, no thanks, Jenny. I have another appointment soon, so I can't stay more than about forty minutes."

"All right then," said her client graciously.

Jenny smiled and motioned again for her to sit on the stiff, formal loveseat. It was a pale green with a curved high-back and gold-painted wood trim. It had several small, pin-cushion pillows of mauve and forest green positioned exactly in the center. The only thing missing were the plastic coverings commonly found in such a living room.

Cora Rae sat but positioned herself uncomfortably at the edge of the cushion, not wanting to disturb the pillows that had been so meticulously placed behind her.

"So, let me start by saying ..." Jenny began.

But Cora Rae quickly cut her off before she uttered another word.

"I'm sorry Jenny," she said, interrupting, "but I don't want you to say anything more unless I ask you a question or I need something from you. It's important that I contact the spirit world on my own without being biased by something you might tell me. That's the only way for me to make a pure connection with the other side, and for you to know that I'm not just telling you what you want to hear."

"All right then," Jenny said again, unperturbed by the approach. "Go right ahead."

Cora Rae didn't close her eyes or clasp hands with her client. There was no Ouija Board or other props. Instead, she looked straight ahead and took several deep breaths. Then, the usual out-of-body experience happened where her brain seemed to enter another dimension and see things not of this world.

"Jenny, I sense that you and your son have suffered the loss of a female figure in the family. It was your son's wife. Is that right?"

Jenny nodded.

"She died recently," continued Cora Rae, "and I sense that she was in an auto accident up the road here, not too far away. And that ..." At that point, Cora Rae held up her hand. "Oh, my!" she said, continuing. "It wasn't *just* your daughter-in-law, was it?"

Jenny shook her head and looked down, trying to keep from crying.

"It was your granddaughter as well. You lost both of them."

It was unusual for Cora Rae to see two deaths happen at the same time; however, in her vision, she saw it clearly—tragically. Both loved ones were killed only a few months earlier when a driver in another lane got distracted and crossed the yellow line in front of them, killing both Cheryl and her daughter Dominique. It had all but destroyed their family. It was Cheryl's husband, Jake, who had answered the door, and now it was clear why he was in such a state of despair. He had still not recovered.

"Can you see them?" asked Jenny, hopefully.

"Yes, Jenny. Cheryl is standing right beside you, and although I don't see Dominique, I know she's close-by too. They are telling me that they are safe and at peace. Everything is good where they are ... that you shouldn't worry. They want you to know that they love you and will be near you the rest of your life. Cheryl says that it's okay for Jake to grieve, but he must move on. They love both of you very much, but it is important that you get back to your lives. You will be with them later when the time is right."

Then Cora Rae's face turned to one of concern. "Yet, they do tell me that ..." However, Cora Rae was interrupted by a buzzing sound coming from near the front door.

Jenny got up and pressed the black, answer button. "Yes? May I help you?" she asked.

"I'm Mr. Mosely," came the voice. I'm here with Cora Rae."

Jenny glanced over at her visitor who rolled her eyes and nodded.

"Yes, he's with me," Cora Rae answered.

When Mosely came to the apartment door, Cora Rae opened it.

"What are you doing?" asked Cora Rae from the couch. "I didn't buzz you." She was irritated at being disturbed during a reading.

"Oh, I thought you had," he said, looking at his portable receiver.

Jenny wiped the tears from her eyes and tried to compose herself. "Well, why don't you come in. I have some biscuits in the kitchen if you'd like one."

"Sure," said the driver, giving her an appreciative smile.

Moseby disappeared into the kitchen while Jenny and Cora Rae finished their session.

"You were saying what, dear?"

"Uh, I was just thinking that ..." Cora Rae stammered, trying to recall exactly what she was going to say. But her connection to the spirit world had been broken; there were no ethereal images hovering about anymore, and she needed to get back to that other dimension. "Let me try to reconnect," she said, this time shutting her eyes. It was another minute before she made contact. "Jenny, your son's wife is asking me why you are involved with the man you're seeing now. She's asking whether you know he's a ..."

"I don't know what you're talking about," said Jenny, suddenly defensively.

Cora Rae listened to the voice in her head and soon understood. "Oh, I see what she's saying. Okay, she says. Never mind."

The medium opened her eyes and closed her folder. Standing up, she said, "I'm sorry about the interruption. I hope what I was able to get you was helpful. Cora Rae reached out and shook Jenny's hand. "It was so nice to meet with you. Again, I hope this helped. You need to tell your son that everything is all right. His daughter and wife are at peace. There was nothing either of you could have done. It was just God's will."

As Cora Rae turned to leave, she saw comfort in the mother's face— even the small wrinkles around her sad eyes appeared to have softened a bit.

Her son entered the room holding a can of beer even though it was only eleven o'clock in the morning.

"Jake, the medium said your family is good and happy on the other side. They are safe."

"I don' want to hear it, Mom," came the distressed voice as her son continued through to the adjacent room. Moments later, the sound of the television coming on told them he had no plans to do much of anything the rest of the day.

Jenny shook her head in dismay. "Thank you so much for coming," she said. "As you can tell, I am at the end of my rope with my son. He's just not coming out of his funk. It's been hard on us both. You understand."

"Yes, I've seen it before. It's a difficult time. If you want another session for you or your son, I'd be happy to come back. My schedule doesn't open up until July, but I might be able to arrange something quick like I did today."

Cora Rae walked across the living room towards the door but then stopped. "Moseby? Are you coming?" she said in a loud voice, not knowing where he'd gone.

Moseby appeared from the kitchen munching on a biscuit. He licked his fingers and wiped his hands on his pants before hurrying out ahead of his employer.

Jenny grasped Cora Rae's hands. "I think it did help me. Now, if I can just reach my son."

"Just talk to him. He needs you and you need him right now. It's going to take time. Comfort each other. Go to the church and ask the priest for help. There are a lot of people and organizations that can give him the support he needs."

"We don't go to church anymore. Even before Cheryl and Dominique's accident, we didn't go as often as we should have. I don't see how I can get Jake to go now. He's so bitter. He thinks there is no God, or if there is one, that He's given up on us. I'm not sure I can bring him back to the church."

"You can. But first, *you* have to try," said Cora Rae.

Getting in the back of the car, Cora Rae motioned for her driver to go down the street to her next appointment. However, there was something unsettling ... something that bothered her.

"How was your session?" Moseby asked.

"Strange," said Cora Rae.

"All your sessions are strange, ma'am," he said grinning.

"No, I mean one of the spirits told me something, and when I asked the client, she didn't want to talk about. I could see in her eyes that what I was about to say was true, though. It obviously struck a nerve."

120

"What was that?"

"Her daughter-in-law asked why she was having an affair with a married man."

"Oh, I see," said Moseby. "I bet that *was* uncomfortable."

"It's more than that, though. He's with the Boston Police Department."

"Oh, wow. Well, that makes it interesting."

"Yes .... very," said Cora Rae.

Cora Rae wouldn't find out until later, but the morning after the reading, both Jenny and her son were found dead in their apartment. Both had been murdered in a most heinous way.

*****

CH 19 –Visiting Claire

2020

Sara paused at the hospital room doorway, thinking about whether to go in. But after opening the door, she changed her mind and let it close. That was when she heard a voice from inside the room.

"Sara?" It was Claire, just opening her eyes but not yet fully awake.

"Yes, Claire. It's me," Sara answered, going back into the room and moving toward the hospital bed.

Claire had the bed scrunched up in a wavy, half-W position. Her head was raised to the highest level and her knees bent almost up to her chest.

"Are you comfortable like that?" Sara asked.

"What do you mean?"

"Well, your knees are so folded up. It's almost like you're ready to be packed into a suitcase," said Sara, grinning.

Claire laughed. "Oh, no. Actually, I did that on purpose. I was stretching my back a bit. It gets so stiff sitting here in the bed. The doctor said I may be able to leave tomorrow."

"That's great, Claire! You look pretty good. It must have been frightful that night. I don't know what happened, but when I heard someone was thrown out of their apartment window at that address, I worried. I tried to call, but I didn't get through and then ..."

"Don't worry about it," said Claire, waving her hand. "I've had my share of visitors since I've been in here."

"Oh, family?"

"Uh, no. Actually, the police and some lady I'd never met in my life."

"Wow, that's quite a combination," noted Sara.

"This woman—she was quite odd, you know. She came in and acted like she'd known me all her life. I'd never even seen her before. She started asking me about what happened that night. I was only saved from her by the detective who came in right behind her. He seemed to know her, but I'm not sure how. The whole thing is confusing.

Ever since you came that day to meet with me nothing's been the same."

"I don't know what to say," Sara said, a little defensively. "Do you think what we did had something to do with everything that's happened to you?"

"I don't know. I wouldn't like to think so, although ...."

"Claire, I've been doing these sessions for years, and I've never had anything remotely close to this happen. There's just no way that ..."

"... that you summoned someone or something other than my boyfriend?"

"No. It doesn't work that way," said Sara. "Tell me what *did* happen to you that night?"

Claire went on to tell Sara about what she remembered from that night—the strange noises, the shadows, the shots she fired, and then being dragged out of the room. Sara listened, trying to make sense of it.

"You say that you felt something grab you by your legs? But you didn't or couldn't see what it was? It was dark, but you don't think it was a person. You think it was ... what exactly?"

"I dunno. It was like some invisible force was pulling on me. It really freaked me out. I reached for my gun and began shooting, but whatever it was ... I couldn't kill it. I must have knocked my head on the floor when I fell from the bed because the next thing I remember, I was lying on my back in the alley below my window."

Sara was quiet for a moment.

"What is it?" Claire asked.

"Did you check to see if you have any marks?"

Claire looked at Sara strangely. "Marks?"

"You know. Do you have any strange lines or marks on your body anywhere? Marks that weren't there before that night?"

"I don't know. I really haven't looked," Claire answered.

"You may want to do that ... just in case."

"In case what?"

"That's all I can tell you right now."

"All you can tell me or all that you *will* tell me?" asked Claire, alarmed.

Sara's cell phone went off, and she looked at the screen. It was LJ's school.

"I'm sorry, Claire, just call me if you find something, okay?"

Sara hurried to the door, purse in hand. She opened it and, without saying goodbye, vanished down the hallway, pushing buttons on her phone to dial the school.

Claire felt uneasy and agitated. *What did she mean by a mark?* she thought. Pushing herself up, she tossed the ugly, floral-patterned sheet to the side of the bed and reached for the cold, protective rail. She jerked it up and then pushed it down to lower it below the level of the bed. A pain shot up through her right side, reminding her of the cracked ribs she'd suffered from the fall, and she grimaced. Finally, she made it out of bed and shuffled toward the private bath. Once inside, she pulled off her gown and began looking.

First, she gazed at the floor where she examined her toes, feet, ankles, and legs. Then, she worked her way up, viewing her hips, buttocks, stomach, and breasts. Pushing her breasts up, she found nothing underneath. There were no marks on her arms, neck or face either.

She sighed. I guess I don't have anything to worry about, she thought as she reached to pick her hospital gown from the floor. But as she started to pull it over her head, she noticed something that hadn't been there before. Just below her hairline on her neck was a red spot that looked like a welt from a bug bite. Claire touched it. It felt hot, like a burning coal had just been pushed against her flesh. She flinched and watched as the spot began swirling in a counterclockwise motion with bands of yellow, pink and black moving inward toward some invisible point in the center. Then, it stopped, and an image emerged.

Shaking, Claire picked up her cell phone to make a call. It was the second in as many days.

"Sara, it's Claire. You asked if I had any marks on my body—you know, ones that weren't there before the accident. Well, I do. I need to see you again—as soon as possible."

*****

(H 20 - LJ's Boyfriend

2020

"Mom, can you come and get me from school?"

It was LJ. Sara had just come out of Claire's room at the hospital when her cell phone went off again. It was highly unusual for LJ and the school to call her in the middle of the day, and when she saw it was her daughter calling, she got doubly worried.

"LJ? What's wrong, honey?"

"I ... I just can't be here right now. Will you come get me?"

Sara drove to the school and went inside. There were other parents there too—all waiting just inside the principal's office. Sara didn't know any of them, but she smiled nervously as she went to the counter to speak to someone.

"Yes?" asked the school principal, Samantha Stevens, a middle-aged woman who had been a fixture at the school for many years. "May I help you?"

"Yes, I'm Sara McLaughlin, LJ's mother. Is she all right?"

The woman didn't smile or nod, she only looked at Sara over the tops of her glasses. "It's been a difficult morning for some of our students, Ms. McLaughlin. I'll call LJ out of class. Perhaps it's best if she goes home today. If she needs counseling, please let us know."

"What's happened?" asked Sara, now alarmed.

"There's been a death, ma'am. One of the students was killed last night. Tragic. I won't get into the details, but those close to him found out about an hour ago. We're allowing some of those students to go home and suggest they talk with one of our counselors later this week."

"Oh, my goodness!" said Sara, shocked.

LJ came into the office, her face smeared with black mascara from crying.

"Mom, let's go home," said LJ, starting to sob once more.

Sara was quiet on the drive back to the house, waiting for her daughter to tell her what happened.

"I just can't believe it," LJ finally began. "Will's dead. He's dead, Mom!"

"Who is Will, honey? I haven't heard you talk about Will before."

"Will Jenkins. He was a friend."

"Oh, well, I'm really sorry, honey. It must be hard on you and the others at the school. How long have you known him?"

"About six months. He was new to the school this year. He didn't have many friends. Kids thought he was, you know, different. But I liked him. Me and a few other kids got along great with him. Now he's ..."

"Oh, honey. Let's get back to the house, and you can tell me all about it."

LJ didn't know a lot about what had happened, only that Will and his mother had been murdered the night before in their apartment. The school principal hadn't gone into details as she had only said that they were disturbing. It was only later that Sara heard more about it on the evening news. The incident not only shocked the school, but it stunned Boston as well.

LJ couldn't eat and couldn't sleep for weeks. She was terrified, and Sara took her to several doctors to get help; however, nothing seemed to help. Sara's husband Vince had also tried to talk to LJ, and they finally decided to take her out of school for the rest of the semester. Home schooling wasn't exactly what Sara had in mind, especially at the high school level, but between the two of them, they managed.

It was during one of her lessons that something got triggered inside LJ, and she broke down crying again.

"LJ? What is it?" asked Vince.

They were working on geometry, when they came across a problem that unleashed the torrent of tears.

"It's a pentagon," said LJ.

"Yes, that's right. We have to find the angles of the ..."

"No, Dad! I can't. I can't go on pretending it's not related."

"Related to what?"

LJ ran upstairs and slammed the door to her room. Vince followed closely behind and knocked. "LJ? We need to talk about this."

He didn't hear anything.

"LJ?"

Vince opened the door. LJ was lying on the bed with a pillow over her head. He could hear her sobs beneath the pillow sheet.

"Talk to me. What's going on?"

It was then that LJ told him that she had continued to be part of the black magic cult at school. She hadn't stopped. She and some others had been leaving school early to go to a clearing in the woods not far from the school grounds. Armed with black candles, charms and a spell book to contact the satanic spirits, they smoked weed and drank whiskey one of the boy's brother bought for them. Will had been the one who had started the group shortly after arriving at the school. Now he was dead.

"So, you see! It's my fault! It's all our faults. We're the reason why he's dead, Dad!" Then she paused. "I loved him, Dad. I really did. He was my soul mate."

Vince was stunned. He didn't know what to say, except, "LJ, it's not your fault. Your friend wasn't killed by some evil spirit. He was killed by an evil human. But dark magic isn't something you mess with. I don't believe in it, but I know your mom does. Still, we told you not to get involved in that shit! Bad people are in those groups—bad people who do bad things. I hope you learned your lesson about that, at least."

LJ continued to cry, and Vince left to go downstairs. He felt helpless and unsure. *Sara will know what to do or say*, he thought—or at least, he hoped so.

But when Sara came home and learned what LJ had told Vince, she was livid.

"No!" Sara screamed. "I won't let her out of the house! She's grounded! I told her to stop! I told her not to do that stuff! That's it," she said catching her breath. "I don't want her involved in *anything!* Do you understand me?"

She wasn't upset with Vince, but she didn't know how else to let go of the emotion. She knew what mysticism had done to previous generations within her own family. She had been told stories over the years from aunts, uncles and others. The last thing she wanted was for her daughter to get involved. Worse yet, the fact her daughter was messing around with forces on the other side—satanic, dark forces—was the worst thing she could imagine.

"Settle down, Sara," said Vince, putting his hand on her arm. "It's not going to help anyone if we're upset too. We have to be calm about this. We have to help her through this."

"I don't know," said Sara. "I can't deal with this. You'll have to handle it, Vince. I ... I just can't."

*****

CH 21 – The Business Card

1970

The late call came into the police station when there was only a skeleton crew working. It was from a curious neighbor who said she hadn't seen Virginia, or Jenny, as her neighbors called her, in days and was concerned. The neighbor, Wendy Sasse, was a twenty-something who generally kept tabs on the older people in her complex. Although a bit of a busybody, Wendy was a kind, good-hearted soul who checked-in on Jenny every day or every other to make sure everything was all right. Jenny and her son, Jake, had been through a great deal as of late, and Wendy wanted to do anything she could to help.

It didn't take long, and another call was received—this time from the building superintendent. Jenny was found, and Wendy's worst fears were realized. She had pleaded with the building sup to go into the apartment after she had repeatedly tried to contact Jenny. She sensed something was wrong.

"Jag," said the dispatcher over the phone, "I've got two DBs at 2309 Brookline Boulevard, Apartment 306. No CIP. Sending a wagon to retrieve but need a detective on the scene to verify it's NC." This was a cryptic message that basically meant, *Go to this address and make sure the two persons who died weren't murdered. There's no crime in progress, so you don't have to rush.* Events like this weren't that unusual in a city of six hundred thousand people.

"Ten four," said John Arthur Gallagher, known as Jag. "Just to confirm that's in Brookline, correct?"

"Confirmed. Brookline. Their police department is short-staffed tonight—thought you could help out."

"I'll take it. It's no problem."

The drive to the apartment was only fifteen minutes, and when he arrived, there were already two other police cars there, restricting access to the building. Jag ran up the three flights of stairs to Apartment 306 and flashed his badge as he entered. The police were inside taking pictures of the bodies and the surroundings—anything that would or could give a clue as to what had happened.

What struck Jag as he entered was the peculiar smell. It was not of a rotting corpse or of garbage or other refuse that had been unattended for days. Strangely, it was the scent of apples. He was familiar with that smell as his family, the Gallagher family, owned an apple orchard not far from Boston. It had been in the family for generations. It was where he, his father and grandfather before him had hired workers to pick the fruit and sell it at local markets nearby. It was a delightful smell that brought back fond memories of his childhood days. However, now he had a new connection with the smell, and this one was wretched and foul.

Yet, the apple smell was not the only thing that was unusual. One of the victims was a fifty-something woman who was found dead on her sofa with the television on, her eyes open, and the expression on her face one of shock and horror. Yet, stranger than that was the fact that her entire body was twisted into a helicoid—a corkscrew shape—like her feet had been held while the rest had been spun into a tight coil. Her son's body—found in another bedroom—was contorted in a similar way.

"What's going on?" asked Jag, coming into the room.

"Got a Caucasian female and a Caucasian male. Looks like they didn't die of natural causes …"

"Yeah, I can see that," said Jag, grimacing while looking at the bizarre contortions of the woman's body. "How the hell did it happen?" he asked.

"You tell us," said another police officer in the room. "That's your job, isn't it?"

"What else do we have?" Jag asked, ignoring the snipe.

"Not much. Nothing else looks abnormal. No forced entry. No stolen items that we can tell anyway. Nothing that seems out of place. It just doesn't make sense."

"It never does, officer," said Jag.

Jag looked around, examining all the rooms: the indentations in the carpeting, the arrangement of the furniture, which lights were on and which were off, the position of the pillows on the sofa, as well as other details. Based on the neatness of the place, he knew from experience that he was looking for something that hadn't been put back in its proper place—perhaps in a hurry. However, nothing leaped out at him. Aside from the bodies, nothing seemed odd.

131

After he finished his preliminary review, Jag closed his black notebook, stuck the yellow pencil behind his ear, and headed out the door.

"Make sure you get pictures of everything," he said, "and I mean *everything!*"

"Say, detective? I found this among the woman's things in her bedroom."

"What is it?"

The officer handed Jag a card. He took it and stood quietly.

"Detective?"

"Yeah?"

"What do you make of that?" asked the officer.

"I ... I don't know ... yet," Jag stammered. "We'll have to enter it into evidence, of course. We'll follow-up to see what the connection is."

The business card read:

Boston City Police Department
Detective Taggert A. Gallagher
Precinct No. C-11
Dorchester, Massachusetts
617-555-2341

It was Jag's dad.

Jag took the white business card and stuffed it into his pocket. It never found its way to the evidence room.

*****

CH 22 - Down in Records

2020

Tommy went downstairs and pulled a cold case file from a long, banker's box along with the bags of evidence that had been collected at the scene. The pictures were snapped using an older model Kodak—likely a Series-16 or Series-20 made during the 1930s. They were somewhat faded but remarkably well-preserved for the length of time they'd been stashed away in a warehouse. The images, however, were another story. These were shocking and grotesque— showing the body of a young woman twisted and bent into a pose that was completely inhuman. Tommy resisted the urge to throw-up and quickly pushed the pictures to the bottom of the stack so they would stop haunting him. Instead, he shifted to digging through other evidence to find the necklace Dag wanted.

Tommy went through each bag. When he pulled them open, a pungent musty smell burst forth, giving credence to the many years they'd not seen the light of day outside their box. But after finishing, he found no necklace.

Going back to the pictures, he did find one that had been taken of the necklace. Far from being valueless, it appeared to be a nice piece with shiny diamond-like stones and a large, blue stone in the center. Like the description suggested, the blue stone was at the center of a pentacle. The notation on the picture was that it was allegedly one of the things stolen from the victim. Whether it was ever recovered was nowhere mentioned in the folder.

This isn't going to tell us anything, thought Tommy.

So, he turned to the police report.

> Case No. ROX80982-45
> Victim: Janice Prodescu
> Incident: Homicide
> Location: 2841 Mulberry Street, Apartment 9G, Roxbury, Mass.
> Reporting Officer: T.A. Gallagher
> Date/Time: June 9, 1945/0600

> *I arrived at the apartment where the first police officers were already at work sealing off the scene. The victim was a 25-year-old Caucasian female. Checked for pulse and found victim to be*

deceased. Body was sitting upright on the sofa in the main living room in front of a radio set that looked new. Body was not yet fully stiffened with rigor mortis.

Vic's eyes were open, head facing toward the radio console. But, the rest of the body was broken and twisted, facing backwards into the sofa. We will await the coroner's report to find out a specific cause of death.

We scoured the apartment. The doors and windows were locked, but a latch on a window in the bedroom was broken. A fire escape ladder outside could have been an escape point, but no fingerprints were found on any part of the window, latch or fire escape.

There was a jewelry box open on the dresser containing only a red lighter. It appeared to be an antique, music-type box. In the bedroom closet there was an open safe, but it too had nothing inside. There were no signs that it had been forced open. Fingerprint dusting in the apartment revealed no prints other than the vic's.

Coroner removed the body. Nothing unusual came from the autopsy, other than the distortion of the body parts.

Detective T A Gallagher

Attached to the report was another.

Case No. ROX80982-45
Victim: Janice Prodescu
Incident: Homicide
Location: 2841 Mulberry Street, Apartment 9G, Roxbury, Mass.
Reporting Officer: T.A. Gallagher
Date/Time: June 9, 1945/0600
Update: December 17, 1945

Further investigation has revealed no more leads.

Case is closed, pending new evidence or leads.

Detective T A Gallagher

Tommy put down the file and picked up another that Ritter had pulled from a special area of the Records Department. Ritter told him it had been misplaced when he initially asked about it. But

Tommy pushed him to look again, and Ritter had found it misfiled in the stacks.

Tommy read the police report which was dated 1995.

Case No. ROX98331-95
Victim: Jose Mercato
Incident: Homicide
Location: 3389 Crawford St., Roxbury, Mass.
Reporting Officer: Z. A. Gallagher
Date/Time: June 11, 1995/0505

Arrived at apartment building at approximately 0505. The incident took place in the basement. The police officers cordoned off the area according to protocol. We had obtained a warrant when neighbors called about noises coming from the place earlier that evening. When no one answered the door, we entered the vic's apartment.

Downstairs was the vic, a 38-year-old Hispanic male. He was priest who was well known in the community and at the local Catholic church, St. Sebastian's. I checked for pulse and found none. The body was rigid, laying flat on his back, his hands stretched out above him, like he was reaching for something. However, there was nothing nearby. His legs were doubled back over his chest—bent completely in the wrong direction to what is natural.

The vic's eyes were open. The body appeared without any other abrasions or wounds. I saw no blood on the floor or loose clothing over the body. The mouth was agape and appeared to be in shock. Pending an autopsy, the body looked to have been dead about two hours—no more.

Nothing else in the apartment seemed out of place. The investigation team dusted for prints around the basement area, the doors, the windows upstairs and other areas, but found nothing other than the vic's.

Interviews with the neighbors revealed that loud noises were heard that evening which prompted their calls. There was one young woman, a Miss Loraine Jackson, who said she heard strange sounds coming from the vic's place many times late at night during the past several weeks. She described them as deep growling sounds but couldn't elaborate.

The Coroner came to remove the body at 0630.

Detective Z A Gallagher

Update: June 13, 1995

Toxicology report was negative. Nothing unusual, other than the bending of the legs backwards, unnaturally, resulting in complete fractures of the knee joints and other bones (see coroner's report) ...

The report went on for several more pages, before concluding. Then, there was one more update.

Update: Nov. 7, 1995

Further investigation revealed no more leads.

Case is closed, pending new evidence or leads.

Detective Z A Gallagher

Tommy flipped to the third case. His heart pounded, as he became more certain of a connection.

Case No. DOR89002-95
Victims: Lenny Pittman and Roger Enright
Incident: Homicides
Location: 8901 Ridgewood St., Dorchester, Mass.
Reporting Officer: Z. A. Gallagher
Date/Time: June 3, 1995/0635

Arrived at the brownstone at 0635. The area was already taped off with yellow crime scene tape.

Vics were upstairs, or what was left of them. Mr. Pittman was a Caucasian male in his thirties. The head was wedged under the bed, while his headless body was still under the bedcovers. There was no blood on the sheets or the carpet around the bed. The officers said the front door had been locked, but neighbors claimed that Mr. Pittman never locked his doors.

In the next room was another male, Caucasian, in his early forties. Mr. Enright was found missing both arms. These were located later inside the kitchen oven. The oven was not on, and the body parts were not cooked.

We dusted the place but found nothing but the two victims' prints. There was a metal box that had been pried open, indentations suggesting someone had used a screwdriver. All appearances are that it was a robbery. However, the state of the bodies suggests something more.

Detective Z A Gallagher

Update 10/6/95

Lab results came back negative on toxicology for both bodies. The report is attached. It indicates a sharp, clean, blade with a very hot temperature was used in slicing the neck of Mr. Pittman, which cauterized the blood vessels. Therefore, there was no bleeding. The tool used in the decapitation is still undetermined. The same tool was used to sever the arms of Mr. Enright.

Detective Z A Gallagher

Update 11/7/95

No further progress reported. Subsequent investigation has ruled out any robbery as the intent. The cause is still unknown. The case will be closed to the cold case file.

Detective Z A Gallagher

The chill Tommy felt earlier when he spoke with the gatekeeper, Ritter, struck him for a second time. *That was an awfully quick close of three horrific cases to the cold case files*, he thought, *and the last two were closed at the same time.*

Tommy made his call again. This time, there was an answer.

"Boss," he said, "I found something here in the files … but first I need to know how far back your family goes with the force."

"What do you mean, Tommy?" Dag asked.

"I found a cold case file with a Tag Gallagher attached to it. Was he your dad?"

"No, he was my great grandfather. He was in the department back— oh—from the forties through the sixties. He was involved in a case that a lot of people said spooked him. My grandmother said it even haunted him. I recall it was a strange case, but I've never seen the case file. They said it was lost. Anyway, my great grandfather was never able to solve it. It was the one thing in his life he said he always regretted."

"What about the ones in the 1990s?" asked Tommy.

"What ones?"

"It's probably better if you come down here, Dag. These look just like the ones we're dealing with."

Dag drove to the police department where he found Tommy at his desk typing on his computer and comparing what was showing on his screen to media clippings and other reports that were scattered about haphazardly.

"Your great grandpa had the same type of case fifty years ago, Dag. Look here," said Tommy, pointing to a section in the file. "This one involved a victim who was a young woman. It says, quote, 'she was twisted like a pretzel in her apartment.' This was in 1945. But when I looked through the media articles written on it, none of them mention the distorted body or anything unusual. They only said it was an apparent homicide.

"So, I kept digging, like you told me to. I found three other cold case files in 1995 that had the same *MO*. Each of the vics was killed and their bodies contorted or dismembered in some horrific way. There was no firm evidence at any crime scene to suggest a motive. However, the detective's early notes indicate he thought they were more than just attempted burglaries. The cases weren't open that long and were pushed off to the cold case files within the same year."

"Is there anything else about these cases?" asked Dag, looking through the files.

"Yeah. The detective on the 1995 cases was ... *Zag* Gallagher."

"My dad?"

Tommy nodded.

Dag looked through the file and the piles of other papers Tommy had stacked on his desk. He remembered his father, Zag, talking about the 1995 case when he was still a small boy. His grandfather, John Arthur Gallagher, Jag, had urged Dag's father not to go into the police business – not to follow in his footsteps.

"There are just too many strange things going on the world these days, son," Jag had said to his son, Zag. "I don't think policing is the thing for us Gallaghers anymore. Let someone else do that. You need to find a career that's just as rewarding but one where your family can be sure you'll come home to them every night. Do you understand?"

Dag scanned the files quickly, looking at the names and dates.

"Yeah, I remember my dad mentioning these cases," said Dag, shaking his head. "They were really upsetting to him. I always thought they were what caused him to have nightmares at night. He was even going to quit the force at one point. He talked about it a lot there toward the end, before he was ..."

"... killed," said Tommy, finishing the thought.

Dag nodded. "He really didn't want me involved in the department either, and I know he wasn't happy at all when I followed him into the family practice."

"Then why *did* you go into the force?" asked Tommy.

Dag shrugged. "Dunno. I guess it's in the blood. I got outta' high school and spent a couple years in college. It just didn't click. It wasn't for me. So, I left and got a job down at the meat packing plant along with some buddies I'd gone to high school with. But that only lasted a year. There was something pulling me away. I knew what it was, but my dad's words kept ringing in my ears. I didn't want to talk to him about it because I knew he'd try to talk me out of it." Dag sighed. "I finally gave in and joined. Dad was very upset with me. I can still remember him yelling at me."

"When was that?"

"I've been active since, oh, 2005. I've had no regrets to this point, but right now I'm beginning to understand what my dad was saying."

"Your grandfather died just a last year too, didn't he?" asked Tommy.

"Yeah, 2019—just before we lost Dad."

"Don't you think it's odd that your great grandfather, Tag, had three in 1945, your grandpa Jag had three in 1970 and your dad, Zag, had three in 1995?"

"You said *three* cases in 1995, but you only have two files," said Dag.

"Here's the other one," answered Tommy, shoving the third one across the desk.

Dag opened this one too. He was beginning to feel sick. He had no answers—only more questions. He also knew what Tommy was thinking.

"What's with this one?" Dag asked, trying to stay calm.

"It's the same but different."

"How do you mean?"

Tommy pointed to a few sections in the report.

"To start with, there was a murder, and it was strange—but in a different way," Tommy began. "The vic was found in an alley."

"Okay," said Dag. "So, what is different about it?"

"Well, two things. It didn't happen in Boston."

"Where was it?"

"Providence."

"Rhode Island?"

"Yeah, just an hour south of here."

"And the other thing?"

"She was thrown from her thirteenth-floor apartment window. The police found the apartment locked from the inside, so they chocked it up to suicide."

"Just like Claire Horwath's case."

"Yeah."

"What was the vic's name?"

"Let me see," said Tommy, flipping open his notebook. "I have that— it was ... a Ms. Abigail Knight."

"Where was she from?"

"Uh, let's see. It says she was from ... well, what do you know ... Boston."

"I think we need to look into that connection," said Dag.

"And what about *your* connection?" asked Tommy. "Your family is connected with this somehow. Your family name is all over these case files." After a moment, Tommy added, "How did your dad die, if I may ask?"

Dag was in no mood to carry on the conversation.

"I think we're done here," Dag said defensively as he steadied himself and left the office. He was angry, upset, and on the verge of lashing out. But he didn't. Instead, he walked away.

Tommy sat alone at his desk with a mountain of folders surrounding him. He wasn't sure what to make of what had just happened. He'd not seen Dag act that way—ever. He could understand why he was upset—his family's involvement and the implications. *But what were they?* He wasn't an experienced detective, yet Tommy knew he was on to something. He was certain that if he could find the connections, he could find the killer.

*****

CH 23 - Mark of the Beast

2020

The hospital corridor was nearly empty, as it was late at night. Visiting hours were over, and Sara felt like a criminal sneaking back into the hospital to see Claire; however, Claire had insisted. She had been frantic on the phone, pleading with Sara to come as soon as possible.

While no one was watching, Sara pushed on the Claire's hospital room door and walked in. But the bed was empty. The covers were pulled down in disarray, and the sheets were crumpled and askew—all thrown off to one side.

"Claire?" said Sara with urgency. "Claire, are you here?"

Then she heard the bathroom toilet flush and saw Claire as she walked out holding her toothbrush.

"What?" Claire asked, stopping when she saw the panicked look in Sara's eyes.

"Oh, nothing," said Sara, relieved. "It's nothing."

"Well, thank you so much for coming. I really didn't know who else to call. You said that I should check to see if I had any marks."

"Marks?"

"Yes, you said for me to see if I had any strange markings on my body."

"Do you?"

Claire turned her back to Sara and untied her gown, letting it drop lower on her shoulders.

"Look just below my neckline ... do you see it?" she asked.

Sara pulled Claire's hair back, lifting it up to reveal more.

"What am I looking for, Claire?" asked Sara.

"The marks. Don't you see the marks on the back of my neck?"

Sara ran her fingers over the skin and up into Claire's hairline in back.

"Claire, I'm sorry. I don't see anything. Are you sure you saw something back here? Maybe it was something on the mirror. Did you use that mirror over there?"

"Yes, I did, but it's not the mirror. I'm sure of it," Claire answered. "I checked myself as soon as you left. There was a red mark on the back of my neck. When I touched it, it became hot. Then, as I watched, the spot started to swirl with shades of yellow and black spinning around inside of it. It was dreadful! I thought it was going to come right out of my body."

Claire was anxious, and the puzzled look on her face now showed even greater concern.

"Settle yourself, Claire. I don't see anything right now. Do you feel something back there?"

"No, I don't. But it was there, I tell you. It was *there!*"

Claire went to the mirror herself and began pulling on the skin around her neck trying to find the marking. Sara continued to look up into her scalp, but they found no remnants. Nothing.

Sara helped Claire to her bed and lifted her legs, swiveling them around and settling them back under the covers before pulling the cotton layers up under Claire's chin.

"You know, sometimes we see things when they're not there just because someone says we might or should," said Sara. "Perhaps because I suggested you *might* have a marking, your brain told you there was one there."

"*No!*" shouted Claire, visibly upset. "I *know* what I saw, and it was *there*. Right *there!*" she said, pointing to the back of her neck.

"Okay, Claire. I believe you. So, there was a red mark on the back of your neck that isn't there now. Could it have been a bug bite ... you know, like a spider or something?"

"Do you know any spider bites that have those colors and swirl around like a cup of hot chocolate?" asked Claire, sarcastically. Then she calmed down. "I'm sorry. I guess I'm just upset over what's been going on the last few days. I don't know what happened to me in my apartment or who or what did it. And when I leave here, I won't know whether the person or thing that attacked me is still out there. Maybe it's waiting for me to come home ... waiting to attack me again!"

143

"It's okay, Claire. We'll figure this out. Trust me," comforted Sara. "Tell me again what the mark looked like."

"It was about the size of a silver dollar, red with a swirling pattern of red, yellow and black. After I touched it, the bands of color began to swirl toward the center, like a pinwheel. The spot was hot on my fingers but not hot on my neck."

"Claire, I really don't think it's anything to worry about, but I don't want to take what you're saying lightly, either. I'll do a little research on my own and see what I come up with. What did your doctor say?"

Claire huffed. "He wouldn't believe me either. He'd tell me the same thing. 'It's nothing' he'd said. Just like the other night. How do you explain that?"

"I can't—not yet," Sara answered. "But let me know if the mark comes back, particularly if you see it on your forehead or right hand," said Sara.

"Why there? What if it comes back someplace else?"

"I don't know. I don't know what that would mean. Let's just take this a day at a time, okay?"

Sara put her arms around her to give her what comfort she could, holding her head as a friend and letting Claire's salty tears wet the soft, white pillowcase.

"We will figure this out, Claire. I promise."

Sara only hoped it was a promise she could keep.

*****

CH 24 - A Young Reporter

1970

Danny Pittman was young and aggressive—a bulldog of a reporter. He had always been that way, even when he was fresh out of college. He wanted to make a name for himself in the big, competitive world of journalism. Having landed a job at the *Boston Globe*, he needed to prove himself to his editor that he was different from the other newbies who had just come out of the sawmill of journalism school.

Short and diminutive, his physical stature didn't share what he thought of himself and his abilities. He was a bit arrogant and headstrong, but there was a core of authenticity to him. He never shirked from tackling a tough story, even if it meant risking everything. Unfortunately, he rarely got that chance.

Assigned to mundane, daily beat stories of everyday life, Danny grew tired of calling local shop owners when they'd been robbed or writing about some weather event that might or might not happen in the Boston area. By the time he'd written his piece and it was edited and re-edited, it looked nothing like what he had put together. Often, someone else's name was even attached, instead of his. Yet he was asked to "buck-up" and put in his dues as had everyone else who worked there.

However, one day in June 1970, Danny turned on his police scanner and heard something interesting.

"Hey, Joe. Just got a DB called in in Brookline. Jag is in route, but you might want to swing by."

"Why?"

"Joe says it's interesting. Just sayin'."

"Interesting? I've seen a lot of DBs. They're all 'interesting' Smitty. That doesn't mean I need to see another one."

"Up to you. The twenty is 2309 Brookline Boulevard, Apartment 306, over."

Danny grabbed his notepad and wrote down the address. Then, with his pen still clenched between his teeth, he hurried out of the newsroom, hoping it would be worth his while.

It took only twenty minutes to get to Brookline at that time of day, and when he arrived he found himself pulling in with two other police cruisers—both black-on-white Chevys with the big red and white lights separated by a siren horn mounted in between. Hoping to get inside the building before the officers blocked things off, Danny ran toward the front door, only to find a sergeant already standing guard. He flipped out his press badge and acted like he'd been authorized to go in, but the officer put out his arm.

"Can't go in, son," said the officer.

"But I was asked to cover the story," said Danny, lying.

"Who approved it?"

"Uh, the chief. The chief said it was ..."

"No, he didn't. Nice try though. You'll have to stay out here. I'm not allowed to let anyone inside."

Danny grinned and climbed back down the cement stairs to the street. However, instead of waiting, he found an alley two buildings down and went around to the backside of the building. There, he found a door not yet guarded and slipped inside. Listening from the entry hall, he heard people talking upstairs and mounted the steep, squeaky steps to find the source.

"I just don't know. I'm shaking. It's horrible—just horrible. Nothing like I've ever seen in my life and hope never to again," came a voice from just above him on the next level. It sounded like a woman of ethnicity and maturity.

Danny cautiously peered up the next flight and saw two older women talking on the next landing. He took out his notebook and pencil and tried to blend in with the other police detectives on the scene.

"Good-day, ma'am, ma'am," he said, tipping his hat to each. "So, what do you make of this incident here? What can you tell me about it?"

One of the women was in her seventies, small and frail. She had long gray hair that was braided and coiled on top of her head. She wore thick, black glasses—coke-bottle-ish, in fact—and her fingers curled around the silver handle of her cane as though she had severe arthritis in her joints. From her accent, Danny pegged her as Polish.

The other woman was younger—not young enough to be her daughter but from their looks, possibly a sister or some other

146

relation. Probably a next-door neighbor, the younger one was also Polish or from that region. She held a baby in her arms and rocked it slowly to keep it pacified. She too was short, but stockier than the older woman. Her face was cherubic, and her brown eyes large and friendly. She wore a simple, flowered dress which flowed in pleats to her knees and black low-heeled pumps that looked aged and worn.

"Oh, officer. It's really something," said the older woman. "The body is all twisted, like it was put through a corkscrew. I don't know what could have done that to someone. And Jenny was such a dear soul. It's just an awful thing. She went to mass every Sunday too."

"Who discovered the body?" asked Danny. "Did you find her?"

"Oh, no," said the older woman. "I just heard about it from Maria here and the landlord who went inside. She said it was the worst thing she'd ever seen. Really terrible."

"It's awful," said the younger woman, whose face was pallid and unnerved. "I ... I can't describe it. I had to help the landlady out of the apartment. She was ready to get sick."

"Was the apartment locked then? Did the landlady have to use a key to get in?"

"Yes. The door was locked. She was still in her bed when we found her," said the younger woman. "At least the parts we could see."

The older woman began to sob. "Oh, Jenny! Poor dear!"

"The parts you could see? What do you mean?" asked Danny.

"I don't know that either, officer. I'm sure you'll see it when you get up there. We just hope you find whoever did this to her. They're a monster. Horrible, horrible person. None of us are safe with someone like that still roaming the streets."

The baby woke up and began crying, so the two women left, going back into their respective apartments. Danny listened for more voices and heard another one the next flight up. He glanced around the corner and up the steps, but there were too many police there to sneak into the apartment and see for himself. Instead, he went out the back door and found a phone booth. There he made a call to the office.

"Hey, Sam, it's Danny. I'm over here in Brookline, and there's been a murder. I want to be assigned to report on it."

"Naw, Danny. That's not your beat," said his boss, a junior editor at the paper. "You have to cover the weather and petty crime stuff. If it's something big, I'll assign Davenport to it."

"No, no, it's not that big, really," said Danny, trying to minimize things to get the story for himself. "It may not be anything at all. I'll follow-up and see, then I'll let you know."

"Well, if it's a murder, we'll find out about it from the precinct. They may want us to cover it so they can get leads to find the murderer. You just come back to the newsroom. We'll look into it later this afternoon after we get word."

Danny hung up the phone and went to the front of the building, waiting for the coroner or police to come out. After about ten minutes, an orange-and-white ambulance van arrived, followed by a second one. Twenty minutes after that, a steel gurney rolled out the front door with a white sheet covering a body. It was quickly loaded into the back of the emergency vehicle and driven away. When a second gurney came out, two other reporters in the crowd muscled their way in to talk with the detective who was accompanying the DB.

"Detective, what can you tell us about the deaths?" said one reporter.

"No, nothing at this time," said Jag.

"Was it a murder-suicide? Was it a family dispute? Was it a gang murder?"

Frustrated with the questions, Jag finally said, "Listen, it was all just an unfortunate accident. We believe the woman just left the gas on in her apartment. Tragic accident, but that's all there is. I'm afraid you won't get much of a story off this one. Sorry."

Danny pushed himself up to the front where the other reporters stood. "Detective, so you're saying there *were* two deaths?"

"Yes."

"A woman and who was the other?"

"There was a young man in the apartment as well."

"And it was just gas that killed them—nothing else?"

"That's about it," said Jag.

"But gas didn't leak out into the rest of the apartment building. How could that be?"

"Others will have to figure that out. I'm only here to find out the cause of the deaths. That's all."

"So, the cause of death was asphyxiation, then?"

"Yes," said Jag, tiring of the barrage, "that's what it appears to be at this point. The coroner will give us more information after the autopsy."

Jag tried to move on, but Danny wouldn't let up.

"The bodies weren't disfigured or mangled in any way?"

Jag looked at Danny with surprise but quickly regained his composure. "No, it was asphyxiation."

"That's not what some ladies said inside the building," said Danny.

"You'll have to excuse me," said Jag suddenly. "That's all we have at the moment," he said, hurrying to his car.

Danny wrote it all down. Something wasn't adding up, and he wanted to be the one who sorted it out and got the headline.

*****

CH 25 - An Invitation

2020

Dag drove up the now-familiar driveway, climbed out and shut the car door. It was another long trip, and one that he really hadn't wanted to make again. However, Patti had called shortly after their first meeting, insisting that her mother and she needed to talk with him. He had tried to discuss things over the phone with her, but she had insisted that a face-to-face was necessary for what she had to tell him. Reluctantly, he had climbed into his aging sedan and retaken the route to Upstate New York hoping his car would make it there and back.

Dag knocked on the door, and, as before, Patti answered.

"Oh, Detective Gallagher, come in," she said smiling, this time more relaxed than the first day they'd met. Her demeanor was oddly easy-going when juxtaposed against what he had seen the last time he'd been there. *If there were a Jekyll and Hyde, this was most assuredly the nicer Dr. Jekyll,* he thought. She was also very casually dressed. Wearing only a white, V-neck sweater and a short, denim skirt, she seemed eager to show-off her great legs and ample breasts of which Dag could see plenty of through the outline of her nipples in the thin, cotton pullover.

The detective walked into the living room and sat down on the sofa, as he had before. He pulled out his notebook tablet and pen, shifting his hips toward the front edge of the cushions.

"So, what is it that you and your mom wanted to tell me Ms. Wilkins?" he asked.

"Before we get into that," Patti began, "why don't I get us some tea. I made some cookies this morning."

"Uh, thanks, but I can't stay long. I just came because you said you had some more information that you wanted to tell me."

Abruptly and without answering, Patti left the room and vanished through the open doorway into the kitchen.

"Ms. Campbell?" asked Dag, raising his voice slightly to get her attention.

"Yes," she answered, calling out from the other room. "I'm just getting our tea ready."

Dag sat patiently, staring at the clock on the wall. It was 4:35 in the afternoon, and he had hoped to get on the road and back to the precinct by no later than 6:30. However, he was willing to be more patient, especially if what they had to say would help him break the case open.

Within a few minutes, Patti returned carrying a platter and tea service set—an elaborate spread of home-baked pastries and packets of tea flavors, all just waiting to be enjoyed. But that wasn't the only thing she had waiting. Gone were the denim shorts and sweater. Now, she had on nothing but a low-cut, devil-red negligee. She looked like a woman in her thirties; not one who was sixty.

She stooped over and handed Dag a cup for the tea. Dumbfounded, he was quickly drawn in, intoxicated by her mysterious spell. He stared, speechless, at her nice, round breasts. Between them dangled her pentagram pendant which held a deep-blue sapphire and small, twinkling diamonds at each point.

"Here you go," she said smiling as she set down the tray.

"Uh, what are you doing?" Dag managed to mumble.

"Bringing you some tea, silly," she said bending over him to pour hot water into his cup and show him more of her cleavage. Raised in a strict, Irish Catholic home, Dag quickly became hopelessly tongue-tied.

Then, Patti opened the tin of tea bags. "See anything you like?"

She took one of his hands and put it on her breast, rubbing it gently so her nipples would be aroused. Dag only sat there in a trance, himself already excited by her and what she was doing to him. Patti leaned in and kissed him, pressing her soft, moist lips onto his. But it was that which broke the spell, and Dag shook his head, turning away from her.

"What's wrong?" she asked, surprised by his reaction.

"Uh, ma'am," said Dag, blinking and taking a breath, "you'll have to stop."

"Why?"

"Is your mother here?"

Patti backed off a few inches, realizing something had changed. "No," she answered, still hovering close, "but why don't we just enjoy ourselves right now?"

Dag sat back, distancing himself from her, but Patti was not deterred. She poured the hot water for the tea into two small cups, but before reaching for any teabags, she again moved close to Dag— this time straddling his leg. She smoothly took his hand and put it on the inside of her thigh, slowly rubbing it up and down.

Dag could feel himself sinking back under her spell, and he was getting aroused again. Then he felt the long fingers from her other hand moving up his inner thigh toward his crotch. Closing his eyes, he struggled between fighting back and yielding to his passions. When he opened his eyes again, she had climbed on top of him, kissing his neck and then unbuttoning his shirt. His resistance was fading, as he felt himself losing control.

But then he saw the pentagram as it dangled before his eyes and heard a tiny voice in his mind telling him to wake up. As the fog cleared, he pushed her back.

"What's wrong?" she asked. "Don't you like it?"

Dag got up.

"Where are you going?" she asked him as he headed for the door.

Dag grasped the front door handle but heard a strange, purring noise behind him. He looked back. Patti was kneeling on the couch, her back arched with her perfectly-shaped ass sticking out provocatively, waiting for a guest. Her head was turned toward him, but there was something unnatural about it. A reddish hue glowed in her eyes and her face was contorted into something foreign, something alien. It no longer seemed human.

Dag started to speak but then noticed the wall behind her. That side of the room—once covered with different crucifixes—now held pentagrams of varying shapes, styles and sizes. In the center was a single triangle encapsulated by a circle—the pentacle. The wall had been repainted too with the white replaced by a deep shade of red.

"Patti, where did you say your mother was?" Dag asked.

"I didn't," she said with a fiendish smile.

"Well, when she gets home, please have her call me."

"But, detective, it's late. You really should stay. It's not safe driving home so late at night with these winding country roads you know."

"No, I really must be going." And with that, Dag let himself out the front door.

The drive back seemed shorter as his mind fixated on what had just happened. This was not the same person he had met only a few days earlier—not at all. He wished that Terri, her mother, her mother had been there. Things most assuredly would have been different.

But where was she? This is odd, he thought. *Very odd.*

***

Patti slumped back on the sofa. She took the glass vase that was on the coffee table and threw it through the front, pane glass window, shattering it and sending shards everywhere inside the house.

"Damn him to hell!" she yelled.

Now, the red in her eyes turned a pale, sick yellow. She got up and went back into the kitchen.

"There Mom! Are you happy? You scared him away! How long will I have to wait for my next chance to seduce a Gallagher? Huh?"

Patti slapped her mother's face as she sat quiet and still at the kitchen table. Terri's body slumped over, unable to answer, her eyes fixed and dilated.

"You just couldn't leave your Christian crap out of this, now could you!"

Patti loosened the black scarf that was tied around her mother's neck, the fibers torn where it had cut through her windpipe. She then unwrapped it from the corpse and flipped it around her own neck, letting the red blood of her mother smear her throat.

"There. Now, doesn't this look nice, mother? I think it completes my ensemble perfectly. Don't you think?" she said with an evil smile.

*****

CH 26 – Digging Deeper

1970

Danny tried to get information out of the police precinct but was making little headway. Instead of facts, he was given more of the same. It was just a "tragic accident," they kept claiming. Even when he went back to the apartment building where the murders had occurred, the neighbors suddenly refused to talk to him. Every door in the place closed, slamming in place once they found out he was a reporter. All, that is, except one.

Mary Littlejoy was another neighbor of the Carters, and she lived on the same floor—across the hall, in fact. Mary told Danny that earlier that day a middle-aged woman with long dark hair had come to the victims' apartment. It was someone she had never seen there before.

"But when I talked to Jenny about it," Mary said, recalling the conversation, "she said it was some psychic she had hired. Jenny said she wanted to get in touch with her son's wife and daughter. So sad. They both died in an auto accident not long ago. It devastated both of them. She said she thought it would help if she could contact them to tell her son they were okay—you know—in heaven."

"What else do you remember about the conversation?" Danny asked.

"Jenny said the psychic was able to contact them and that she had felt better about things after it was over. She said the woman told her that her granddaughter and daughter-in-law were there with her and her son all the time and that they were in a good place. The woman said they told her they were sorry for causing them so much pain, but they should know that it happened for a reason—it was supposed to happen that way. There was nothing they could have done."

"Supposed to happen? Why would that make any sense?"

"Jenny didn't tell me. I'm not sure she knew what they meant by that," said Mary.

"Do you know who the psychic was? Did she give you a name?"

"She said the name Cora Rae, but I didn't get a last name."

"Cora Rae?"

"Yes, I'm sure that's what she said."

The psychic world was a small community, and it wasn't hard for Danny to track down the only Cora Rae who fit the description. She lived not far away in Roxbury. Another psychic he talked to, a Ms. Theresa Turner, gave the reporter the address and phone number for her.

"I'm sure Cora Rae will talk with you," Theresa had said. "She's very open about what she does. Personally, there are many of us who believe she's a bit of a charlatan. She doesn't have the abilities the rest of us do. It's a tough business. Some people fake it to get clients and make a living. That's a travesty as far as I'm concerned. It does our profession a disservice. But I'm always happy to help law enforcement, and if I can do that through you, that's great."

"So, she's a competitor," Danny had said.

"Well, she makes a lot of money doing those sessions, and those of us who are truly connected with the other side aren't so sure that she is. She's never able to do it when we're around. That's usually a sign that someone is, well shall we say, a pretender. But don't tell her I said that. It's a small community, you know. I wouldn't want her to know that's what was being said about her."

Danny smiled. "I'm not in the business of spreading comments and opinions of others. I'm just a reporter, and all I'm trying to do is gather the facts."

He tried to reach Cora Rae by phone but received no answer. So, he drove to Roxbury hoping to find her at home. Luckily, she was on her front porch sipping an iced tea, as the temperature in Boston had climbed into the 90s that day.

"Ms. Taylor?" Danny asked, walking up a line of brown, brick pavers that cut through the front yard to the porch steps.

"Yes?" the woman had replied.

"I'm Danny Pittman from the *Boston Globe*. I'd like to ask you a little about the session you had with Virginia Carter."

Cora Rae got up from her seat and started to go inside the house, but Danny rushed up the steps and put his foot in the door jam.

"I'm sorry, but you can't come in," she said firmly.

"I'm only trying to get your side of the story, ma'am," said Danny.

"There is no *my side* of the story, mister," said Cora Rae. "There is no story to tell."

"According to the police, you were at the apartment the day the woman and her son were murdered."

"Murdered? You mean died. I read that they died from a gas leak," said Cora Rae.

"Not from what I understand, ma'am. I heard they now believe she was murdered, and since you were there that day, I thought you could tell me more about that. What was your appointment about?"

"That was between my client and me," said Cora Rae, her arm shaking nervously as she clung to the door.

"So, you were there?"

"I have to go. Get your foot out of my doorway before I call the police!"

"You're a psychic, right?" Cora Rae looked at the reporter with mild surprise. "That's what I've been told," he said.

"Who told you that?" Cora Rae asked.

"Other psychics. You live a small world, Ms. Taylor. People talk and the smaller the group, the more people talk."

"So what. Yes, I gave her a session. That was it. We connected her with loved ones, and then we left."

"We?"

"Yes, I have someone with me for protection—just in case."

"Just in case what?" asked Danny, as bull dogged as ever.

"Just in case," said Cora Rae, not giving him anything more.

"Is he your driver, then?"

"He's my bodyguard, if you must know."

"So, he was there too?"

"Yes, he was there. He's always there to give me protection in case I need it. I've had problems in the past."

"What about complaints from your clients that they were burglarized? I've heard several of yours were broken into shortly after their sessions with you. Is there any truth to that?"

"I don't know what you're talking about," said Cora Rae, crossing her arms.

"I looked at the police records for some of your previous clients, and there does seem to be a correlation between …"

"You don't know who my clients are," said Cora Rae, now defiant.

"Again, Ms. Taylor, it's a small community—you and your psychic friends."

Cora Rae slammed the door and drew the shades, while Danny closed his notebook.

There is more to the story, he thought. *I think I'm on to something.*

*****

CH 29 – Another One Dead

1970

Danny was working on his multi-part story on the deaths of Jenny Carter and her son when he received a phone call.

"Hey, Danny? Weren't you talking to that Cora Rae lady last week? She's the psychic you think was involved in the death of Virginia Carter and her son."

It was Danny's editor, Jacob Landman. Danny's first story had raised great interest and circulation had increased significantly since the time the first part was printed.

"Yeah, I spoke to her. Why?"

"She's dead."

"She's dead?"

"That's what my lips said when they moved. Yeah, she's dead, Danny. I think you need to look into it right away. I'd say you have another story to tell."

Danny visited the police precinct and talked to the investigating detective about the connections and what they had found.

"It's an ongoing investigation, so I can't discuss it," said Jag.

"But Virginia Carter was brutally murdered only a few weeks ago. Now, Cora Rae? They were both together on the same day. What happened to Cora Rae?"

"I said, I can't go into the details," said Jag. "And as of right now, the Carter deaths are still labeled an accident."

"You expect me to still believe that?" asked Danny.

"Yes," Jag answered.

Danny thanked the detective and left, but he didn't leave the building. Instead, he went downstairs, nosing around to find information from anyone who could give it to him. The central files were in the basement where the man in charge was a man named Ritter, Leroy Ritter. At home, he had a young son named Nathan— the very same who would work with his dad at the precinct for a few years before taking the reins himself.

"Can I help you with something?" asked Leroy, watching Danny come down the walkway.

"Yes, I was wondering if you had anything more on the Cora Rae Taylor case. It just came in. I'm from the state office," said Danny, lying, "and I'm helping out."

Leroy had the file on his counter. It hadn't yet been filed and checked in.

"This is all I have so far," said Leroy, pushing the file to him.

Danny opened the cover and flipped through the pictures. They were ghastly. The first was of the bed's headboard across which were the blood-smeared words: *Hello Plottar*. Other photos showed parts of the body as if they'd been put through a meat grinder with shredded pieces hanging from the bone. The reporter felt his stomach heaving. Feeling light-headed, he thanked Leroy and handed him back the files.

"Is there anything else you needed?" Leroy asked.

"No. I'm good for now," Danny answered, hurrying back upstairs before he lost his lunch inside the building.

The case of Cora Rae had sent another shockwave through the police department. It had been gruesome, and only the strongest among the coroner's office had been selected to collect the pieces for examination.

Danny continued to dig, contacting Theresa Campbell once again.

"Mr. Pittman," Terri said, greeting him warmly, "it's good to talk to you again. What can I help you with?"

"It's about Cora Rae."

"Oh? What about her?"

"She was murdered two nights ago. I was wondering if you had any information on that."

"Well, I'm sorry to hear that," said Terri, not appearing overly distraught. "I didn't know her well—had met her only a few times. Why would you think I would know anything about that?"

"You're in the community of them—psychics, that is. I just thought you might have heard something. Do you have any sense for who might have done this? The fact that Jenny Carter and she were both killed and both so violently. It seems too coincidental. But it's obvious now that Cora Rae didn't have anything to do with Jenny Carter's death."

"Why do you say that?" asked Terri.

"Well, because she was killed too. I'm assuming they were both killed by the same person."

"You don't know that. Maybe Cora Rae had Jenny murdered and the hitman turned on her so he wouldn't be found out."

"Is that what your psychic ability tells you?"

"Maybe," Terri answered coyly.

"What else does it tell you?" Danny asked.

"Why don't you book a session with me, and I'll tell you," said Terri.

Danny scheduled his session with Terri and hoped it would gain him more information. He didn't believe in the medium mumbo-jumbo, but perhaps that was a way for Terri to tell him what she knew without incriminating herself. *You never know*, he thought.

*****

CH 28 - Deep Dive

2020

For the next several weeks, there was little activity in Boston and its precincts, which was a good thing. Murders and other violent crimes were down in the city and nearby suburbs, which the mayor attributed to "the increased money he had allocated to law enforcement." The reality was that September temperatures had fallen to below-normal levels, calming agitation in the masses and reducing violent outbursts. It was a well-known fact that hot summer nights brought out the worst in people, and by the same token, extremely cold weather forced crime rates down as fewer people ventured out and got into trouble.

The extra time also allowed Tommy to continue his work on the cold case files. He looked at all the homicides and unusual deaths that occurred between 1920 and 2020, the year Dag's father, Zag, had died. Although many could have been homicides, they also could have been accidental deaths or suicides. Tommy didn't waste time on those; rather, he focused on, as he put it, "the more interesting cases."

There were a few unusual murders in 1920, but the bodies had been found in remote areas outside of Boston, not within the metropolitan area. From 1921 to 1944, nothing unusual surfaced. It wasn't until 1945 that things got "interesting."

It certainly was an interesting time historically too, as the second world war came to an end in Europe and the Pacific. President Roosevelt had also died that year, and the new president, Truman, had been handed the task of ending the war against millions of Japanese soldiers who were willing to die for their emperor, Hirohito.

Aside from the Janice Prodescu case in 1945, two more cases stood out, and while the notes taken at that time were not as thorough as those in 2020, there were enough to piece together what had happened. Both cases involved gruesome murders on the south side of Boston; both cases involved people found alone; and both cases involved a Gallagher.

In the summer of that year, the police were called to the basement of an apartment building in Medford. There, a local resident had found the body of one of the tenants, referred to as a Mr. Rosco Arthur. Tommy quickly flipped to the detailed report that contained the detective's notes.

Case No. MED76312-45
Incident: Homicide
Victim: Rosco Arthur Pending
Location: 4456 Crawford St., Medford, Mass.
Reporting Officer(s): Det. Al Bondino/Det. Taggert A. Gallagher
Date/Time: June 6, 1945/0600

Received the call at 0550 and arrived at the apartment building at 0600. The building sup, Jonathon Whitmore, showed me to the lower level, where the trash from the building shoots gets deposited.

Behind the gray trash bin were the outstretched legs of the vic, a Mr. Rosco Arthur. Later confirmed to be in his mid-twenties, Mr. Arthur was wearing only white briefs at the time of death. It is unclear why he went to the garbage room as there was no sign of a trash bin that he might have carried with him.

Mr. Arthur suffered a blow to the back of the head, which the coroner's report said was not the cause of death. More baffling was the body. The torso, head and arms were found separated from the legs, as if someone or something had somehow torqued the upper part of the body one way, while turning the bottom part the other, causing a brute force separation of the two. We loaded the body parts onto a gurney and brought them back for examination by the coroner.

I questioned all the tenants in the building (see list attached), but none had seen anything. Investigation of the deceased's apartment found nothing significantly out of place. However, we did discover that two guns from a rack and some money may have been taken.

Note: The initial response was made by Detective Tag Gallagher, who recused himself from the case as he knew the victim. Detective Al Bondino assumed the case at that time.

Detective Al Bondino

Update: December 18, 1945

Further investigation revealed no more leads.

Case is closed pending new evidence or leads.

Detective Al Bondino

The second case was equally strange.

Case No. DOR1230045
Incident: Homicide
Victim: Dumitra Prodescu
Location: 10201 Ridgewood St., Dorchester, Mass.
Reporting Officer: Det. Taggert A. Gallagher
Date/Time: June 23, 1945/0630

Received the bulletin over the radio and proceeded to the cited address with my partner, Det. Randall Thompson. The building was a duplex brownstone. Neighbors reported hearing screams in the middle of the night.

We knocked on the door, but when there was no response, we forced entry and went inside. Starting in the dining room, we went through the first floor, going from room to room. There was nothing out of place downstairs that we noticed.

Upstairs, we found the vic. in her bedroom. It was Caucasian female, in her fifties, named Dumitra Prodescu. The body was still under the bedcovers, or at least the top portion was from the torso up. The bottom half was found in the guest bedroom down the hallway, also under the covers of the bed in that room. Strangely, there was no blood on the sheets or the carpet around either bed or in the apartment hallway.

A neighbor heard a muffled scream at about 0330, no other witnesses were found. There was no forced entry as the front door had been unlocked, but neighbors claimed the vic never locked her doors. She generally kept to herself but would sometimes bring neighbors chocolate chip cookies she baked for them. They also said she had a granddaughter, who was less than a year old and was being cared for by a sister of hers. As for other family, none have yet been identified.

The deceased was divorced and lost her daughter a few months earlier. Neighbors said she closed herself off after that.

We checked for odd fingerprints, but none of the prints came up in our files. We will continue to investigate.

Update December 2, 1945

No further progress reported. The case will be closed to the cold case files.

Detective Tag Gallagher

Tommy had a strong constitution, but the pictures were horrible. Although there was no blood, the body of the woman looked completely drained of it.

Between 1946 and 1969, Tommy again found no other cases that were like them; however, another surfaced in 1970 with similar characteristics. Reading the description, it was just as gruesome as the others.

Case No. BRK12300-70
Incident: Homicide
Victim(s): Virginia (Jenny) Carter (mother)
*   Jacob (Jake) Myron Carter (son)*
Location: 5410B Patriot Way, Brookline, Mass.
Reporting Officer: Det. John A. Gallagher
Date/Time: June 8, 1970/0630

> *... Female vic was found ... the body was mangled ... such force required to commit the crime would have been significant.*

> *... Male vic was found in a similar state. His body was ...*

> *... There was no sign of forced entry, and no indications of a burglary. The doors were locked from the inside – all double-bolted ...*

> *... The female victim was a fifty-something. She held a job at the local police precinct as a trans-scriber. The male was in his late twenties—the son of the female. He was unemployed and living at home.*

Detective Jag Gallagher

Update: November 4, 1970

No further evidence has been identified. Case moved to the Cold-case files.

Detective Jag Gallagher

Tommy shuddered—another case moved quickly to the cold case files. But he set it, along with the other cases, aside for later. That was about all he could take in one sitting.

He looked at his watch. Unfortunately, he still had another hour to kill before his shift ended, and he thought he might as well make the most of it. So, he moved to something else. Starting with the Internet, he typed in searches for all articles related to Zeller Arthur Gallagher, Zag, who was murdered earlier in 2020. Most newspapers had obits that lionized the man, holding him out as a hero and patriot.

Boston Police Chief Murdered

Boston – Zeller Arthur Gallagher, better known as Zag, was murdered Saturday night. Born July 4, 1961, he died suddenly at the hands of criminals he spent his life trying to arrest and put behind bars. Graduating from Alsip High School in 1979, ... He joined the Boston PD in 1983 and became a detective in 1995 and chief in 2001... He worked on some of the most challenging cases the department faced during the 1990s. He is survived by his wife Trudy, his father, Taggert, his son, Douglas, and his grandson, William.

Grandson? thought Tommy. *I didn't know Dag had a son.*

But Tommy kept looking, hoping to find something more substantial.

It took another two hours—well past the end of his shift—but he was getting used to that as a detective. Finally, he stumbled on something even more interesting during his Internet search. It was a reference made to the disappearance of a Boston police officer back in 1995.

... as there have been a few notable missing person cases as of late. The most notable, unsolved case involves a Boston detective, Jessie Davis. Detective Davis was a partner of Zeller Gallagher, otherwise known as Zag. It is still unknown whether foul play was involved or whether he merely left town after divorcing his wife. The couple lived in Boston and have a young son, Bradley.

Date: June 30, 1995

165

Tommy pressed further, hoping to find something more. Going downstairs to the cold case storage area, he found his friend Ritter, who was just packing up for the day.

"Hey there, Tommy? What's shakin'?" said Ritter, who was in good humor.

"Ritter, I have to ask you another favor. I know you've already done a lot for me, but this one is ... well ... sensitive."

"Okay. I'm listening," answered Ritter, being non-committal.

"I need to find out everything I can about the disappearance of Jessie Davis. It happened back in 1995—about the time as those other murders. I've gone through all the stuff on the Internet, but it's all sanitized."

"Sanitized? What do you mean?"

"I mean, it's been scrubbed of anything of substance. It's a bunch of stuff that could have been taken from any missing person's file. It's like somebody went through it with a black marker blocking out anything that would look suspicious or out-of-place. Do you understand? Most of the stuff says he just disappeared—like *poof.* They act like it's normal for police detectives to just go missing. Do you have anything more on that?"

Ritter drew a deep breath. "Boy, I don't know about this one, Tommy. You're diving into deep water here."

"Come on Ritter. If you know somethin', just tell me."

Ritter looked at him and then said, "Well, okay, but you didn't hear it from me. Understand?"

Tommy leaned in closer so as not to miss a word.

Ritter began. "They say there's a file somewhere here at the precinct. I don't know where it is. I don't have access to it. But ..."

"But what?" asked Tommy.

"But word has it that it's a case Jess was working on at the time of his disappearance."

"You think it's connected, then?"

Ritter didn't answer.

"How do I get the file?"

"The only person I know that has access to it is the *boss.*"

"You mean the captain?"

"No, even higher up—the District Attorney's Office. I'm not even sure the DA knows he has it; it's been so long. 1995 is eons ago now. New DAs come and go, you know," said Ritter.

"Not this one," said Tommy. "This one's been with us for a while. I bet he knows something."

"You may be right, but I wouldn't do it, Tommy. It's a CEM if I ever saw one."

"CEM?"

"Career-ending move, and it's something I know nothin' about. Got that?"

Tommy made a gesture of sealing his own lips and then said, "Thanks, Ritter."

However, secrets were the least of Tommy's concerns. He was young and wanted to make a mark for himself, even if it involved less-than-virtuous means. He would get that file—whatever it took.

*****

CH 29 – Lunch with Mitzie

2020

Sara couldn't help but think about the girls in the photo she had found in the yearbook in the attic. Mitzie had told her their great grandmothers had been close friends and they had shared the same line of business; both were psychics. After reading her great grandmother's entries in her personal journal, Sara felt sure one of the girls in the picture was the friend and Mitzie's great grandmother. *But even if it were true, what difference did that make?* she thought. *Why would Mitzie contact her and bring it up?*

Sara hadn't written down the number when she'd gotten the call, but she had a good memory for things like that. The number on her mobile screen came back to her in an instant: *555-904-8093*.

For someone who dealt with the spirit world, been assaulted in a private apartment, visited some very shady parts of town, and fought nightmares on a regular basis, it was odd that Sara now hesitated before picking up the phone to call Mitzie. Her finger pushed the last number, and she pressed the phone to her ear waiting as the buzzing at the other end beeped on and off. Finally, there was an answer.

"Hi, you've reached Mitzie's phone. Leave your message ..."

Sara began to put the receiver down when she heard another voice.

"Hello?"

"Yes, hello. Is this Mitzie?" Sara asked, startled to be talking to a live person.

"Who's this?"

"This is Sara McLaughlin. I'm sorry to bother you, but ..."

"Oh, Sara! No, it's no bother at all. I'm glad you called back. I figured it would take you a little time to process what I told you. But I knew you'd find that what I was telling you was true. So, are we still on for tomorrow?"

Sara was a bit put-off by the Mitzie's pushiness, but this time she relented.

"Sure," Sara said. "At 12:30, right?"

"*Oooooh*, I can't do it at 12:30 now. What about, say 1:30 at the Village Bistro near Beacon and Charles?"

"Uh, sure. I'll see you tomorrow," said Sara, still uncomfortable with the arrangement but willing to see it through.

The next day, Sara drove to the popular bistro, finding a parking place in one of the garages nearby. She took the elevator down to the mezzanine floor and went out through the side door onto the street. The restaurant was only a block down, but the sidewalks were crowded with the hustle and bustle of weekday businesspeople hurrying either to or from their important lunch meetings.

Sara pushed the brass handle of the restaurant door and went inside. Almost immediately, the hostess came up to her and smiled.

"Welcome to the Village Bistro. How many in your party?"

"Sara!" came a voice from a corner table toward the back. "I'm over here."

Mitzie, as loud as ever, was motioning with one arm and holding a martini glass in the other.

"That's my party there," Sara said, somewhat embarrassed and pointing to the lady with red hair who was already very animated.

Sara went to the table, grinned stiffly and sat down.

"Hi, Mitzie, it's so good to meet you," Sara said shaking hands.

"Sit, sit!" Mitzie commanded, continuing to gesture broadly.

"How did you know it was me?" asked Sara. "I mean, I just walked in, and you knew who I was."

"I looked you up on the Intranet—your *Facebook* page—and saw your photo. I try to do a little homework before I meet someone, especially a new client."

"A new client?" Sara asked. "I'm not here as a client."

"Not yet," said Mitzie, smiling again.

"So, are you two ready to order?" the waiter asked coming by and pulling out his order book.

"Not yet," said Mitzie. "Why don't you give us a minute."

The waiter huffed and strode off to another table to see if he could offer his assistance elsewhere.

169

"I'm not completely sure why you think we have something in common," said Sara, pulling off a piece of bread and using her knife to scrape a sliver of butter from its dish. "Did you say that our grandparents knew each other?"

"No, it was our great grandmothers, actually. My mother's name is Patricia, and her mother is Teresa."

"And your great grandmother, what was her name?"

"What *is* her name, you mean. She's still living. Her name is Beatrice, but we always just called her Bessie."

"Really? Your great grandmother is still alive? That's amazing!"

"Her last name is Belzikov. Like I said earlier, she went to school with your great grandmother."

"Janice Prodescu," said Sara. "So, it *was* your great grandmother in the picture."

"What picture?"

"I found a photo in one of my great grandma's high school yearbooks. It was an old sepia-toned picture that showed six young women enjoying themselves some night in 1938. That was when she graduated."

"Since my great grandma graduated in the same class as yours did, I bet I have the same picture at home," said Mitzie.

Sara smiled. "*Now* I understand the connection you were talking about. Sometimes I'm just a little too cautious about things. I wasn't so sure about you or this meeting, but after I saw the picture, I had to ask."

"Do you have it with you?"

"Actually, I do," Sara answered. She dug through her over-sized purse, pushing things to the side and rummaging to get to an inside pocket. "Here," Sara said, handing the group picture to Mitzie. "This is my great grandma Janice," she added, pointing to the young, dark-haired girl in the middle. "And these were their friends at the time. On the back it says Best Friends Forever, June 3, 1938. I guess that was back before the shorthand we use today ... you know BFF and all of that."

Mitzie giggled. "Yeah, and that's my great grandmother right there beside Judy. Believe it or not she hasn't changed that much, except for more wrinkles. That sparkle in her eye is still there."

"What do you know about their relationship?" Sara asked, "Your great grandmother and mine, that is."

"I remember my mother saying some things that she'd heard as a child. She said those two ..." Mitzie paused, her finger moving between the faces of Janice and Bessie, "... were the troublemakers at school—something each denied, but often with a wink and a grin."

"What do you mean?" asked Sara.

"Mother told us of the time when they got sent to the principal's office for burning up the science lab. Those two were supposed to have cleaned up and put everything away. They swore they had, but still, there was a strange fire in that room after the teacher closed the lab for the night. The firemen never figured out what caused it either. The next time was at one of the high school dances. Several of the teachers who were chaperoning couldn't get out of the teacher's lounge. It was locked."

"So ..."

"Yeah, but the lock was on the inside where *they* were; the door just wouldn't open. And then there was the time when a girl they really disliked fell down some stairs during school and broke her leg."

"What's so odd about that?" asked Sara. "That happens all the time."

"Well, you might be right. But then again, the day after that, they found a doll in Janice's locker dressed like the girl with pins stuck in its leg."

Sara was quiet. "I don't know. It sounds like a lot of coincidences to me. The only story I heard was the one where they were at my great grandmother's for her birthday. They had gotten this crazy idea to make a Ouija board, when your great grandmother, Bessie, said she already had one."

"I didn't know they made them back then," said Mitzie.

"Yeah, they started making them back in the 1890s. Anyway, the girls got it out and began trying to contact the dead. They didn't know anyone close to them who'd died, so they just started asking any spirit to step forward and talk to them."

"What happened?" asked Mitzie.

"From what my aunt told me, there was a sharp, loud noise, and the door to the room where they were doing the séance buckled, as if someone or something was trying to get in. They all hid under the bed. Auntie said it was the most scared her grandmother had ever been in her life. I know that sometime later the two of them spent a lot of time doing more with the Ouija board and practicing their medium skills. They read a lot about it too. Auntie said it was too dangerous for them to play with stuff like that when they didn't know what they were doing."

"I heard it a little different," said Mitzie.

"Oh, yeah? What did you hear?"

"They had several incidents that they could never quite explain."

"Like what?"

"My great grandmother told us her life was never the same after that night with the séance and their girlfriends. In fact," Mitzie said, pointing at the picture, "it was probably when this photo was taken."

Sara had read her great grandmother's version in her journal, but now wanted to hear what Mitzie knew about it.

"How was her life different?" asked Sara.

"Grandma Bessie said she would wake in the middle of the night hearing voices and feeling something near her in the bed. Once she was sleeping and got panicked, unable to breathe. She felt like something was sitting on her chest, and when she opened her eyes, she saw a dark shadowy figure on top of her. She screamed and tried to push it off, but her hands went right through the black mist. Then, it just dissolved back into the darkness."

The waiter stopped by the table again and stood behind Mitzie, but they didn't notice him until he cleared his throat. "A, ladies, are you ready to order?" This time, he put on a fake smile and let his pen hover over the small, black book to await their choices.

"I'll just have the garden salad; oil and vinegar on the side," said Mitzie, not even looking at the menu. Then, while handing the menu back to the waiter, she added, "Oh, and give me another martini— double olives, please."

Sara flipped quickly through the menu, but rather than hold things up, she said simply, "I'll have the same, except make mine a Chardonnay."

For the next hour they traded stories they had heard about their great grandmothers, grandmothers and about their mothers. All held a similar theme. Strange things had happened to these women—things that couldn't be easily explained.

Then, Mitzie stopped and stared at Sara. The look on her face was stony and cold.

"What?" asked Sara, a little unnerved by the sudden change.

"There's another reason I asked you to lunch, Sara."

Suddenly, the warmth and the camaraderie Sara had felt evaporated. Sara sat waiting … waiting for a punch line that would knock the wind out of her sails. *Things were going too well—too smoothly*, she thought.

"I am a psychic, just like you. It runs in our families," said Mitzie. "There are too many coincidences between us. There's no denying that. Just listen to us … the way we've talked about our families. You've obviously known that you were psychic from a young age."

"I'm listening," said Sara cautiously.

Mitzie reached for her purse and pulled out a piece of paper. She unfolded it and pushed it toward Sara.

"Back in 1945, your great grandmother and mine got together again. They lived in the same town but had drifted apart after high school. Grandma Bessie said she received a handwritten note from your great grandmother, but I also heard that your great grandmother got a similar one from Bessie. Odd, though. Neither claims to have sent one.

"Anyway, it was the spring, and they agreed to get together and go out to dinner to talk about what was going on in their lives and, mainly, to reminisce. Grandma Bessie said they had a great time and went back to Janice's to have a glass of wine and relax. They got talking and laughing again, when Aunt Janice suggested they break out the Ouija board just for fun. And they did."

"What happened?" asked Sara.

"Not much, apparently. Grandma said the pointer moved, but it didn't say anything they could understand."

"But what *did* it say?"

"I think she said it spelled out *Hello Plottar* or something like that. Since nothing else seemed to happen, they didn't take it seriously. They didn't know what it meant or who or what *Plottar* was at the time. They didn't know anyone by that name."

"What on earth would it mean?" asked Sara.

"I don't know. They were both in their twenties. Bessie was married by then, but your great grandmother was still single at the time, I think. Yes, it's true that she had a child out of wedlock, of course ..."

"My grandmother, Cora Rae."

"Yes, but it wasn't well accepted back then, as I'm sure you've heard by now."

"Of course," said Sara wanting to change subjects, "but back to the Ouija board, you still don't know what it meant?"

"No. Grandma Bessie only had a part-time job at JC Penny, and I think Aunt Janice was clerking for a law firm downtown. Anyway, Grandma Bessie never figured out what that Ouija message meant. To this day, she still doesn't understand it."

"Well, that's an amazing story, but I don't see what ..."

Mitzie stopped her in mid-sentence. "Your great grandmother ..." she began before hesitating, "... she *died* that night."

"*That* night?" Sara repeated.

"That very night," said Mitzie.

Sara stopped to think. It was true; in 1945, her great grandmother had died, but she had thought it was later in the year—not in the springtime. She had always been told it had been from a heart attack. That's what her aunt had always said.

"I thought Grandma Janice died in June or July of 1945—not during the spring," said Sara. "She died of a heart attack."

"Oh? Is that right?"

"Yes, I'm sure of it. Auntie said she died of a heart attack."

"When she was in her twenties?"

"That's what my Auntie told me," said Sara.

Mitzie shook her head. "I don't know, then. Grandma Bessie says she's blamed herself all these years. She knew there was nothing she could have done, but she always felt it was something they had done that night that caused it—something with the Ouija board that triggered it. She's done readings for hundreds of people during her life, but she said she's never felt the cold chill that she felt when she and Janice did the board that night. The room grew frigid, as if all the life had been sucked out of it."

The sudden chill, the feeling of death, and the sense of an abject wickedness in her presence—she had experienced those same feelings and more. During a session, she would sometimes feel a bone-cold finger touch her soul, as if it were trying to steal it from her and run.

"Mitzie," Sara said suddenly, "it's been nice to meet you, but I ... I need to go."

"Is everything alright?" Mitzie asked, perplexed by the abrupt change.

"I really haven't been feeling one hundred percent lately. It's probably just a cold coming on. Thanks again."

Sara placed a few bills on the table and left quickly, hurrying past the front check-in booth and out the etched, glass door. Mitzie sat dumbfounded, still in the middle of sipping her martini.

Sara, too, wasn't sure what had just happened. It shouldn't have bothered her, but it did. It was just one more strange thing that reinforced her feelings. There was something wrong—something dark and unnerving—and it was exercising its will over her more freely every day.

*****

CH 30 – In Too Deep

1970

Danny knew there was something going on in Boston, but the death of Cora Rae had temporarily derailed his story. Trying to get it back on track, he answered the door of his apartment where Terri Campbell had arrived to give him a promised reading. Initially, Danny had resisted having her come to his place, but she had explained that the surroundings of his personal affects and other vibrations were critical for her to give him a good session. He had reluctantly agreed.

"Danny, so good to see you again," said Terri. "I'm glad you could take time out of your busy schedule as a reporter to have a session with me."

"I'll tell you upfront that I grew up in a family that didn't believe in this kind of stuff," Danny answered, pulling up a metal chair in his kitchen and gesturing for Terri to do the same.

"That's okay. Most people don't," she said, "but I'm glad you're giving it a try with an open mind."

Danny wasn't sure he had an open mind, but what he was sure was going through a session with Terri would help him understand the world they lived in and the type of business they were running. If it were a sham, he figured he would see that pretty quickly. *Perhaps it would lead to another article or even a column in the paper for him*, he thought.

Terri pulled a cigarette out of its case. "Do you mind?" she asked.

"No, go right ahead," said Danny. "Let me get you a light."

"No, I have one right here," she answered, flipping open her red, metal lighter and igniting the stick. She took a drag and blew the blue smoke out the side of her mouth as Danny fetched an ashtray. "So, who do you wish to talk to?" Terri asked getting settled at the table.

"My father passed away a few years ago, and I wasn't able to say goodbye to him," said Danny, lying. His father was still quite alive and living elsewhere in Boston.

"Let's see what he has to say to you," said Terri, closing her eyes.

Danny grew restless as it took Terri several minutes before she said another word to him. Her breathing slowed and her eyes went into REM mode, flashing back and forth, left and right, quickly under her eyelids. Finally, she took a deep breath.

"I see your father," said Terri.

Ah! thought Danny, *so she* is *a fraud!*

"Yet, I don't understand. Why do you believe he is dead? I see him in his kitchen making lunch for himself. He seems quite alive to me."

Danny froze. *How could she see that? How could she know?*

"Uh, well, uh, maybe you're seeing my ... my father-in-law," said the reporter, wincing at how lame that sounded.

"I didn't know you were married," said Terri, opening her eyes.

Danny now felt trapped. He wasn't married, and he was stumbling in search of another excuse. But thankfully for him, a rescue was near at hand. Terri quickly shut her eyes again.

"But there is another who is coming through," said the psychic. "It is Cora Rae who wants to speak to you," said Terri. "She is standing behind me now, and she says that she is sorry for the pain and suffering she caused while she was alive. She admits that she had Virginia Carter killed, and she feels bad about that."

"Why? Why did she have her killed?"

"She says that Virginia Carter was sleeping with someone she knew—a good, close friend—and that disturbed her. She had her killed because she couldn't bear the thought of them being together."

"Who was she sleeping with?" asked Danny, leaning forward, now more interested.

"Someone on the police force. She won't tell me who it was."

"On the Boston police force?"

"On either the Boston force or one of the nearby towns. She doesn't want to get specific."

"What does she say about *your* involvement?" Danny asked.

Terri's face changed, contorting itself momentarily before resuming the session. "You mean Terri's?" asked the psychic, now speaking in the third person.

"Yes."

"Terri had nothing to do with Virginia and her son's murders. She is only with you today trying to give you help on your story. She is channeling me now."

"But how does Terri know so much about the murders?"

"That comes from me, Cora Rae," said Terri. "She's the one telling Terri all these things."

"Who am I talking to now? Cora Rae or Terri?" asked Danny, confused.

"You are talking to Cora Rae right now, so I can tell you something important," said Terri.

"I see. Is there anything else Cora Rae can tell me?" Danny asked.

"Yes."

"What's that?"

"You don't need to find my killer—Cora Rae's. The one who killed me did what he should have done. I deserved to die for what I did. It ends with me."

"He? You say it was a man who killed you?" asked Danny.

"Yes."

"Who? Who killed you?"

But Terri came out of her trance. She blinked as though she had just awakened from a deep sleep and was trying to regain her bearings.

"Did you get what you needed?" she asked as if she knew nothing of the conversation.

"Almost," said Danny. "I had one more question, but you woke up."

"Oh, well sometimes that happens. I hope your other questions were answered."

"I think I'm understanding those better too," said Danny smiling weakly.

Danny told Terri he appreciated the session and that he would stay in touch with her. After she left, he straightened up in the kitchen putting away some dishes. On the counter next to his gas stove, he found her red lighter. *She must have left it,* he thought. *I'll get it back to her tomorrow.*

But the next morning, Danny's body was found. It had been brutally mangled—just like Jenny's, her son's and Cora Rae's before him.

*****

(H 31 – A Horned Image

2020

Dag was sitting in his office when Tommy walked in, notepad in hand. But this time, he sat down and merely waited for Dag to say something.

"What do you have?" asked Dag, impatiently, but not looking up. He was busy on his computer trying to research other gruesome, cult-like murders that had occurred outside of Boston—anywhere in the country.

Tommy threw a picture on Dag's desk; it was of a corpse from one of the cold case files he'd been looking into. He waited for Dag's reaction. Dag finally glanced at it but didn't seem to react.

"So, what's special about that?" Dag asked, returning to a case in Providence, Rhode Island in 1995 which Tommy had brought to his attention earlier.

Tommy was surprised. "You're kidding, right?" he asked. "Look at the body here. Do you see anything strange?"

"Yeah, it's missing a head. So what. We've seen that before—now as a matter of fact. What case is this?"

"I'm sorry, but I think decapitation qualifies as unusual for a murder. Wouldn't you agree?"

"Yeah, but it's no more twisted than the other things we've seen." Tommy smiled at Dag's pun but didn't pursue it. "So, what's the case?" Dag asked again.

"It's from 1995—a priest by the name of Jose Mercato. He was found in Roxbury."

"A priest, eh?"

"So, what do you see in the pic?" said Tommy, waiting for a different reaction.

Dag glanced again at the photo, holding it closer to his face. He studied it, looking for something unusual on the page and then shrugged.

"Dunno. What is it?"

"What is *that*?" Tommy asked, pointing at something within the frame.

Dag flipped the picture around toward his partner and pointed to the same spot on the picture. "Right here?" asked Dag.

His index finger hovered just below a dark image on the wall, just behind the severed head of the victim.

"Yeah. There."

"That's just a smudge on the window, I think," said Dag.

"I don't think so," said Tommy. "Look at the way the light reflects off the wall here." Tommy circled another section of the picture with his finger. "The light from the window must have been from behind the photographer, over his shoulder, and reflecting the image in the window behind him on the wall in front. You can see the faint outline of the tree here too, but then there's this ..."

Tommy thumped the photo with his finger.

"Uh, I ..." Dag's face grew pale.

He immediately saw what Tommy was pointing at. Inside the imaginary circle was the fuzzy image of a head—two yellow eyes, a long face, white fangs, and something else.

"What *is* that?" asked Tommy, already knowing.

"What do you think it is?" asked Dag.

Tommy hesitated, wondering whether to say what he really saw. "It looks like ... well ... it looks like two horns?"

Dag nodded. "Yep, that's what I see too. You're not seeing things – at least I don't think so. But maybe it's just an animal of some kind— like a wolf-goat, I think. It's probably an animal from another exposure in the same camera. That's probably it. It's just a double exposure."

Tommy didn't answer, letting him ponder his own words. Finally, he said, "If that's what you think, Dag. I'll leave that to you, but I would ask what an animal would be doing looking through the window behind a photographer at the scene of a horrible homicide. And the other question is ... the head has horns like a goat but if you look carefully at the face ..."

Dag looked again. "... it looks human."

"Yeah. This is just too creepy for me," answered Tommy, taking back the picture.

"What other pictures do you have?" asked Dag, now interested in what had been found.

Tommy hesitated again. He wasn't sure he wanted to bring anything else up after that.

"Come on, Tommy. You must have something else. You didn't spend all this time and only find this one picture."

Tommy finally relented.

"Okay, I've got some evidence from the murders in 1970 and 1995. There was another I found dating back to 1945. All seem to have the same MO—unusual positions of the body or missing or separated body parts. There were a few murders in 1920 too, but the bodies were dumped in the woods around the Mansfield area—pretty far from Boston."

Dag flipped through what Tommy shoved at him, sorting out the things he thought were worth following up on later. But as he parsed the pile, he stopped once again.

"Look at this," Dag said.

Dag held up another picture from the Pittman murder in 1970—the one that had happened just after Dag's great grandfather left the department. In it was the body of the reporter or pieces of it. But in the background was a bookshelf with some white ceramic plates and several trophies and awards. One of the awards was a faceted, glass globe with a black marble base.

Tommy reviewed the picture carefully, trying to meet the challenge thrown up by his partner.

"I don't see anything," Tommy finally said. Then, he paused. "Wait, you mean right here," he said correcting himself and pointing to the picture.

"Yeah, so you see it too."

"Now that we've seen the other one, this one is pretty hard to miss," said Tommy.

Dag threw the picture on the desk. Reflected in the facets of the globe were the images of the same horned animal's face staring at the body from the side.

The realization of what they were seeing shook Tommy. "Jesus," he said. "This was no animal."

"… not one that walks the earth during the day, anyway," answered Dag. "You still thinkin' fame and glory, Tommy?"

Tommy shook his head. "I don't know what to think anymore," he answered.

*****

CH 32 – The Attic – Part 3

2020

Ever since her lunch with Mitzie, Sara had become increasingly on-edge. Before that meeting, the incidents of somberness and melancholy had only crept into her mind periodically; now it was constant.

Sara pulled on the red, plastic tip that dangled with a cord from the ceiling square above her. The folded, aluminum stairs clung tenaciously to the board inside before she extended it down, planting the gray, rubber feet on the carpet so it wouldn't move. She knew where to find the other things of her great grandmother's that were stored up there. Her aunt had given her boxes of stuff from her side of the family, but she'd never gone through them. Instead, she'd just shoved them in the attic and procrastinated sorting through them. Now, she wanted to go back to things she had already seen—things she needed to see again. The first she found quickly.

"Ah, here it is," Sara murmured, as she set aside the music box and uncover the personal journal. In it, she had read about the frightful experience during a séance with her great grandmother's friends. But after reading the entry, she had felt unusually sick and tossed it back into the box. Now she was interested to know what else was in that journal.

The diary fell open to the spot where Sara had stopped—at the time of the séance. Not wanting to relive that traumatic episode, she flipped to the next page.

The next date was April 4, 1939, but skimming through the note, she didn't find much there—nothing bizarre or otherwise noteworthy anyway.

> April 4, 1939
>
> I haven't felt myself for several months, especially after what happened during the séance. I've tried to be upbeat and cheery, but even Bessie told me today that I seemed glum and out of sorts …

The pages that followed were about finding a summer job and babysitting for the Gallaghers who lived just down the street. Janice said she didn't want to babysit all summer but wanted to find a real job at a restaurant or shop in town.

Growing weary of the mundane entries, Sara put the journal in her jacket to carry with her to read later. She found other journals and notebooks too and packed those in her coat along with the first one. Next, she gently pulled out the yearbook with the title *Boston English High School -- 1938*, opening the page to the picture of all the classmates. Inside it, someone had placed other sepia photos—one of which was that of the six young ladies who had participated in the séance that night back in 1939. This time they were standing together in the chemistry lab in the school—the very same one that had caught on fire earlier in the year.

The photo was slightly faded, but Sara held it close to her face to make out any details she might otherwise miss. Of the six girls, two were smiling broadly, while the other four who sat side-by-side in the center had only faint expressions of amusement on their faces. These four were dressed in dark—almost black—skirts and sweaters with white blouses underneath. Around each of their necks was a pendant. The two girls in the center were Bessie and Janice.

Sara had brought a magnifying glass up with her, and now she grasped its long handle to see if it would reveal any more secrets for her. Partially covered by their sweaters, the girls' pendants showed a rider and horse of different colors. The girls on either side of the four had solid pendants with red flames in the center. As for the middle four, one had a white horse's head, another had a black one. Janice's pendant revealed a red horsehead and Bessie's, one of pale green. *But there's something else there*, Sara thought, moving her magnifying glass up to see what the shadow was behind Janice's and Bessie's heads.

"Oh, my god!"

Sara dropped the magnifying glass. It hit a wooden plank and cracked the glass down the middle. She was trembling as a something cold clawed at her heart—at her soul.

Just above the girls' heads was a faint shadow. It had two distinct yellow eyes, a long, animal-like face and two horns. It was the head of a goat. It was haunting and menacing at the same time.

Sara took a deep breath. *Breathe ... breathe ...* she thought to herself. She stuffed the picture back into the journal and forced herself to go on.

The next thing she needed to see again was that old jewelry box. This, she pulled out from under other things she had frantically tossed back into the crate the last time she'd been in the attic.

The old jewelry box given to her by her aunt on behalf of her mother was beautiful, but there was something foreign about it. Sara picked it up and felt a tingling run up her arms just as she had the time before. There was nothing warm and comforting about the box, quite the contrary. There was something that seemed to draw her energy away from her—like a leach sucking the life force of blood from its host.

The wooden box had three, pull-out drawers. The carvings on the outside were of strange animals with woodlands and rivers all around them. Some creatures had horns like a giant elk; others merely had spikes—both long and short—on their heads. All were four-legged and hooved with matted, black fur. Yet, each held a hungry gaze with its eyes of yellow, red or black and fangs that protruded down the sides of its mouth. All were enough to give a small child nightmares well into adulthood.

As for the box, it had copper braces on the corners and a metal latch with a small, hourglass-shaped keyhole. The top was painted, but it was difficult to tell what the painting was supposed to be, as much of it was faded and worn. There were two-headed cows and donkeys with humps like camels along with shepherds with horns of their own tending them on a pastoral mount. Above all of them were three, angel-like beings wearing red robes and floating down from the sky. However, instead of donning golden halos, they wore a headdress of writhing snakes, as if they, themselves, were figures of the Medusa. If she looked hard, Sara could make out crosses on their chests, yet these were upside down.

Sara opened the box. Instantly, there was a rush of cold air and the sound of a raspy, almost guttural, voice coming from within.

Hellooo Plottarrr ... it seemed to call out.

Sara slammed the lid closed, shaking. The words coming from the music box echoed in her head; they were the exact same ones Mitzie claimed had revealed themselves on Bessie and Janice's Ouija board. But there was something more—something inside her, challenging her to press on. She did and reopened it. This time, there was no wind, no cold, no voice.

She took out the red lighter and set it on the floorboard of the attic. Inside the music box was a mirror that was attached to one edge and could be tilted up. However, the mirror was broken; beneath it were two pieces of jewelry. Sara picked up a necklace, twirling it with her fingers. It was mesmerizing, yet hauntingly so. It had a small clasp which was supposed to open, but when she tried, it wouldn't move. Attached to the gold chain was a pendant. It was a round cameo, but instead of the traditional robin's egg blue and white, it held the image of a red horse's head. This was the very same necklace Janice had worn in the school picture. As Sara held it, she felt it get hot in her hand—so hot that she dropped it back into the box before it burned her palm. Rubbing her hand, she hesitated to pick up the second one. This too was a piece that had been in a picture she had seen: the signet ring used to inflict burns on its victims. She didn't touch it, fearing it would try to burn her as well.

Yet, no sooner had she dismissed it, than the signet ring began spinning on its own inside the box. Faster and faster it gyrated until the red velvet lining of the box began to smolder. Just as she began to slam the lid closed, the inside of the box burst into violent flames.

Sara closed her eyes and pushed away the dark shadows trying to pry open and enter her mind. *No,* she thought. *No!* She sat back breathing deeply, her head spinning. *Breathe. Just breathe!*

But this time, the darkness overtook her.

*****

(H 33 - Reassigned

2020

Early in the year, there was a series of murders in and around the near suburbs of Boston. The average number of homicides during an entire year was between fifty and sixty. Causes ranged from domestic disputes, gangs, robberies and burglaries, and various other reasons. However, it had been the seventh murder of 2020 that had been the most sensational—that of the police chief, Zeller Arthur Gallagher. It had received wide-spread attention and wall-to-wall news coverage.

The flurry of investigative activity in the police department had been unprecedented. Almost every detective had become involved—all except one: Dag. As the son of the chief, he was forbidden from being on the case. Rules prohibited it to avoid any possibility of prejudice or personal bias.

But the case had dragged on for days, then weeks, and then months. The newly appointed police chief, Patrick Malloy, had struggled mightily in the giant footsteps of his predecessor. Time was also working against him, and he had no leads, no clues, and his career looked like it had no chance. He needed something—a life raft—and he needed it fast. The months passed, and the chances of solving one of the most horrendous and news-breaking stories of the decade, were growing slimmer. The press had been relentless in resurrecting the story every few weeks, asking the chief what was being done and what progress was being made. Yet, he had no answers. Frustration turned to angst and then to panic. Finally, the chief got the dreaded call from Richard J. Johnson.

Dick Johnson was the district attorney for the city of Boston. He was well-respected and had held the elected position for over eight years. He and the mayor, Jack Gryzbowski, were tight. They'd been together since the very beginning when Johnson had run Gryzbowski's first campaign for city council. But now, a new election was in the offing, and this time the mayor had his sights set higher; he'd decided to run for the governorship. Since Johnson had tied his fortunes directly to the coattails of the mayor, the election was crucial for both of them. Both men knew how important image was to a politician; it meant everything. And one vital part of that image as mayor was to show a city with a low or at least declining crime rate.

However, with the new year starting off with strange murders capturing the headlines, the news media showed a grimmer picture—one the mayor was doing everything he could to avoid. If a mayor couldn't control the crime in his own city, voters would not reward him with an even bigger job. That was a fact.

"Malloy? It's Johnson."

"Yes, sir. What can I do for you?" asked the police chief, talking to his DA.

"You got anything on the Brookline, Dorchester or Needham Heights investigations?" asked Johnson, coolly and impersonally.

"We're working on them, sir. We have some promising leads."

"Yeah, what about Zag's murder?"

"Uh, well, we're looking into some cold cases that might be ..."

"Cold cases? So, basically you're wasting time. You're not going to find anything from some old case files—at least not within the time we need. Why aren't you out talking to witnesses and collecting evidence? I need a police chief who takes charge, Malloy. We need this case solved, and I don't care who you find or what you have to do to find someone."

"Well, sir, we're doing those things too. But we're also looking at old, cold cases with similar MO's—bodies distorted, twisted, dismembered ... you know."

"No, I don't know, Malloy. I think you're spending valuable time going through cases that couldn't be solved then and won't be solved now. As I said, you should be spending more time analyzing what you have in front of you. We have more technology now than ever before. We've spent millions of taxpayers' dollars on it. We're able to do a hell of a lot more with a hell of a lot less these days. That's what we're telling voters. Do you understand? So, I suggest that you do *real* police work instead of screwing around with crap that doesn't matter. I want Zag's cases solved by the end of the month. Do you understand?"

"But sir ..."

"The end of the month. I want someone arrested! Do you hear me!"

189

"Yes, sir. Got it," Malloy answered.

He put down the phone and stared out the window. It was a cool, rainy and overcast day, and the temperatures the rest of the week didn't promise to be any better. The showers had started as a cold front had come through the area the day before. Fall was always a time of unpredictable weather, and these days, everything seemed to be unpredictable—especially for the new police chief.

Malloy's next call was unusual but not unexpected.

"Dag? It's Chief Malloy."

"Hi, Chief. What can I do for you today?" asked Gallagher.

"I need a favor."

"You need a favor, sir?"

It was rare that a chief would start a conversation with that statement, but Dag had seen many things during his career. Yet, even so, this surprised him.

"Yeah, I realize this may be counter to things we're supposed to do here in the department, but it seems the investigation into your father's death is going nowhere."

Dag was quiet. Now, he wasn't sure where the conversation was headed.

"I know that may disappoint you," the chief continued. "I know it disappoints me. I want to see the killer or killers found and put away like everyone else. But the team working the case just hasn't been able to come up with anything. They don't even have any good suspects. Worse than that, the DA is breathing down my neck."

Dag waited for the punchline.

"This is between you and me. It can't go beyond us," said Malloy.

"What do you want me to do?"

"I want you to look over things in the case. I know it will be rough, and as hard as it will be, I think it will be less emotional than going the rest of your life not knowing who did this. Am I right?"

Dag knew he was right, but he wasn't sure he had it in him to look at the evidence.

"What about Tommy?" Dag asked instead. "What do I tell him?"

"That's fine. We'll include him too. But this can't get out. It would look really bad and would jeopardize any case we have against whoever we eventually find that did this."

"I understand, sir," said Dag.

"Good. Then, as of now, unofficially, you're on the case. Stay in the shadows. I'll get any information you need so you don't have to ask Larson for it. Got that?"

"Yes, sir. We'll do what we can."

"Oh, and I need you to find the killer within the next thirty days. Not a day more. I told the DA we were close. It can't go longer than that."

As soon as Dag hung up the phone, he got an unexpected visitor.

"How's it going?" asked Tommy, barging in.

Dag didn't look up at him, instead he stared out the gloomy window of his office that was caked with rain droplets and self-pity.

"Dag? Are you okay?"

"Yeah, yeah. Just got a call from Malloy. He's a piece of work. He wants us to bail his ass out on a case. He's given us thirty days to find the killer."

"Which case?"

"My dad's."

"What! Are you nuts? The entire department's been looking into that for months. Besides that, won't it screw up the case?"

"Yeah, that's why this can't get out. You can't tell anyone," replied Dag. "So, what do you know about it? Anything? I've been banned from asking until now." The melancholy in his voice mirrored his sad reflection in the gloomy windowpane that was his only portal to the outside world.

Tommy pulled up a chair and threw his feet up on the other side of Dag's desk to get comfortable. However, one stern look from Dag was all it took for him to take them off, realizing he'd overstepped his boundaries.

"I don't know much, Dag. All I know is there aren't any clues—none. The detectives are stumped. They found your dad's body in the alley. His service revolver hadn't been fired, but he'd been beaten to death.

Nothing was taken either. Whoever did it didn't take his gun, his wallet—nothin'. So, the guys think it was something personal."

"Yeah, that's what I've been saying all along. It was someone with a grudge. Did they look at all the ex-cons who'd been let out of jail recently?"

"Yeah, and all had alibis."

"Maybe the people they were with are lying?"

"They may be, but nothing has shaken them loose yet," said Tommy.

"What about family members of the ex-cons? Sometimes they have hard feelings too—you know, vengeance."

"So far, nothin'. Same deal. All have alibi's, weren't around Boston, or were in prison someplace else."

Dag shook his head. "I'm sure there's something they're missing."

"Well, before you get started on that, we have another case to solve too, you know—the Jenkins case."

"Maggie and Will?"

"Yeah," Tommy began, "I followed up on that psychic lady who came into the precinct looking for someone to talk to about their murders. I think her name was Mitzie Wilkins."

"Yeah. I talked to her too."

"She's the one who told you she thought a psychotic killer was on the loose, right?"

Dag smiled. "*Psychic* killer, not psychotic. *Every* killer is psychotic, Tommy."

"Okay, well, I found *twelve* self-proclaimed psychics in Boston who advertise their services."

"Why are you wasting your time with this garbage?" Dag asked. "You're chasing after leads coming from a psychic or even a *psychotic* psychic woman who came into the precinct telling me she had a dream about these murders and that I should believe her? *Please.* Is that the best you can do?"

"You have to admit these are really strange cases, and for someone to just suddenly come into the department and tell you it's all about psychic stuff, well, you have to wonder, don't you?"

"Wonder about what, Tommy? I don't understand where you're going with this. I've been in the business a long time. You can't believe *everything* you hear from a witness—even so-called 'reliable' witnesses. A lot of times, you can't tell who is reliable and who isn't. You have to go by the proof—the evidence. That's why we're here, right? We go by the evidence we collect, and then we make a call on whether somebody is guilty or not guilty. When we are reasonably convinced the evidence points to their guilt, we arrest them. It's pretty simple."

"Yeah, you're right about that. That's why I talked to every one of 'em—all those psychotic psychics. No one would tell me who their clients are or who they talked to during the last six months. So, I thought we could get a court order."

"Are you serious?"

"Yeah, we can get a court order to search their houses and collect evidence on their clients. One of them *has* to be connected to one of our vics," said Tommy.

Dag grunted. "You don't know that Tommy. You'd be wasting our time and squandering any remaining credibility we have left with the judge. That's the last thing I need right now—to piss-off a judge, especially after what the chief just told me."

"My dad knows Judge Crosby pretty well. I bet he'll give us the warrant," said Tommy.

"Not if you're asking for warrants on twelve different addresses," said Dag. "You have to narrow it down to one or two and have really good reasons to show why the warrants are justified. They don't just give them out like candy on Halloween, you know. It doesn't work that way."

"Okay, so how do we do that?"

Dag pouted. "I really don't want to go down that path, Tommy. It's a dead end."

"Come on man! You gotta' give me somethin' here, Dag. I've been bustin' my balls down in the Records Department. I think this is our best shot."

"A psychotic psychic. That's our best lead. Really?"

"Let's bring that Mitzie lady in for questioning again=. Let's find out if she knows anything more," said Tommy.

"Fine. You go bring her in. I need to find out something on my dad's case by the end of the day too. We're running out of time on both of 'em."

"Today? By the end of today?" asked Tommy, taken aback by new deadline. "For the Jenkin's case too?"

"The chief wants something by the end of the month. As of today, we have eight days left—tomorrow, only seven, the next day six. Do you see any trend here?" Dag asked sarcastically.

"Yep. I think I got it," Tommy answered.

*****

Part III

CH 34 - Bad JuJu

1995

Abby had gotten home late that night and kicked off her shoes. She'd had another one of those sessions with a client where odd things had happened, and she'd felt unnerved.

First, Dwayne Fletcher, her driver, had been late getting her to her appointment with an older man named Leonard or "Lenny" as he preferred. Dwayne had written down the wrong address and ended up on North Salem Avenue instead of South. Next, the middle-aged man who answered the door wasn't Lenny; he was Lenny's partner, Roger.

"My partner is out," Roger explained, "but I'm expecting him back shortly."

Unfortunately, the "shortly" grew to an hour, as Lenny had gotten confused with the change in daylight savings time and forgotten to reset his watch. Finally, Lenny arrived, and he began telling Abby about his father who had died many years earlier. He had been murdered in 1970, but the police had never found the killer or killers.

"I just need some closure," said Lenny. "What happened to dad was such a terrible thing, you know. The police never tracked down the murderers, and it devastated our family."

Handsome with meticulously trimmed black hair, prematurely and rapidly going gray but still with solidly black eyebrows, Lenny's face was narrow, coming to a pointed chin. His long-sleeved, designer shirt was starched and pressed perfectly, and his olive wool pants were creased neatly down to their precise one-and-one-quarter-inch cuffs at the bottom.

"That's awful," Abby replied. "We've had things like that in our family too, so I know what it's like."

"Do you think we can reach my father and talk to him?"

"We can try," said Abby. "But I can only contact him if he wants to be reached. Sometimes the spirits don't want to talk to us."

"Why?"

"I don't know. Each has a different reason, I think."

"I'll tell you now that he might not want to talk to me," said Lenny, who was in his thirties.

"Why is that?"

"My dad was a very strict man. He was very religious and practical. By trade he was a reporter, and he followed stories that were a bit unusual. I think because of his faith and views on life, he wouldn't approve of my lifestyle."

"Because you're gay?"

"Yeah. I've known I was gay since I was a little boy. I never married, and as I got older, my mom wondered why. I never told her I was gay; I thought that would crush her. Mom suspected. My dad died when I was young—only five. I really didn't know him, but Mom talks about him all the time. I feel like I knew him."

"I find that those who have departed us are usually quite forgiving, Lenny. I'm sure it will be all right. Having said that, do you still want to talk to him?"

"Yes. I want to make sure he's okay, and to make sure he understands who I am. I'm not looking for his approval—just his understanding. I want to be sure it's okay with him."

Abby understood. She didn't have many gay clients, but she did know the friction within some families—especially parents who grew up in a different generation.

She sat up straight and began to take a series of deep breaths, each intended to bring her to a lower state of relaxation and higher vibration to tune-in to the departed souls.

"I see a man standing behind you, Lenny. He's about your age now, actually, and he's dressed casually in a light jacket and gray trousers. He's got dark hair and a mustache. It looks like his eyes are a dark brown and are deeply set."

"That sounds like Dad," said Lenny.

"I'm sharing with him your concerns, and he's nodding. He's telling me he's in a good place. He's fine, and you shouldn't worry about him. He calls it a 'safe' place, in fact. He's also smiling and telling me that he understands you. He loves you—no matter what."

196

Lenny smiled in relief. "So, he's okay with who I am?"

"Yes, Lenny. He's proud of you and only hopes that you can continue to be happy. He says life is a challenge, and finding the right partner is important in that journey. He says that if you believe Roger is the one for you and you're happy, then that's all that matters."

"Good. I'm glad," said Lenny.

But Abby suddenly paused. Her face changed—contorting and turning crimson. She began gagging, coughing madly, and grabbing her throat as if she were choking.

"Can I get you some water?" Lenny asked, standing up and becoming concerned.

"Yes," she managed to say, continuing to cough with her arm over her mouth.

Lenny rushed back with a full glass, and Abby took long, deep gulps.

"Any better?" he asked.

"Yes, thanks," she answered. Then, she returned to her session. "I'm asking him more about what happened to him—how he was murdered."

Lenny leaned forward, anxious to hear the answer.

However, Abby continued to cough, and when she opened her eyes, she saw a diseased and bony hand reach toward her. It tried to grab her around the neck. This wasn't Lenny's father; it was another being who was standing where Danny's spirit had been.

Abject fear seized her for the first time. It was a cold, numbing sensation that held her by the throat. Again, she began coughing, clutching her neck as the icy fingers of the malevolent spirit tightened its grip around her windpipe.

"I can't breathe!" she managed to say, her words thin and dyspneic. Her eyes grew large, bulging from their sockets as she bent over the coffee table in front of her, heaving.

Lenny grabbed her by the shoulders, lifting her out of her seat and spinning her around. He clasped his arms around her midsection and squeezed sharply, forcing her diaphragm to push out whatever was choking her. She coughed again, but nothing came out; however, Abby was suddenly able to breathe again. Unsteady and quivering, she clung to the back of the sofa for support as she tried to calm herself.

"Are you all right?" Lenny asked, scared for his guest.

"I'm not sure I can continue, Lenny," said Abby, shaking her head. "There are spirits here that don't want me in this house. Do you understand that?" she said, trying to compose herself.

"Uh, I guess so," he answered, never having experienced anything like this before. "There are evil spirits in my house?"

Lenny was nervous. He had worried about the session for many weeks prior to that day. His father's death had been a mystery, and the gruesome details of the murder had not been released to the family for many years afterward. In fact, Lenny had never told his mother about them fearing she would never be the same if she knew.

"Yes, I'm afraid there are, Lenny," Abby began, "but I'm sure it has nothing to do with you or your father. It may be something that was just here before you moved in."

"What can I do?"

Abby got up. "I think it best if you sought a spiritual cleanser— someone who can rid your place of dark spirits. That's not something I can or will do. I'm sorry." Abby tried to be professional; however, she could feel something strong and demonic stirring in the house.

"Please, can we try again?" pleaded Lenny. "I really want to speak more to my father. Will you please stay?"

Abby reluctantly nodded and took another deep breath. This time she focused on getting the demons out of her meditation, blocking them from getting inside her.

"Was your father a nice person?" she asked.

"Yes, of course," Lenny said. "He wouldn't hurt anyone."

"I ... I'm just trying to be sure I have the right energy that has returned to speak to us," she answered. "I'm blocking bad energy, bad spirits, so if he wasn't very nice, I may not be able to connect with him right now."

"Yeah, he was very nice."

"I see him again. He's here. He says again that he is very proud of you, Lenny. You are a good son. He says …"

"Yes?"

"… he says your mother feels the same way, even though she is still with you on earth. Perhaps she hasn't told you this, but this is how she feels."

Then, Abby coughed violently again and put her hands back to her throat.

"I'm afraid, that's all I can do," she said continuing to hack and trying to catch her breath. "I'm sorry. I have to go."

Uncharacteristically, she got up and walked straight toward the front door.

"Here's my contact information," she said, handing Lenny her business card. "Call me to reschedule any time. There's no charge for your session. Now just isn't a good time."

"But, but …" Lenny started once more.

By this time, Abby was nearly to the car with Dwayne scurrying behind her, trying to keep up. Dwayne was still munching on something he had pulled from the refrigerator as he helped her get inside. Once in the back, she crumpled into the corner of the soft, leather seats.

"Take me home," she told him, pushing her head back and closing her eyes.

It was a long ride home.

*****

CH 35 - Visiting the Priest

1995

Abby Knight had been having terrible nightmares for years, but more recently they had escalated into something more intolerable. Insomnia and nightmares are one thing, but when those terrors begin seeping into the daytime hours—particularly during her sessions—she could find no relief.

Like her mother and her mother's mother, Abby had certain abilities that most others did not. She too could connect with the dead, and like her mother, Cora Rae, and grandmother, Janice, she had learned to create a small business out of helping others reach across the divide and get in touch with loved ones who had departed.

Although she had not had problems with aggressive or dangerous clients, Abby knew from others in the business and her own family that certain precautions were needed when going to someone's home to conduct a session. She was much more comfortable having her own shop, but increasingly she found she had to make "house calls" to bring in the extra money they needed to make ends meet.

However, as it turned out, Abby had more to fear in her own home than she did in any customer's. Now, tormented day and night, she gradually began to break under the stress. An old friend of the family, Terri Campbell, suggested she see a priest. Abby was Catholic and went to Sunday mass most weeks although not as religiously as she knew she should. Reluctantly, Abby called and talked to the priest, telling him only that she had a serious matter that was bothering her and wanting to talk to him. He suggested she come to confession, but she asked if he would see her in his office instead.

"Father Jose, thank you for seeing me," said Abby, coming into his office and trying to be deferential. She sat in the colorful and broad armchair, covered in a rich cobalt with a series of bright, colorful suns depicted, glowing across the seat and back.

"It is no problem, Abigail," he said, not knowing her well.

"Call me Abby, Father, please."

"All right, Abby. So, you were telling me something serious was bothering you."

"Yes, I have these terrible dreams. They're about demons and horrible beasts. I thought maybe I should go to a doctor, but a friend told me they were so disturbing I should see a priest. She said they sounded demonic."

"Tell me about them."

"It's the same every time, Father. I'm walking through a dark forest. There is snow on the ground, and it's at night. All I can see is the white ground and the towering black branches of the trees shooting over the top of me like a scary, dense spider's web. I feel as if they're trying to reach down and grab me, so I run. The wind is howling, and the snow is heavy, pelting my face and stinging my eyes. I'm cold, lost, hungry, and afraid."

"*Um hum*," said the priest, listening carefully.

"Well, I keep running through the woods trying to find my way out, when I see that my footprints in the snow lead me right back to where I started. All I'm doing is making a giant loop. The faster I run, the faster I come back to the same place."

"That certainly would be unnerving, but it isn't unusual. Many people with high stress and anxiety have those dreams. You said there are a lot of things happening in your life right now—your young daughter, your job—all sorts of stresses. It's no wonder you would have dreams like this."

"But it's not just that, Father."

Father Jose sat and put his hands and fingers together, leaning forward.

"After three times around the loop in the woods, I look up into the high branches of the trees. There I see a stiff, frozen, and mangled body."

"Of some animal?"

"Of a person, Father. Its eyes are light brown, and they're not blinking—frozen open with snowflakes falling on its eyelids. Its arms and legs are wrapped around the tree trunk backwards. It looks like it's screaming because the mouth is open, but no sound is coming out."

"My, my! How horrible, indeed," said Father Jose, now making the sign of the cross.

201

"Then, the dead body comes alive and begins reaching down for me from the tree. Its arms, hands and fingers are only bone, and they stretch—like rubber bands—down to where I am. I can feel it try to grip my neck and squeeze my throat. I can't breathe. Then, I look into its face."

Father Jose waited, wondering what was coming next. Then, he said, "And?"

"It is *my* face, Father. *Mine!*"

Father Jose shook his head.

"All around me are horned beasts, snarling and baring their teeth," she said. "They look like a combination of different animals—a lion's head, a snake's body, and a scorpion's tail. Their eyes are yellow with black slits like a dragon's."

"I have heard of such things before, and they usually lead down a very dark path. This may be the early stages of a possession, so we cannot take this lightly." Father Jose rose from his desk and moved some books to the side, revealing a large, flat calendar beneath. "I want to schedule an exorcism for you. I'll need time to make the arrangements and contact my bishop. There is a priest I know who specializes in this sort of thing. He'll need to be there. When can you make yourself available?"

"I ... I ..." Abby was stunned. She knew her situation was bad, but this was almost worse than being told she had four weeks to live. It was the survival of her soul, not just her body.

"I should be able to have things lined up within the month," said Father.

"Why so long?"

The priest shook his head. "I'm sorry, but it takes time—the church, the red tape, the authorizations, etcetera—they all take time."

"How long will it take—the exorcism?"

"I don't know. Sometimes it takes an hour; sometimes many hours or even days."

"Days?"

"Yes. If the demon is particularly strong or resistant, it can take a lot of time and energy. Exorcisms can be dangerous, but they are sometimes necessary. We must trust in God. He is the One who will help us through to the other side. If we believe in Him, you will be cured."

"I'll have to check, Father. As I said, I have a young one at home. I will have to find a babysitter," said Abby.

"Abby, don't wait too long. The demon will only get stronger, and as it does, it will be harder for us to exorcise it. Eventually, it could take over you and your soul completely and then you'll be beyond our reach. You'll be lost."

Abby left the church shaking. She would have to think about what Father had said. She was terrified by the thought of an exorcism, yet she was terrified by the thought of a demon possessing her soul as well.

I'll think about this more tomorrow, she thought, even though she knew that meant another night—and possible day—of terror.

*****

CH 36 - Questions for Mitzie

2020

Tommy waited in Dag's office for Mitzie to show up. She was supposed to be there by 1730 hours or 5:30 PM, but she was late. By 5:40 Tommy was getting annoyed; however, a few minutes later, she arrived.

He had never seen her, and from what Dag had said, Tommy fully expected her to be wearing something more appropriate for a circus act than a police questioning. However, he was surprised when she entered the precinct wearing blue jeans, a long-sleeved, pink blouse and a deep, plum cashmere sweater—much more high-class than he had imagined.

"Hello, you must be Detective Walcott?" she said smoothly, almost gracefully.

"Yes, and you must be Ms. Wilkins."

"Yes, but call me Mitzie."

"I'm heading up the investigation of several cases—one of which you came in to discuss with my partner some time back," said Tommy, stretching the truth. He motioned to the hard, wooden chair beside his desk. "Please ..."

Mitzie sat down and gently placed her plum purse on the scuffed, dull floor beside her.

"So, you came in ... what, a couple of months ago? And you spoke with Detective Gallagher about the homicide in the ... which case was it now?" he asked, testing her.

"The Dorchester murders. I told him about my dream—the one I had about the man with the knife—a bloody knife. And ..."

"... And what exactly did Detective Gallagher tell you at the time, ma'am?" asked Tommy, cutting her off and making sure he stayed in control of the meeting.

"Well, he said that he didn't believe me. Or at least I think that's what he was saying to me anyway."

"And why *should* we believe you, Ms. Wilkins?"

"I have more information on the case—information that you need to solve it; that's why," she said. Mitzie gave him a strange, mischievous grin that had a dash of seduction and intrigue to it.

"And what would that be, exactly? I mean, we really can't prosecute a case based on a dream, now can we?"

"Oh, I said that just to get your partner's attention. It was really the *symbols* in the dream that were important, you see. But I've had other dreams since then, some that were much clearer. Some that told me exactly what happened at the murder scene."

"Symbols … in the dream, you say?" said Tommy, now wondering he had gone back to this source. *She is going to be a waste of my time*, he thought.

"Yes, symbols are powerful."

"I'll need more than that, Ms. Wilkins."

"But in my dream, I saw another form leaving the scene of the murder. It had been there earlier in the day, and I believe it too was a psychic."

"A form? You mean a person?"

"I believe it was a woman, and I believe she does readings for people—you know, connecting them with their deceased relatives. But this one … well … I think she did a little more."

"Such as …"

"It seems to me that when I saw her return later in the day—in my dream that is—she went there to get a *bonus* check for her work, if you know what I mean."

"To burglarize the place," said Tommy.

"Yes. I think she went back to the house with someone else, and they burglarized it, killing the woman and her son."

"I see."

"Not only that, but I had another dream where the same woman and her partner did the same thing to another one of their clients. That one was in Needham Heights. They ended up throwing her out the window of her own apartment."

"Claire Horwath," said Tommy, completing the thought.

"Yes. That's why I went to see her. I had this dream about her getting attacked. I thought I could help, but no one would take me seriously. But when you called, I wanted to come back and try again. I sensed that you, at least, might understand me. You can see things for what they really are, I think. I'm afraid your detective partner can't see much of anything. Perhaps he's been at his job too long. I'm not sure how he calls himself a detective when he can't seem to 'detect' anything."

"Ms. Wilkins," said Tommy, ignoring her slight toward Dag, "all I've heard you talk about are your dreams. You realize that we're the police, which means we have to find evidence—hard evidence. I need *facts*, ma'am. I don't do well *detecting* things that are in dreams either. Do you have any information that is not in a dream?"

Mitzie seemed to squirm in her chair, but then she said, "Well, I know what you're saying, but in my world, dreams, feelings, and the dimensions beyond are all part of *my* reality. In fact, they *are* reality. But if you're interested, I do have a name that I see in my dreams."

"Humor me."

"All right. It's Sara."

"Sara. Did you get a last name?"

"There was a last name. I think it started with an *M C*. Maybe it was McDonnell or McKenzie or McLaughlin or something. I think it may have been McLaughlin, though. You can check on that one."

"Is that all?" asked Tommy, ready to wrap up the meeting.

"She has a driver too. I don't know his name, but I think he is the other one who's involved."

"A driver …"

"Yeah, he acts as a bodyguard for her."

"I see," said Tommy. "Well, at least that's something."

"That's a lot," said Mitzie slyly. She smiled, knowing she had planted a seed. "I'm always having dreams about things, so I may have more for you later. Can I call you?" she asked, as she got up from the chair.

"Sure," said Tommy insincerely.

She handed him her card and smiled again before leaving down the busy hallway.

Tommy pulled out the list of psychics he had found during his research. There was no particular order to it, but with only twelve names, it didn't take long to find a match. It was the fifth name … Sara McLaughlin … just as Mitzie had said.

Tommy placed the call. "Hello, may I speak with Sara McLaughlin?"

"Just a minute," was the answer.

"Hello, this is Sara," came a different voice on the phone.

"Yes, this is Detective Walcott downtown. I need to ask you a few questions about a case we are investigating down here. But it would be better if you came down to the precinct, say tomorrow morning at 8 AM?"

Sara wasn't sure he heard it right. Both shocked and surprised, she stammered. "Excuse me. What was that again?"

"This is Detective Walcott—Boston police. We need to talk to you down at the station," Tommy repeated curtly.

Sara's body shook. The last time she'd interacted with the police, things had not turned out well. It had been several years earlier, and she had been both younger and more naïve. She had tried to volunteer her psychic services to the police to help them solve a particularly vexing case—a missing-persons case. The police chief at the time, Zag Gallagher, hadn't given her the time of day. He hadn't even feigned an interest. However, when the district attorney and then the mayor got involved, the chief changed his mind and called her back.

Zag had offered her a chance to work on the case—that of a seven-year-old boy, Daniel Gibbons, who had gone missing fifteen months earlier. The police had found a few leads, but all had led to dead ends. The alibis of the family members had checked-out, and both the father and mother seemed to be truly in agony over their loss, offering rewards and generating local community and media support in trying to find their missing son.

Sara had taken the case, coming into the precinct to read over the case files and touch, smell and see the evidence. There had been a small, red tennis shoe left at the park where the boy had been last seen. His mother had taken him there to play with his younger brother, who had been five at the time. She had struck up a conversation with a neighborhood mom while sitting on a bench next to the swings. Daniel had been over by the monkey bars, climbing in and around the thin, steel tubes that were bent in all different directions to make the ascent more challenging.

Daniel's mom told police later that she was talking to her neighbor for only a few minutes when she looked up to see where her boys were. Jack, the youngest, was going down the slide, but she couldn't see Daniel. At first, she thought he was hiding someplace amongst all the playground equipment. But when she couldn't find him, she panicked and called police.

The police investigation discovered little. Daniel's red tennis shoe was found near the monkey bars, but there was little other evidence. None of the children remembered seeing anyone else at the park other than the other kids they knew. There was a gate nearby, and it had been open at the time of the disappearance.

Nothing like that had ever happened at that park—or that neighborhood—before.

One six-year-old girl thought she saw Daniel get off the monkey bars and walk to the fence, but she wasn't sure. When asked if there had been anyone else outside the fence, she couldn't remember. She really hadn't paid that much attention to the whole thing, as she had been more interested in playing with her own friends. But she was only six; it was hard to ask anything more of her.

The entire case upset Sara. She had a young daughter of her own, and she couldn't imagine losing her—even for a minute. She had thrown all her efforts into helping the police get a lead, a break— whatever she could that might move the case along.

But it was a vision she had that broke things open.

She remembered exactly when the vivid images came to her. She was downtown, leaving the police station, when she saw a street vendor selling hotdogs. She was hungry, and she walked briskly over to the stand to purchase one with chips and a *Diet Coke*. Just as she was paying for the lunch, there was an overwhelming flood of pictures and emotions that filled her mind.

She thought it had been the smell of the hotdogs that had triggered it. But the street quickly enveloped into a thick fog where she saw a little boy. There was a smell of hot dogs coming down from upstairs, but in the basement was a dingey, dirty bed. Chained to the bed was the little boy, curled up and crying. It was dark, damp and filthy dirty. The boy was sick, perspiring with fever and scared to death.

He was thin, and his hair was long and unruly. It was clear he hadn't had a bath in weeks.

During the next several days, she had other visions, but it was only when she passed the hotdog vendor on the corner. As she focused on the details of her visions, she noticed that the "basement" room where the boy appeared was actually a lower-level apartment within a three-story brownstone. There was a man who came in and out of the room. He was tall, thin and wore a major-lead baseball cap, although she couldn't see the name.

What was the connection with the hot dog vendor? she thought. *Why did she get her visions then?*

Each day she came to the precinct, Sara struck a conversation with the hotdog vendor outside, asking him about his business and his family ... anything that would give her a clue. But there was nothing—nothing abnormal or telling in his stories. He was an amiable man—older and seemingly sincere. He had a wife, two children, and six grandchildren. He was sixty-four and hoped to retire in another five years or so. He was hardly the type that would kidnap and keep a young boy hostage.

Finally, she asked him about other vendors—whether he knew others who sold hotdogs on other corners. He said he knew a few, but he wasn't close to any of them. Most were younger guys who had tried to horn-in on his corner. He was getting old, and it was harder every year to chase them away and protect his turf. Sara asked if there was anyone in particular with whom he'd had recent run-ins. He told her about a Hal Reynolds who, for years, had tried to push him off his block.

"Yeah, he's a pain in my ass. Every year, I have to tell him to *fuck off* and go find another corner. I've got a wife, kids and grandkids to support. He don't have nobody but himself—the bastard. He's just a prick. Finally, I told him that if I ever caught him around my block again, I was callin' in the police chief, my good buddy Chief Gallagher."

"Oh, so you know Chief Gallagher?" Sara asked him at the time.

"Well, no, not really," the vendor said. "I've sold him a lotta' dogs over the years. He comes up and asks for his with mustard and relish. He usually wants the ones that 'er mushy—you know, really cooked through. So, I always keep one in the bottom of the cooker for 'im, just in case. I think he appreciates it. Anyway, I told Reynolds

209

I was gonna' have the chief on his ass if he didn't cut the *shit* out. He only swore at me, folded up his cart, and moved down another block. Ya' know, there's enough business 'round here, you don't have ta' steal it from another guy."

"What does he look like?" she asked, but before he got the words out of his mouth, she already knew. The image was strong, and it popped into her brain so fast that she knew it couldn't be anyone else.

The police found Reynolds at his downstairs apartment with the boy in his back bedroom. He was arrested and eventually convicted. The boy was returned safely to his parents and to a grateful community. However, Chief Gallagher had taken the full credit, not even mentioning her name or involvement. That would have been fine for Sara, except for the fact that he had her followed for six months after that, suspecting she may have been involved because she was able to lead them to the perp. After that, she vowed never to get involved with the police.

Now she was being called in again. This time, it was not to help, but as a suspect in a crime.

"Uh, I'm not sure I can get down there tomorrow morning, detective. I have to get my daughter off to school, and then I have to ..."

"Sorry, Ms. McLaughlin. Perhaps I didn't make myself clear. You *will* be here at 8 AM—whether you come down willingly or I have to pick you up in a squad car. It's your choice. Which will it be?" His tone was unyielding—even threatening.

"I'll make arrangements, then," she answered solemnly.

"Good. I thought you'd understand," said Tommy, pleased with himself for strong-arming her.

Sara felt sick as she turned off her cell phone.

"Who was that honey?" her husband called out from the other room.

"Uh, nobody, Vince. It was just somebody trying to sell something. You know, the usual."

"I thought they couldn't do that anymore, what with the Do Not Call List and all," said her husband.

Sara didn't answer. She was worried. Afraid now that Claire had somehow implicated her in the accident. All she could do was wait and see. Eight o'clock would come soon enough, and she would get an answer, whether it was one she wanted or not. *****

CH 39 – Interrogation

2020

It was early when Sara came into the precinct. She was nervous, and it showed. Her hair and makeup, normally perfect, were mussed as if her alarm clock had failed to go off and she had dashed from her bed to the car to make the meeting.

Pushing her hair back behind her ear, she signed in at the front desk and followed a police officer to Dag's office where Tommy had arranged the interrogation. Tommy wasn't in yet, but Sara waited patiently for him. The meeting was scheduled for 8 AM, but that time came and went with no sign of anyone coming to see her. At 8:45, a middle-aged man walked into the room, surprised to find a strange guest sitting in front of the desk, as Tommy had failed to inform him of his arrangements. Dag threw his tan, London Fog on the steel peg on the back of the door, closed it and then stared curiously at Sara.

"Did we have an appointment?" he asked.

"Why yes. You asked me to come down to the station for questioning," she answered, not knowing she had the wrong person.

"Who are you supposed to be meeting with?" Dag asked.

"Detective Walcott. Isn't that you?"

"Oh, Tommy. Sure, he's been working on some cases with me," said Dag. Then, hesitating, he added, "And what is your name?"

"I'm Sara. Sara McLaughlin."

Dag smiled and extended his hand.

"I'm Detective Gallagher. Tommy is my partner. I'm sure he'll be here any minute. What time was your meeting?"

"Eight," said Sara, still managing to keep a pleasant grin on her face.

"Hmm, well it's nearly 8:50. I wonder where he is?" Dag asked, looking around. He pulled out his cell phone and dialed Tommy's number, but no one picked up. "I don't know, he must be running late."

"If this is about the Horwath incident ..." Sara started, "... I'll tell you that all I did was have a session with her earlier in the day. That's all.

She is a nice lady, and I was just trying to help." Sara volunteered in the hope of avoiding a long and tedious meeting—or worse.

"Ms. McLaughlin, I'm sure Tommy will go over all that with you once he comes in," said Dag, trying not to interfere.

"Well, he was rather brusque on the phone," she added. "I did visit Claire in the hospital to see how she was doing. I felt bad about what happened. She seemed to be doing fine, though."

"How long have you known Ms. Horwath?" Dag asked, opening a drawer and picking up a plastic container of breath mints.

"Only a month or so. She called me for a session, and that was the only time we met, you know, before her incident."

"What kind of 'session' are you talking about?"

Sara became quiet, but then said, "Well, I'm sure you already know that I'm a medium. I help people."

"And how did you help Ms. Horwath?"

"I helped her communicate with her boyfriend who died. He was killed in Boston, downtown, earlier this year. She was really torn up about it, as you can imagine. I guess she just wanted to be sure he was okay, like most of my clients."

"I see," said Dag, skeptically.

Yet, he found a morsel of pureness, an innocence, about her. His job had done much to callus his emotions over the years, and at some level, Dag thought he was immune to any feeling of empathy or softness. *However, she was different somehow*, he thought.

"So, you saw Ms. Horwath in the hospital. When was that?" Dag asked.

"It was only a day or so after her accident. She was still trying to deal with the trauma. Claire told me she didn't know what it was that attacked her. She said she had heard noises, and then was dragged from her bed. She had grabbed her gun and fired some shots, but she hadn't hit whatever it was."

"*Whatever* it was or *whoever* it was?"

Sara shook her head. "That's what she said, detective. That's what she told me. Then, she blacked out. She didn't remember anything

213

after that. The next thing she said she remembered was lying in the alley."

"Sorry, I'm late," came a voice from the doorway. It was Tommy who directed his apology to Dag, not Sara. He came in and took a seat next to his visitor. "It looks like you started without me," said Tommy, making himself comfortable. Then, he glanced at Sara and said, "Thanks for coming," but his tone was flat and insincere.

"As if I had a choice," Sara said under her breath.

"I'm sorry. What did you say?" asked Tommy, not hearing her.

"Oh, I said it's my pleasure."

Dag had heard it all and just grinned.

"I was just asking Sara about her relationship with Claire Horwath."

Tommy pulled a file from his briefcase and plopped it down on Dag's desk. Flipping open the cover, he perused the information before beginning.

"Ms. McLaughlin, how long have you known Claire Horwath?" asked Tommy, jotting down notes on his computer pad.

"I just went over this with Detective Gallagher," she said, annoyed.

"Yes, but I need know it directly from you. How long ..."

"Tommy, you were late. I started without you. Let me just fill you in on what we've covered so far," said Dag, giving Sara the benefit of the doubt.

He caught Tommy up with their conversation with the calmness and smoothness of someone who'd been doing it for a few years.

"... and I think that's about where we are, isn't it?" Dag asked, looking at Sara.

"Yes, I think so."

"Did Ms. Horwath not pay you for your services, Ms. McLaughlin?" Tommy asked bluntly.

"What?"

"I asked if Ms. Horwath had paid you? It's a simple question, Ms. McLaughlin," Tommy said, sarcastically.

Sara bit her lip and answered. "Yes, she paid me."

"Where were you on the night of July 8?"

"I was at home with my family, I'm sure," she said.

"You're not sure?"

"I said I was sure!" she said, rather forcefully.

"Can your family back that up?"

"Of course, they can!" said Sara. Then she asked, "Am I suspected of doing something here?" She looked over at Dag, hoping for his intervention, but he only sat stoically watching the game as it unfolded.

"I'm just asking questions, ma'am," Tommy continued. "I'm just trying to find out who did this to Ms. Horwath."

"Do I need a lawyer?"

"That's up to you." Tommy looked at her suspiciously, giving her no sense of comfort.

"Then you're not arresting me—because if you are, you need to read me my rights," she said firmly.

"No, Ms. McLaughlin, we are not arresting you at this time," interjected Dag.

"Who else was with you when you visited Ms. Horwath?" Tommy asked.

"It was just me and my driver."

"Your driver? You have a driver? You must be doing pretty well if you can afford a driver. People must be paying you quite a bit to talk to their dead relatives."

"Tommy," Dag said sternly, fed up with his partner's behavior. He was quickly crossing the line of professionalism and that was something Dag couldn't tolerate.

"It's for my protection, detective," answered Sara.

"Protecting you or the scam your running?" he asked with a snippy voice.

"Tommy!" Dag admonished again, this time louder.

"Listen, I'm answering your questions," said Sara. "You don't have to give me an attitude."

215

Tommy glared at her. He had always thought highly of himself, and now, playing detective, his ego was growing rather quickly.

"I don't appreciate the way you're talking to me, Ms. McLaughlin. I am an officer of the law you know," Tommy snapped.

"And I'm a law-abiding citizen, whose innocent until proven guilty, right? I don't care for the remarks you're making about me."

"Law-abiding? Innocent? We'll see about that, won't we?" Tommy said back at her.

Sara stood up and looked at Dag. "May I go?"

"We won't force you stay at this time," Dag answered.

"But don't leave town," shouted Tommy before the door had closed.

After she left, Dag turned to his partner. "What the hell was that?" he demanded. "Since when do we start by convicting people before we've even begun questioning them?"

"She's the attacker, Dag! Or an accomplice at the very least! I bet we can place her at the scene the night of the crime. Then, we'll connect her to the other murders. I'm sure she was involved in those too."

"Tommy, that's not how we investigate crimes. We don't form a conclusion and then create the evidence around it! We don't get rough with suspects to coerce them into a confession! It's the quickest way to get them to clam-up, and it's the fastest way to get our case thrown out of court. If you do this, she'll lawyer-up, and we'll get nothing more out of her. Unless she's demonstrated that she isn't going to cooperate, we need to take this slow and easy. She was cooperating with me just fine before you got here."

"You handle it your way; I'll handle it mine," said Tommy, slamming his file closed and storming out of the room.

This was the first time Dag had seen this side of his partner, and it was a surprise. To this point, Tommy had been helpful and accommodating in working with Dag on the cases. Now, however, it was clear he was no longer happy with that backseat role.

Meanwhile, Tommy marched down the hall and punched the button on the elevator. His next stop was the fifth floor and Chief Malloy's office.

*****

CH 38 - Lenny and His Bat

1995

All was quiet as Lenny turned out the overhead light in the family room. The only sounds came from the crickets that were outside chirping excitedly, hidden in the shrubbery surrounding the small plot set aside for a garden. Roger was supposed to go away on a business trip, but at the last minute had to reschedule as his customer had a conflict and couldn't meet with him until the following day.

So, Lenny and Roger spent the night watching television until Roger yawned, deciding to turn in early. He had a 7:35 AM flight to catch and didn't want to oversleep and miss it.

Later, after watching another movie, Lenny trudged up the narrow staircase heading straight for the bathroom. There he did his business, washed his face and brushed his teeth. He opened the medicine cabinet and took down two plastic containers with white, child-proof caps. He'd always had trouble opening them because of the arthritis in his right hand, but this time they seemed to pop-off easily. He jiggled the first container, allowing two green capsules to slide into his palm, and after rinsing these down, he shook a white caplet from the second container. He grimaced as he placed it on his tongue and emptied the rest of the water from his clear, bathroom glass. Flipping on the bathroom nightlight, he went into the bedroom where Roger was already asleep.

The comforter was thick and quilted with fine stitching that had a mosaic pattern of bright colors. However, it had been warm that day, and Roger had neatly folded it into thirds and placed it at the base of the bed. With the windows open and the balmy air blowing lightly across the sheets, he didn't need any extra layers.

"Crap!" Lenny muttered, realizing the television remote wasn't resting conveniently next to him on the nightstand.

Lenny flipped off his sheet and leaned over to retrieve it. After picking up the remote, he climbed back into bed, turning on the set and then fidgeting with the channels until he landed on *The Tonight Show* with Jay Leno.

With drooping eyelids, he made it through the monologue but started to doze off during the following commercial. Time passed, and the next think Lenny heard was the sound of someone slowly coming up the stairs.

Creak ... Creak ... Creak!

Alarmed, Lenny reached for his cell phone, but again it wasn't next to him on the nightstand. He looked over at Roger; yet his partner hadn't moved and was sound asleep. Not wanting to wake him unnecessarily, Lenny quietly groped for the bat he kept under the bed. He slid his hands from side to side under the box springs to feel for the hard, smooth surface of the Louisville Slugger. But the footsteps kept coming, reaching the top of the stairs before moving down the hallway toward their bedroom.

Frantically, Lenny rolled out of bed onto the floor and stretched to grab the bat. Lying on his stomach, he put his fingers around the knobbed handle and began pulling it out. But just as he started to get up, he felt a sharp pain in the back of his head. Instantly, his vision blurred before going dark.

Frantically, Lenny rolled out of bed onto the floor and stretched to grab the bat. Putting his fingers around the knobbed handle, he began pulling it out. But just as he started to get up, he felt a sharp pain in the back of his head. Instantly, his vision blurred before going dark.

***

Lenny felt a stabbing pain in his brain. He touched the back of his head and felt a gooey slickness, and as he pulled back his hand, he looked at his fingers; they were covered in his own dark, crimson blood.

Now on the television was a horror film of the 1940s, shot in black and white. While a young couple was kissing beside a creepy tombstone covered with black, stringy vines, the blurry image of the mausoleum behind them came into focus. A creaking noise, like that made in his house only moments before he blacked out, groaned from the cold, gray stone building as the iron, grate door swung open. Two green eyes appeared suddenly, piercing the blackness and evil within.

Lenny staggered to get up. He could feel the blood now trickling down his back. Again, he heard a creaking noise that he thought was coming from his study down the hall. He didn't know how long he'd been unconscious, but he pushed himself down the corridor anyway and toward the study. Bat in hand, he listened for anything coming from that direction.

Reaching the study door, he stopped. It was ajar—a small gap showing a bizarre flickering of light streaming through it, as if there were a television in the room like the one still turned on in his bedroom. Yet, he knew there was no TV inside. He pushed open the door, bat in hand. His heart pounded, and he could feel every muscle in his body tense-up. Taking in a breath, he raised his bat and flipped on the light.

But there was no one there. The room was exactly as he'd left it earlier that evening. He glanced around once more, just to be sure. *No,* he thought, *there was something different. There was something that wasn't quite right.*

He moved slowly around the back of the old, walnut desk holding up his bat. There he saw that the lower drawer had been pried open, then closed to try to make it look untouched. Carefully, he opened the drawer. His simple, metal cashbox, where he kept his extra reserves, was gone. There had been several thousand dollars in it, and he hadn't told anyone about it or the cash he kept there—not even his partner.

Lenny slammed the drawer closed, cursing that he'd been robbed. His arms and hands were still shaking from the trauma as he grabbed the railing to go downstairs to get his cell phone. Picking it up, he dialed 9-1-1.

"This is 911, may I help you?" asked the calm, female voice on the other end.

"Yes, this is ..."

Just then, Lenny again heard another noise coming from upstairs.

"I'll call you back," he said, gripping the baseball bat once more and heading back up the stairwell.

He was angry. Ticked-off at whoever had violated his home and hit him over the head. *It is payback time,* he thought.

Lenny reached the door into his bedroom and pushed it open. He raised his bat—then, he dropped it on the floor.

"Oh, my God!" he shrieked.

On top of the television was the half-torso of his partner, Roger. His eyes were open, and mouth agape. A fine stream of blood trickled down the middle of the screen which now showed an apple orchard with an unmanned tractor rolling through it.

Scratch ... scratch scratch

The sound was coming from the closet door. Lenny flung open the door.

Screeeeeeeeeeeeeeeeeeeech!!!

Downstairs, the voice on the cell phone came back online.

"Hello? Hello? Is anyone there?" asked the 911 dispatch agent.

*****

CH 39 - Father Jose

1995

Father Jose was troubled by what he had heard from Abby. That night, after her confession, he prayed for her and her family. He had only been at St. Sebastian's church for a few months, and he was just beginning to get to know the congregation and the community. Prior to that, he'd been assigned to the St. John Kanty church in Buffalo where he spent five years as the associate pastor.

A young priest of only thirty-five, he was devout. He had a zeal for the faith and was uncompromised in his beliefs in the orthodoxy and doctrine of his religion. At the same time, he believed in the Devil and the powers that Satan could unleash on those poor souls who found themselves vulnerable or even open to the dark suggestive temptations from the other side. However, not all priests held the same view. In fact, his parish priest in Boston, Father Latner, did not. He came from a school that believed people were the source of their own evil—from Original Sin. Father Latner really didn't believe there were evil spirits out there that could take possession of one's soul—only man's embellishment of the power of evil to make it appear like that.

So, instead of trying to convince his monsignor, Father Jose talked directly to the bishop of his diocese, Bishop Dolan. He knew the bishop had grown up in the rough and tumble area of the Bronx and had witnessed much during his seventy years. In fact, he had allegedly participated in several exorcists during that time.

"Father, thank you for seeing me," said Father Jose, kneeling and kissing the bishop's ring.

"What is on your mind, Jose? You sounded troubled when you called. Is everything all right at the parish?"

"Yes, Father. It's not that. I had a parishioner come and give me her confession last week. She told me of terrible dreams she was having." Father Jose went on to tell of the horrid scenes Abby had described.

Bishop Dolan bowed his head and made the sign of the cross. "Have you discussed this with Father Latner?"

"No, Father. I don't believe he has as open a mind as you do on this subject."

"You are speaking of bodily possession, then?"

"Yes."

"I see. You think this woman is possessed."

"Yes, Father. I think she is very troubled, at the very least, and I'm afraid for her soul. I'm not sure there is much I can do to help her. I think she may need an exorcism."

"Does she communicate with the dead?"

"She said she does."

"Did you tell her she should not do that? She will only be opening herself up to more evil that is out there."

"I know, Father, and yes, I told her. She is a medium. That is her line of work. She said it will be difficult for her to stop—apparently it's something that just comes to her. She has a hard time shutting it off."

"I don't think there is anything I can do to help unless she ceases that communication. Even if we exorcise the evil within her, it can easily come back through her channeling."

"We must do *something* for her, Father. She has a young daughter."

Bishop Dolan sighed. "If you can get her to pledge never again to initiate communication with the dead, then I will consider pursuing an exorcism for you. However, that is the only way I will do it. It is far too dangerous as it is, and if she is a medium, the risks are that much greater."

"I understand, Father. I will talk to her and convince her."

"Go in peace and with God's blessing," said the bishop, making the sign of the cross.

***

Abby was unnerved by what Father Jose had suggested. When she got home, she threw the keys on the kitchen counter and walked into the family room, where her husband was asleep on the couch with his glasses askew on his forehead and the television screen showing a rerun of *Hogan's Heroes*. He said he'd watch their daughter when she went to her appointment but likely fell asleep after getting her to bed. She kissed his forehead and laid a soft blanket over him to make sure he didn't get too cold. Then, she turned off the light and the TV and went upstairs.

Climbing into bed, Abby pulled up the covers hoping they would keep out the bad spirits that seemed to be following her. The haunting image of the decaying hand wouldn't let her go to sleep. Try as she might, she couldn't get settled. Hours passed, and eventually her eyelids grew heavy. They began to droop when the telephone rang, jolting her awake once more.

"Hello?" Abby answered, in a groggy stupor.

The sound on the other end was a low guttural growl—something she had never heard before in her life. She felt a coldness, a blackness—the same sensation she had gotten when she was at Lenny's.

Suddenly, a gray mist began bubbling up through the receiver of the phone and encircling her neck like a noose. Abby felt it tightening just as it had at Lenny's—choking her like she'd lodged a green grape in her windpipe. She tried to scream, but nothing came out.

***

The next morning, the alarm sounded upstairs, and Abby's husband, Chris, rolled off the sofa to trudge up the stairs to the second floor and past his daughter Sara's room where she was still asleep in her bed.

"Abby? It's time to get up," Chris said, coming into their bedroom to silence the alarm.

However, the sheets were pulled back, and there was no one there. The phone was off the hook, dangling by its cord on the floor. The light buzzing sound of the disconnected line was the only thing stirring inside—pulsating with a haunting warning.

But Abby was gone.

Days, weeks, months passed and there was no sign of her. She had vanished without a trace.

***

Father Jose tried to reach Abby several times but had no luck. Finally, he went to her home. She was not there, and neither were her husband and daughter. The house was empty.

*****

ᑕᕼ 1ᗝ - Uᑭ ᖶᕼᕮ ᖇᔕᔕ

1995

The police report showed that there had been a break-in, and that something had been stolen from the metal lockbox. The body of Lenny Pittman was found stuffed under the bed with his bat wedged up his rectum. Like one of the previous victims, his head had been turned completely around to face his backside, thereby breaking numerous vertebrae and other bones. Roger's torso was found resting on top of the television. His bottom half was still in the bed.

Detective Zag surveyed the crime scene, noting the similarities with the others he had recently added to his growing list of homicides. He walked into the study, finding the fresh scratch marks on the lower right drawer of the desk. Opening it, he found the broken metal money box which was empty. The first arriving police officers had found the bodies.

Above each of the beds were the same words scrawled in chilling, blood-smeared letters: *Hello Plottar.* Although a recurring theme for these incidents, it was new to Zag. After taking pictures of the scene, the police lifted the frame to take pictures and survey the position of the corpse relative to the box springs and end board.

"I've heard the term 'shove it up your, you know what' but this is taking it a little too far," said one of the cops, jokingly.

"Real funny," said Zag, not at all amused. "Sanders, go over this place with a fine-tooth comb. I want to know every fingerprint, carpet fiber, and dust particle that is out of place.

"Yes sir."

"And where is Murphy? He needs to be here too. There's a lot of potential evidence here for us to look at. These crime scenes must contain something that the killer left behind – something that will lead us closer to who he is," said Dag. "It's just too messy not to."

"Who he is or who *they* are," said Murphy, Zag's long-time partner, coming into the room.

"What's that supposed to mean?" Zag asked.

225

"It means that maybe more than one person was involved in this."

"Maybe. We need to collect the evidence first."

"And people like this ... well, you just never know what sorts of things they can get into," said Murphy.

Grant Murphy came from a solid Catholic family with straight-laced virtues and ideals. With six kids of his own, he and his world were black and white. You were either God-fearing and lived by the Book or you didn't. And the way he saw things in this case, Lenny didn't abide by those rules.

"You know. It's pretty obvious the guy was a fag. The pictures show the two of them together—you know, like a couple. Two homos living in the same apartment—well something bad was bound to happen to them."

"Really, Murphy? Who made you king?" said Zag, annoyed. "Take your sanctimonious comments outside or leave them at home. They have no place here. We're here to solve a crime, not be the judge."

"Suit yourself," said Murphy. "But I'm tellin' ya', it just ain't right."

"You're right," answered Zag. "Being stuffed under your bed with a baseball bat up your ass just ain't right. We just need to find out who did it. I think we can agree to that, can't we?"

*****

CH 41 - Missing

1995

After finding no one at the Knight home, Father Jose followed up on his own before going back to the bishop.

"Father, I haven't been able to reach that woman I told you about who I believe is possessed or flirting dangerously with evil spirits. She's not home and no one seems to know where she is. I talked with Chris, Abby's husband, who is with their daughter and staying at Abby's aunt's place. However, it's been over three days, and no one has been able to reach Abby. She's gone missing."

"Have you contacted the police?" asked Bishop Dolan.

"No, but the husband did."

"Is he involved in her disappearance?"

"I don't think so. I spoke with him, and he seems just as worried. There must be something we can do to find her. Can you contact some other parishes around here? Maybe she's still in the area and is attending another church. I have a picture of her right here."

Father Jose handed a picture to the priest. It was an older photo—one when Abby was younger. But Bishop Dolan didn't take it. He pushed it back to Jose and said, "There is nothing more we can do. She has blasphemed the church by her actions contacting the dead. She has sinned and not sought to repent. There is nothing I can—will—do. Her soul is in God's hands now."

"I don't accept that," said Father Jose, angered by the bishop's attitude. "Christ didn't reject people because they sinned."

"True, but they came to Him for forgiveness. She did not."

"Yes, she did, Father. She came to me for help!"

"She did not ask to be forgiven for her sins, did she?" asked the bishop.

Father Jose was quiet.

"Go on with your life, Jose. You worry too much about others who do not care about the Church and its teachings."

Dissatisfied with the answer he got, Father Jose went back to his parish and began preparing his homily for the following day's mass. He had a strong message for the congregation, but he also wanted to open his arms to them—to those who needed him and the church but were afraid to reach out.

"Today's second reading was from the Acts of the Apostles," Father Jose began, "which talked to us about black magic. Acts 19: 19 through 20 says, '*And a number of those who had practiced magic arts brought their books together and burned them in the sight of all. And they counted the value of them and found it came to fifty thousand pieces of silver. So, the word of the Lord continued to increase and prevail mightily.*'"

"The Bible is clear on this. Anyone who practices black magic is to be condemned to eternal damnation! He or she will be thrown into the depths of Hell from which no salvation is possible. That is what we believe.

"Now, I have come to understand that some of you in this very congregation participate in occult activities. You believe they are harmless and are only entertainment or diversions. You don't understand the power that the Dark One has over you when you open up these kinds of portals into your soul. Ouija Boards, Tarot Cards, Psychics, Channelers, Palm Readers, and others are all under Satan's control. They are there to capture your spirit and drag it into the blackness of the pits of Gehenna.

"It is clear from scripture in the New Testament, and several times in the Old Testament, that such practices will enslave you to the Devil. I found many references in the Old Testament: Deuteronomy 18:10–14, Exodus 22:18, Leviticus 19:26 and 31, 1 Samuel 15:23, 2 Kings 21:6, Micah 3:7, and Micah 5:12.

"In Deuteronomy, it says, 'There shall not be found among you anyone who burns his son or his daughter as an offering, anyone who practices divination or tells fortunes or interprets omens, or a sorcerer or a charmer or a medium or a necromancer or one who inquires of the dead, for whoever does these things is an *abomination* to the Lord.

"Throughout its pages, you will find these admonitions. Therefore, you must heed the word of the Lord or you will be cast down amongst the others who violated His laws."

Father Jose glanced up from his homily. "These words are harsh, but these are not my words. They are the words of the Lord. Are they to strike fear into you—perhaps, yes. However, I am also here to tell you that the Church and I are here to help you find your way. We are here to guide you back onto the path of righteousness. You need not suffer. You need not feel hopeless in trying to fight evil. Christ is our savior and the One who can defeat any and all demons, including Satan. Put your faith in Him. He will not let you down."

Father Jose finished his sermon and sat down, feeling a sense of satisfaction with how he was serving his God.

At fifteen, Sara sat in a pew with her aunt listening. She felt uncomfortable with what the priest had said as she already knew she had the ability to communicate with the dead. But she said nothing to her aunt about it. It had been only a few months since her mother had disappeared, and weeks since her father had committed suicide over her loss. Now, Sara left the church even more confused.

***

Monday morning—the day following the mass—Father Jose was found dead in his small apartment. His head had been detached from its body. Across the apartment in the bathroom was found a severed hand. It was clutching a broken and bloodied crucifix.

*****

CH 12 - Hogan's Heroes

1995

Abby didn't remember the long ride home, but once there, she threw the keys on the kitchen counter and walked into the family room, where her husband was asleep on the couch with his glasses askew on his forehead and the television screen showing a rerun of *Hogan's Heroes*. He said he'd watch their daughter when she went to her appointment but likely fell asleep after getting her to bed. She kissed his forehead and laid a soft blanket over him to make sure he didn't get too cold. Then, she turned off the light and the TV and went upstairs.

Climbing into bed, Abby pulled up the covers hoping they would keep out the bad spirits that seemed to be following her. The haunting image of the decaying hand wouldn't let her go to sleep. Try as she might, she couldn't get settled. Hours passed, and eventually her eyelids grew heavy. They began to droop when the telephone rang, jolting her awake once more.

"Hello?" Abby answered, in a groggy stupor.

The sound on the other end was a low guttural growl—something she had never heard before in her life. She felt a coldness, a blackness—the same sensation she had gotten when she was at Lenny's.

Suddenly, a gray mist began bubbling up through the receiver of the phone and encircling her neck like a noose. Abby felt it tightening just as it had at Lenny's—choking her like she'd lodged a green grape in her windpipe. She tried to scream, but nothing came out.

***

The next morning, the alarm sounded upstairs, and Abby's husband, Chris, rolled off the sofa to trudge up the stairs to the second floor and past his daughter Sara's room where she was still asleep in her bed.

"Abby? It's time to get up," Chris said, coming into their bedroom to silence the alarm.

However, the sheets were pulled back, and there was no one there. The phone was off the hook, dangling by its cord on the floor. The light buzzing sound of the disconnected line was the only thing stirring inside—pulsating with a haunting warning.

But Abby was gone.

Days, weeks, months passed and there was no sign of her. She had vanished without a trace.

*****

The police report showed that there had been a break-in, and that something had been stolen from the metal lockbox. The body of Lenny Pittman was found stuffed under the bed with his bat wedged up his rectum. Like one of the previous victims, his head had been turned completely around to face his backside, thereby breaking numerous vertebrae and other bones.

Roger's torso was found still resting on top of the television. His bottom half was still in the bed.

Detective Zeller Arthur Gallagher, or Zag as they called him, surveyed the crime scene, noting the similarities with the others he had recently added to his growing list of homicides. He walked into the study, finding the fresh scratch marks on the lower right drawer of the desk. Opening it, he found the broken metal money box which was empty. The first arriving police officers had found the bodies.

After taking pictures of the scene, the police lifted up the frame to take pictures and survey the position of the corpse relative to the box springs and end board.

"I've heard the term 'shove it up your, you know what' but this is taking it a little too far," said one of the cops, jokingly.

"Real funny," said Zag, not at all amused. "Sanders, go over this place with a fine-tooth comb. I want to know every fingerprint, carpet fiber, and dust particle that is out of place.

"Yes sir."

"And where is Murphy? He needs to be here too. There's a lot of potential evidence here for us to look at. These crime scenes must contain something that the killer left behind – something that will lead us closer to who he is," said Dag. "It's just too messy not to."

"Who he is or who *they* are," said Murphy, Zag's long-time partner, coming into the room.

"What's that supposed to mean?" Zag asked.

"It means that maybe more than one person was involved in this."

"Maybe. We need to collect the evidence first."

"And people like this ... well, you just never know what sorts of things they can get into," said Murphy.

Grant Murphy came from a solid Catholic family with straight-laced virtues and ideals. With six kids of his own, he and his world were black and white. You were either God-fearing and lived by the Book or you didn't. And the way he saw things, Lenny didn't abide by those rules.

"You know. It's pretty obvious the guy was a fag. The pictures show the two of them together—you know, like a couple. Two homos living in the same apartment—well something bad was bound to happen to them."

"Really, Murphy? Who made you king?" said Zag, annoyed. "Take your sanctimonious comments outside or leave them at home. They have no place here. We're here to solve a crime, not be the judge."

"Suit yourself," said Murphy. "But I'm tellin' ya', it just ain't right."

"You're right," answered Zag. "Being stuffed under your bed with a baseball bat up your ass just ain't right. We just need to find out who did it."

*****

CH 43 - A Talk with Bessie-Part 1

2020

In addition to his dad's murder, Dag was now tasked with finding answers for the other cases he was working on too. So, he took home a stack of case files to go through one more time. He flipped open the first one dated 1945. The Janice Prodescu case had been reviewed time and again by countless people, but all had failed to make much progress on the murder. Even Dag had read it several times and not spotted anything worthy of pursuing—until now.

Jack Davis' notes:

> *"I spoke with Mrs. Turner on September 5 about the homicide. She claimed that she had a meeting with the victim the previous day, but it was solely about some service work she was doing. Given the situation, no further investigation of Mrs. Turner was deemed necessary."*
>
> *Officer: Jack T. Davis*

Really? thought Dag. *He took her at her word without any follow-up? What was the "situation" that required no further investigation?*

Dag knew the officer who later became a detective. His family had been friends of the Gallaghers for years. Their families had once been very close, in fact, but had drifted apart. He remembered someone on the force saying that Jack was still alive, living at a seniors' home just outside the city. *He had to be in his nineties*, Dag thought, *so it was hard to know if he would still be able to recall details of the case.* Even if he could answer, Dag wasn't sure how reliable his answers would be.

Detective Davis had been married to a woman named Ivona; however, he had split with his wife after many years together. His time on the force had taken its toll on the marriage. Jack was later diagnosed with Alzheimer's, or at the very least, severe dementia. They had five children together, all of whom were grown with children and even grandchildren of their own.

Dag got on his computer and looked up the address of the seniors' home, finding it was located not far from his house, near Dedham, Mass. He decided to swing by on his way home. *It's worth a shot, he thought. At the very least, I'll be able to see him and, maybe, cheer him up a little.*

Dag got to the seniors' home just before it was time for the first dinner seating. He approached the front desk and showed the young lady his badge, hoping to talk to Jack before he left his room for supper.

"Hello, I'm Detective Gallagher. I'd like to speak to Jack Davis, if I may."

The young woman looked at Dag curiously. "Jack Davis? Do you know Mr. Davis?"

"Not directly. I just had some questions to ask him about a case I'm working on. It's an old case, but I thought he might recall some things."

The woman shook her head. "I'm not sure about that, but you're welcome to try. He's in Memory Care. I'll need to have someone escort you back there."

"Oh, I see," said Dag, realizing the dementia must have progressed during the intervening years. "Well, I'll see if anything sparks a memory, I guess."

A young woman came to the front and motioned for Dag to follow her. They arrived at the door of the Memory Unit, and she punched in a code to open the door. Inside, Dag saw a long table with several residents all pushed up to it, putting together puzzles or sadly staring across the room.

"The detective is here to see Jack Davis," the young woman said to a middle-aged woman in charge.

"Mr. Davis? Well, all right."

She got up and went to one of the older men at the table. His hands were trembling uncontrollably as he tried to fit a puzzle piece into position. His frail body was slumped over in the wheelchair, and his eyelids drooped, barely able to stay awake.

"Mr. Davis, there is someone here to see you," said the woman, gently getting his attention.

Dag took a look at the gentleman and smiled. He had enjoyed a long life, and now was not the time to disrupt it. There would be nothing to gain from asking him questions. Any answers had long escaped him, evaporating into the aether all around.

"Mr. Davis, I'm Detective Gallagher. Our families knew each other once. It is so good to meet you. I've heard a lot of good things about you on the force."

The old man raised his head and smiled. He didn't understand what was being said, but he realized someone was there talking to him.

The woman glanced up at Dag, but she didn't have to say anything. Dag nodded and put his hand on the man's shoulder. "It was good to meet you, sir. You served your city and your community well."

Dag left the unit and walked back down the hallway. But it was there that he spotted a nameplate on a resident's door that he recognized: Beatrice Belzikov.

"Excuse me," said Dag talking to his young escort, "but would it be alright if I visited with Beatrice Belzikov for a moment?"

"Let me see if she's available," said the woman.

She knocked on the door and pushed it open after hearing someone say, "Come in." Dag could hear murmuring inside before the young woman returned, this time holding the door open.

"She's asking if she's in trouble," said the woman laughing.

"No. Tell her it's nothing like that. I just have some questions for her. That's all."

The woman conveyed the message and waved him inside.

"Ms. Turner?" Dag asked, greeting the elderly woman in her room.

She was in the assisted living facility rather than the nursing home portion of the complex. She had her own apartment and could fix her own meals when she wanted, or she could go down to the dining room and join the other residents for supper.

"I go by my maiden name now. It's Belzikov."

"Oh, yes. I'm sorry. I knew that. Ms. Belzikov," Dag said, correcting himself. "I'm Detective Gallagher from the ..."

"... from the Boston PD," she said with a broad smile. "It's good to meet you. Please come in and have a seat. Is there anything I can get you to drink? They have an excellent tomato juice here."

Dag could tell she was still sharp as a tack, articulating things as she probably had twenty or thirty years earlier.

"No, no thanks. I won't be too long. I just wanted to ask you a few questions about a case I've been working on. Do you mind?"

"As long as you don't arrest me and put me in jail for the rest of my life," she said without laughing. "Of course, that might not be that long anyway, so I'm not sure you'd get your money's worth."

"No, I'm not here to arrest you, Ms. Belzikov."

"Call me Bessie," she said, sitting up straighter.

Bessie was all of five foot two and wafer-thin. She was spry and energetic for her age. Dag thought she didn't look much over seventy but knew she was a centenarian. Her gray hair was still thick and bushy and looked like she'd just had it quaffed earlier in the day.

"Okay, Bessie," said Dag. Then he stopped and added, "May I ask you why you are living in an assisted living facility? You seem so independent and energetic—so young for your ..."

"... for my age? Yes, I know. I'm told that a lot. But I think there's a law or something about reaching the age of one hundred. That's when they have to lock you up to protect you from yourself." She laughed.

"You're over a hundred?" Dag asked, kindly.

"I'll be a hundred and one in three months. Sharp as the day I turned eighty."

"You've got good family genes," said Dag.

"Well, it's not from my clean livin'," she said. "What can I help you with detective?"

"I'm looking into some cold case files, ma'am. There was a homicide in Roxbury in 1945. The victim's name was ..."

"... Janice ... Janice Prodescu," Bessie answered without prompting. She sighed. "That was one of the worst times in my life. We were friends, you know."

"Yes. I did."

"Yes, we were good friends. I still struggle with how we grew apart so quickly."

"The files said that you met with her the night before she died. Can you tell me about that? Do you remember?" Dag asked.

"You see, I knew your great grandfather, Tag Gallagher," she said, not reacting to his question. "He was a great man—honest and meticulous. He was a good cop. And as I recall, he was young and handsome too." Her voice trailed off in thought.

"I'm sure he would have appreciated having someone remember him like that," said Dag, grateful for the words. "Now, what do you remember about the case?"

"It's been a long time—almost seventy-five years. Jack was on the squad then too, but it was Chief Gallagher who spearheaded the case."

"Jack Davis and my grandfather, Tag?" said Dag, clarifying.

"Yes, of course, Jack Davis. He married my sister, Ivona. I'm sure you knew that. And I knew Tag too, but I'm talking about Michael Gallagher, Mag. He was your … let's see … your great, great grandfather, I think. He was the police chief at the time. He and your great grandfather, Tag, were on the force together until Michael retired—I think around 1948 or 1949. Then, Tag went on to become chief after that."

"So, you were questioned about the Prodescu case by my great, *great* grandfather, Michael?"

"Yes, and some from Tag too. I remember that I was very upset over the chief's questions. He just kept going on and on. Relentless, he was."

"Had you known the victim long?" Dag asked.

"No. Dumitra wasn't a friend. Dumitra was a client. That's all. I had known her only a short time before she was found."

"No, not Dumitra," said Dag. "I meant Janice. You said you were friends."

"Oh, Janice. Yes, yes. We went to high school together. Did I say that I saw her just before she died?"

"Yes," said Dag, trying to keep the conversation straight. "But you say you knew Dumitra *too*?

Dag's mind was beginning to spin with all the new information.

"Dumitra, why yes. She was a client. I had a session with her."

"A session?" asked Dag.

"Yes. I was a medium back in those days. I don't do sessions anymore, of course, but it runs in the family. My daughter is a psychic, and so is my granddaughter. Mitzie, my great granddaughter, tells me that she is one as well, but I've never had a session with her. I believe her, though. Don't get me wrong."

"Mitzie? Mitzie Wilkins?"

"Yes, she's my great granddaughter," answered Bessie.

"I think I understand. So, you had a session with Dumitra. Who was she trying to contact?"

"If I recall, she was trying to reach her daughter who had died suddenly. She was really overwhelmed by grief and hadn't been able to move on. That's what I do ... well ... that's what I used to do, anyway. So, I met with her."

"Did you reach her ... the daughter, that is?" asked Dag.

"No, I don't think we did. I'm not sure why, but no."

"Did you know that Janice was her daughter?"

"I always liked Janice. Well, that is, until after we graduated from high school."

"Oh?"

"Yes, she made me unhappy then. It was hard for me to get over, really."

"What was that?" asked Dag.

"You're a skeptic," Bessie said, again changing the subject. "I can tell. You don't believe anyone has the ability to contact the dead, do you?"

Dag hesitated, suddenly realizing how sharp and perceptive this centenarian still was. "Not really. I don't. I'm sorry."

"So, you think we're quacks, I suppose. Don't you?"

Dag had been taught growing up never to disrespect his elders, and he found himself fumbling for the right words. But, before he could find them, she answered for him.

"I thought so. It doesn't matter. I've met many people like you during my lifetime. I've learned to accept it. There are those who believe in such mysterious things and those who don't—and can't. What I've never understood is how some of those skeptics can be so religious and believe in their mysticism and not in what we do."

Getting back to the point, Dag asked, "Do you remember what happened *after* the session with Dumitra?"

"What happened was what usually happens. I remember that Dumitra thanked me for connecting the two of them and asked when I could come back. I probably told her it would be a few months, at least, as I usually had other appointments. You see, you don't want your client to book regular sessions with you. It's not good for them. They become obsessed with it, and if they are to move on in their lives, they need to do that ... not rely on the next session with me."

Dag was surprised. He'd expected that most mediums milked their accounts, generating as many bogus sessions as their clients could afford.

"So, you went home? What did you do then?"

"I don't remember now. I know that I was married and had a daughter. I probably went home to them. I didn't think anything more about it until I read it in the papers a few days later."

"You weren't anywhere near Janice's or Dumitra's homes the nights of their murders, were you?" Dag asked, point blank.

"No!" she said forcefully. "I thought you weren't here to arrest me?"

Dag laughed. He realized he was pushing as he did with current cases and current suspects. This case was decades old.

"Sorry, you're right," he answered. "I'm just trying to find out what happened those nights; that's all. But I do have a couple more questions. Do you mind?"

"I don't think I have much of a choice," she replied, a bit more sharply.

"Ms. Belzikov, you don't need to worry. I'm sure everything is fine. But you mentioned the name Jack as your brother-in-law. We're talking about Jack Davis?"

"Yes, of course, Jack Davis. He's in the other wing here at the center. He married my kid sister and they had five brats. Oh, I'm sorry, didn't mean to say that—I meant, children." She rolled her eyes.

"Were you close to Jack then?"

"Not close, but we knew him well, sure. I'm surprised you didn't know him better. It sounds like you didn't."

"No, but I'm sure my father and grandfather did," said Dag.

"Well, you should. He was a half-brother of Rosco's. Didn't you know that?"

Dag's head was spinning.

"Wait a minute. You mean to say that your husband, Rosco Turner, had a half-brother—Jack?"

"I thought everyone knew that," said Bessie, blinking as if dazed through her thick, wire glasses.

"Your first husband, Rosco, was apparently murdered too. That also happened in 1945—the same year of Janice's and Dumitra's murders."

"Like I said, it was the worst year of my life," said Bessie.

"In the statement you gave to my great grandfather, Tag, you said that you met Janice that night to talk about "service work." What was the service work? Was it something more than just talking about psychic stuff?"

Bessie was quiet.

"Ms. Belzikov, are you all right?"

Finally, she looked back at him. "So that's why you're here—to arrest me for lying seventy-five years ago."

Dag was startled.

"You got me, detective. I lied about that. I only channeled for her. I told the detective about those 'other services' because ... well ... because psychics—especially back then—were considered quacks. I thought that if I had told him I'd had a séance with Janice that day he would have thrown me in prison."

"I understand," said Dag.

"But, as for that night ..."

241

"Yes?"

"... I had a five-year-old daughter at home and a husband." She started to tremble. "But my husband wasn't home that night."

"Where was he, then?"

"He was with yet another woman. He was cheating on me. It was something I never forgave him for."

Bessie started crying. It was all coming back to her, as fresh and painful as it had those many years ago.

"I believe you," said Dag.

He could feel that she was telling him the truth. And after so many years, there would be no way he would bring a centenarian to trial based on what she did or did not tell police back then. She was not admitting to killing Janice, Dumitra or anyone else. She was merely cleansing her conscience.

Dag jotted some notes on his pad. He knew his questions had taken a lot out of Bessie, and he didn't want to press things any further.

"Thank you, Bessie. Thanks for meeting with me. If I have any more questions, is it okay if I call you again?"

"Sure," she said, dabbing her eyes with a tissue. Then, she added, "As long as you don't come back to arrest me."

Dag laughed. "I don't think that will be necessary."

*****

CH 11 – Slow Progress

2020

Dag went to the basement and rang the little bell. "Ritter? Are you in today?"

Ritter came out from the back holding the last quarter of a baloney sandwich he was still working on. He swallowed, wiped his mouth and said, "Hey Dag. What's happenin'?"

"Ritter, here's approval from the chief for me to look at the evidence they have on my dad's murder. I need to see what they've come up with so far."

Ritter looked at the slip and then at Dag. "Are you sure you want to do this? There are pictures in there that ... well ... I wouldn't want to see if it was my dad."

"No, I don't ... but I do. Ya' know? I want to find out who killed him. Chief thinks I may be able to help in some way."

Ritter shook his head and went back to get the file. He returned with an armful and pushed the sign-out computer tablet across the shelf. Dag scribbled his initials and took the file.

"You can't say I didn't warn you, Dag," said Ritter.

"You can't tell anyone I was here getting these either, Ritter. Chief's orders."

Dag took the files upstairs with him and closed the door. He opened the first and began sifting through the pictures and reports. Ritter had been right. It was really too much for him to bear, so he put away the pictures and focused on the notes.

> ... the chief was bludgeoned with a crowbar-like tool ...
> ... autopsy revealed two deep gashes in the back of the skull ...
> ... attack was so vicious it appears to be emotionally driven ...
> ... head nearly separated from rest of body ...
> ... service weapon not drawn ...
> ... angle of attack so high, it's difficult to see how anyone under eight feet tall could have done it ...

What? thought Dag. He re-read the last point. *No one under eight feet? How could that be possible?*

Dag continued looking. There was a reference made to a video. The notes said there were two cameras in the alleyway and that each had taken footage during the night of the murder. Dag looked inside the container for them, but they weren't there. All he found were a few extraneous things: a couple business cards, a pen, and a red cigarette lighter. The rest of his personal stuff had been returned after being examined by the lab and dismissed as not evidentiary.

But what's he doing with a lighter? thought Dag. *He didn't smoke, or at least not that I knew.*

Dag rang the lead detective on the case. It was Kyle Petry, someone he had known for years and someone for whom he had a lot of respect. Under normal circumstances, he would have obeyed the chief's admonition about contacting someone on the team directly. However, in this case, he understood Petry was a good cop. He would toe the line as he needed to and wouldn't say anything.

"Kyle, this is Dag. How are you doin'?"

"Good Dag. Haven't heard from you in a while. How are things?"

"Fine, Kyle. Listen, Chief asked that I look at a couple files on my dad's murder. I know it's not protocol, but apparently they're getting a little heat to get things resolved. You know how it is."

There was no sound on the other end.

"Kyle? Are you still there?"

"Yeah, I'm here, Dag. I'm sorry you're in the middle of all this. Chief's right in a way, but we're doing everything we can to figure it out. It's not been easy. You know those kinds of cases."

"Yeah, I sure do. Listen, Kyle, I saw a note in the file that suggested the killer had to be over eight feet tall to strike my dad the way he did. Is that true? Is that the belief of the team right now?"

"Dag, you know there are plenty of people who speculate in their notes just to get some fresh thinking into the case. I don't remember who suggested that, but no, it's not a favored opinion."

"Why would they say something like that then?"

"The coroner said the blow from the crowbar or whatever hit him was at such a sharp angle that it had to be someone very tall or standing on something."

"Were they on stilts or hanging out a window?"

"No, we thought about that too, but the body was so ripped apart it would have been nearly impossible to do on stilts or from a window."

"Unless there was an accomplice."

"Of course. That's always a possibility."

"Any sign there was more than one attacker?" asked Dag.

"No. Not that we found."

"And one other thing," said Dag. "The file refers to two videos taken by cameras in the alley. They weren't in the tub with the other evidence."

"Yeah, I have those," said Kyle, knowing he shouldn't have taken them without checking them out. "I guess it's good that they weren't in there for you to see anyway. They were pretty shocking, Dag. Not something you should see—your dad and all."

"What did they show?"

"There were two cameras, but the angles were bad. All you can see is a single shadow at a distance. You can't make out faces or anything—all pretty blurry."

"You said a shadow—as in one? Only my dad's?"

"That's what's so baffling, Dag. Yeah! We only see *one* shadow which is Zag's. We don't see *any* other person or shadow in the pictures."

"But I thought you said there may have been two attackers. Shouldn't there have been *three* shadows?"

"Yeah, but no. There is only *one* shadow in the alley. *One*, Dag."

"Well, I know you're doing everything you can, Kyle. I'm sorry to bother you with this, but like I said ..."

"... yeah, I know—the chief," Kyle answered.

"Yeah. Talk to you later."

Dag got off the phone, but he didn't feel any better. Were there two attackers or none? Were the attackers high-up or at some other angle that couldn't be seen from the alley cameras? He now had many more questions and was beginning to understand why the team had run up against a brick wall. It was a wall without bricks.

*****

CH 45 - Diary Entries

2020

It had been over a week, and Sara finally decided she should go over her great grandmother's diary again. She started to open it but felt her stomach get queasy, and she closed it. Taking a breath, she put it aside for later and sorted through some of the other old notebooks she had brought down with her from the attic. Musty and yellowed, many were notes from classes Janice had taken in high school. However, there was one that caught her eye—one with an apple-red cover marked simply "Notes."

Quickly she flipped through the pages. It was similar to her daily journal, but it had other odds and ends, such as recipes, phone numbers, meeting dates, and other things. But it was on page eleven that she found an odd entry which read:

RA—EX2-2987

Following that entry was the note:

Forbidden Love
From the Apple Orchard

Forbidden Love? Sara thought. *Back in 1943? That was almost unheard of—at least it was never talked about. Perhaps that was her great grandfather.*

Sara knew that her great grandmother, Janice, had not been married when she had her daughter, Cora Rae. It had been scandalous that Janice had gotten pregnant out of wedlock—instead, trying to raise her daughter on her own. However, with her tragic death, the family had wanted to send Cora Rae off to an orphanage. That never happened. Instead, Dumitra's sister, Ivanna, had insisted on taking the child and raising it in her already-full family with six other children. It had been a miracle the day of Janice's murder. Only by chance had Janice taken little Cora Rae to her aunt's to spend the night. There, she had remained.

But who is this RA? Sara wondered. *And the EX2-2987—what was that? Was it a license plate? A telephone number?* More ominously was the reference to apples and an orchard. *How could that be?* she thought.

Sara continued flipping pages in the book, hoping to find other information about the mystery man, but nothing stood out. The strange EX2-2987 did not reappear, and there were no obvious connections or references to it made on later pages.

Another entry talked about the time when Janice received a jewelry box from Bessie Belzikov. That entry read:

> *"My best friend in the whole, wide world gave me a beautiful jewelry box for my birthday today. It's so beautiful, that I'm sure I will keep it for the rest of my life. I'll give it to my daughter, and she will give it to hers. It will be one of those treasured family heirlooms, I hope—something we can pass from generation to generation."*

Sara knew exactly the box to which she was referring. She had discovered it the last time she'd been in the attic and brought it down with her. She had found a place for it on her dresser in her bedroom.

Sara glanced across the room to look at the box. She felt like the piece was talking to her, but it was as if they were both underwater. She heard the sounds but couldn't understand what it was saying. After what had happened with the box upstairs, she was afraid to open the lid. Yet, her nose began picking up a familiar smell wafting over from it—the scent of apples.

*****

CH 46 - Another Disappears

1995

Jessie Davis had been at the police precinct about as long as Zag had—perhaps even longer. He was a few years older but had gotten his detective's badge at the same time as Zag. As younger detectives in the late 1980s, they had been assigned to older, more seasoned men on the force who could show them the ropes of investigation. However, now that they were older and more seasoned, they were being asked to offer advice to the youngsters coming up through the ranks.

Like Zag, Jessie came from a blue-blood cop family. It ran in his family just like it did the Gallaghers. Jessie's father, Jack, had been involved in several murder investigations during his long career with the department. On several, he had teamed up with another Gallagher to look into the deaths: Zag's father, Jag. These were the bizarre killings during 1970—ones that greatly affected, and disturbed, both men.

But in 1994, Jessie and Zag were assigned to help a task group investigate strange sites being uncovered in Purgatory Chasm State Park—just outside of Boston. Near the rock formations known as The Coffin and Lovers' Leap, police found the burned carcasses of dead animals which appeared to have been offered in sacrificial rituals. Circles of stones and rings of salt were found as well as the obligatory pentagons and drawings of goat heads.

Fearing the use of the park as a late-night rendezvous spot for black magic or satanic worship, the state police asked for help in investigating the incidents. Jessie and Zag were both chosen based on their years of experience. However, when the other cases came up in Boston that required Zag's attention, he had been taken off the task force well before it had even started. Jessie had remained and become the head of the group. He had previous exposure to ritualistic murders earlier in his career. That assignment involved a serial killer. He had been on loan staff from the Boston PD to the one in Hartford, Connecticut.

Five women had been killed during a two-year period—all with the same MO: strangulation and death by a razor-sharp piano wire. Eventually, he tracked the killer down—living in a small house just outside of Hartford in the town of Rocky Hill. There, Jessie had linked the killings to a maladjusted plumber who worked for a company in town. The young man used his access to homes in Hartford to commit the terrible crimes. As a youth, the man had tormented and killed his neighbors' pets during his high school years. He was also involved with a local satanic cult. Without friends or any living family, he was left to fend for himself and kill "whenever the voices in his head told him to."

"How are the witches and warlocks?" Zag asked, smiling as he saw Jessie on his way into the precinct.

"Very funny, Zag," said Jessie. "We haven't found any cauldrons lately, if that's what you're wondering."

"No broomsticks either, I take it."

Jessie smirked. "It's a bit creepy though, especially when you go on a stakeout at the park at night. You get there after dark and wait for someone to show up, but we have yet to catch them in the act."

"So, what's creepy about it?"

"I don't know, exactly," said Jessie. "You just get this feeling that you're being watched. The other night we were sitting in the unmarked and we heard branches breaking all around us. We turned on our spotlight and shined it into the woods, but there was nothing there. So, we went back to our lookout, thinking it was a bear or deer or something. An hour later, something rammed against the side of our car."

"What was it?"

"Yeah, we jumped out and shined our lights all around, but again we didn't see anything. *Nothing.* My partner got out and took his flashlight into the woods, but he didn't find anything there either. When he got back to the car, he told me to get out and take a look at something. He pointed his light at the side of the car. You won't believe what we saw."

"What?" asked Zag.

"There was a long crease in the side of the car—from the rear fender to the driver's door. The paint was scratched too, like from a nail or from a claw or something."

"That's strange."

"It scared the crap out us!" said Jessie. "We looked at each other and got the hell out of there."

"Have you been back?"

"No, not yet. I don't want to go back without reinforcements, but I'm told we have to go back out tomorrow night. I'm not looking forward to it."

"Well, I'd be happy to go for you, but I have a date to wash out the gutters on my house," said Zag, smiling.

"Very funny," said Jessie. "If you change your mind, let me know."

***

Jessie continued on the case for several more months, and by 1995, he was following up on a group that was known for satanic worship and holding rituals. Surprisingly, they weren't younger youths but rather middle-aged adults who were involved in an established and known cult with a long history.

By 1995, Zag was up to his eyeballs with the strange murders going on in the Boston area. He was busy with his cases, and Jessie was buried with his. They hadn't talked for a number of months before some troubling news reached Zag's desk. It was John Bricker, another detective at the precinct, who stopped by to tell Zag.

"Yeah, did you hear that Jessie's gone missing?"

Zag looked up from his desk and put down his pen. "What? Jessie's missing?"

"Yeah. They don't know what happened to him. He went out to Purgatory by himself to stakeout the ritual spot. They found his car, but no traces of him. He just vanished."

"No. There must be an explanation," said Zag. "He didn't just disappear."

"Almost the entire force is out there now looking for him, but Ted told me that they're baffled. There aren't any footprints, any pieces of clothing, any communication from him last night—nothin'."

"My god," said Zag. "I'll ask and see if I can help."

Zag put aside his work and helped with the investigation to find Jessie. But after months, nothing was found. In fact, nothing was ever found. *****

CH 49 - The DA Gets Tough

2020

The DA called and left an urgent message for Dag. Normally, important messages like that would have been forwarded to him on his cell phone. But the young officer at the front desk had forgotten, and the note lay unaddressed in the answering machine queue. Later that morning, the officer realized her mistake and routed the message, making sure it got to him.

Dag picked it up, noting it had been left nearly three hours earlier. He was angry, but he figured it wouldn't do any good to yell at the young woman officer. He just told her never to let it happen again. Then, immediately, Dag picked up the phone and dialed the DA's number.

"Yes, Dick. Sorry. I just got your message. What can I do for you?"

"Dag, I spoke with Chief Malloy last week, and I made it clear that I wanted the cases in Dorchester and Brookline solved by the end of the month. I *assumed* he told you that." There was disgust in his voice.

"Yes sir, he did."

"Where are you on the cases? I *assume* you're about ready to make an arrest?" The condescension was almost more than Dag could take.

"Uh, well, sir, we are still working on that. I think we're a lot closer than we were last week."

"That's not telling me a *damn* thing!" shouted the DA. "I told the chief that if you weren't making real progress by this week, I'd have to take action on my own."

"But we're making progress, sir. We ..."

"It doesn't sound like it, Dag," said the DA, cutting him off. "I'm going to have to remove you from the cases if you can't figure things out. This is too important to the mayor, and therefore to me. We can't let it go on any longer. We need cops who *solve* crimes—not twiddle their thumbs at their desks. The mayor needs a stellar record of crime fighting going into this next election. You're a cop. It's your job to find and arrest criminals, is it not?"

"Yes, sir."

"It's your job! That's what you're supposed to do. That's what we pay you to do—find criminals!"

Dag wanted to tell the DA to save the political speech for another time, but he didn't.

"I understand, sir."

"I don't think you do. Things have gotten worse, not better. In recent months, homicides are up, robberies are up, other violent crimes are up. This isn't good. It's not good for the chief, the mayor, or me. And Dag, it's not good for you or your career either! Am I clear!"

"So, what do you want me to do, sir?"

"I have information that you've been questioning a Sara McLaughlin about several of these cases. Is that correct?"

"Yes sir."

"She's a suspect, I *assume*. She's been involved in some way with each of the murders?"

"We don't know that for sure, sir, but we think there may be a connection there."

"Then *arrest* her!" the DA said bluntly.

"What?" asked Dag, incredulously. "I thought you said to arrest her, sir?"

"I did. We need an arrest, and she's the most likely candidate at the moment. We can find the evidence we need later to bring her to trial."

"Find the evidence? I'm not sure ..."

"You know perfectly well what I'm saying. Don't play dumb. Now make that arrest, or you'll be removed from the case and ... and possibly every case going forward! You'll never see a retirement check either. In fact, if you don't arrest her this afternoon, I'll bust you back down to beat cop."

"Yes, sir. I understand."

Click.

The line went dead. Dag couldn't believe what he'd just heard. He knew detectives got pressure from time to time, especially on high-profile cases, but never to this extent. A few years earlier, he'd gotten an important case and taken heat on it too. It was not nearly as high-profile as the current cases, and it took several months before Dag had fingered the culprit. He'd broken the case open when he discovered the prime suspect had replaced the tires on his car only days after the murder. The treads on the old tires matched those at the crime scene. However, he never imagined that a DA would go so far as to push for an arrest without *any* evidence.

"Hey, boss," said Tommy coming into Dag's office. "I have more info on those cases we're looking at."

"Save it," said Dag, coldly. "We've been told to arrest Sara McLaughlin."

"Good."

"Good? What evidence do you have that you're not telling me about?"

"She's guilty, Dag. You and I both know it."

"We don't have any evidence, and you want to arrest her too? The DA just called. The mayor and DA want—no, *demand*—an arrest. He didn't say it directly, but everyone knows the mayor is going to announce he's running for governor, and he doesn't want these cases hanging over his head during the campaign. He just wants them wrapped-up—out of the way."

"All right, then, so I'll go arrest her," said Tommy, without flinching.

"You don't seem bothered by this," said Dag. "You realize we have *no* evidence. We can't just go and arrest someone when we have no evidence."

"No, it doesn't bother me. It's what we have to do."

"For our careers, you mean."

"Yeah, of course. I'm not sacrificing my career over something like this. No way," Tommy exclaimed.

"I don't know how you can be so cavalier about it. We're talking about destroying someone's life!"

Tommy shrugged. "I met with the chief yesterday and told him all about it. He called the DA and gave him the same message. He told me right there and then that he wanted her arrested."

"Chief Malloy? You met with him?"

"Yeah. And I told him where we were on the cases. When he pushed me on solving the case, I gave up the name of Sara. I know she's guilty. It wasn't hard for me to give her up. When it comes to me or her ..."

Dag had known the chief a long time, and he couldn't imagine his boss agreeing to something like that. But for Dag, everything seemed to be upside down. The old chief had been more principled. He would have resigned as chief rather than compromise his beliefs in the judicial process. At least that was the old chief he had known and respected—his dad. *Maybe Malloy wasn't the same? Maybe Malloy was as weak as some had said. Maybe his dad and he weren't cut from the same cloth as he had always thought?*

"Why would you go behind my back like that?" Dag asked, furious at what his partner had done.

"Listen, Dag," Tommy answered, now dropping all pretenses, "this is *my* chance to shine in this department. If you're not going to push on this case, then I will. The DA and mayor want an arrest in these cases, and by God, *I'm* going to give it to them. I want to make something of my life. I want to be *that* detective everyone talks about. If you want to just sit back and float through life, then fine. I don't want to end up in a dead-end job like you. Someday, if I play my cards right, I'll be the police chief, then the mayor and then the governor. Who knows, maybe even go to Washington. That's what I'm shootin' for."

Dag listened. There was a lot he wanted to say—a lot he wanted to teach this young kid who thought he already knew everything—but he didn't. He held his tongue.

"Dag, you've got a lot of baggage in your family. Your father was killed mysteriously this year. Wasn't he supposed to retire this year too? That's what I heard. He's had a bunch of strange cases like the ones we have now—ones he never solved either. Your grandfather had some cases like this too, didn't he? Seems like both of 'em covered up some of those for some strange reason. Those cases are the ones still in the cold case files, aren't they?

"They failed, Dag," continued Tommy, on a roll. "Your family failed. I'm *not* going to fail. I'm not going to let this opportunity pass me by like you're doing, and for what? Out of duty? Morals? Scruples? I'm seizing the moment—you know, carpet deem, or whatever that saying is," said Tommy.

"It's *carpe diem*, and it means 'seize the day,'" corrected Dag.

"Whatever," said Tommy.

"I get it, Tommy," said Dag. He put his hands behind his head and stared coldly at his young partner. "Maybe you're right. I mean, how stupid can I be! I always thought that being a police officer meant, what, upholding the laws of the city, county, state and country. Boy, was I wrong. It's about .... me, I guess."

"Me?"

"Yeah. It should all be about *me!*" said Dag, pounding his finger against his chest. "I shouldn't really give a *damn* about the people I'm supposed to be serving in this town. Why should I give two shits about them anyway? As long as I take care of myself, that's really all that matters. What's the harm in that? If I'm taken care of, then all's good, right?"

"Hey, if I don't take care of *me*, nobody else will," Tommy said crossing his arms defensively.

"Again, you're right. Of course! What was I thinkin'? I need to live by the Golden Rule—*fuck* over others before they *fuck* you!"

"Sometimes you do, Dag."

"So, I guess I had you pegged wrong, Tommy. I thought you were better than that. I realize that others sometimes get ahead by shafting the other guy, but I didn't think you were one of them. The question I have for you is whether you can live with yourself when you make those kinds of decisions? When you're a hundred and on your deathbed, will you look back and smile, counting all the people you fucked over to get what you wanted in life? Will you smile knowing you screwed ole' Dag all those years ago? I suppose I won't be around to see that day anyway," said Dag, getting up and starting to walk out of his office. But before he got to the hallway, he added, "Is it worth selling your soul to the Devil? Will that bring you lasting happiness? Will a big promotion and a lot of money make your life worthwhile--meaningful? Maybe for you it will, Tommy, but not for me. It's not the way I want to live my life. But hey, it's your life, not mine. Best of luck with that."

"You're a naïve old man," Tommy shouted back, defiantly. "Dag, you have to understand how the game is played in the real world—in the big leagues. That's why you're still a lowly lieutenant. At the end of the day, you're only one thing, Dag ..." Dag stopped in the corridor while Tommy finished his thought. "... you're a loser. You and the rest of your miserable family have been losers for a long time—from your great grandfather to your father to you. I'm going to be police chief one day. Then the mayor and then the governor and then, who knows. I'm going to get their 'cause I know what it takes. I know you have to sacrifice things and sometimes people who get in your way.

"Will I look back and regret it later in my life? I don't think so. When I'm sitting in my big house with my fancy car and servants, I'll be thinking about you, Dag—you and your miserable retirement in a trailer park somewhere."

Dag's fist was clenched by his side, but he counted slowly to ten and relaxed his hand. He continued walking away and didn't look back. At that point, Tommy was talking to himself. It was as if he were trying to convince himself—argue with himself—that what he was doing was right. It was an argument even he realized that he was losing.

Tommy shook his head and left the office. He walked down the hall to the precinct cafeteria and got himself a small, brown paper cup full of Joe. It was cold and tasteless, like just about everything else he'd touched that day.

*****

CH 48 - Mitzie's Warning

2020

Mitzie had been surprised at her lunch meeting with Sara when her guest had gotten up abruptly and left the restaurant. Mitzie knew she was pushing but didn't think she had pushed that hard. She called Sara a few days later, hoping to keep the channel open.

"Sara? This is Mitzie. I couldn't help but think that you were upset about something when you walked out of the restaurant. Is everything okay? Call me."

However, Sara didn't return the calls.

Finally, Mitzie called her just as she was leaving the house. Sara had been in a hurry and hadn't looked at the number before answering it.

"Hello?" she answered.

"Sara, it's Mitzie. I've been trying to reach you. Is everything alright?"

"Sure, fine," Sara said bluntly.

"Well, I was just calling to be sure you are alright. I didn't mean to upset you the other day at lunch."

"No, really. I'm fine," said Sara, hoping to get Mitzie off the line.

"All right, but there was one more thing I needed to tell you. This is pretty urgent, that's why I thought I should get in touch with you again."

Sara took a breath. "Yes?"

"It's not something I can share with you over the phone. But it is something that has to do with the welfare of your family, I'm afraid."

"Welfare of my family?" Sara's voice became strained and squeaky.

"Yes. It is of some importance, I should think. Can I stop over now?"

"*Now?*"

"Sara, it's *important!* I've had visions lately, and I think they're warnings—warnings I'm supposed to tell you about before it's too late."

"What kind of warnings?" Sara asked dubiously.

"It's not something I can share over the phone. Sara, just let me stop by."

Sara thought for a moment and decided there was no way out of this. If it were a ruse, she'd find out soon enough. If it weren't, then she would hate herself if anything *did* happen to someone in her family and she hadn't gone through with the meeting.

"Fine, but I have someplace else to be soon. I have to leave here within the hour."

"It won't take long. I assure you," said Mitzie.

It took Mitzie nearly the entire hour to get there, but when she finally arrived, she parked her new, bright-red Porsche in the driveway directly behind Sara's car, making it impossible for her to leave.

"Such a quaint place. Very charming," commented Mitzie, half-heartedly, as she came in the front door.

At the same time, Vince strolled in, crossing from the family room into the kitchen to get a beverage from the refrigerator.

"And this must be your husband," Mitzie said with a twinkle in her eye.

She extended her hand. Vince saw they had a guest and came over to take her hand. He smiled, not knowing who she was or why she was there. Mitzie took his hand and gave it a sensual squeeze before letting go. Sara didn't notice, but Vince did. He drew back slightly but tried not to be too conspicuous about it.

"I don't believe we've met," Vince said, being polite.

"I'm Mitzie Wilkins. I'm a friend of your wife's."

"Yes, well, Mitzie just came over to drop off something. She won't be long," said Sara, trying not to get her husband interested or involved in the meeting.

"No, I don't want to stay too long," Mitzie answered. "I just appreciate your seeing me on such short notice—especially due to the seriousness of what I have to discuss with you."

"Seriousness?" asked Vince, now drawn in. "Is there something serious that I need to know about?"

Sara sighed.

"Your wife didn't tell you?" exclaimed Mitzie. "Well, I'm a psychic, like Sara here. We have a lot in common. Do you mind if we go into your family room here and chat?"

Worried about what Mitzie might say, Sara started the conversation right away after they got settled.

"Vince, Mitzie told me that she's had visions lately. They involve us—our family. I thought it was important that she come over and talk to me—us—about it." Then, turning to her guest, Sara asked, "So, what did you see in your vision that was so important you needed to talk to us about it?"

The jovial expression on Mitzie's face softened quickly. "They haven't been the same twice," she began. "The first one I had was about a month ago. I saw my Great grandmother Bessie and your great grandmother sitting in a room with several other girls." Mitzie turned now as an aside to address Vince. "As Sara knows, our great grandmothers were friends back then. Anyway, they were joking and giggling in what looked like a party to me. Then, a black shadow came through the doorway. It just floated through the closed door like a spirit. Then, it sped up and rushed over to your great grandmother, grabbing her by the throat and raising her body toward the ceiling, stretching her neck until it almost broke. Your Grandma Janice tried to scream but nothing came out."

"My God! How horrible!" Vince said.

Meanwhile, Sara sat quietly, waiting patiently to hear everything before making a judgment.

"Yes, it was!" said Mitzie, nodding. Then she turned back to Sara. "But I had another one just a few days ago. In it, you and your driver were having a session with one of your clients."

"Marvin?" Sara asked, surprised his name was brought up.

"Isn't that your driver's name?"

"Yes, it is."

"Then, it *was* Marvin. He looked to be about five feet two or so, stocky, muscular, with short dark hair and a goatee."

"That's him," said Vince, surprised at the detail and the accuracy of her vision. "So, what happened in *that* vision?"

259

"Sara and Marvin held a session where several very strange things happened. In the one in my vision, you got up and walked out," she said talking directly to Sara.

"I had told you about a few of those lately. I'm sure that's all it was. You just remembered that as part of your dream. That's all."

"Maybe, but Sara, what worries me is what happens after that. In both visions, I hear the breaking of glass inside the client's house or wherever you had your meeting. But this happens *after* you and Marvin leave. It's late at night, and I see someone dressed in dark clothes and a black ski mask going into the place. He's short and stocky and has a tattoo on the back of his right hand."

"Does it have a bunch of triangles kind of nestled together?" asked Vince, pointing to the back of his own hand.

"Yes. But in my visions it's dark, and I can't see anything else except that he's carrying a green, canvas duffle bag. He's going through your client's drawers and closets searching for jewelry and valuables."

"Marvin? No way! He'd never do a thing like that!" exclaimed Sara.

"I don't know honey. He is kind of strange," said Vince.

"Yeah, he's strange, but he would *never* steal from one of my clients. He just wouldn't!"

"Do you notice anything unusual about him when you're doing your sessions?" Mitzie asked.

"No, not really," Sara answered. "He's usually not around that much."

"Not around? What do you mean?" asked Vince.

"I mean, he's usually in the kitchen trying to find a soda in the refrigerator or ..."

"... or casing out the place?" said Vince.

Sara shook her head. "Marvin wouldn't do that."

"The rest of my visions are equally foggy, but there was another one I had a few weeks ago. That's when I decided to call and talk to you at the restaurant. I thought that bringing up our mutual interests— our great grandmothers, for example—would help me get through to you. But you left the restaurant in such a rush, I didn't get a chance. Then, when I had the same vision yesterday, I called again."

"What was that vision?" asked Vince, eagerly.

"That one was really strange. I think it was supposed to be symbolic. It's why I haven't been able to sort through it very easily. In it, I am wandering through an arcade like the ones they used to have at the circus or at a state fair. There are all sorts of side-shows at the place: bearded ladies, three-headed dogs, elephant men—those kinds of things. However, there is one show where a man is outside hawking tickets. It's Marvin. He catches my attention and waves at me to go inside and see his show. He gives me an insincere smile and says, 'You of all people will certainly enjoy my entertainment. It's so much more exciting than anything else here.'

"So, I buy a ticket and go in. Pulling the tent flap open, I find it pitch-black inside. But I walk in anyway and instantly feel a hand grip my arm and push me forward. Then, the bright lights come up, and I realize I am in the middle ring of three setup like stages with bleacher seats all around me. The lights hurt my eyes, and I want to scream. But then, more spotlights come on, shining on each of the stages. In my ring there are three tall stools. Seated on those are three, life-size dolls with faces. They're faces that I recognize."

"What did the faces look like?" Vince asked, now completely drawn into the story.

Mitzie put her hand over her mouth. Then, she said, "Sara, maybe I shouldn't have come. Forgive me."

Mitzie began to get up, but Sara motioned sternly for her to sit down.

"Mitzie, you've come this far; you'd better tell us what you saw," she said Sara, wanting to bring it all to a merciful end.

"One of the dolls had your face, Sara. The other had ... Vince's."

"What about the third face?" Vince asked.

"I haven't met your daughter, but it was that of a young girl."

Sara looked at Vince, but he was still focused on Mitzie and her story.

"So, that was your vision about our family?" asked Sara. "We're just sitting in the middle of a circus tent?"

"It's what I noticed about each of you—each doll—that frightened me. You see, each of the dolls' arms and legs were twisted around their bodies like pretzels. It was like you were all made of silly putty. You all had bizarre smiles on your faces too, like you were enjoying all of it. I screamed, but no one heard me. Then, when I thought it couldn't get worse, the dolls began to move. Their arms and legs continued twisting around their bodies until their heads fell off and rolled across the ground, ending up at my feet. It was horrible."

Sara was in shock. Her mouth gaped open, and she shook her head. "I don't believe in such things," she stuttered. "It was only a dream. That's all."

"I don't know what it means, but I know about the murders the police are working on right now—the ones where the bodies were all twisted and contorted. It was just like what I saw in my dream. I'm sorry, but I did want to warn you. That was all." Mitzie got up and continued to the front door. "Again, I'm sorry I troubled you."

She was out the door, in her car and driving off before Sara could collect her thoughts.

"She's talking about the case that was in the paper lately, right ..." asked Vince, "... the one where they say the bodies were mangled?"

"I think so," Sara answered, still staring blankly across the room.

"Well, then you and LJ need to leave town," said Vince. "You should pack your bags and go—at least for a few days or even weeks. I'll call my mother and tell her you're coming later today."

"I can't Vince. I had to go down to the police station today. I can't leave the area."

"What? You went to the police station? Why? Why didn't you tell me?"

"I didn't want to worry you," she said. "But I guess there isn't much more that could worry you—worry us—now."

"Sara, what's going on?" Vince's voice was loud and angry.

Sara told him about the interrogation at the precinct and the discussion she had with Detective Gallagher. She told him about the session she had with Claire Horwath and what happened to her in the alley.

"The police are trying to tie all this together," said Sara.

"What about the strange murders of LJ's friend at school and his mother?" Vince asked.

"That too. They were grilling me all morning," she said, leaning into his arms and crying. "They were accusing me and Martin of being involved in their murders too, Vince. I don't understand any of this."

"But you haven't done anything, Sara. It's all just a misunderstanding," he said, defending her and trying to make her feel better.

"Mitzie called me several weeks ago," Sara admitted, wiping the tears from her eyes. "At that point, I didn't even know who she was. We met at a restaurant in town, and she talked about our two great grandmothers. I thought it was strange, but I went along with it. Then, I went to the attic to look through some of Grandma Janice's stuff to see if what she was saying was true. Vince, it was. I found a yearbook with their pictures in it and another with a group of girls who apparently were all good friends at the time. Then, there was this journal."

"What kind of journal?" Vince asked.

"A diary—you know, where she wrote down things that happened every day. Vince, it was scary. There were things in there that she never should have written down—things that frightened me. She and some of her girlfriends were into Ouija and black magic, I think. I don't know for sure, but she wrote about some of her seances and other sessions she had in that journal."

Vince put his arms around her as she sobbed. He placed his hand behind her head, kissed it and held her close.

"We'll figure this out, Sara. We will."

"How?"

"I don't know right now, except that you and LJ need to get away from here."

"You have to come with us, Vince. You were in those visions too, you know!"

"Yeah, but I can't lose my job, honey. I don't have much vacation left, so I really can't," he said. "I'll be all right. Don't worry. I'm a big guy. I can take care of myself."

Sara wiped her nose on his shoulder. She didn't want him to lose his job, but she still worried for him. Either way, she knew nothing she said would make a difference. He was stubborn like that.

"If there's something going on with Marvin, you may not be safe anyway," he said. "So, I'll call Mom and tell her you two are coming for a few days ... until this blows over?"

Sara stared at Vince, unsure.

"At least do it for our daughter," Vince added. "She's been through enough lately with what happened at school and all."

Sara nodded. She hurried to the base of the stairs to call out to LJ who was up in her room.

"LJ!" she shouted, "you need to put some things in a suitcase, honey. We're going to your grandma's for a few days."

Sara glanced back at her husband. "Vince, we'll go, but this isn't going to blow over quickly. The police will wonder where I've gone. They'll think I left to escape being arrested for those murders. They'll come looking for me."

"No, they won't. I'll call them and tell them you had to leave and where you'll be in case they want to find you."

"I don't know. You should have been there yesterday when that officer grilled me. He warned me not to go *anywhere*."

"They'll have to understand. Your safety and LJ's are more important."

Again, Sara knew not to argue. There wasn't enough time for that now anyway.

"And what about you?" Sara asked, "How are you going to keep yourself safe?"

"I can take care of myself. Since I know what might happen, I'm prepared for it. I'll just make sure I keep the doors locked before I go to bed. You need to call me when you get to Mom's. I want to know that you made it there safe."

Sara and LJ left for Pennsylvania later that night, arriving at Vince's mother's place at about midnight. It was a long drive, but Lilly was happy to see them.

***

When the doorbell rang that same night, it was late. Vince climbed out of bed, coming down the stairs to see who was calling. He figured it was Sara coming back for something she'd forgotten. But looking through the peephole, he found another woman standing there staring back at him—one very short and very familiar.

"Mitzie? What are you doing here?" Vince asked, half asleep. "Did you forget something?"

"No, but I think you did," she said, forcing her way in.

"What?"

Mitzie came in and threw her jacket down on the chair in the entryway. Then she came towards him, putting her arms around his neck and kissing him passionately on the lips and rubbing him with her hand.

"What are you doing?" Vince asked, pulling away.

"Sara's gone, isn't she?"

"Yeah, she and LJ left to go to my mother's place."

"I want you," Mitzie said in a breathless tone. The look in her eyes was sensual and wild—like a hypnotic spiral disk, rotating and sucking him in. She again grabbed him by the crotch and pushed her lips up against his, opening her mouth for a lustful kiss.

He hesitated, but feeling the warm pleasure of her mouth and her tongue, he couldn't help but draw closer to her. She continued rubbing him and making him hard.

"No," he said finally, stepping back. "You need to leave, Mitzie."

She looked at him and smiled. The slick redness of her lipstick was a visual Siren's song, and she licked her lips slowly trying to entice him back.

This time Vince didn't bite. Instead, he walked to the door and opened it.

"You need to leave," he said firmly, standing his ground.

She pouted, play-acting the part of a hurt lover, and when she didn't move, he grabbed her jacket and led her to the front door.

"Are you sure?" she asked one more time, grabbing him again through his robe. "You're hard, and you want me, don't you?"

"Yes, I mean no!" Vince said, trying to resist her. "Get out!"

Mitzie took her jacket from him and walked out. Vince shut the door quickly behind her and listened as the Porsche outside revved its engine and then drove off down the street. When it was quiet, he started back upstairs but saw she'd dropped her red lighter on the carpet by the banister. He picked it up and instinctively turned the wheel to light it to see if it worked. The flame ignited, so he closed the lid and threw it into the waste basket nearby before going up to his room.

***

Early in the morning, Sara's cell phone rang and rang, but no one picked up. She had left it downstairs at her mother-in-law's while she and LJ were sleeping in the queen-sized bed in the guest bedroom. It was three in the morning.

As the sun was streaming through the bedroom window, Sara yawned and threw off the covers. She saw that she'd gotten a voice mail. It was from Vince. Quickly, she pushed the buttons on the phone to retrieve the message.

"You have one new message. To play this message ..."

She skipped the instructions and pushed one to play.

"Sara, it's Vince. Sorry to call so late. I was having the weirdest dream and wanted to call to make sure you and LJ are okay."

In the background of the call, Sara heard another noise but couldn't tell what it was.

"Just a minute, sweetheart. I hear something downstairs ..." said Vince. Then there was a sharp *click* on the recording as he set the phone down on the nightstand. But what she heard next was deeply disturbing. In the background was a low, growling noise.

"No! No! Get away from me! No!" It was Vince, shouting from some distance away—likely from the base of the stairs.

She heard a banging noise, and Vince screaming—this time in terror.

"No! No! *Ahhh!*"

The guttural, animal-like snarling grew louder as if a huge tiger were downstairs mauling him. Sara's hand quaked as she held the phone to her ear and listened, wanting to drop everything and run to help him. But they were over four hours away.

"Vince!" she cried out, even though it was just a recording. "Vince!"

Suddenly, the banging in the background stopped.

"No ... no ... get away ... get away! Let go of me!"

The banging continued until she heard what sounded like the splintering of wood. Fading into the distance she heard Vince yelling, "No! Get away from me! No!" Then the line went dead.

Sara's heart stopped beating for a moment as terror gripped her. She thought about calling the police but didn't think they would take her seriously since she was violating their order. Instead, she gently pushed on LJ, who was still asleep next to her.

"Honey, I have to go home right now—just for a little while. I'll be back, okay? You stay here with your grandma. I'll call you later."

LJ mumbled something and rolled over, pulling her white, down pillow closer to her. Quickly, she fell back asleep.

Sara changed her clothes and ran downstairs. Her mother-in-law was grilling bacon in a small pan on the electric oven she had used for the previous thirty years.

"Oh, you're just in time for an early breakfast, I see," said Lilly, smiling while holding a fork in her hand. The gray plumes of smoke from the bacon curled up from the pan, rising effortlessly and unwittingly into the humming, churning fan blades overhead.

"Mom, I have to go. I'm sorry," Sara said, visibly distressed. "I have to get back to the house."

Startled, Lilly put down the fork and came over to her.

"Sara, what's wrong. You're trembling, dear. What's happened?"

"I don't know. I got a message from Vince last night. I think he may need me. I don't know any more than that. I'll call you when I get there. Take care of LJ until I get back."

Lilly started to ask her more questions, but Sara waved her off, closing the screen door behind her and jumping into her car.

Sara hated to leave her mother-in-law that way, not knowing what was going on at her home. She had panicked her many times before, earlier in her marriage to Vince. Looking back, she had felt remorseful and stupid. None of those times had been important or dire; not like this one—not even close. *I'll call her later,* she promised herself, *once I get to the house and see how Vince is.*

The trip seemed to take twice as long as it had the previous night. Sara could feel terrible anxiety welling up in her. She pounded on the steering wheel each time she called the house to talk to Vince but got no answer. Pushing harder on the accelerator, she watched as the speedometer shot past seventy, eighty, then ninety. The telephone poles and farmhouse mailboxes flew past her like wagon spokes turning at high speed. Even through the smaller towns, where the speed limit dropped to thirty-five, she barely backed off the throttle.

But it was in the town of Troy on State Road 6 where she saw flashing lights in her rearview mirror. Then came two, short blips of the siren.

Whooooooo .... Whooooooo

"Shit!" she said, pulling over to the side of the road.

The police officer came up to her window and tapped on the glass. Grudgingly, she rolled it down.

"Yes officer?" she asked as calmly as she could.

"Ma'am, do you know how fast you were going?"

"Uh, no officer, I'm afraid I don't. Was I going over the speed limit?"

The cop had his midnight blue uniform on and wore stylish, aviator sunglasses that were so dark Sara could only see her own reflection in them. On his left breast pocket, he wore a silver badge that read *County Sheriff.*

"I need to see your license and registration," the officer said coolly.

Sara got her purse and handed her license to him. Then, she rummaged through her glove box to locate the car's registration. The glove box was a mess, and it took time to sift through the napkins, car repair receipts and other garbage to find what she was looking for.

The sheriff looked at her license and then said, "Stay here. Remain in the vehicle. I'll be right back."

While he returned to his squad car, Sara pulled out her cell phone and made another call. This time to someone else.

"Hello?"

"Mitzie? It's Sara. I'm sorry to bother you so early in the morning, but I need a favor ...."

The police officer came back. This time, he stood back from the driver's door and put his hand on the grip of his gun, even though it remained in his holster.

"Ma'am, it appears there is a warrant out for your arrest." His voice was stern and demanding. "I'm going to ask you to get out of the car and put your hands over your head."

"What?"

"You heard me ma'am. Now!"

Sara got out of the driver's seat as the officer roughly grabbed her wrists, forcing them behind her and clipping on a pair of cold, steel handcuffs. He pushed her toward his squad car and opened the back door before pushing down on her head and shoving her inside. Then, he took off his hat, threw it on the passenger seat and got in.

Turning around he said, "Apparently, you were told not to leave the Boston area by the local police department, and yet you're out here. You are in violation of that order, ma'am," he said, reaching again for his radio to call in the incident.

He got on his squad phone and gave the dispatcher details of the arrest, citing Sara's name, driver's license information and the make, model and year of her car. Sara wanted to cry, but she knew that wouldn't accomplish anything. Still, she fought back tears as they drove to the police station. Her nightmare never seemed to end.

*****

CH 49 – A Talk with Bessie–Part 2

2020

Tommy Walcott was charging ahead with his arrest, or more precisely, the DA's arrest. He'd contacted Dick Johnson directly, unusual for a first-year detective. It also miffed the police chief, having been side-stepped by the brash youngster. However, the DA was sympathetic to the breach in protocol, as he was desperate for a quick resolution to the heinous cases that were pending with the police department. He was eager to hear directly from anyone willing to do move his agenda forward.

To Dag's chagrin, the arrest warrant was issued without delay, and the police chief alerted his force to find Sara McLaughlin and arrest her as soon as possible. But finding her was suddenly a problem. They had called the house and her cell phone to ask her to turn herself in, but they had gotten no answer. In another snafu, the front desk had again failed to forward a message from her husband, Vince, who had called the precinct earlier that night telling them she'd gone to his mother's with their daughter, LJ.

The next morning the call came in from the Troy Police Department, which had just pulled her over for speeding. At about the same time, the DA released Dag from the case and promoted Tommy to lead detective, putting him in charge. As soon as Tommy got the word of Sara's arrest, he jumped into his squad car and squealed his tires, speeding off to Troy to pick her up and bring her back to face charges.

Dag knew Tommy had no real evidence; what he had was hardly even circumstantial. But despite the lack of evidence, Dag's experience and gut also told him they were wrong. Sara wasn't the perpetrator. She had committed no crime, as far as he could tell.

Despite being off the case, Dag drove back to the nursing home to visit Bessie again. He thought he had messed up during the earlier conversation and that there was more she had to offer. *He would try again,* he thought.

When Dag arrived, he talked to the same young woman at the front desk who had helped him before. But this time, he only needed to show his badge and sign in, walking back down the now-familiar hallway to where the independent living units were. But before he reached that section of the complex, he heard his name called.

"Dag?"

Dag stopped in the hallway and peeked into one of the rooms—it was a critical care unit. Inside, he found Bessie, sitting up in her bed and watching TV. By her bedside was her granddaughter—Patti.

"Well, hello again," said Patti, as Dag entered the room. "Twice in just a few days. That's a record—even for me, I think."

Dag didn't smile. His last experience with Patti had been less than pleasant. However, he did nod to Bessie as he entered.

"Ms. Belzikov, it's good to see you again. We spoke yesterday," he said, unsure whether at her age she would remember.

"Yes, of course I do," said Bessie, annoyed by the suggestion.

"You've moved," said Dag, looking around the room. "Different digs, I see."

"She had a little episode last night," said Patti. "They brought her over here to give her some special attention."

"You don't give me any special attention," said Bessie. "I have to get it from someplace." Then, Bessie turned to Dag, who was being eyed by her granddaughter. "Gallagher ... Gallagher," Bessie mumbled to herself, "wasn't that the name of the detective you were having a fling with?"

"Excuse me?" Dag asked, taken aback.

"No, grandma," said Patti, you must be thinking of someone else." But Patti's buoyant personality was suddenly replaced by a cool aloofness.

"No, I'm almost certain of it, Patti. You and that detective ... what was his name? It started with a 'J' I think."

"Jag?" said Dag, blurting it out without thinking.

"Yeah, that was it. You had this thing for him. I remember. He was a lot older than you. That was it ... Jag. I knew it was an unusual name," said the old woman.

"That ... that was my grandfather," said Dag haltingly. "You and my ... my *grandfather*?"

"No!" Patti said, sternly. "Grandma, you're getting old, and forgetful. You often get mixed up in the head, don't you?"

Bessie looked at Patti and said, "Perhaps you're right, dear. I'm almost a hundred and one, you know. You have to give me a little break if I don't' always get my facts right anymore." Then, turning back to Dag, she said emphatically, "But what I *do* remember is that I didn't have anything to do with that murder case you talked about yesterday."

Patti chimed in. "What murder case?"

"He was asking about Dumitra Nicolescu," said Bessie. "But you know her maiden name was Prodescu, right?"

"Prodescu? Yes. Her daughter was ..."

"Janice Prodescu," said Bessie. Then she laughed unexpectedly. "Of course. Dumitra was her mother. They were both killed for the same reason, you know."

"Grandma, I think you need some rest. Her head is rattled," said Patti. She then looked at Dag. "I think she needs her rest. If you'll leave us, please." Patti's face was now steely and harsh.

Dag shook his head. "I only have a few more questions."

"Maybe later," said Patti sternly.

"Listen," said Dag, "I know your grandmother wasn't involved. I'm only trying to gather some facts, Patti. It's an old case, and it's difficult to find many people who are ..."

"... who are still alive?" Bessie said, finishing his thought.

"Yes."

"Well, detective, I can assure you that my grandmother wasn't involved in the case with that Janice woman or the Dumitra woman—either of them."

"Janice? That witch! Hell no!" Bessie shouted, exploding. "There's no way I'd have anything to do with her!" she said with contempt rolling off her tongue. The sudden and dramatic change was unnerving to Dag who stepped back from the bed.

"Oh, grandma, come on. You don't mean that. She was a good friend of yours. You told a lot of stories when you two were younger and how you were best friends. You went to school together. You hung out together."

"No! She was a *bitch*! A *whore*! She was the one who got all the attention. She got the boys; she got everything she wanted. She had it all."

"I think you may be confusing her with someone else, grandma," said Patti, trying to steer her grandmother into a different memory.

"Janice was the one who had the greatest psychic powers of any of us. She's the one who could contact just about anyone at any time. It was effortless for her. For me ... it was hard. You know that. I wanted to be just like her. I did. I wanted to be able to go right into a session and connect. For the rest of us, it always took time if we could do it at all. It wasn't until after ..."

Bessie stopped and nervously looked over at Dag.

"... after what?" he asked.

"Never mind," said Bessie. "It wasn't anything. It was all a long time ago. When you're young you do things that you shouldn't do. Some of them don't matter."

"And the others?" Dag asked.

"When you're my age, those don't matter either," said Bessie.

"Grandma, don't worry. We all understand that your memory isn't that good anymore. It's okay. The detective won't be staying and bothering you any longer today, will you detective?" Patti suggested, staring coldly at him.

Patti took her grandmother's hand.

"You felt bad about what happened to your friend Janice," said Patti. "You've told us about it for years. You still feel guilty, even though you had nothing to do with it."

Bessie's eyes teared, droplets welling up and making her lids puffy and red.

"It's okay, grandma," comforted Patti. She looked at Dag disdainfully and said, "I think she's had enough for one day. If you don't leave, I'll call the nurse."

Bessie began to sob. She covered her eyes with her arthritically-racked hands.

"Yes. She was and will always be my friend," said Bessie, now changing back to her more mild-mannered self. "We were there together through thick and thin growing up. She was the one with the talent. I was the one with the curse."

"Grandma, that's not true. Now, really. There, there ...," said Patti, stroking her grandmother's arm.

"She was like a sister to me, you know. Then, the day before she died, I got a call from her. She told me there were things going on that were *getting* out of control or was it beyond her control? It was something like that. I told her she was just stressed. She'd had a lot of appointments, and each one took a lot out of her. People always asked for her. She had a great, welcoming personality which made them feel good and safe. She told them the good news and the bad news, but mainly she just wanted them to feel that their loved ones were in a good place. She was like no one else I ever knew."

"Where were you when she died?" asked Dag, hoping this time to get the straight story.

"Actually, I had been to see her that very day. We'd had a nice time together, sitting by a fountain in the park, having sandwiches we'd bought from a café nearby. We laughed and giggled most of the afternoon before we went back to her place for a glass of wine before I left."

"Did you do any psychic readings that night?"

"We got out the Ouija board and tried to contact some of our departed classmates who were with us in high school. Strangely, even though Janice was always able to reach people, this time we couldn't. The only thing we kept getting from the Ouija board was the phrase, '*Hello Plottar*.' That was the same message we'd gotten those few years earlier when I'd tried it. It scared the crap out of me when I saw those words."

"So, you don't know who killed her?"

"Of course not. I've even tried to do a session to reach out to Janice, to ask her what happened, but I could never get through. There was something blocking me. I gave up on that a long time ago." Bessie shook her head sadly.

"Dag! Please!" The look in Patti's eyes was now becoming incensed.

Dag could tell it was time to finish the conversation.

"Ms. Belzikov," said Dag, "Thank you for your time. You've been very helpful. I'm sorry I had to bring up some unpleasant memories."

Dag left the facility with more questions than he had before. And then there was that other issue that troubled him even more. *Had Patti had an affair with his grandfather? What was* that *all about?* It seemed he had yet another unsolved mystery on his hands. Instead of making progress, he felt he was only falling further behind with even more questions than answers.

*****

Part IV

CH 50 - A Secret Affair

1980

Jag had been married nearly twenty years. It was a good marriage, but not a great one. He had been absorbed with his case load, especially since being promoted to detective a few years earlier. Then, he had been challenged by the horrific murders in 1970, when he had been young and inexperienced doing investigative work.

He and his wife, Nancy, had a son Zeller soon after Jag joined the force. Now, Zag had just turned twenty and was looking to join as well. But Jag had discouraged it, and even though he had fought his dad over the same issue, he hoped his son would heed his advice.

Yet, there was something in the Gallagher bloodline that was drawn to law enforcement. It was the Siren that called each of them until they gave in.

The year was 1980, and Jag had met a vivacious, pretty and very young woman who had come into the precinct wanting to help the police with some of their unsolved cases and missing persons files. Her name was Patti Campbell.

Full of energy, she had offered to help Jag, and although he had been reluctant, he had finally succumbed to her charm and agreed. During the next several months, she was able to assist in finding two missing girls and the body of a third. She helped piece together how the one young women was killed and who might have done it.

Jag took Patti to where the body was found—in the back part of a landfill near a utility substation. It was surrounded by high fences and barbed wire—a place difficult to access. There, the psychic began to have visions of the woman being abducted from a convenience store near her home. She had gone there to purchase a quart of milk, some dishwashing soap, and a bag of bagels. Cameras outside the shop showed her leaving at 9:44 PM but there was no one with her. She never returned to her apartment.

Just across the street from the parking lot of the convenience store, a man waited in his car. Patti's vision was of a middle-aged man wearing a gray overcoat and black baseball cap with a red-letter *B* embroidered on it. At the substation, she took police to another area where they found a discarded orange, utility vest. It was torn and had blood on it that matched the victim's. What was unusual about the vest was its size: a 6XL. These were enough clues to let the police focus their attention on one man: Manuel Hernandez. Hernandez was a huge man—six feet, three and over three hundred pounds. He was an avid Boston Red Sox fan and had several articles with the logo. Although this wasn't enough on its own to charge him, they found matching DNA on the victim that matched his.

During this time, Jag became emotionally involved with Patti which put a strain on his marriage. Still, he tried to make both work. When they finally brought charges against Hernandez, Patti led Jag and a squad of his officers to the perp's home, surrounding it. Jag used a bullhorn and broadcast that he should come out and surrender himself. Moments later, they heard a gunshot and rushed the house with their guns drawn. Inside, they found the man's body with a single shot through the temple. The house was filled with pornographic pictures and many of minors. It was clear to Jag they had gotten their murderer.

Jag had thanked her and told her they would have to break-up the relationship, but Patti would have nothing of it. Jag had relented too, and so they had continued with the affair.

It wasn't until later that year when Patti told Jag she was pregnant that Jag finally terminated the relationship. He wanted her to get an abortion, but she refused, insisting on having the child.

Fuming, Patti never forgave or forgot Jag's turning on her and leaving her. But in return, she did bear a child—a beautiful girl. She named her Maria. However, soon she would get a nickname: Mitzie.

*****

CH 51 – No Free Ride

2020

Sara waited impatiently in a cloistered room within the Troy police station. It was labeled Interview Room B, but it looked more like a WWII interrogation room. Gray, barren, and cold, it had all the warmth of a funeral home. She was required to turn-in all her personal belongings, including her purse and cell phone. She had asked for her one phone call, but the over-zealous deputy in charge had only told her, "You'll get your chance—but not now." Then, he had opened the door to the cell and pushed her inside before closing it and letting the haunting sound of the latch clicking shut echo through the hallway.

An hour passed before the door finally reopened. This time, another deputy walked in.

"Get up!" he barked.

"You have to let me make a phone call," she insisted.

"Later," said the officer.

"No. I know my rights. I want to make a call!" Sara said, not moving.

The deputy didn't answer and, instead, pulled her arms behind her and ratcheted the handcuffs tightly around her wrists.

"What's that for?" she asked, surprised and humiliated.

"You're going for a little ride back to Boston. Apparently, they're so anxious to get you back that someone drove all the way out here to pick you up. You must be some sort of celebrity," he said sarcastically.

"They want me? What do you mean? Who is *they?*"

At that moment, Sara saw another person walk into the room. It was Tommy.

"I'm Detective Walcott," said Tommy, flashing his badge as he came in. "And you must be Officer Mullins. I appreciate you processing the transfer so fast." Then, he looked over at Sara. "Well, well. If it isn't Ms. McLaughlin," Tommy said with derision. "So, what did they get you on? Did you kill someone else that we should know about?"

"She was doing eighty in a forty-five zone," said Officer Mullins as he handed Tommy the case file. The young detective flipped it open and lifted the top sheet to read.

"Looks like you *were* speeding, ma'am. Oh, that's not good," he commented, shaking his head. "In Boston that just might get you ... well, a life sentence—if you know what I mean." His expression was smug and aloof.

Sara was angry. "What else am I being charged with then?" she asked him, her face flushed with rage.

"The murders of Margaret and William Jenkins of Dorchester, and the attack on Claire Horwath in Brookline. And, if you're really lucky, we might be able to stick you with the murder of Zag Gallagher too. That would be a bonus. But the more we can pin on you, the more famous you'll be. Think of it that way! And if you're famous, well, then so will I, 'cause I was the one who caught you."

"You know damn well I didn't kill anyone!" Sara spat back at him.

"Maybe yes. Maybe no. It's not up to me to decide, though, is it? But, you have the right to remain silent. Anything you say or do may be used against you in the court of law. You have the right to consult an attorney before speaking to police and to have your attorney present during questioning now or in the future. If you cannot afford an attorney, one will be appointed for you before you answer any questions, if you wish. If you elect to answer any questions now without an attorney present, you will still have the right to stop answering any questions until you talk with an attorney. Knowing and understanding these rights as I have explained them to you, are you willing to answer my questions without an attorney being present?"

"No!" said Sara, emphatically.

"Not a problem," said Tommy.

"Are you finished, then?" asked Sara.

"Yes," Tommy retorted.

"Then I want my phone call."

***

The ride to Boston was quiet. Tommy listened to his police radio, while Sara looked out the window as the countryside whizzed by.

She wondered if she would ever get to see the beauty of the rural country again. If convicted, she knew she never would. When they arrived at the Boston police station, Sara was processed, her paperwork prepared, photos snapped, and fingerprints taken. A female officer escorted her to the back of the precinct building where she was strip-searched and given a new set of fashionable, orange, coveralls—all provided free-of-charge by the goodwill of the city.

"Can I call my attorney again?" Sara asked. "I asked him to go to my house. I haven't been able to reach my husband."

But Tommy shook his head. "Sorry, but you've had your one call. Those are the rules."

"Come on!" pleaded Sara. "Just one more."

"Nope," he said.

Sara was going to call her husband again too, hoping he would pick up. She was worried about Vince, worried about LJ, worried about everything. And now she found herself alone—this time in a barred cell. She wondered whether her daughter would ever come and see her in prison. She wondered whether she would ever see the light of day again. She wondered too if being on the other side—in the spirit world—would be a better place for her.

*****

CH 52 - A Second Affair

1995

When the terrible murders hit Boston in 1995, Patti again went into the precinct. This time, the son of Patti's former lover, Zag, worked with her to try to track down the people who committed the crimes.

They had three bodies by July. The first, Lenny Pittman, was the son of a reporter who had been horribly murdered twenty-five years earlier. Along with Lenny was his partner Roger Enright who was killed the same night. Even stranger was the murder of Father Jose Mercato, a local priest. No connection had been found between the two murder scenes, and no one could figure out why anyone would want them dead. The evidence pointed to burglaries gone bad; however, the mangled mess of the bodies suggested something else—something more sinister.

At first, Patti had been very helpful. She had identified another woman, Abby Knight, as someone of interest. Patti claimed that Abby was a psychic too but was involved in black magic. She alleged that Abby was connected to a group that was meeting in Purgatory Park and conducting ritual killings of animals there.

Zag had followed up on all her leads but could never tie anything back to Abby, the park, a cult ... or anything. Once Abby Knight disappeared, the cases went completely cold.

***

"But Patti, what you've been telling me doesn't add up."

"Why?" she shouted. "Of course, it does. You're just not looking at it the right way."

"Abby Knight has been missing for a month. No one has seen her. She left her husband, Chris, and her daughter and hasn't been seen since May 7."

"That would be the perfect alibi then, wouldn't it? 'I went missing, so I couldn't have done the killings'. Isn't that what she'll tell you if you find her?"

"That's not what I meant," said Zag.

"Then what did you mean?"

"I don't know. I've talked to her husband, her sister, her friends ... it just doesn't sound like someone who ..."

"Someone who left her only daughter ... why wouldn't she be capable of doing this then?"

"Leaving your daughter isn't the same as murdering people."

"Not in my book," said Patti. "Both are about as cruel as it gets."

"I don't know. I'll have to look into it some more," said Zag.

"Come back to bed, honey," said Patti, stroking the sheet. "We can talk about this later. Can't we?"

Yes. Patti had found another Gallagher to seduce.

*****

CH 53 - Dag and the Cult

2020

Dag again poured over the files Tommy had given him—cold case files from the 1940s, 1950s and 1960s. He came across two Tommy had talked about that were cult-related—ones in 1948 and 1958. Then in 1995, there was that investigation into burned animals in Purgatory Chasm State Park. It was on that case that Detective Jessie Davis had disappeared while on a stake out there.

Maybe it's time to take another look, thought Dag, opening the files. After reviewing the details, he decided to go to the park and search for himself. He wanted to see if there were any ongoing charred remains of animals that might be a sign the cult was still active.

Dag arrived at the park and hiked directly to where the previous animal remains had been found. There, he began his search. He didn't find what he was looking for after the first day or the second, but on the third, he struck gold. Next to a steep cliff was an abandoned fire pit with the small bones of what looked like cats or dogs or some other small animals. The stones were pushed around to make it look haphazard, but Dag saw one configuration that smacked of what he was looking for: a circle with a pentagram inside it.

Now Dag was determined. He took pictures of the site and then committed himself to a prolonged stakeout. The DA had relieved him of most of his duties as a detective, so he had the time, and as God knew well, he had the will.

It took over ten days before Dag and his surveillance got a hit. Sitting in his unmarked car, he saw several dark cars pull into the park's lot but continue down a side road and drive deeper inside the park grounds. But it was then that Dag also got a call from the precinct.

"Yeah?" he said, answering the police cell he used.

"Dag, it's me, Smitty."

Smitty was the nickname of Arnold Paul Smith, the senior technician who worked at the Boston police lab.

"Yeah, Smitty, what's up? I'm kind of in the middle of something right now. Can I call you back later?" asked Dag.

"Sure thing. I just wanted to let you know that I got back the results of my analysis of those charred remains you asked me to examine—to see which animals they were."

"Yeah, right. Well, if it's the standard wild animals of a park, we can talk about it when I'm back in the office."

"That's the thing. There were a lot of those, but there was also something else."

"What do you mean?"

"DNA from a human, Dag. A dead body was cremated there."

Dag felt sick. But there was little he could do at the moment as he continued watching cars ramble into the park.

"Dag?" Smitty said again, not hearing any reply.

"Yeah, Smitty. It's bad—really bad. But I have to go right now. I'll get back to you."

Dag got out of his car and followed on foot through the dark woods. He was thankful for the thick cloud cover; otherwise, the forecast of a gibbous moon would have given him away.

It was nearly midnight when the last cars found their way to the rendezvous spot—their rear red lights brightening as their mysterious owners parked them in the make-shift lot. Out of each car emerged someone wearing a black or burgundy, hooded cloak. Their faces were covered, and they wasted no time leaving their cars behind and taking the same narrow trail deeper into the woods.

Dag followed quietly. It was too dark to get pictures, but he did have his service pistol and a taser if he needed them. Patiently, he watched as the enigmatic group gathered in the very same area under the cliff where he'd found charred remains. They drew lines in the earth and lit black candles, placing them around the perimeter of a large circle. Then, to Dag's shock, one led a white goat into the center of the arena. In unison, the worshipers of the cult began chanting with one beating a primitive, animal skin drum. As the pounding grew louder and faster, one in a bright red robe pulled out a long knife.

"To the Dark One, we offer this sacrifice so that we may become richer and more powerful in our magic and dominion over others," said the figure. "May we cast aside and trample those who might get in our way. May we take no pity or remorse for any deed we do in your name. May we revel in the misery and despair of others and work toward the utter denigration of mankind. May we further your desires and aims to crush all goodness in the world and bring about total darkness in every corner. May your evil be supreme and live forever!"

The figure then slit the goat's throat, letting the blood splash over the robes of the others and into the circle itself. Those splattered by the ritual licked their arms and hands of the blood ... and smiled.

Dag grew closer holding his service revolver and ducking behind one of the old-standing trees nearby. It was then that the goat's neck was held over a gold cup to let more of the blood run into it. When the goat was dead, the person in the red robe took the cup and passed it around the circle, letting each member drink from it. Dag was sickened by what he saw.

But the ritual was not yet over. A fire was lit, and the goat head and its body were laid on the burning, pyre-like altar. The flames quickly enveloped the wood stack, shooting ten or fifteen feet into the air and casting glowing embers far up into the night's sky. And as the goat burned, the cult chanted.

"Satan is our king ... Mammon reigns supreme ..."

Dag tried to use his cell phone to request backup, but there was no signal so deep in the forest. *His only choice,* he thought, *was to go back to the grassy lot and take down the license plates of those attending. He would then take those back to the precinct to match against their owners.*

But before he could rise from his cover, the ritual ended, and the members began disbursing from the ceremonial circle, returning to their cars.

Dag spotted the leader, now wearing a red robe stained with the blood of a sacrificial goat. Crouching behind trees and thick bush, he followed stealthily, hoping to catch the person in an isolated area of the path where he could arrest them without a confrontation from the others. However, that opportunity never materialized.

Instead, they reached the parking area, and Dag stopped just at the perimeter, watching to see which car the leader got into. The leader clicked the remote, flashing the headlights on one of the vehicles. Then, after opening the rear driver's side door, he pulled off the cloak.

"No ...." Dag stammered.

It was not a he.

"Patti? Patti Campbell?" mumbled Dag.

Dag felt his knees buckle, and his head spin. She looked over in his direction as if sensing someone was watching, but she couldn't see him in the darkness. Then, like everyone else, she started up the car and drove quickly out of the park, leaving Dag with a sense of emptiness and lost opportunity.

*****

CH 54 - Morrie Investigates

2020

At the Troy police station, Sara had used her one phone call to reach Morrie Blum, an attorney and long-time family friend. Since she'd been unable to reach Vince, she had asked him to go to the house and check on him. Gladly, Morrie had agreed.

The day had started with fog, but had quickly devolved into a cold, steady drizzle. Morrie put his windshield wipers on intermittent and then clicked it up to the middle setting to keep his view clear enough to navigate the slippery roads. He watched with annoyance as the huge, rubber blades whisked back and forth, leaving a singular streak of water down the middle of his line of sight.

As the big Mercedes sedan pulled into the driveway, a UPS delivery van backed out, having dropped off a package on the front porch. The overhang of the porch was just large enough to keep most of the packages dry, but others were being pelted by heavy raindrops that would soon make whatever was inside them damp and soggy.

Morrie knocked on the front door and then rang the doorbell for good measure. A full minute went by without an answer, so he left the porch, stepping over the downspout that had come loose from the side of the house and continuing along the flagstone walkway, through the open wrought-iron gate, and into the back yard. Well-kept with beds of flowers all neatly pruned and mulched, the yard was small and cloistered by a fence shared with the neighbors. In the center was a large, rather-ugly, stone birdbath that stood beneath a gnarly bark, hickory tree that had seen many families come and go from the house with which it shared the lot.

Morrie tried the back door, but it was locked; so, he climbed the wooden deck stairs to the double sliding doors that connected the wrap-around porch between the kitchen and family rooms. The first sliding door was locked too but not the second. There, he gently slid the door open until the end nudged the white, rubber bumper, bringing it to a stop.

"Morrie?"

"Mike, what took you so long to answer?" asked Morrie, coming into the kitchen. "I saw your car out front, and I began to worry when the front door was locked and neither you nor Vince came to answer it. What's going on?"

"You don't want to come in here," said Mike, looking visibly shaken. "It's a mess, Morrie."

Mike Strom had been with Morrie for seven years—first as a paralegal and then, after graduating from law school, as an associate. He was being considered for partnership, and Morrie had every intention of making him one once he had the prerequisite experience and demeanor.

"What's the matter, Mike?" Morrie said.

Morrie walked through the kitchen and then into the dining area in front. The counters, sinks and kitchen table were clean; the cabinets neatly closed; and the chairs, sofas, tables and other furnishings in the dining and family areas undisturbed. Everything seemed to be in place. Then, he heard a tapping noise and felt a blast of cold air on his face. He looked up, realizing it was air coming through the ducts above him as the air conditioner had kicked on. But the tapping noise continued.

"What's that noise?" he asked Mike.

"It's bad, Morrie. Real bad," said Mike pointing up with his finger.

"Upstairs?" asked Morrie, swallowing stiffly.

Mike nodded.

Morrie walked to the staircase; it had deep cuts in the banister running two or three feet long—more like gouges than scratch marks. At the top of the stairs, he found the hallway leading to the master bedroom and two other bedrooms at the far end. The doors were closed making him feel uneasy and vulnerable.

Morrie looked back to the bottom of the stairs where his associate stood and motioned for him to come up. However, Mike only shook his head. So, Morrie continued down the corridor, passing the first two rooms and moving toward the master bedroom door from where the tapping sounds were coming. He pushed on it and instantly got another cold smack of air blowing across his face and shoulders. As he started in, he noticed something else—the door was splintered down the middle, cracked in half.

As he pushed on the door, he felt it resist as if fighting back. Then, putting his shoulder against it, he prepared to force it open the rest of the way. But instead, the door suddenly flew open on its own, ramming the brass doorknob into the wall behind it and making a deep dent.

"Vince?" said Morrie. "Vince, are you here?"

It was then that he could feel it. There was something else in the room—something that made the hairs on the back of his neck stand up.

Stepping nervously inside, he saw that the bed covers were pulled down and the sheets crumpled in mounds. Near the headboard were two white feather pillows, one on top of the other. The top one had three slit marks that were burned around the edges as if a fiery-hot poker had ripped, then shredded them. A few feathers stuck out through the tears—all were withered and black. But it was what was on the headboard above it that shocked him. Written in blood were the creepy words *Hello Plottar*.

"Oh, my God!" he said.

Morrie held his hand over his mouth. On the side of the bed were more scratch marks grooved into the planks of the hardwood floor. One had a lone fingernail, pulled from its owner, set deeply into a break in the boards.

As he stood there, the floorboards under his feet began to shake. Within seconds the shaking became violent. He ran for the hallway opening, but before he could reach it, the door slammed shut—shattering the already broken piece into two separate pieces as it hit the doorframe.

Morrie stood frozen in disbelief.

Staring back at him from inside of the door was Vince's severed head—speared through the forehead and impaled on a spike coming out from the top of the door. Its eyes were closed—its skin now mottled and putrid with a growing purple tint.

"Mike! Get up here! Mike!" shouted Morrie, frantically trying to open the door.

Mike reached the door and shook the handle from the outside to force it open. But it wouldn't move.

"Mike! Get me out of here!" shouted Morrie.

Mike backed up, ready to kick-in the door, when it opened on its own as mysteriously as it had closed—this time slowly and creaking as it eventually bounced against the rubber stopper.

A shocked and stunned Morrie rushed out.

"My God!" he said, looking at Mike and shaking.

"The rest of the body is in the next room," said Mike, his face pallid and ghostly.

Indeed, it was in the next room where police would find the rest of Vince's body. It was hung on the ceiling fan in LJ's room, spinning around slowly as the fan rotated. The tapping noise Morrie had heard had come from there instead—from Vince's feet scraping the bedpost of LJ's bed each time the fan made one revolution.

Thump ... thump ... thump ... thump ...

*****

CH 55 – In Handcuffs

2020

Morrie called 911 and asked for a police car. Within ten minutes the navy and white sedan pulled up with its lights flashing, and an officer got out.

"Did you call in a possible problem with this residence, sir?" asked the patrolman, coming to the door.

"Yes, I'm Morrie Blum. I'm the attorney for the family who lives here. The wife, Sara, asked me to come over and see if everything was all right with her husband. She had problems last night getting a hold of him and was worried that something might be wrong."

"There are three cars in the driveway," observed the policeman. "I assume one is yours?"

'Yes."

"And the other cars in the driveway?" asked the officer. "Who's are they?"

"I believe one is the husband's—Vince. The one in back of it is that of my associate, Mike Strom; he's inside. He arrived first and knocked on the door, but no one answered. The husband didn't pick-up calls on his cell phone either. The front door was locked when my associate arrived, but Sara, the wife, told us where to find the spare key. So, Mike went in, you know, just in case there was a problem."

"Well, let's take a look," said the officer, starting toward the front door.

Morrie held out his hand. "It's bad, officer. The woman's husband is dead inside. You'll need to call the coroner and a detective unit. You'll also need more than one body bag."

The policeman went in and quickly discovered the remains of the husband. He radioed for backup and proceeded throughout the rest of the house. Two other squad cars arrived, and more officers went inside. After several minutes, the first officer on the scene came out.

"I'll have to hold both of you for questioning. Gentlemen, you'll have to come with me," said the officer, harshly.

Moments later, a detective's car pulled up just as policemen proceeded to cordon-off the entire house with yellow crime tape. The detective jumped out of his squad car and strutted over to where the first officer on the scene and Morrie were standing.

"Are you Mr. Blum?"

It was Tommy Walcott.

"Yes," answered Morrie.

"I understand you and your associate were the first ones on the scene."

"Yes."

"Do you realize you may have corrupted the crime scene? Did you touch anything?"

"Detective, any prints would be limited to a few doorknobs. We were very careful. You'll be able to distinguish those from ..."

"I know how to do my job," said Tommy bluntly. "Your being here will certainly make our job harder."

"Am I being charged? I *am* the attorney for Ms. McLaughlin you know," said Morrie, defensively.

"Not yet," said Tommy, enjoying a brief sense of superiority over such a distinguished man. "But all the same, you have to go down to the precinct for questioning."

"We've been informed," answered Morrie, tiring quickly of the brash detective.

Morrie got in the back seat of the police cruiser along with his associate, Mike. He wasn't worried about himself. He'd been through much worse in his life, not to mention the things he'd endured in Korea. No, now his thoughts were with Sara. How in the world would he be able to tell her?

*****

CH 56 - Charred Remains

2020

Dag got back to the precinct and plopped into his office chair. It had been a long and nerve-wracking night. Angry at himself for missing the chance at arresting the cult members and nailing its leader, Patti Campbell, he strummed his fingers on the desk top thinking about what to do next. However, slumber came to him quickly, and his head bobbed twice before, dropping into a deep sleep.

"Dag, Dag, wake up," came a voice.

He opened his eyes and sat up in his chair. Rubbing his face with the palms of his hands, he answered, "Yeah, yeah, what time is it?"

He had slept through the night in his office. Standing in front of his desk was Smitty holding a data stick.

"Were you here all night?" Smitty asked.

"Uh, no. Only since about two."

"Two this morning?"

"Yeah, it's a long story. What do you have for me, Smitty?"

"We talked last night, remember? You said you were in the middle of something, so you couldn't talk. I brought this by so you could look at it. I tried sending it over our internal system, but the file was too big. Here, take a look."

Smitty handed Dag the stick which he promptly slipped into his computer's old-styled USB slot. Then, booting up the system, he opened it.

"What am I looking at?" Dag asked.

"Like I said, we found human remains among those in the sample you brought in from the park."

"Was there any good DNA in it?"

"Yeah," said Smitty. "We were able to find some that hadn't been exposed to the flames. I went ahead and ran the sequence against our database to see if we had anyone in it that matched."

"And?"

"We do."

"What was the vic's name?" said Dag still glancing through the file.

"Jessie Davis, I'm afraid."

Dag looked at Smitty and shook his head. "I was afraid you were going to tell me that."

"Yeah."

"We'll need to go back out and scrub the area to see if we can find other fragments or bones. There may be other pieces of the body in the woods too—ones that weren't put in the fire."

"Yeah. And someone will need to tell his family."

"Yeah. I'm afraid so," said Dag.

"Dag, how do you tell a family that their loved one was murdered or even worse killed as part of a satanic ritual? How do you tell them that they were then burned beyond recognition and left in the woods where they might never be found? How do you do that?"

Dag sighed. "You don't, Smitty. You tell them he died honorably and in the line of duty. That's what you tell them. Because that's the truth."

*****

CH 59 - About Demons

2020

The library was open late, and Dag spent the time pouring over texts that discussed demons, exorcism, the occult, wizardry and witchcraft. He read as much as he could, finding tomes covering the markings of the Devil, the signs of its presence and the aftermath of its visits.

In one book, *The Reality of 666*, he read ...

Demons are known to live inside human beings, sometimes for years without manifesting themselves until the time is right. Other times, they come and go, changing the person's demeanor and character into something unrecognizable before letting the person reclaim their body. Eventually, with fury and malice, they break through the consciousness of their host and seize control, forcing the host's character and soul deep into hiding.

Another chapter read ...

The destruction that can be wreaked upon human flesh by these demons can defy description. Their impact on the human soul can be even worse. The conditions of bodies found that have been attacked by demons are almost never reported in the press. The horrific nature of these attacks would likely cause civil unrest, if known.

Demons will sometimes use their hosts to commit heinous crimes. However, other, more virulent forms of demons, are capable of physical violence on their own—without the need of a human host. These types of evil spirits are far stronger and deadlier and are greatly feared inside and outside the Church. They range from the incubus and succubus that are only interested in sex with their victims to those with powers able to inflict bodily injury.

Dag wasn't sure he wanted to read anymore. His Catholic upbringing was shouting at him to stop; yet his Boston PD badge was pushing him to continue.

Demons from history that have displayed great power come from the Lesser Key of Solomon, particularly the Ars Goetia.

Listed within are seventy-two powerful demons who rule under Satan in Hell. Ones specifically cited through the ages include Satan's four cardinals: Urieus (East), Amaymon (South), Paymon (West), and Egin (North).

Bodies of victims attacked by these demons have been found contorted beyond recognition. Limbs have been turned in directions against the torso that make the human shape almost unrecognizable. Heads and other limbs often become severed or separated from the rest of the body, and it is not uncommon for the sexual organs to be missing altogether from the cavities left behind."

Dag shuddered. He knew well the police reports from the 1945, 1970, and 1995 cases where the bodies were twisted and contorted in this fashion. As he jotted down the dates in the margin of his notebook, it struck him that there was a sequence.

Every twenty-five years, he said to himself. Then he looked at the next series of crimes, in *2020. Exactly—twenty-five years after the last ones.*

Dag shut the reference book and put it aside. He couldn't handle any more occult talk. Just reading about demonology was making him sick—mentally and physically. Yet, the possibility of all the murders being connected through this bizarre and unimaginably evil strain of spirituality was something he couldn't ignore.

He felt the vibration of his cell phone calling him on his hip. "Detective Gallagher," he answered.

"Dag, this is Steve Yeager." Dag knew Officer Yeager well. They had gone to the police academy together and been assigned to several of the same cases. He was a good man—dedicated and religious. But Dag could hear trouble in his voice.

"What's up Steve?"

"Dag, you've got to come back to the station right away. You know that lady you were investigating for the bizarre murders we had on the south side the last few months? They just found her husband. It's not pretty."

"I'll be right there," said Dag, jumping up from his chair.

Dag knew he wasn't on the case anymore, but a fellow officer asked for his help and that was something he would never refuse. He knew few officers who trusted Tommy, and he wasn't surprised that they would turn to him first for help, whether or not he was on the case anymore.

Dag got to the precinct and entered just as two other officers came in behind him, escorting an older man dressed in an expensive, Italian-cut charcoal suit.

"Morrie?" asked Dag, looking curiously at Sara's attorney, who appeared as if he'd been through a sleep deprivation test. "What are you doing here?"

Dag knew Morrie Blum from other cases he had worked on. Their relationship was cordial and professional. Dag had always respected the attorney for his level-headedness and ability to conduct a deep and thorough analysis of the evidence.

"He's with me," said one of the attending officers coldly.

"I just need a quick word with him, officer," said Dag.

"I'm afraid not, detective. Detective Walcott told us that under no circumstances was anyone to talk to these two gentlemen until he got here."

"When is he supposed to get here?" asked Dag.

"Don't know. He didn't say," said the officer.

"Then, I'll take over from here," said Dag firmly.

"But I can't let you ..." stuttered the officer, trying to protest. "The detective said ..."

"Well, I can always go to the chief's office and see if we can get him involved. Would that be better?"

The officer backed off knowing that bothering the chief on such a petty matter would be suicide. Dag put his hand on the officer's shoulder.

"Officer Phillips," said Dag, looking at his name badge, "I'll take full responsibility if there is any problem. You're completely off the hook on this one. You can go."

Phillips winced but decided not to go up against the veteran detective. Dag smiled disingenuously as the officer turned to leave.

"Thank you, Detective Gallagher," said Morrie, with urgency in his voice, "I *do* need to talk to you."

"Why are you here Morrie?" Dag asked. "Why are you being questioned by Detective Walcott?"

"It's about Sara ... Sara McLaughlin. Tommy Walcott is there at her house now. I was the one who called the police."

"It's her husband, right?"

"Detective, her husband is dead—murdered. My associate and I were only stopping by at the request of Sara. She's being brought in too to face questioning."

"Where is she now?"

"She called me from this precinct, so I assume she's still here. Either Tommy or one of your other officers brought her in."

"There isn't much I can do, Morrie. You know that."

"Yes, but the one thing I do know is that my client is innocent. She hasn't done a thing. She wouldn't hurt anyone—especially Vince, her husband. They had a good marriage. I know that from personal experience."

"So why are you here?" asked Dag.

Morrie looked at him with surprise. "I realize some of you detectives think we attorneys are all crooks, but I assure you it's not true. And no, I had nothing to do with Vince's death either. After you see what happened to him, you'll wonder who on this earth could have done such a thing. It's, well ..."

"I'll stop in and see Sara," said Dag, cutting him off as politely as he could. "They're probably holding her in one of the cells in the back."

Dag went to the front desk officer to see what he could find out.

"Hey Victor," Dag said to the officer on duty at the desk. "Say, could you tell me where they are holding a ..." he paused, acting as though he were looking at his note pad, "... a Ms. Sara McLaughlin? Is she here anywhere?"

The officer looked at the computer screen on the desk. "Let me see," he said, clicking on different areas of the screen. "Uh, she's in Lockup Block B, cell four."

"Thanks, man."

Dag went to the security gates that sequestered the prisoners being held in Block B. It was a higher area of security and one with grimmer accommodations than those for the petty criminals in Block A. There was a buzzing noise at the gray, steel gate as Dag was let through the security airlock that separated the free, outside world from the dark, cold cells where those suspected of violent criminal activity were temporarily being held.

Sara sat staring at the dingy cement wall of her cell but turned her head when she heard someone coming down the dirty linoleum hallway. She looked through the small bars in the door, but once Dag arrived at her cell and showed his face, she turned back to stare at the wall.

"Sara?" Dag said, trying to get her attention.

She ignored him.

"Sara, I know you don't want to talk to any of us cops right now, but I have to ask you some questions."

Dag sensed that somehow she knew about Vince.

"Go away!" she said, sobbing.

Dag unlocked the cell and came in, yet he kept his distance.

"Sara, I'm afraid I have some bad ..."

"Vince is dead," she said, interrupting and starting to cry. "I could feel it when it happened. I could sense it. I already knew."

"I'm sorry."

Sara only continued to cry. She buried her head in her hands as tears rolled down her cheeks. With her hair matted and snarled around her face and shoulders, she was a pitiful sight. Even with his years of experience on the force and having seen just about everything, Dag's heart was being pulled apart. He felt sympathy for this woman. Her attorney, Morrie, hadn't needed to tell him. He knew, deep down, that she was no criminal. Instead, she was a victim—a political one.

He moved toward the window and stood beside her.

"Ms. McLaughlin, I need to know everything you know about these cases. I believe in you, and I want to help."

"No, you don't," she snapped.

"I understand why you might feel that way."

"You don't understand anything!" she shouted. "How can you stand there and tell me you understand? My husband is dead. My life has been taken from me. I have nothing left but emptiness."

"What about your daughter?" asked Dag. "I'm sure she loves you. What about her?"

Sara stopped crying to wipe her nose on the back of her sleeve. She still didn't look at Dag, but instead, shook her head.

"My mother can look after her," she said. "She'll have to now. I may never see her again."

"Okay, that's fine for you, but what about your daughter? Is that fine for her? Is it fine for her not to have her mother—especially since she's just lost her father?"

Sara was quiet.

"So, what good does that do anyone? It certainly doesn't help your daughter. It doesn't help you, and it absolutely does not help me."

"You? What does this have to do with *you*?" Sara barked.

Dag drew closer to her.

"Sara, listen to me," he said with a serious, fatherly tone. "Other people are going to die a horrible death unless you help me. You know that, and I know that. Someone out there is killing people, and only you can help me stop them."

"Someone?" asked Sara.

"Who do you think it is?" asked Dag.

"Detective, you have no idea what you're dealing with here. It's obvious to me, but if you don't believe in the spirit world, then there's no way I can help you with this."

"Convince me," said Dag. "And while you're at it, tell me about the significance of the twenty-five-year cycle."

"Twenty-five-year cycle? I don't know what you're talking about."

"I've gone back and looked at other murders that are similar to the ones we've been seeing here in Boston during the last several months. This is not the first time it's happened here. Our records aren't that good before the turn of the century, and they're spotty through the 1920s and 30s. So, the first cases I found were in 1945. The first was ...

"My great grandmother, Janice."

"Yes. And what's strange about that is your great grandmother was with a friend that very day—the day she was murdered. The second involved a Mr. Rosco Arthur—a Mr. Rosco Arthur Turner, to be exact. We dug his last name out of the files. He was found dead in his home under similar circumstances. Later that year, they discovered a third, Ms. Dumitra Prodescu. All the victims had the same thing in common – Bessie Belzikov."

Sara's head was spinning. "Wait, wait!" she said. "Rosco was a Turner?"

"Yes, and Bessie Belzikov's married name was Turner. She was married to Rosco Arthur Turner?"

"The very same Rosco Arthur? You're sure?"

Dag looked at Sara without comment. She knew there was only one Rosco Arthur; she just couldn't believe he was married to Bessie.

At this point, it was hard to believe Sara could look any worse than she already did, but now she appeared as if she'd seen one of Satan's prime demons.

"Rosco Arthur Turner--Bessie Belzikov Turner," she mumbled, trying to get a grasp of it.

"Yes. Apparently, Bessie was the close friend of your great grandmother, Janice Prodescu. They went to high school together and ..." Dag began.

"I know all that," Sara shot back, interrupting him. "I just didn't know he married Bessie. And both he *and* my great grandmother were murdered the same year?"

"Yes."

"Was he killed the same way too?"

Dag hesitated. Then, he admitted to her. "Yes."

"And so was my great, great grandmother, Dumitra," said Sara, thinking more clearly. "She was killed with her body all twisted up in knots."

"Yes. And similar murders happened after that—all within twenty-five years of each other. In 1970, there were three more murders—

the circumstances were similar to the victims in 1945. In 1995, the same thing. And now in 2020."

"Who were the others?" Sara asked.

"There was Virginia Carter and her son Jake, Danny Pittman—a reporter—and, of course, your grandmother, Cora Rae Taylor in 1970."

"Yes. Grandma Taylor was killed in 1970. That's true," said Sara, nearly catatonic. Her eyes were dazed, and her expression flat.

"Then we move to 1995," Dag continued, "twenty-five years later. We find three horrible murders in the same west and south suburbs of Boston—one in Roxbury, one in Dudley Square and one in Dorchester. Those are the same general areas where the other murders were committed."

Sara continued to stare—this time unresponsive.

"Sara! Sara! Are you listening to me? I need your help on this," said Dag, clicking his fingers in front of her eyes.

"I don't know," she responded, hardly moving.

"The first ones were in 1945 and Bessie. The next were in 1970 and ..."

"I don't know," Sara repeated.

"... and 1995 and now 2020," Dag repeated, still pressing.

"I just don't know any more," said Sara with despair.

"I think you do, Sara. This year, in 2020, we've had two more murders." Dag snapped his fingers again. "Sara, who was involved in those?"

"I ... I don't know," she finally answered. Dag had succeeded in getting her back with him.

"It was Maggie Jenkins and her son, Will. Her son went to school with your daughter, LJ. Do you remember that?"

"Yes, yes!"

"And the next one, we already know," said Dag, his voice dropping.

Sara broke down in tears.

"Is there one more to happen in 2020? Is there a *third* I should know about?"

"I don't know!" Sara screamed finally, sobbing.

Dag realized he had gone too far. He had pushed too hard. He was frustrated, but he stepped back, now seeing he has only making things worse.

"What do you know about the Belzikovs?" he asked her.

"All I know is what Mitzie Wilkins told me."

"You know Mitzie?" Dag asked.

Sara explained how she was contacted by the woman and the encounters they had had since then.

"I see," said Dag, thinking. "Is that it?"

"Well, I found a diary of my great grandmother's in the attic of our house. Grandma Janice made an entry in it about a séance she and her friends had when they were in high school. It was 1939—six years before the first murders."

"I assume that séance included Bessie Belzikov?"

"Yes, but ..." She stopped.

"But what Sara?" coaxed Dag.

"It was something strange that Grandma Janice said about Bessie in her journal. She said that ..." Sara hesitated again.

Dag raised an eyebrow, hoping she would continue on her own without more prompting.

"... no," she said finally.

"Why not?"

"Because you won't believe a word I say anyway, so what's the point?"

"Try me. Just this one time," encouraged Dag.

Sara sighed. "Well, the entry said that my great grandmother went into a trance to contact the spirits from the other side. But at the end of the session, she saw something strange in the room with them. Looking up at Bessie and she saw a ... a ..."

"A what?" asked Dag.

"A demon. She said there was a demon standing right behind Bessie. It was unmistakable. She fought the vision, thinking it was just an aberration. But it was the same every time she blinked."

"Do you believe that?" Dag asked, skeptically.

"I didn't at first, but now ..." said Sara, "... now, I'd say yes. The two remained friends after that. However, later in the diary, Janice noted she was surprise by Bessie's ability to perform these séances herself too and do other things she hadn't before. She wrote that Bessie had always been jealous of her since she was able to contact the dead with relative ease and Bessie couldn't. But after the séance, Bessie could do that and more very easily, somehow. It was a mystery to my great grandmother."

"Strange," said Dag.

"But there's one other thing," Sara said.

"What's that?"

"You're not going to want to hear this."

"Try me ..."

*****

CH 58 - A Talk with Bessie-Part 3

2020

It had been two days since Dag had been home. He'd been at Purgatory Park waiting up all night on a stakeout, hoping to catch another meeting of the cult he'd discovered. It was five in the morning when he staggered up his front porch, opened the door and collapsed on his sofa.

He glanced over at the mantel where there was a row of picture frames. The first was a young girl with blonde hair, not more than thirteen, smiling on a beach while packing sand over her younger brother who was laughing, half-buried by millions of grains. The second was that of the boy taken more than ten years later the prior Christmas, standing with his new .22 caliber rifle. Dag had hoped he wouldn't become a police officer, and thus far, he hadn't seemed interested. Of course, Dag hadn't taken that advice from his father either. It was true that he had tried, but that had only lasted a few years. Eventually, he too had succumbed to the calling and gone into the family business.

The last picture on the mantel was of the entire family at Christmas. It was older, taken three years earlier. Both children were seated in front with Dag and Gloria—now his ex-wife—standing behind them. They were all dressed in emerald green—a green sweater, blouse or shirt—anything they had that was green. It was a formal, family portrait, but by then both Dag and his wife knew it would probably be their last.

She had left him to marry someone else—a local ophthalmologist. She now lived in New York City, having moved there after remarrying. Dag was lucky to see the kids three times a year, including the major holidays of Thanksgiving and Christmas and what few vacation days he could take. He had sacrificed a lot for his job, his career. He always feared his family would be one of those sacrifices, and, unfortunately, it ended up that way.

Dag got up and poured himself a single-malt Scotch. Deciding that one jigger wasn't enough, he continued to pour a second, popping three half-moon ice cubes in the glass and swirling it around a few times to let it mellow. He went back to the couch to lay down and take a long sip.

What was left of his life? he thought. *He didn't have a family, many friends or any hobbies. Now, he didn't have much left of a career.* Policing had been his life, and at that point, that was pretty much over too. It was likely he would be chained to a desk job until he retired in another twenty-five years or so. He hated desk jobs and wasn't sure he could bear it.

Twenty-five years, he thought. *There's that number again. Will I be shuffling paperwork on another series of these gruesome murders in 2045?* He couldn't bear the thought of that either.

He took another swig of the Scotch and put the glass down on the end table without a coaster as its bedding, letting the condensation stream down the side and onto the wood finish. Soon, he dozed-off with the tumbler continuing to cry beside him and on his behalf.

The next thing he heard was his cell phone, still in its belt holder. Groggily, he rolled over to grab it before it went silent.

"This is Dag," he answered.

"Dag, it's Tommy. I need those cold case files for us to tie all this together. We're charging Sara McLaughlin with three counts of first-degree murder and one of attempted murder."

"I already know what you plan to do, Tommy," Dag said sarcastically. "I'm so glad you've spent all this time and resources arresting the wrong person."

"Come on, Dag. You and I both know she was involved, even if we don't have all the evidence we'd like to make it air-tight. But, as we both know, that doesn't really matter."

"Why's that?"

"We'll make up what we don't have."

"Now, you're going to *manufacture* evidence?" asked Dag, stunned at how far his partner was willing to stoop.

"The higher-ups want a conviction. So, you do what you gotta' do. That's something you were never willing to do and look where you are now."

"I have my conscience, Tommy. I *will* be able to live with myself. Will you?"

"No problems there, buddy. Once I move into the mayor's office, I'll give you a call and remind you of that."

"You do that."

"Just make sure you get me those case files within the hour," said Tommy, hanging up.

Dag pulled out the cold case files one more time. Rubbing his eyes, he reopened the 1995 file on Abigail Knight—the missing person's file. His eyes flew over familiar lines he'd read many times before, but this time they stopped. He went back to the middle of a paragraph he thought he'd absorbed the first five times he'd read it, but now he spotted something he'd missed.

> *... according to a witness, she saw a woman leave the apartment earlier in the day. She was asked who had come to visit the missing person that day, and she said it was her daughter and her husband.*

Dag looked at the sentence again ... *her daughter and her husband.*

Whose daughter? Whose husband? It was unclear from the sentence who she was talking about. Then, it struck Dag. The daughter and husband were not Abigail Knight's daughter and husband. They were the *witness's.*

He quickly went back to the beginning of the note. *Who was the witness?* he asked himself. Quickly, he found his answer.

Terri Campbell. Terri Turner Campbell.

So, it had been *Terri's* daughter who had gone to the victim's apartment the day of the murder.

Dag flipped back through his notes, finally coming to the page where he'd outlined the genealogy.

> Bessie (Turner) Belzikov – Mitzie's great grandmother
> Terri Turner Campbell – Bessie's daughter – Mitzie's grandmother
> Patti Campbell Wilkins – Terri's daughter – Mitzie's mother
> Mitzie Wilkins – Patti's daughter

So, it *was* Patti who was at the scene.

Dag sketched out what he thought he knew about the cases, the witnesses and how it all related.

Okay, he said to himself. *So, what I have is this.* He drew it out on a piece of paper to line up the sequence of events that he believed had happened.

1945 – Medford – victim Rosco Arthur Turner – connection with Bessie: husband.

1945 – Dorchester – victim Dumitra Prodescu – connection with Bessie: Janice. Connection with Janice: daughter.

1945 – Roxbury – victim Janice Prodescu – connection with Bessie: best friends.

1970 – Roxbury – victim Cora Rae Taylor – connection with Bessie: Janice. Connection with Janice: daughter. Possible involvement -- Terri Campbell. Connection: daughter of Bessie.

1970 – Brookline – victim Virginia Carter and son Jake. Connection – unknown.

1970 – Mission Hill – victim Danny Pittman. Connection: reporter investigating murders.

1995 – Roxbury – victim Father Jose Antonio Mercato: Connection: unknown.

1995 – Dorchester – victim Lenny Pittman and gay lover Roger. Connection: son of 1970 reporter.

1995 – Dudley Square – victim Abigail Knight. Connection: daughter of Cora Rae Taylor. Also, Sara's mother. Also, possible suspect: Patti Campbell Turner. Connection: daughter of Terri Campbell.

Jag (grandfather) possible affair with Patti Campbell.

2020 – Downtown Boston – victim Dad (Zag). Connection: unknown.

2020 – Brookline – victim Claire Horwath. Connection: client of Sara McLaughlin.

2020 – Dorchester – victim Margaret Jenkins and son Will. Connection: unknown.

2020 – Dorchester – victim Vince McLaughlin. Connection: Sara's husband. Sara knows Mitzie Wilkins.

Dag amended his notes on the 1995 Pittman entry, writing:

'... witness – Terri – cites her daughter Patti and her husband coming from dwelling.'

It had been obvious, but this put things in perspective for him. Everything pointed toward these two families: the Belzikovs and the Prodescus—and specifically, the daughters. *But what was the source of it all? What was the cause?* he thought. *Wrong place at the wrong time? Or was there something more? How could these Belzikov women have perpetrated such horrific crimes—ones that required immense strength and special cauterizing and other tools? And what was Sara's role in all of this? She wasn't a Belzikov. It was her family—the Prodescus or those related—who were being murdered.*

Dag didn't have much more information, and one of his best sources was over one hundred years old. Bessie had started to tell him something, but Patti had stopped her. He had agreed, but now he knew he needed to hear the rest—especially without Patti in the room.

***

It didn't take him long to return to the senior care facility, and when Dag asked at the desk to see Ms. Belzikov again, he was surprised when he was told she was still in the intensive care wing of the building.

Hurrying down the hallway, he pushed through the double doors to the wing and approached the nurses' station.

"I'm Detective Gallagher," said Dag, showing the nurse his badge. "I need to have a word with Ms. Belzikov."

"I'm afraid she's not able to see visitors at this time, detective," said the young woman, holding a computer pad and scribbling down some notes.

Dag read the upside-down screen the nurse was holding, making out Bessie's name and the diagnosis—*cerebral hemorrhage.* Dag's spirits fell. He saw her as his last chance to tie all the pieces together, and now they might be beyond his grasp, lying in the other room, unlikely ever to be retrieved.

The nurse looked back up at him, wondering why he was still standing there.

"Can I just stop by her room? I won't go in," he said.

"No, I'm afraid not," she said firmly.

Dag walked slowly back toward the double doors but waited until the nurse left the station. He had seen Bessie's new room number on the chart. She had been moved to another one which he had read upside down on the tablet: Room 43. He redirected his approach down another hallway, avoiding the gurneys and pill trolleys along the way before finally reaching Room 43.

Dag peered inside. There, Bessie was resting, her eyes closed and a breathing tube taped just below her nose giving her oxygen. But somehow she sensed someone was there, and she turned her head to look at him, her piercing blue eyes wishing to be heard one more time.

"Um, it must be ..." Bessie mumbled, her lips barely moving.

Dag glance both ways down the hallway, and seeing no one there, walked in.

He went to her bedside and smiled at her. "Ms. Belzikov. I'm so sorry to disturb you at this time. But I was just wondering if there was something else you wanted to tell me? We were a bit hurried last time, and I wasn't sure whether you'd shared everything with me."

"No," she answered in a low, gravelly voice. Dag's heart sank. She was his last hope. "There's more," she added. "There's much more."

"What is it, then?" asked Dag anxiously.

Bessie took a couple deep breaths. Then, she said, "There's so much that I just don't know where to start."

She was struggling to breathe, and each breath was a heavy exertion for her.

"How about the beginning," Dag asked with a smile.

Bessie smiled back. "You're a good man, detective. Deep down, so were your father, your grandfather, and even your great grandfather. We all have our flaws, you know."

"Thank you. They all tried; I'm sure."

"Well, Janice Prodescu and I were once friends. Like I told you before, she had talent. I ..." Bessie's voice weakened, and she stopped. Dag waited patiently, not interrupting. "... I married Rosco Arthur—an old high school flame. I thought Janice was jealous of me and my husband. I always thought that."

"I don't know," he answered, trying not to offend her.

"That's good enough for me," she answered. "But there's one more thing. It's my daughter and granddaughter."

"Terri and Patti?" Dag asked.

"Yes. Patti always did have a thing for you Gallaghers," said Bessie, curling her lips into a slight smile.

Dag was quiet for a moment. Then, he asked, "Gallaghers. Plural?"

"Yes," said Bessie. "But the rest is for you to find out. You're the detective, after all."

"Yes."

"And, as far as I can see, you're a damned good one. But there is one thing you won't easily find out on your own, so I will share that with you."

When Bessie had finished, Dag had to take a moment. It was more than he could absorb. It changed everything, yet nothing.

"So, if that's all, I'd like to rest," said Bessie, closing her eyes again.

Dag could tell she was tired from talking, and he got up to leave. "Ms. Belzikov, they say you had a stroke. Is that right?"

Once more, she made an effort to smile. "If you want to call it that. I would call it something else."

"What?"

"You wouldn't understand, detective. I believe it's payback for what I've done in my life."

"I don't believe that."

"You may believe as you wish," she answered.

"Well, I'll check back with you later this week," he said as he was leaving the room.

She raised her hand as if to stop him. "You and I both know that won't happen. I won't be here. But I appreciate the thought."

Dag left. There was an emptiness in his heart that he couldn't explain. He felt bad for Bessie, even though he'd known her for only a short time.

***

An hour after Dag left the room, Bessie received another visitor—her granddaughter, Patti.

"Hi grandma. How are you feeling today?" Patti asked, coming over to the bedside.

"As if you're concerned."

"Of course, I am, grandma."

"I know what you did, Patti. I saw you with the book—my old book. I saw you mouth the words."

Patti smiled. "Grandma, grandma. I think the stroke must have affected your brain and your memory. We need to get you some medication for that. You're just not thinking straight."

Bessie smiled. Patti was always trying to divert blame, even though she never denied her involvement in satanic practices.

"We both know what caused it, dear. My memory is perfectly fine. Don't act like you had nothing to do with it. It was a conjuring I've used before. You can't fool me."

"Has anyone else been here to see you?" asked Patti, ignoring the comment. "Has Mitzie come by?"

"No. I haven't seen her—not since the summer. She doesn't call or stop by. I haven't seen Terri, either. Why is that Patti?"

"I dunno, grandma. I guess they're both just busy."

"Well, tell them I'm in the hospital. Tell them I want to see them, okay?"

"Sure grandma."

"Oh, by the way, there *was* someone who came in to see me—that Detective Gallagher fellow."

"He did?" asked Patti, now more serious than before. "And what did he want?"

"He asked me some more questions, that's all."

"And what did you tell him?"

"I told him, Patti. I told him," said Bessie.

Patti looked seriously at her grandmother. "You did, did you?"

"Yes, dear. I told him about our secret ... our family secret."

"Did you tell him about Mom and Tag?"

"No."

"She should have killed him when she had the chance," said Patti. "And what about me? Did you say anything about me and his father and grandfather?"

Bessie shook her head. "It would do no good to tell him those things."

"You're right, grandma," Patti said, breathing out slowly. "Jag was another one who escaped our wrath."

"You must let it go, child," said Bessie. "You must let go of the family's rage and anger. I have, and so has your mother."

Patti smiled at her grandma, stroking her hair as if to comfort her.

"Yes, you both have, grandma. But everything will be all right," said Patti. "It will. I'll get through this just as I have everything else with our family. I've had challenges like this before. You've been the matriarch of our family for a long time, you know. Almost one hundred and one years! Think of that! How many people live to be that old? Not many, I imagine." Patti continued to stroke her grandmother's thin gray hair. "It's too bad you're not going to see that birthday, though" Patti said calmly. "There's just too much at stake—for all of us."

"What do you mean?" Bessie's eyes grew wide.

But before Bessie could reach the call button, Patti took the pillow from under her head and viciously pushed the pillow down on her grandmother's face. The centenarian struggled with what strength she had left, but it wasn't nearly enough. She fought her granddaughter, scratching at her with her fingers, but soon, her thrashing stopped. Pulling off the pillow, Patti lifted her grandmother's limp head and replaced the pillow.

"There now, grandmother. Isn't that better?" Patti continued to stroke her gray hair with her fingers.

Bessie was peaceful and still—perhaps the first time she had been at peace in a very long time.

***

Downstairs in the visitors' area of the nursing home, Dag sat at a small desk to collect his thoughts and get them down in writing before he left the building. Finishing his notes, he got up to leave after switching off his computer. Yet before the computer screen went dark, something flashed across the screen. They were words written by an unknown source.

The first line read: *Goodbye, Detective Gallagher.* This was followed by a second line which added three more words: *... and good luck.* It was strange. But Dag only shrugged. He didn't know what had happened only a few hundred feet away in a critical care unit where Bessie lay in her bed growing ever colder.

She was dead—never to see her one hundred and first birthday.

*****

CH 59 – Legal Defense

2020

Sara sat in a four-by-six-foot cell. The metal bench was hard and cold. She felt like the criminal others were saying she was, but then again, she felt like the widow she was too. Her attorney, Morrie, and his associate had been hauled down to the station for questioning in connection with Vince's murder too. Tommy had interrogated them separately for nearly two hours before Morrie stood up in his session.

"I am walking out of here," he said resolutely. "Unless you are arresting me for the murder of Vincent McLaughlin, I'm not going to sit here and answer any more of your stupid questions. You and I both know I had nothing to do with the murder. So, are you arresting me?"

Morrie got up and left the room as Tommy shuffled his papers, knowing he had nothing more to cover. After collecting Mike, Morrie went to the chief's office and found him inside wrapping up a call.

"Chief Malloy! It's good to see you again," said Morrie going in and shaking the chief's hand as he hung up his line. It was highly unusual for someone like Morrie to get so far into the building and be able to walk in on the chief. However, he knew the chief well, having worked as defense counsel on shared cases with him before he became chief.

"Morrie, how are you?" asked Malloy, getting up from his desk and extending his hand.

"Been better, but hey, what can I expect when I have to deal with some of your greener detectives." He laughed. "But that's all right, they'll get the hang of things soon enough, I suppose."

"So, I take it you're here to discuss a case with one of my detectives?" asked the chief, now puzzled.

"Sara McLaughlin. She's my client."

Malloy's expression changed instantly. "Oh," he said, sitting down. "I'm sorry to hear that."

"Sorry because you're afraid of my defense?" Morrie said it light-heartedly so not to raise the chief's ire.

"No. You're a good lawyer, Morrie. I've always thought that," said Malloy.

"But the reason I stopped in is that I'm not getting much help from Detective Walcott. I have a right to see my client, as you know. Is there any way I can find out where she's being held? You know me; when I want something, I usually go right to the top." Morrie laughed again, and this time, Malloy smiled.

"Sure," said the chief, "I'll find out and take you there myself."

It wasn't long before the chief and another officer had located Sara's cell.

"There you go, Morrie," said Malloy, turning to leave. "It was good seeing you."

"Thanks Chief. I appreciate the help," the attorney answered.

"Morrie. Thank God you came!" Sara exclaimed as she heard his voice and saw him come through the door.

Morrie had known her mother and her grandmother and had helped both through similar instances with the police. He was still practicing after over forty years after graduating from Harvard law school. A short man—only five feet, six inches tall—he was still a man of great stature. With a full head of gray hair that he kept meticulously trimmed and combed in place, he had penetrating brown eyes and a nose like a Bloodhound's for sniffing out a falsehood. A bit puffy around the eyes and sporting multiple chins, he looked like he had enjoyed the finer things in life and had so for several years. His nose was narrow and pointed with fine, red, spider lines running through it, suggesting that he liked an occasional bottle of Bordeaux or perhaps a brandy. Over the years, he had accumulated his many wrinkles and other battle scars in the performance of his juridical duties. On his neck he had a scar where a client had attacked him with a ballpoint pen after he lost the case for him. But for Morrie, law was a passion, and his clients his wards.

Morrie sat down with his client to go over the charges brought against her. He pulled out his reading glasses and balanced them on the end of his nose. Then, he opened the folder he'd been given and reviewed the papers inside. After several minutes, he closed them and took off his glasses, folding them and putting them back in his jacket pocket.

"It looks like they are accusing you of attempted murder and murder in the first degree on several counts, Sara. Pretty serious stuff. Did you know the victims? Let's see ... uh ..." He opened the folder again and fumbled around for a name before finding one in the papers, "... uh ... yes, uh, Margaret and William Jenkins and the attempted murder of Claire Horwath."

"Yes, apparently I've been quite busy killing or trying to kill people according to the police detective," Sara said sarcastically.

"I see you didn't have enough time with Claire Horwath, apparently, as she was only severely injured. So, you're quite right, young lady, you have been busy," said Morrie, but not laughing. "So, why don't you tell me what really happened. Or, if you prefer, just tell me what I need to know to prepare a robust defense."

"I may need a robust defense, Morrie, but it's not because I'm guilty. It's because I overheard outside in the hallway that the mayor is running for governor and he wants those cases wrapped up as soon as possible. He needs a conviction so he comes away looking like a hero instead of the mayor who couldn't catch a terrible, vicious, serial killer like me. He's willing to throw just anyone under the bus to save his own skin."

"I assume that would include the district attorney. He's always been a sycophant of the mayor's."

"I don't know, but he's got a new recruit—a young detective who's clearly ambitious."

"Tommy Walcott," said Morrie, interrupting.

"Yes. That's him. He's a guy I don't trust at all. He's in it for himself and doesn't seem to care about finding the real killer or killers."

"Okay, Sara, so tell me your side of the story."

"Before we do that, I need you to take care of things with ..." she broke down.

"With Vince?"

She nodded, letting the tears roll down her cheeks.

"I got a call from him late last night. I left in the afternoon to take LJ to her grandmother's in Pennsylvania. He called me early in the morning and left a message on my cell. I don't have it with me to show you, but it sounded like he was being attacked. It was really horrible."

"And you have that on your cell phone?"

"Yes, but the police have that," she said. "Oh, and one more thing, Morrie. Would you mind calling my mother-in-law, Lilly? I want to be sure LJ and she are okay."

Morrie nodded. "What do you want me to say to her?"

"Just tell her I was speeding and brought into the police precinct. That's the truth—at least part of it. Don't tell her about her son right now. I think it would be too much for her, and I don't want LJ to know right now either. It's been a really hard time."

"Will do. Now, tell me what you know."

Sara spent the next hour telling Morrie all she knew about the incidents, her relationships with each of the victims and where she was on the nights they were attacked. Morrie used his cell to record her words so someone in his office could type them for him.

Once Sara finished, Morrie leaned back and put his hands behind his head, thinking. The look on his face was blank--expressionless.

"That's quite a story, Sara," he finally said. "Now I understand why you thought you would need a robust defense."

"What are my chances, Morrie? What do you think?"

Morrie sat and pondered that for a second, putting his fist to his chin.

"I won't lie to you. I think we have an uphill battle. But there are a lot of things in your favor. For instance, I don't know how you, physically, had the muscle to do what they said you did to those victims."

"Perhaps they'll say I had help," she answered.

"They do state that in the allegations. They claim your driver helped you. But still, it would take a lot of brawn to pull off those crimes. The other thing is the problem with the blood. They didn't find any spattering anywhere other than the words written above the bedframes. Yet, the police reports state that the bodies were drained. Did you take a few pots with you on those nights or did you get them from the kitchen?"

Sara shook her head, unamused with his culinary reference.

"Well, we have several things we have to look into," said Morrie. "Let me kick things into gear. I'll get back to you, first thing tomorrow with my thoughts."

*****

CH 60 – Visit to the Prison

2020

Sara sat in her cell. The darkness in her life seemed to be all around and closing in on her—suffocating her with its gloom. When she tried to sleep, she had terrible dreams, but it didn't end there. When she was awake, she either had more frightening visions or was anxious about having another one. By the third day in jail, the haunts and terrors of previous medium sessions began to flood back into her thoughts. She believed she was going mad—no, she *knew* she was. It was as if a terrible virus had invaded her body and her brain and was slowly taking over. She was losing control, no longer able to know what was right, what was real, what was true, or just what was.

It was on the fourth day that Sara received a visitor.

"Hello, Sara," said Claire Horwath, coming up to the glass window.

It was the area where prisoners and those held for trial could talk with people from the outside world. The two women weren't forced to use a phone to talk, but it was still unnerving having to communicate through a thick, glass partition with a round, metal "vent" into which to speak.

Sara sat down, embarrassed to be seen in the bright orange jumpsuit she'd been given.

"Hi, Claire," Sara said in somber tones. "Thanks for coming to see me." She looked stressed and gaunt. Dark circles under her eyes revealed the fact she hadn't slept since she'd been locked up.

"How are you doing?" asked Claire, sympathetically.

Sara was tried to smile, but it was futile. She couldn't pull it off, so she didn't try. Instead, she shrugged.

"I brought you something," said Claire, reaching into her purse. She pulled out a small box. "I know I can't give this to you directly, but I'll give it to the guard."

"Okay," said Sara, both curious and confused.

Claire handed the box to the guard, who looked at it suspiciously. He took it to the back to have it examined, analyzed, and X-rayed.

"So, how have *you* been?" asked Sara. "It looks like you've recovered."

"Yes. Within the last few days, I've healed very fast. At least that's what the doctors tell me. They're kind of amazed, actually. I had two cracked ribs, a broken wrist, and a concussion," said Claire, holding up her casted hand. "But all in all, I'm lucky to be alive."

"Yeah, I think you're right, Claire."

"I've had this feeling ever since our session that my former boyfriend truly is my guardian angel," Claire said with a hopeful, but forlorn, look in her face. "He is looking out for me. He's taking care of me—protecting me. It was a special relationship that we had. It just felt right from the moment we met. Do you know what I mean?"

Sara thought back about the time she and Vince had first met. It had been over fifteen years earlier. They had attended the same church, the Cathedral of the Holy Cross in Boston. She had just graduated from high school and thought she would return to the church where her aunt had taken her as a child. It was a large church with a sizeable congregation. At first it was nice going back to a familiar church, but when she became involved in the young adult's group, it got even better. There, she met Vince.

Sara had been struck by Vince's sensitivity and warmth. He cared about others—not just himself. He was also very dedicated to the faith. Like her, he had grown up in a strong catholic household and had gone to church every Sunday as a child—come rain, snow, or shine. They had married not long after starting to date, and soon came little LJ, the darling of their lives.

It was a lot to take in, but Sara finally acknowledged Claire's reflection. "Yes," Sara answered, "I do know what you mean. I felt the same way about my Vince." Her face then turned melancholy.

"You don't look like you feel well?" Claire asked.

Sara reached behind her neck and rubbed it with her hand.

"I can't complain," she answered.

Claire looked at her curiously as Sara removed her hand.

"What's that on the side of your neck?" Claire asked.

"What?"

"Right there, where your hand was," said Claire. "Turn around and let me see. Pull your hair back."

Sara did as Claire asked, turning around and exposing the back of her neck.

Claire gasped.

"What is it?" Sara asked.

"Oh, God!" Claire said, putting her hand over her mouth. "You've got the same marks I had—those red marks that look like swollen, bug bites. You have the same ones."

"Can't be," Sara said. She swiveled to face the female guard who had been standing against the wall behind her. "Do you have a mirror or something?" she asked the guard, but the guard only ignored her.

"Sara, look over this way," said Claire. "Maybe I can show you through my compact."

Claire positioned her makeup mirror so Sara could see the reddish, irritated spots on her neck—the ones she had been rubbing unconsciously for days.

"It's probably just because I've been touching it for the past several days. It's been bothering me."

"What does it feel like?"

"It's hard to describe."

"Coarse, itchy, bothersome, annoying—like a mosquito bite you can't stop scratching?"

"That's it, yeah," Sara replied, surprised at Claire's answer. "It's like a mosquito bite that just won't leave me alone—just like that."

"And it won't. Trust me. I rubbed mine until it started bleeding. You told me to watch out for them, especially if they were on my right hand or side. They would have made it there if I hadn't done something."

"What did you do?" Sara asked, worriedly.

"I went to see my priest. He rubbed them with blessed, sacrament oil. I'm fine now. The marks are gone."

"So, you think they're the marks of the beast?"

"I don't know, Sara. That's an area you're more familiar with than I am."

"Well, what did the priest tell you?"

Claire hesitated, but when she saw the fear in Sara's eyes, she relented.

"He told me that he'd see those marks before—particularly during an exorcism he had performed a few years ago. He said the victim was wracked by demons, and they had to strap him to a chair to perform it. When the priest put holy water on him, those marks appeared on his chest and arms. They looked like claw marks, but they were deeper and a bloody red."

"What happened to the man?" asked Sara.

Claire grew quiet.

"Claire, what happened?"

"He died," she said, looking down. "The priest tried to release the beast from within him, but ... you know sometimes, I guess, it doesn't always work. Sometimes people are so entwined with the demon that they can't be separated. At least that's what my priest told me. He said they tried to expel the beast. But the demon was too strong, and it killed him."

Sara sat quietly. She had heard of difficult exorcisms, but none that had resulted in the death of the person possessed.

"You should have a priest help you with those marks," said Claire, suddenly uncomfortable in her chair.

"I'm afraid the only way I'm going to see a priest in here is if I'm awaiting my execution," said Sara. "The way things look, it won't be long." At this point, Sara saw she was dragging down the conversation, so she changed subjects. "Well, I'm glad *you're* feeling better, Claire.

"Thanks," said Claire. "I am feeling better. But there is one thing I want to tell you."

"What's that, Claire?"

"Last night, I had a dream. In it, I saw you sitting under a big oak tree in the middle of Boston Commons—you know, the large park downtown."

Sara nodded.

"Anyway, it was the dead of winter, and there was snow all around. You were just sitting there, while snow piled up all around you—until you were almost completely buried in it. Then, an elderly woman rolled past in a hospital bed. She was in bad shape and had an air tube running to her nose."

"That's strange," asked Sara. "Was it anyone you know?"

"No, I'd never seen her before. She had short, gray hair and lots of wrinkles—like she was at least ninety or even a hundred."

"What did she do?"

"She gave me a box like the one I just gave you," said Claire.

It was then that the guard brought Claire's small box to Sara, setting it next to her on the counter. It had been unwrapped, but the lid had been put back in place. Sara picked up the box and looked at it, unsure what to do next. It was square and white with a red ribbon dangling from the side.

"The woman in my dream gave me the box and said, 'Let this protect you against ill winds and dark spirits—for there are many.' At that point, the snow stopped, and the temperature grew warmer. I could see the clouds parting overhead and the sun struggling to break through. When I looked back where the woman had been, she was gone."

"What was inside the box?" asked Sara, holding hers.

"I don't know. At that point, the dream ended."

"So, you never opened your box to see what was inside?"

"No," Claire said, pausing. "Sara, there are some things that I didn't share with you when you did my session."

"We talked to your mother and your boyfriend. Isn't that right?"

"Yes, and it's about my boyfriend. I'm not sure this makes any difference, but it's something you should know now that they've arrested you. It might help your case."

"What's that?"

"My boyfriend—the one you spoke to during the session?"

"Yes."

"He was Zell Gallagher, chief of police. He went by the nickname Zag. He was having an affair with me. As you know, he was murdered earlier this year in the most brutal way. I don't know if there is any connection, but for what it's worth, I thought I should tell you."

Claire got up to leave, but as she did so, she said, "Sara, you gave me some things that mean more to me than anything I can think of—fond memories of my closeness to Zell and knowing he's okay."

Claire walked out of the room, letting the guard close the gate quietly behind her.

Sara looked down at the small, white box. She pressed her fingernails under the lid and pried it off, setting it to the side. A thin layer of fluffy cotton covered whatever was beneath, and she lifted that off as well. Seeing the gift, she smiled. It was *exactly* what she needed, and something she would keep close to her the rest of her life.

*****

CH 61 – Driver's Interrogation

2020

The old city government building was dingy and drafty. Its high ceilings made it nearly impossible to keep it uniformly heated during the winter and cooled during the summer, so every room always seemed either too hot or too cold. The pale green walls had recently been repainted with a fresh coat of the same drab shade, but with the dim, florescent lights flickering overhead, they still looked old and dated.

Tommy walked down the hall and pushed through the door marked *District Attorney* which also had *Richard J. Johnson* in smaller print right below. He knew this was not going to be the congratulatory meeting he had originally expected after he had arrested Sara McLaughlin. That bubble had burst shortly thereafter.

After he had driven Sara from Troy, Pennsylvania to the Boston PD building, Tommy had received a call from Johnson demanding to be filled in on his case against her. Tommy told him all the particulars believing he would be praised for his decisive action. Instead, Johnson berated him for the weak case he had.

"But I thought that's what you wanted us to do," he told the DA. "I thought you *wanted* us to arrest her."

"Yeah, but with a solid case of evidence! I thought you had a stronger case against her than this," said Johnson, the ire in his voice escalating. "You have to come up with something more; otherwise, you're—*we're*—really *fucked*! Do you understand me!"

"What do you mean—do something more?" Tommy asked.

"I'm not going to spell it out for you, son. Your career is on the line. You need a stronger case than this one if you want me to win this in court. And I'm telling you right now, I'm not even taking it to court with what you have—not with the election coming up. This is a *capital* offense we're trying here! We have to have our ducks in a row!"

Tommy was confused. Young and ambitious, he had yet to understand fully how those in positions of power had perfected the art of manipulation and mastered the ability to accept no responsibility. What he was learning the hard way was that those types of people got someone else to do their dirty work without being tainted. Innocent people like Tommy were used as expendable firewood just to keep the engines burning and wheels churning on the city's machine. It was a jungle. It was ruthless. And it had its own rule book for survival.

"Okay, sir. Can you give me some direction?"

"Walcott, grow up. You live in the big leagues now. There's no one out there to protect you. You have to do what you have to do if you want to get ahead in this world. Boston's a big city with big-time players, and that's the way they play the game here. Either you pitch a no-hitter and get a big contract or you strikeout and are benched forever. Which do you want?"

Tommy understood what the DA *was* saying, but he didn't grasp what the DA was *not* saying. He would have to find a way to skirt the system and, perhaps, do things illegally without getting caught. No one would be defending him. There would be no paper trail of approvals.

If he succeeded, he wouldn't get the glory, but he wouldn't be benched either. If he failed, he'd be blamed and fired, if not prosecuted. It would work that way until he rose to the summit of the mountain. Then, he would be the one making others choose whether they wanted to risk everything on the climb toward power, money and fame.

"Got it, sir," said Tommy, following the message.

Tommy hurried back to the precinct and went over the case again. The most glaring weakness in his case was just as Morrie had pointed out to Sara—the muscle required to commit the murders. The actions taken against the bodies of the victims were almost superhuman. It would be hard to convince a jury that someone as small and petite as Sara could have accomplished that—even with the help of her driver, Marvin. And then there were the alibis. Sara had said she'd been nowhere near the scene of the crimes when they had occurred. Indeed, she'd been with her husband, in bed, in the middle of the night. Her husband, Vince, had corroborated that fact.

But wait, he thought. *Vince was dead now. He wasn't around to testify on behalf of her as to where she was on those nights.*

He pulled out his lighter and flipped the thumbwheel to set it ablaze. The flame fired up long and clean. He tore the pages out of his pad related to the questioning of Vince and watched as the flame caught the papers' edges, engulfing the entire bunch. Tommy quickly dropped the ball of fire into his metal trash can, throwing a full glass of water over it to extinguish the flame before it set off the fire alarms overhead.

He looked at the black molten mass at the bottom of his trash can. There was no pang of guilt—nothing that brought him to his knees. No thunderbolts erupted from the sky and struck him down. *Yeah, what he'd done was wrong, but so what*, he thought. *I'm sure this stuff happens all the time. What's another corrupted court case? I'll be done with this, get what I want, and then never have to do it again.*

Yet, he'd fallen off a cliff and just not realized it—yet. The cliffs would continue to come, and in the future they would only grow increasingly taller.

Some words from Dag now came back to him, ringing in his ears.

> *"So, I guess I had you pegged wrong, Tommy. I thought you were better than that. I realize that others sometimes get ahead by shafting the other guy. The question I have for you is whether you can live with yourself when you make those kinds of decisions? When you're a hundred and on your deathbed, will you look back and smile, counting all the people you fucked over to get what you   wanted   in   life.*
> *...*
> *Is it worth selling your soul to the Devil? Will that bring you lasting happiness? ... Maybe for you, it will, Tommy, but not for me. It's not the way I want to live my life. But hey, it's your life, not mine."*

Tommy shrugged it off or at least tried to.

Dag doesn't know what the hell he is talking about, he thought. *He's an old guy, and anyway, what has he accomplished in his life? He's a loser. I'm not going to end up like that.*

Yet even though Tommy had an uneasy feeling inside him, he bit his lip and pressed on. He looked through the rest of his notes, Finally, stumbling on another entry ....

> *After the session concluded, she retrieved her hat from Marvin, her driver, and waited by the curb while he got the car. It had*

been cold that night, and Marvin had gone to get the car. He had pulled up, gotten out and opened the car door for her.

"Marvin has been good to me. He always has been." "He'd do anything for me." Quotes. "Why once I called him at 2 in the morning to take me to the airport. It was an emergency and I had to catch a flight out. He was there right on time and got me to the airport for my flight. That's just the way he is."

He'd do anything for me, thought Tommy. That was a pretty strong statement.

I think I need to give Mr. Marvin a quick call. Like the DA said, there are things you have to do to move ahead, and this is one of them, he thought, rationalizing what he was doing.

Tommy spent the next three hours researching the department's files on Marvin Fletcher. And just as he'd hoped, there was a bonanza of information to be found. Not only had Mr. Fletcher been involved in a juvenile case when he was seventeen, but it was a case where he was accused of raping his sixteen-year-old girlfriend. As a juvi, he was sent to a detention center where he spent a year in confinement until he was eighteen, when he was released. It was not on his official record, but there was enough there to connect the dots. He was also arrested later for embezzlement from an employer, two DUIs, and the forging of a check.

Tommy found the address and rounded up a police squad car to accompany him to Marvin's house which wasn't far from the precinct. Tommy had told the officers that this was a potentially dangerous suspect—wanted for multiple murders. He didn't have to tell them twice, and they drew their 9mm pistols as they approached the house. Another squad car pulled around back to cut off any escape route.

"Police!" the detective announced after going up the two wooden steps to the porch and pounding on the front door. "We have a warrant for the arrest of Mr. Fletcher." There was a rustling noise inside. "Police! open up!" Tommy yelled again.

He heard the back door open and slam closed, so he jumped off the porch and ran to the side of the house where he spotted a stout, young man in a T-shirt and jeans trying to sprint down the alleyway. At that moment, the squad car blocked the way, and an officer leaped out, drawing his gun. Tommy pulled his pistol as he came down the narrow walkway between the neighboring houses and entered the alleyway.

"Police! Don't move!" Tommy yelled, assuming the Weaver-style firing position.

The young man didn't twitch. He held up his hands, not wanting them to think he was reaching for anything. The police officer came up behind him and pushed him to the ground, grabbing his arms and cuffing his wrists behind his back. They frisked him on the ground to see if he were armed, but they found nothing.

"What's your name?" asked one of the officers.

"Jerel, sir."

"Jerel what?" asked Tommy, putting his gun back in his holster.

"Jerel Fletcher, sir."

The police searched Jerel and found two ounces of marijuana on him.

"Where's Marvin Fletcher?" Tommy asked.

"That's my dad."

"Where is he?"

"I dunno."

They took Jerel down to the station where he was thrown into one of the tiny, Spartan rooms for questioning. Tommy walked in and sat across the table from him.

"Jerel, you know you're in trouble, right? Possession, evading an officer, and all that. Those will put you back in the slammer for a while. Is that what you want?"

"No, sir."

"Then, give me your dad's cell number. Perhaps we can work something out if you can get him to come in."

"What's he done?" asked Jerel.

"That's police business. Just give me his number."

A few moments later, Tommy dialed.

"Marvin Fletcher?"

"Yes, who's this?"

"This is Detective Walcott with Boston PD. We've got your son down here at the station. I suggest you come down now."

It took over an hour, but Marvin arrived at the station and was immediately ushered into a separate interrogation room.

"Where's my son?" Marvin asked.

"He's in another room being questioned by detectives," said Tommy.

"About what?"

"Murder," said Tommy, lying.

"What! He didn't murder anybody!" exclaimed Marvin.

"How would you know that? Are you home all the time to watch him? Apparently not, since you weren't home when we stopped by today."

"No, but I know my son. He wouldn't hurt anybody."

"Then what about you, Marvin. Who did you murder?"

Tommy threw a thick folder of papers down on the plain, metal table. Marvin didn't know it, but none of the papers had anything to do with him. Still, the effect was the same.

"We've got a lot of evidence against you Marvin, my friend. And, from your perspective, it doesn't look good."

"I didn't do nothin'" Marvin mumbled, trying to be as uncooperative as possible.

"Three murders there, Marvin!" Tommy shouted, taking stabbing jabs at the stack with his finger. "I think you're looking at the death penalty for at least one, if not two, of them, Bud. Doesn't look good at all. If you're lucky they'll give you lethal injection, and you won't feel a thing. At worst, they'll give you the electric chair—you know, where they hook up them electrodes to your shaved head and send a bunch of electricity through them. Your brain fries, just like we put it inside a deep fryer and cook it a while. Kind of like a Thanksgiving turkey, you might say. It comes out nice and crispy!"

Marvin didn't react at all, as if he'd been through the drill before.

"Tell you what, Marvin. You tell us everything you know, and we'll try to get you a reduced sentence ... say, life without parole. I can't promise anything, but I'll do what I can. Do you understand me?"

Marvin stared at Tommy, unsure what to make of him.

"You're the driver for Sara McLaughlin, right?"

"Yeah," he answered, awkwardly.

Tommy could tell Marvin's hands were shaking a bit—now more nervously after knowing the unpleasant options he was facing.

Growing up, his single mom had three younger kids to care for, and he was left to fend for himself. Before the incidents when he was seventeen, his record had been clean. He hadn't even gotten a traffic ticket until then. In that year, he'd been pulled over for speeding and busted for a bag of marijuana in the glovebox, a misdemeanor. But it was the ugly break-up with his girlfriend and her calling the cops on him that got him in real hot water. The arrest had forced him to drop out of high school.

He'd gotten a few jobs after that—mainly in retail, helping unload boxes from delivery trucks and restocking shelves. At twenty-one, he'd decided to go back and get his GED. It took another two years, but he had saved enough and scored well enough on the standard aptitude tests to get some scholarship money to attend the local community college. There, he spent his first year in general studies. But the schoolwork and his evenings working at a local restaurant took its toll. He wasn't able to keep his grades up, and eventually he dropped out.

Years passed, and he had been in and out of jail. But something clicked one day, and he decided to turn his life around. That was when his brother, Ramsey, was shot and killed by another gang member in the neighborhood. That's when he ran into Sara.

They were both waiting at the Department of Motor Vehicles when they struck up a conversation. Sara was there renewing her license plates, while Marvin was applying to get his chauffer's license and earn a living driving. By coincidence, they discovered that Marvin's father, Dwayne, had driven for Sara's mother, Abby, and a brother-in-law, Moseby Wright, had driven for her grandmother, Cora Rae. *Small world*, Sara had thought at the time.

Within two weeks, Marvin was working for Sara helping her in her business by driving her to meetings and, more importantly, being her bodyguard in case of trouble.

"What kinds of things do you do for Ms. McLaughlin, besides driving?" asked Tommy.

"I drive. I sit. I wait. That's it. That's what I do," said Marvin, curtly.

"Do you murder people?"

'What?"

"Do you murder people for your employer?"

"What kind of question is that?" asked Marvin. "I'm askin' for a lawyer. I have a right to a lawyer."

"So, when you go with Ms. McLaughlin to these sessions with her clients, do you stay outside and wait in the car?" asked Tommy, ignoring his request.

"I said, I want a lawyer," Marvin said again.

"If we go there, I'll have to read you your rights and arrest you, Marvin. Is that what you want me to do?"

Marvin shook his head.

"I didn't think so; otherwise, my questioning may have to get really ugly if you know what I mean."

"Are you threatenin' me?"

Tommy pointed to the camera in the corner of the room and the two-way mirror behind him.

"That camera is turned off. I turned if off myself. And there's no one in the other room watching. So, there won't be any evidence of what I might do to you because I use soft, rubber which doesn't leave a mark but hurts like hell. My superiors just said, 'Do what you need to … just don't leave any marks.'"

Marvin began sweating. "Sometimes," he said finally.

"Sometimes you do extra things. Not always?"

"No," said Marvin, "not always."

"Sometimes, then, you go in with her—inside the house?"

"Yeah."

"Why would you do that?"

"She told me she'd been threatened by a client a few years ago. That's why she hired me—to protect her, man."

"Do you carry a gun?"

333

"No."

"So, what do you do when you're inside the houses of her clients while she's doing her thing. Do you burglarize the place while the owner's tied up with your employer?"

"What? Are you kiddin' me? I'm not sayin' anythin' else until I get my lawyer," said Marvin.

"If you do, I'll have to arrest you here and now on first degree murder charges. Is that what you want?" Tommy asked, trying to scare him.

"Why?"

"Because," said Tommy, violating multiple codes in the law books, "getting a lawyer will make you look guilty. If you just answer my questions, then I'll think you're innocent, and we can get past this and get the real person who killed these people. Do you understand?"

"But I know my rights, and I know I have the right to a lawyer," asked Marvin. "I know my rights, man."

"You just need to answer my questions, and then we can all be on our way. Understand?" said Tommy, playing with his words.

"So, you're tellin' me I can't have a lawyer?"

"Of course not, Marvin. I'm only trying to do what I think is best for you, even though you don't know it right now. You're too wrapped up in everything to see it. You've got to trust me, Marvin."

Marvin sat motionless and waited for the next barrage of questions to hit him.

"Tell me where you were on the night of March 15 this year."

"What day of the week was that?"

"Uh, let's see ... a Monday," answered Tommy.

"I was alone in my apartment watchin' football on TV, probably. I always do that on a Monday night."

"Was anyone around who can corroborate your story then?"

"No, I was alone at home."

"You didn't call anyone, and no one called you?"

"Not that I remember."

Tommy smiled slightly. "So, it is possible that you *were* at the home of Claire Horwath in Brookline and that you did enter the building to burglarize and then try to murder her. Is that night?"

"What? No, man! I wasn't there. I swear!"

"But you don't have any alibi for that, do you?"

"I told you. I was at home watchin' football. I wasn't there."

"Did Ms. McLaughlin put you up to it? What was she after—money, jewelry, what?" taunted Tommy.

"I'm not sayin' nothin' now," said Marvin. "You're goin' down the wrong track on this one, man."

"I don't think so, Marvin. In fact, I think you and your employer do this on a regular basis. You two go to her clients' houses; she gives them some phony séance; and while she's doin' that, you scout their places for valuables to steal. Then, you both go back and rob them later that night. Isn't that how it works? Isn't that the scam?"

"No!"

"The problem is that you got caught a few times. Wasn't that it? The people were at home in bed, and they heard you. They came out to see what was going on, and you killed them, right?"

"No! I'm not sayin' nothin', but you got it wrong, man."

"Marvin," said Tommy moving closer, to within inches of his face. "Like I told you earlier. You could fry for this. Don't you get that?"

Marvin sat in his chair, unmoving.

"We execute people who do things like this. In fact, we execute people for a whole lot less than this."

Marvin blinked stiffly as little beads of sweat began forming on his forehead.

"Let me describe how you'll die, Marvin. They'll take you and put you in a hospital gown, so they don't have to do it later after your body is blue and stiff. They'll strap you down onto a gurney tying both wrists to the metal bars on either side and then binding your ankles to the braces at the bottom. Then, they'll roll you down a cold, dim hallway with dingy white tiles to a small, square room. In there

335

will be a man preparing syringes with the chemicals that will kill you."

Marvin's eyes stared at Tommy, both out of contempt and fear.

"The man won't even look at you as they wheel you in. He won't really care who he kills. That's his job, and he can do it legally. But he'll wait until the others leave and lock the door behind them. There will be a large window in the front of the room so the witnesses sitting outside can watch you as you die.

"The man will pick up the first syringe and insert the needle into a little, glass vial. Then, he'll pull back the plunger, drawing in the sedative that will be the last thing you will ever remember in your miserable life. All those memories of your happy childhood, the birthday parties, the dances, the times drinking and smoking with your friends out at night—all those things will soon be erased forever. The man will then grab another vial from the stainless-steel tray next to him. This vial holds the poison that will kill you. He'll fill the second syringe with that little concoction of his and push on the plunger to squirt a little out of the needle.

"Your heart will be beating about a hundred eighty times per minute and your brain will be going nuts. You'll get light-headed and dizzy, scared beyond your wits as you think about your impending death. All that will be going through your pathetic mind is terror—a terror that you will no longer exist in a few minutes. Your life will be over. *Poof!* Just like that. And there won't be anything after that but darkness—endless darkness for all eternity!

"But perhaps it won't be that way for you. Perhaps there is a hell, and if there is, then certainly your soul will be tossed into its fires forever—writhing in endless pain for endless years."

"No!" shouted Marvin. "Shut up!"

"You'll watch as the man ties up your arm with a rubber cord to catch a vein. He'll plunge the first needle into your arm and begin pressing down on the syringe, pushing the sedative into your system that will set the stage for the final injection. At this point, your brain will check-out, and you'll become unconscious. You'll never see the second needle go into your arm."

Marvin closed his eyes. He couldn't take any more.

"Within seconds, your heart stops pumping blood to your brain, and all of your systems shut down. Your body shakes in a nervous reaction as it dies, and then it goes limp. After that, another person comes into the room to check for a pulse, and they record your time of death. All the witnesses get to go home as they throw your body onto a gurney and cart it off to a pit to be tossed into with a bunch of other rotting corpses."

Marvin was horrified—speechless.

"Or ...."

"Or what?" asked Marvin, eagerly.

"You can tell me that you did it and that you did it with your employer, Ms. McLaughlin. If you do that, then I can probably get you out in twenty years or so—for good behavior, of course. So, which will it be, Marvin? Do you want to see the light of day again in twenty years or end up dead in cold darkness for the rest of eternity?"

"So, all I have to do is tell you that me and Sara had a thing goin'?" Marvin asked. It sounded to Tommy like he was weighing his options pretty seriously.

"Yep," Tommy answered.

"Okay. Well, if you can cut the sentence to five years, you gotta deal."

"I'll see what I can do," said Tommy, knowing he wouldn't be able to make good on it.

Tommy made an appointment and then went to Johnson's office, eager to share his latest conquest and gain favor back with a man whose coattails he hoped to ride for a while. He waited patiently in the lobby, tapping on his cell phone before resorting to looking through a few magazines that were scattered in a mess on a side table, including *Good Housekeeping* and *Kitchens & Bathrooms Today*.

An hour passed, but still there was no sign of Johnson. Tommy looked again at his watch and then got up to talk to the secretary who was doing work on the computer.

"I'm sorry to interrupt, but will the DA be much longer?" he asked her.

She shrugged and only said, "Don't know. It's hard to tell. He'll be out when he comes out. Nothin' I can do about it."

Finally, the door opened. The DA came storming out, shouting on his cell phone.

"What do you mean you don't have a building? We need a campaign headquarters that's down near the Commons! He's going to be the next governor of Massachusetts, for God's sake! Now get that lease signed today!"

Johnson walked past Tommy, hardly noticing he was standing there.

"Uh, Mr. Johnson?" said Tommy, trying to catch his attention.

The DA only glared at Tommy, pushing him out of the way. "Not now. Can't you see I'm busy?" he growled.

"I'm sorry to interrupt, but I thought you might want to know that I got a confession out of a guy who works for Sara McLaughlin. He's confessed to everything—the murders, the robberies, everything. We'll have those murder cases wrapped up in days. You'll be able to bring it to trial and get your conviction."

Johnson looked at Tommy with disdain.

"Do you really think I need to know this now? Can't you see I'm in the middle of something?" he said with a nasty edge to his voice.

"Uh..."

"I didn't think so," said Johnson. "So, why don't you go back to your hole and make an appointment to see me like a good little soldier. I assume you know how to do that?" His condescension was obvious.

"But I did, sir," replied Tommy. "This is what you said you needed— a more solid case against Sara McLaughlin on those three murders in the city this year. You told me we needed to wrap those up fast to clear the air for the mayor's election campaign."

"You're young and naïve, kid. That's not the way it works. As far as I'm concerned, you're only doing your fucking job getting that confession. If you want me to say thanks, then you'll be waiting a long time. The mayor and I expect you to do your *fucking* job. You got that?"

"Uh, yes sir."

"So, don't get all high and mighty running up here like a sixth grader to tell me what you've done. You haven't done *shit!* And whatever you do get done, don't expect a ticker-tape parade out of it. Got it?"

Tommy took a breath. He'd been berated by the DA before, but this was different. Although young and naïve, he was starting to learn. He was slowly understanding why they called it *the jungle.*

Johnson began walking away, punching buttons on his phone to heckle someone else on his list.

"I'll make another appointment with you for tomorrow, then," said Tommy, backing away. But his words fell on deaf ears. The DA didn't respond. He was already yelling at his next victim.

Tommy stood with a clenched jaw and his anger building. Now he realized that at best he wasn't going to get a magic ticket to the top; at worst, he had simply been duped into doing dirty work with no hope of any payoff at all. He wasn't going to be treated any differently than before. He wasn't going to just do a few favors for the elites and vault to the top. If anything went wrong, his career would be over. However, if things went well, he still might find his career in jeopardy. Those who knew too much were often expendable if things got rough. No longer was he in the shallow end where he could touch bottom. He was in the deep end, and no one was standing nearby with a life preserver.

Taking out his cell phone, he started to make another call, but he changed his mind and stopped it.

Let's not be hasty. Keep your cool. You can still do this. You're just as smart and crafty as they are. You'll be fine, he told himself.

*****

CH 62 – "I'm Afraid Not"

2020

Dag pulled up in front of the nursing home where Bessie was living. He had more questions than ever now that he had talked with Sara. Bessie would be the only one who could clear things up, he thought. He only hoped she hadn't deteriorated any more from the previous day when he had last seen her.

"May I help you?" asked a different young lady sitting behind the desk in the visitor's area. She was wearing a black sweater with a white name tag that read "Peggy." Her highlighted brown hair was pulled back into a ponytail and dangled lifelessly over her shoulder.

"Yes, I'm Detective Gallagher. I was here yesterday and spoke with Bessie Belzikov. I was hoping to ask her a few more questions. I'm investigating several cases that I think she could help me with."

"No, I'm afraid not," she said in a monotone voice.

"Oh, I know it's not visiting hours, but this is very important. I need to see her right away."

"Detective, I'm afraid she's not here."

"Oh, has she been moved back to her residence?"

"Uh, no. I'm afraid she died last night. I believe it was peaceful, but her granddaughter is here right now taking care of her things."

Dag was surprised.

"But she seemed fine yesterday."

"She passed in her sleep, sir. She was over a hundred, I think."

"Yes, she was going to turn one hundred and one in a few months," said Dag.

Dag looked down the hall and spotted Patti walking the other way carrying some of her grandmother's things.

"Would you buzz me through? I'd like to speak with that woman there in the corridor."

Dag hurried to catch up with Patti before she went out the back service door. There, he called out to her. "Patti, it's me, Detective

Gallagher." Then, catching up to her, he added, "Say, I'm sorry to hear about your grandmother. It seemed pretty sudden, didn't it? She seemed fine yesterday."

Patti shrugged. She hadn't been crying and didn't appear too broken-up over it. Her manner was very matter-of-fact, which struck Dag as odd.

"I don't know. I got a call shortly after I left last night. The center called me and said she'd passed away. I was surprised, but, *hey,* she lived a long life. Can't complain too much about that."

Patti started to walk away, continuing through the gray, double doors.

"Just a minute, Ms. Wilkins. I have a few questions for you," said Dag.

Patti turned around impatiently. "How long will this take?" she asked. "I need to get my grandma's stuff out of the room and make the funeral arrangements."

Dag pulled out his notepad and clicked to get a fresh screen.

"What do you know about your grandmother's talents for contacting the dead?"

Patti laughed. "Are you kidding? Is this your new line of interrogation—asking questions about whether someone can talk to the dead?"

"No. But there are a lot of coincidences between your family and these murders that go back to the 1940s. They seem to happen about every twenty-five years—about every generation."

"I don't see your point," said Patti.

"Did your grandmother ever talk about when she became a medium?"

"She was born with it. It runs in the family."

"Not according to a diary left behind by Janice Prodescu." Patti's cavalier attitude changed abruptly. "According to it," said Dag, "Bessie Belzikov wasn't able to perform séances or contact the dead until late in her senior year in high school. Ms. Prodescu's diary says it was "sudden" and "quite remarkable.""

Of course, Dag was only giving Patti hearsay evidence—what he had gotten from Sara.

341

"I don't know anything about that," said Patti, defensively.

"And when did you get *your* ability, Ms. Wilkins?" Dag asked pointedly.

"Like I said, I've had it all my life."

"And your daughter, Mitzie?"

"I don't know where you're going with this," said Patti.

"And your daughter, Mitzie?" Dag repeated the question, hoping this time for an answer.

"She doesn't have the ability. She's not a medium."

"Then why does she have cards that say 'Psychic' on them," said Dag pulling one out from his folder and showing it to her.

Patti bit her lip. "That's just a promotional thing. You know how companies often do stuff like that. It's marketing; that's all. It doesn't mean anything, really."

"And why isn't your mother Terri here? I would think she would come to help with the affairs of her own mother," Dag asked, suddenly realizing that she was not with her daughter.

"She's not well, detective. My mother is no spring chicken. She couldn't make it today, but she said she'd be coming out soon to help. She was really upset this morning when I told her the news. She couldn't bring herself to even get out of bed."

"I see. Well, I'll be following up with her soon to help put the missing pieces together. Thank you for your time," said Dag. Then, he added, "And again, I'm sorry for your loss."

Patti glared at him. He could see the enmity in her eyes, and it was just as well that he couldn't see any deeper.

*****

CH 63 - Ghost

2020

Patti had waited until the next morning to call Mitzie about Bessie's death. Her daughter had taken the news hard. Losing her great grandmother was a blow to her as they had been extremely close. Without a caring mother herself, Mitzie had been brought up by her grandmother and great grandmother. But as Mitzie fell further and further under the influence of her mother, the relationships with Terri and Bessie had grown cool. Terri's conversion to the faith had also put distance between them, and Mitzie had found more excuses not to go visit her. Eventually, she had stopped seeing both of them at her mother's insistence. Still, she had feelings for them.

It was almost midday, and Mitzie could hardly find the energy to get out of bed. Patti called, wondering where she was. She had told her daughter to come to the nursing home to help her with Bessie's things. After being harassed all morning, Mitzie finally complied, pulling herself together, climbing into her Porsche, and heading off to the assisted living facility to help her mother.

The nursing home was operating as if nothing had happened the night before, and, indeed, the death of a guest was not unusual. Mitzie found Patti alone, sitting in the dark in her grandmother's room. There was no TV on or radio playing; there was only quiet.

"It's about time you got your ass over here to help me!" said Patti caustically. "But you're already too late. I've cleaned everything out. I hope you didn't want anything 'cause I threw it all away in the dumpster out back. All the religious crap she had—it's all gone. So, thanks for the help, Mitzie."

"I'm just not myself right now," said her daughter. "I never thought it would affect me like this—her passing, that is."

"Well, get over it. We have to move on with our lives."

"What about the funeral?" Mitzie asked.

"I'm just going to cremate her," said Patti. "We'll stick her on the mantel or something. We can figure that out later."

Mitzie just shrugged. "So, is there anything else to do?"

"Not now. I've pretty much handled it. I'm going down to the administrator's office and fill out the termination paperwork and then stop by the dining room to get something to eat. Do you want anything?"

"No."

"Well, I'll be back in a few minutes."

After Patti left, Mitzie sat on the edge of the empty bed, staring at the cold walls and feeling alone. Her eyes filled with tears. She would miss her great grandmother; that much she knew.

"Why are you crying my dear?" came a voice from the doorway.

Mitzie turned. Standing there was an old woman holding a cane. The image was fuzzy, but it was speaking to her in a clear voice.

"Yes?" Mitzie asked.

"I said, why are you crying?" asked the woman again.

"My great grandmother passed away last night. We are just here gathering her things—my mother and me."

"I see," said the woman. "But I haven't been gone that long. You miss me already?"

"Great grandma? But ..."

"But what? You've never talked to a spirit before? Sure you have. You've done it many times ... or at least your mother has."

The spirit of her great grandmother stood before her. She was dressed in a long, white blouse with a matching bow that was tied in front of her neck. There were little images on the blouse, they were red and green, but Mitzie couldn't make them out. Bessie had a crimson cardigan on, buttoned neatly to the top, and her black pants were cropped just above the ankles, just like she used to wear them.

"You can't really be there," said Mitzie.

"Why not? We've had the ability to see spirits in our family since 1945 my dear. You know that. However, some of us broke free of that dark bondage, like your Grandma Terri and me. Your mother did not. It was a curse, after all."

"I don't understand?"

"It's simple, child. There's good, and there's evil," said her great grandmother. "You need to understand that. Does good always win over evil? Well, I'm learning a lot on this side of the veil, and it looks like it does. But as for you and those still living in the physical world, you must make a choice every day. You must choose between good and evil. You are given that choice. Your mother has made her choice. However, I'm hopeful you will reassess where you want to end up."

"I ... I don't know. Mother is so ..."

"... demanding. Yes, she is. She's also very controlling, and if you follow her, you will be following a dark and sinister path indeed."

"It's always been that way in our family, hasn't it?" asked Mitzie.

"Our family ... ah, yes," said the specter. "You do know that I could not have children of my own, don't you?"

It was a bombshell, and Mitzie wasn't sure she had heard the spirit correctly.

"What?"

"I was barren, child. I could not have children of my own."

"I don't understand. You had Grandma Terri."

"I *raised* your Grandma Terri."

"Then, how ... where did you ..."

The old woman smiled. "It's another one of our family secrets. It's one even your mother doesn't know."

"What!" exclaimed Mitzie. "Grandma Terri has been my grandmother all my life!"

"I passed the demon within me to Terri and Terri passed it on to Patti. It was a ritual, and one we did gladly every twenty-five years. However, your mother does not wish to share the demon; she does not wish to pass it on to you. That is a good thing."

"How did you become possessed by it?"

"Unfortunately, it was at a séance when my wish was granted. You could say it was a Faustian bargain—a deal with the Devil. And you always lose when you do that. I just didn't understand that generations after mine would also lose. I just wanted it to stop. For a long time, I wanted it to stop, and it didn't. Now, it's time it did. It's

345

gone on long enough. The Devil has gotten more than his pound of flesh from us Belzikovs."

"I still don't understand," said Mitzie.

"I became possessed with a demon in 1938 when Janice and the rest of us girls had a sleepover. We had a session that night. It started off as a joke, but Janice revealed to us that she really *could* contact the spirit world—she'd always been able to see them and talk with them. She had gotten that skill from her mother too.

"We got out a Ouija board. There were a lot of strange things that happened to us that night—a night we vowed never to talk about again. But it was during that Ouija session that I asked the spirits to give me the same ability as Janice—to be able to contact the dead. I was jealous and desperate to be able to do what she did.

"Suddenly, there was an utter coldness that swept through my body, and I thought as if my heart had stopped beating. The sensation seemed to dissipate, but in reality, it never did. From that moment on, I was able to see things and hear things I'd never experienced before. I could see long-dead ancestors and talk to them. But there were also many dark spirits out there that flooded my body and soul. I fought to keep them out, but they grew stronger every day. Eventually, after a few years, I don't remember much of anything. I had ceased being me. Something else had taken over; I was no longer in control of myself. Then, the Silver Jubilee came—a special meeting of the coven I belonged to. It was there that I passed along my powers to your Grandma Terri. At the moment of the transfer, I felt like a fever had been lifted, and I could see again."

"And you weren't killed?" asked Mitzie.

"No. I was supposed to die, but I made a deal with the Devil that everyone in my family be spared that. In return, the curse on each generation involved others."

"Others? You mean others being murdered?" asked Mitzie.

"Yes. But now that I'm gone, maybe the cycle will be broken."

Mitzie nodded. She was beginning to understand now.

"In the upper, righthand drawer of that dresser there, you'll find something that I want you to have," said Bessie's spirit.

Mitzie went to the dresser and slid it open. Inside was a book with a black, leather cover. It was upside down, and she couldn't read the title. So, she pulled it out and turned it over.

Mephistopheles by Johann Georg Faust.

"This is dark," said Mitzie. "Why would you want me to have this?"

"Look inside," said Bessie from behind her.

Mitzie cracked open the cover, but instead of reading the opening passages to Faust's timeless story, she read another one:

Genesis

The Beginning

1 **In the beginning, God created the heavens and the earth. 2 Now the earth was formless and empty, darkness was over the surface of the deep, and the Spirit of God was hovering over the waters.**

"That's odd," said Mitzie. "How did you get a book like this? I mean, the cover says one thing and inside is the Bible?"

She looked over her shoulder, but there was no one there. The room was empty.

"Who were you talking to?" asked Patti coming back into the room.

"Uh, I was just, uh …" Mitzie said stuttering.

"What's that?" her mother asked, pointing to the book she held in her hand.

"It's about demons," said Mitzie, holding it up to show the title. "I found it in the dresser. I guess you missed it when you were cleaning things out. This is what I want of hers."

Patti smiled. "Fine. It's yours."

They left the room and went into the hallway.

"Mitzie, I have another job for you. It's a new client of mine. Since Sara is out of the way, I've had to go back to developing my own clients instead of profiting from hers—that is, until you start catching on yourself."

"Out of the way? What do you mean?" asked Mitzie.

"Oh, the police picked her up yesterday. They're holding her at the police station downtown, I think. Word has it that she's being brought up on murder charges. Three to be exact. I think they picked up Marvin too. So, you'll be on your own for a while. We don't need to worry about her as our competition anymore."

Mitzie clutched her book more tightly. "I see," she said. "You *really* think she did those things? I thought you were just trying to hurt her business by getting the police to follow-up on her."

"No doubt in my mind that she did it. You never really know someone, do you? They can look one way and be someone totally different," said Patti. Then, she added, almost as an afterthought. "Oh, and her husband was murdered last night too. She's had a bit of a rough patch. Don't you think?"

"Vince?"

"Yeah, he's dead. Why? You were supposed to go over there and seduce him after Sara was gone. I guess you never made it over there."

"I ... I don't remember," said Mitzie. "You know how I blank out once in a while."

"Yeah, you've always had your moments," said Patti, knowing full well what was causing it. "Anyway, hop in. I'll give you a ride home."

However, when they got to Patti's car, Mitzie stood back. "You know Mom. I think I'll leave a little later. I've got my car here anyway. You go ahead."

"Suit yourself," Patti answered, climbing in. She revved up the engine and screamed out of the nursing home parking lot like she was trying to get to her next ritual sacrifice.

Mitzie opened her book again.

... [3] **And God said, "Let there be light," and there was light.** [4] **God saw that the light was good, and He separated the light from the darkness ...**

*****

CH 64 - Sschooled by the DA

2020

The pace of the case against Sara McLaughlin proceeded with unusual haste. She was quickly arraigned on charges of fraud, intention to commit fraud, breaking and entering, assault, aggravated assault, conspiracy, attempted murder, and first-degree murder. Most had multiple counts attached to them, one for each of the victims, except only two charges for first-degree murder, as Claire Horwath was not killed, and the case file on the last victim, Vince McLaughlin had not yet been concluded. Instead, they brought attempted murder charges against her for Claire's case.

Marvin was also arraigned. His charges were the same, except for the murder charges. Those were lessened from first- to second-degree as the DA believed Marvin was only a patsy in the bigger scheme arranged by Sara to steal from her clients and, if they resisted, kill them. He was also willing to provide testimony against Sara.

The plausibility of the allegations was suspect, but that didn't deter either the mayor or the DA from pursuing them. They needed arrests and arraignments—which they had—and a trial—which they were about to begin. It didn't matter to them whether Sara and Marvin were innocent or guilty. They just needed a conviction—*any* conviction. Timing was everything as all politicians knew well, and the election was just around the corner.

"Good job," said Johnson, the DA. "The mayor sends his regards."

Tommy nodded and smiled, surprised with the sudden appreciation. "We'll make this happen, sir."

"Oh, I know we will, son," said Johnson. "The mayor's election to the governorship is counting on it."

They were in the DA's office. After the cold shoulder Tommy had gotten only days earlier, he was afraid this day would never come. He knew Johnson and the mayor could be brutal with anyone who opposed them or who might be a liability for them. Worse treatment was reserved for those they felt were of *no* use to them at all.

Johnson's office was impressive and expansive with a large piece of corner-office property on the thirty-third floor of the state building downtown. Thanks to the mayor, Johnson's suite was prime real estate. From there he could see Boston harbor and across to Logan Airport. It was a spectacular view, and one which Tommy could easily see himself having someday.

"So, after we take them to trial, I assume I'll be taking over Dag's office as a senior detective. It will only be a matter of time before I'm chief of police," Tommy said with an air of superiority and cockiness.

Johnson chuckled.

"What's so funny?" Tommy asked.

"Oh, just watching you young kids. You're such damned idealists."

Tommy looked confused. "I don't know what you mean."

Johnson stood up and reached for his humidor. Pulling out two cigars, he handed one to Tommy. It wasn't legal to smoke inside the building, but the DA ignored such petty rules. Tommy took the brown, cappa-wrapped stogy and clipped-off the end before lighting it. Johnson did the same and sat back in his chair, blowing smoke rings that glided effortlessly across the desk and into Tommy's face.

"What I mean, my dear chap, is that we all have our ambitions," said the DA. "The difference is that you youngsters believe you are the only ones that do and that yours somehow supersede everyone else's. Well, it doesn't work that way." Johnson paused to take another puff, exhaling the blue smoke slowly and deliberately. "You have to wait in line for your turn."

"I never said that my ambitions should come before anyone else's," said Tommy. "I just meant that there are things I want to achieve in my career. I assume that loyalty and dedication mean something to you and the mayor, right?"

"Of course."

"But?" said Tommy, baiting something more from the DA.

"But there are a lot of people who've given their souls to benefit the mayor and his career over the years. You aren't the first, and you won't be the last. Some go back twenty-thirty years, like me."

"They haven't done as much as I have, even if it didn't take me as long."

"Son, you're naive. There's a long line of detectives and other politicians who have sold out for years. Each of them thinks that he or she is at the front of the line. They *all* do." Johnson laughed again. "It's a game. It's all about who plays it best. And I have to tell you there are others who play it far better than you *ever* will." The color drained from Tommy's face even though he tried to maintain his cool. "But hey, Tommy. You can keep on trying. At least you earned a free cigar out of it."

There wasn't much more to be said between the two men. Tommy took a few more puffs on the cigar and put it out in the tray next to the solid-brass light fixture on the DA's desk.

"Let me know if there is anything else I can do to help," said Tommy, as he took his leave.

"Don't worry. I won't hesitate to ask," said Johnson, merely waving and swiveling back in his pin-cushioned, leather chair so he could take in the grand view outside is office.

Tommy had just gotten his second taste of it—heavy politics in the real world. *How many more bites did he need to take?* He asked himself. *How many more* could *he take?* Realpolitik was the name of the game that was played. This was an initiation rite for him—a rite of passage for all who were gutsy enough to attempt it. Most who tried failed, but for those who could successfully navigate the map of the political jungle, reaching the pot of gold would make it all worthwhile. *Wouldn't it?*

But what neither men understood was that life in a satanic cult was much the same. Only the strongest survived. The weak became chum for those at the highest levels of their game too.

*****

CH 65 - "Come Forth, My Child"

2020

Mitzie drove in the direction of the precinct building. She planned to talk with Detective Gallagher. There were things he needed to know.

Her red Porsche zipped across the wet pavement as she hurried downtown. The weather was cool and drizzly, with low, stratocumulus clouds acting like a shroud to keep out the warm, uplifting, brilliance of the sun's rays. She crossed over the Charles River toward Fenway Park before passing by the Church of St. Botolph with its massive stone facade and Gothic-arched doorways. The street sign pointing to the church streaked by her window, but it was then when she suddenly had the impulse to turn around.

Mitzie took the next street—an unplanned detour—and doubled back down a few side streets until she reached the empty parking lot next to the church. There, she turned off the engine and sat, staring up at the majesty of the structure.

Before her was the magnificent, Gothic window that arched gracefully up the facade, taking up the entire back of the church. Soaring into the sky at the front of the church was a tremendous stone tower that rose like a watchman's turret on a grand castle. She hesitated, wondering if she should go in, wondering if it would help, and wondering whether lightning would strike her dead if she tried. Something moved inside her, and she got out of her car, pressed the auto lock button on her keychain and let the door latch closed.

The nave was dim as little sunlight filtered in through the beautiful stained-glass windows that graced the walls like works of fine art hanging in the Louvre Museum. Along one side was a bank of votive candles—all in standard white—that were offered to parishioners for a dollar a piece to remember loved ones who'd passed before them.

Mitzie glanced around to see if anyone were there. In the back row, hunched over on a kneeler, was an older gentleman holding a rosary. His eyes were closed, but his lips were moving, presumably reciting the *Hail Mary's*. It had been a long time since Mitzie had been in a church. The last time she could remember was with her grandmother Terri who took her many times when she was older—

in her twenties. Her grandmother was always going to church, it seemed—sometimes every day during the week, except Saturdays. Sundays were a requirement.

Her mother, Patti, on the other hand, had scoffed at her mother's futile 'rituals' as she called them. "What's the point?" Patti would say. "There ain't no Heaven anyway! But there sure is a Hell!" When asked about it, she would add that "Hell ... Hell is a place where Satan's worshipers are rewarded for their bad deeds on Earth—the more horrible, the better."

Mitzie walked toward the front of the church where the altar was draped in purple, and there were red geraniums in gold foil pots lining the pulpit and the choir section.

"May I help you?" came a voice from a doorway to the side of the church.

It was an older priest, wearing his black shirt and collar but also dressed in khaki pants and loafers. His hair was gray and cut short, and his glasses were simple, black, plastic frames that underscored his position as a wise elder.

"I ... I ... I think I'm in the wrong place. Sorry, Father," said Mitzie, turning to leave.

"Are you sure you're in the wrong place?" he asked, with a sympathetic look. It was as if he could tell she was in pain and seeking relief. He had been a priest for many years—he knew that look when he saw it. He had seen many tortured souls during his lifetime.

Mitzie turned back and stared blankly at the priest.

"Are you Catholic?" he asked.

"*Uh*, I think so. My grandmother brought me to this church many years ago."

The priest smiled and extended his hand. "Come. Why don't you give me your confession? There doesn't seem to be a queue this afternoon, so I have time." She hesitated. "Come forth, my child," he said, coaxing her.

Mitzie walked into the confessional and sat down facing the slatted, wooden divider. The priest slid the solid partition on his side across so he could hear what she had to say but couldn't see her directly.

"Do you remember how to do it?" he asked, kindly. Then, without waiting for an answer, he prompted her. "You say, 'forgive me Father for I have sinned.'"

"Forgive me Father for I have sinned," she repeated.

"Tell me then, what is troubling your heart."

"There is too much for me to tell, Father. I don't know where to start."

"Just tell me a few things. You have the rest of your lifetime to catch up on the rest," he said, comfortingly.

"I believe that my mother is possessed. It's an evil that's been passed down from generation to generation. It is trying to attach itself to me ... and ..."

She stopped, unable to speak the words.

"... and you're afraid that it will?" the priest said, completing her sentence.

"Yes. I've done some things."

"That's why we're here."

Mitzie continued. "My great grandmother passed away yesterday. I saw her spirit in the room where she died at the nursing home. She told me about that and many more things. You see, my mother is a devil worshipper. She said it runs in the family—just like our ability to talk to the dead. But then she always laughs and says the two are forever linked."

"I see," said the priest grimly.

"I felt it coming over me less than a year ago," Mitzie exclaimed. "I could feel myself going down the same path. I don't remember everything I do, Father. There are blank spots in my life. I'm afraid to ask ... I'm afraid to find out what I've done. I think my mother has something to do with that."

"Well, I hope you're not coming here for an exorcism. I'm afraid that would be extremely complicated and very much out of my area of expertise," said the priest.

"No, I'm not sure why I'm here, really," she admitted, starting to get up.

"Well, as you know, the Bible forbids contact with the dead. You are likely to become possessed by evil spirits when you do that." There was little sympathy in his voice.

Mitzie hesitated. "What can I do, Father? My mother wants me to continue this—to follow her down this evil path." Then, she said, "Isn't there a commandment that says 'Thou shalt honor thy father and thy mother'?"

She could hear a sigh from the other side of the confessional. "Yes, that is true, but in this case it is not an act of honor to thy mother by violating one of the other commandments. What if your mother said, 'Go kill someone'? Would you do that?"

Mitzie had nothing to say. With the gaps in her memory, she didn't know whether that too had happened.

"You need to say twenty Hail Mary's, ten Our Father's and do forty hours of community service," said the priest. "You should also pray to Jesus Christ for your redemption. You have sinned against God, but there is salvation if you are truly sorry for your transgressions."

Mitzie nodded. It was a lot of religious-speak, but this time she didn't mind. She felt she had it coming.

She left the church and got back in her car. She did feel better somehow. Maybe it was a selfish notion, that all she had to do was dump some of her problems on the priest and everything would be fine. But she knew it didn't work that way. There had to be more sincerity than that. She was getting there, but she hadn't yet arrived. She had another stop. And this one would be no easier.

*****

CH 66 – The Trial

2020

Sara's trial date was fast approaching, and Marvin was still refining his testimony with the improper coaching from the district attorney. Johnson had told Marvin that he would be lenient with him if he cooperated with the conviction of Sara. Marvin had gladly obliged. The problem Marvin had was keeping his story straight from version to version. He wasn't going to tell the truth, and he had a difficult time remembering exactly what he was supposed to say. The DA also worried about it, making him rehearse his story many times to ensure he could be convincing to a jury.

When first interviewed, Marvin had talked at length about his involvement in the thefts but not the murders. Initially, he said he acted with someone else. The DA had assumed he had meant Sara, but with further questioning his answer became more confused. However, after several days of "discussing" it with the DA, his story became clearer. What he meant, he eventually said, was that Sara had masterminded the entire thing and forced him to help her steal to remain in her employ as her driver. He told the DA that Sara and her husband Vince were the ones who were breaking into their client's homes after he cased the places during Sara's sessions with them. Together, they had stolen many of them blind, particularly taking advantage of their age and emotional vulnerability.

Marvin's involvement eventually became diluted to the point that he was merely the driver who had taken them to the victims' homes. He had known about what went on, but he hadn't gone in and done the burglary directly. With that plea deal, he would end up with, at most, five-to-ten years in prison—far better than the life sentence the DA had originally threatened.

However, the DA never had any intention to reduce Marvin's sentence. Johnson needed to wrap Marvin up with the burglaries *and* the murders directly. That was the only way to get the jury to believe in their ability to mangle the bodies like they were.

After jury selection, the trial began, and Johnson gave his opening arguments. His harangue was a blistering condemnation of Sara and her choice of occupation. Labeling her psychic work as "snake oil" for a "gullible public," he quickly framed her as an opportunist who preyed on the sick, emotionally distraught and elderly.

"Not only did she take their money for the session," he said, "but she went back to 'double dip' and take all the rest. It is repulsive. To think someone would be so depraved of morals and ethics to do such a thing—and then mutilate their bodies after killing them. Not even a wild animal would do that.

"Ms. McLaughlin was in the business of manipulating her clients' emotions to her greatest benefit," continued Johnson. "She created the illusion that the spirits of their loved ones were returning as sympathetic entities who 'understood their pain and suffering.'

"It's the oldest con game on the books. Get the shill to feel like someone is on their side; let them drop their defenses and trust you; and then hit them when they least suspect it!

"But that wasn't good enough for Ms. McLaughlin. No! She had to take more. Fearing they would be able to identify her for taking their money and belongings, she killed them. Why would she choose to do it in a most horrific and heinous way? I can't explain. Only she would be able to tell you that, and I'm sure you'll never hear any such explanation cross her lips."

Johnson was good. He was a forceful, powerful man, and the shear strength of his presence and deep voice was enough to convince most jurors of the guilt of the defendant sitting in the courtroom.

Next, it was Morrie's turn. He took off his coat, unbuttoned his cuffs and rolled up his sleeves. It was symbolic if nothing else. He wanted to bring his polished professional image down to the level of the common man. He wanted to connect with the jurors. In this way, he wanted to gain their trust.

"Now that we have the fictional account of the story from the opening remarks out of the way," Morrie said with an amused grin, "let's get down to what *really* happened."

Morrie came around in front of the jury box and put his hands on the railing separating the twelve jurors from the rest of the courtroom.

"The defense will show that Ms. McLaughlin had witnesses to her whereabouts on the evenings when the murders occurred. That is undeniable. And as most rational people understand, it is impossible for one human to be in two places at the same time—at least with today's technology. However, you will also be shown graphic photographs of the crime scenes where the murders occurred. These will be difficult to view. They are, as the prosecutor says, horrific and heinous. Yet, it will be obvious to all of you," he said, speaking directly to the jurors and making eye contact with each of them, "that it was physically impossible for my client—all five feet, one hundred and five pounds—to do what the prosecution is accusing her of. She has been called a strong woman to be sure. Yes, she *is* strong-willed, perhaps, but hardly one with superhuman strength. What happened to those victims required super-human strength. Likewise, even with the help of another person or persons, she could not have done to these people what was done.

"Then there is the lack of blood. Cauterizing the cuts and-or draining the blood of each victim would require tools, supplies, and time. None of these were available to my client, and there was no evidence that the actual tools and supplies needed were in those apartments at the time of the murders. It would have taken hours, if not days, to set it all up."

Morrie backed off from the railing and gestured toward Sara.

"You are already aware of my client's occupation. She is a medium— a psychic. That may be problematic for some of you. It may offend some of you. But she did not choose that vocation. Contrary to what you or others may think, she was born with the talent. What she did, however, was use those skills for good rather than bad. She chose to help people reach their loved ones rather than cast dark spells or curses upon them."

Since these were opening remarks, the prosecuting DA could not object even though he seethed at what Morrie was saying. However, Sara's attorney would need to be more careful during the trial when describing her abilities and what was and was not possible at each murder scene.

"As a psychic, she is able to connect her clients with recently departed loved ones." Morrie paused. "Please understand that I am not here to persuade you one way or the other on this matter, and that is not the point of this trial nor should it be weighed as to whether she is innocent or guilty. She is *not* on trial for providing a psychic service and receiving money for it. There are no counts filed against her by the state on that matter. The days of witch hunts are long behind us. Therefore, you must *not* consider it. What she *is* being charged with is assault, attempted murder, and murder—

none of which she did. We will show you clearly, and without any doubt, that she is innocent of these charges."

Morrie began to sit down but then stopped. He smiled and pointed his finger, adding, "Oh, and there's one more thing. We would just like to call your attention to the fact that this is an election year. I'm sure the DA would want me to remind all of you to vote in the upcoming election. It is, of course, the patriotic thing to do, and after all, his boss is running for the governorship, if you didn't know."

And with that, Morrie sat down.

Sara smiled. *That was good,* she thought, *but they still had the whole trial ahead of them. Let's just hope his closing remarks are just as strong. Only time would tell.*

The DA gritted his teeth. It was a below-the-belt punch, but he would have his share of those moments during the trial too. He was certainly not above stooping to that level or lower. That was just the way the game was played, and he always played every game to win.

*****

CH 69 – Some Advice

2020

Dag went back to the evidence room and pulled out all the trace samples and bagged remnants of evidence that were collected from the macabre murders in Boston that year. He knew the Belzikovs were somehow the link connecting all of them, but proving their guilt was another matter. He was frustrated by the obvious implications he knew were there, yet without proof, it made little difference. His meeting with Sara had been enlightening, as had his conversations with Bessie. They had added new pieces to the puzzle, but they still weren't enough. The puzzle was far from solved.

Think! he told himself, striking his forehead. *It's got to be here someplace! Then, he* heard a knock at the door and looked up. "Come in," he said. "The door's open."

Tommy came in and sat down. It was late—after hours—and he'd brought a six-pack of beer, chilled, but sweating. He dropped it not-so-gently on the table as a peace offering.

"I didn't expect to see you," said Dag, choosing to ignore the gesture.

Tommy pulled a beer out of the cardboard container and twisted the top off, tossing it into the garbage container next to him. He took a swig, and then pulled out another one, taking the aluminum cap off before handing the cool, brown bottle to Dag. Dag took it and downed a couple of gulps before setting the bottle back on the table, continuing his review of a file.

"You know, Dag," Tommy finally said, tilting on the back legs of his chair, "Sometimes things aren't exactly as they seem. Do you know what I mean?"

As soon as Tommy started talking, Dag could tell he'd already had several beers before he'd arrived at his office.

"Yep, Tommy. I do indeed."

Tommy took another sip and placed the bottle in his lap. Using one hand, he gestured to Dag, forming a circle with his thumb and index finger.

"Life's a vicious circle, isn't it?" he began. "It's like that symbol—you know—the one where there's a snake in a circle and it's eating its own tail. You've seen it, I'm sure."

"Yep. I know the one," said Dag.

"But, in the whole scheme of things, we're not much of anything, are we? You and me—we're just animals eating our own tails. We think we're eating somebody else's, but we're not. We're devouring ourselves, you know. It's like we're our own worst enemy or something."

"Maybe, Tommy. But then again, maybe greed, lust, and desire push us to devour what we see in front of us—whatever is dangled as bait—even if it turns out to be ourselves."

Tommy sat back, putting his hands behind his head. Then, he leaned forward again, using his right hand to point his finger at some unseen figure in the room.

"*They*," the young detective said, missing Dag's point and raising his voice, "*they* have all the power, don't they? And they don't give a rat's ass about us or anyone else."

Dag sat nodding his head only slightly to acknowledge the comment.

"I thought that by doing what they wanted me to do—what you *wouldn't* do—they would reward me somehow. They would give me the big raise ... the big promotion ... another step along the way to the corner office. You know, like the DA has." He stopped and took another full gulp of his beer. He turned to look Dag squarely in the eye. "Have you ever been up to his office ... the DA's?" he asked.

"Yeah, pretty nice," said Dag.

"*Pretty* nice?" Tommy said sarcastically. "Un-friggin' *believable*—that's what it is! I don't think the mayor has any nicer of an office."

"He does," said Dag. "His is about *twice* the size of the DA's. And you should see the governor's mansion. It just gets better and better as you go up the food chain."

"*Shit!*" said Tommy. "So, how do we get a piece of that?"

"Is that what you want, Tommy? Do you really want a piece of what they have?"

"Yeah!"

"Haven't you realized that what they have isn't enough for them? It will *never* be enough for them. They will *always* want something more. It's an unquenchable thirst. It never goes away. *Never!*. Is that what you want?"

361

"But they got it all, Dag," Tommy answered, still not understanding. "Why should they get it all and we get nothing?"

"They have nothing, Tommy. What they have is meaningless. Just look at the mayor. He wants the governorship because his mayoral office and position isn't big enough. Once he has that, he'll want a U.S. Senate seat ... and on and on.'

"Or the presidency? That's what I want."

"Good for you, Tommy. And if you can raise great, loving children, and have a wife who loves and supports you as well as a family with a strong faith and belief in God and His goodness, then I'd say you're right. You will be wealthy beyond your wildest dreams."

"I don't know, Dag."

"But what have they sacrificed to get there? Have you thought about that?"

"Nothing! They haven't sacrificed a thing, Dag. We're the ones sacrificing, not them."

"Really? Did you know that the DA's wife filed for divorce from him six months ago? His daughter is in rehab and his son has been kicked out of high school more than once. The mayor's family isn't much better, but his secrets are more tightly kept. His wife is an alcoholic—she's been arrested several times on DUIs, but the charges, of course, are always dropped. They have no children—either by choice or because they can't. They can't experience the joy they bring and the love that you can only get from them."

"Really?"

"Yeah, really. Seizing the top spot by crooked and shady means always comes with a price. Look at history," said Dag.

"I hated history in school," mumbled Tommy.

"Well, you should brush up on it. It will tell you about what people have done to get to the top. It will also tell you how much worse it gets once they got there. You've seen how nasty the game is to climb to the top. Well, it's even nastier when you're there. Many other people—nastier and cleverer—are constantly trying to bring you down. They want to topple you, to destroy you and your family to get what *you* have. Like you, Tommy, they will do *anything* to get what others on the top have. You will be the target, and as long as you're on top, you'll always be one. It's a game where you're constantly looking over your shoulder. It's a game that's been played for thousands of years, so don't think they're going to change the rules just for you."

Tommy finished his beer and popped another one. Dag wasn't sure his partner was listening, quickly got his answer.

"I don't know," Tommy finally said. "I'm as smart as them. I can play the game just as good."

"Okay, let's say you can," said Dag. "You further your own cause. You get to be mayor ... maybe governor ... maybe more. That's great. But what *is* your cause, Tommy? *Yourself?* Is that a worthy and noble cause?"

"*Hell* yes! They always say to value yourself. They tell you when you're little to have confidence and believe in yourself. Well, that's all I'm doing."

"So not giving a shit about your fellow man is okay with you?"

"Hey, it's every man for himself, Dag. It's a jungle. You know that."

"You need to protect yourself—that's true. But can't you do that and not hurt other people in the process?"

"I don't think so, Dag. I think it's the only way to get to the top. It's eat or be eaten. I prefer to be the one eating."

"Well, if that's your viewpoint on life, I can't change it. I don't think it's true. I think goodness can still win the day. That's how I'm living my life. I want to make this a better place when I leave than how it was when I got here. Is that asking too much?"

Dag began to take another slurp from the bottle but instead put it down on the table. "Do you have any morals, Tommy?"

"What's that supposed to mean? Of course, I do. That's pretty damn insulting, Dag."

"Okay, fine. Then where do you draw the line? You said you're willing to do just about anything to get to the top."

"Yeah."

"Would you commit murder for them?"

"No! Of course not!"

"Would you kidnap or steal for them?"

"No!"

"Alright, then. What about accusing and convicting someone of something they didn't do when you know they didn't do it?"

Tommy stared at Dag. He knew what he was saying.

"As I said before, when you look back at your career, will you think about the grand 'ole days when you had someone convicted and executed for murders she didn't commit? Wouldn't that be a form of murder, Tommy?"

Tommy looked away from him.

"Or even later, when you're breathing your last breath, will you feel comfort and a sense of well-being knowing that she and her family suffered for years for something she didn't do? A woman with a daughter who had to grow up without both her mother and father."

Tommy picked up his beer and emptied that one too, letting the last few drops drain into his mouth.

"So, what do you want from me?" Tommy asked, becoming increasingly uncomfortable and irritated.

"I'm not going to tell you what you should or shouldn't do. You can make your own decisions. Deep down, you know what's right and what's not."

"Hey, a man's gotta do what a man's gotta do, Dag. Nobody's gonna' look after *me*. Nobody gives a shit about *me*, so why should I give a shit about them?"

"So, it's you against the world, is it?"

"Yeah, pretty much."

"Well, I'm sorry you view life that way. I guess the last ten minutes of my trying to convince you otherwise shows how much I really don't give a shit about you and your life. I wish I had those ten minutes back."

Dag pushed his chair back for a moment and put his hands behind his head.

"You know, my father once said something to me. He said, 'Son, what goes around comes around. What you put into life is what you'll get back. If you deal out a bunch of crap to other people to get ahead, you're going to end up with a bunch of crap in sitting in your lap in the end. It's just the way life works.'"

"Not always," said Tommy. "It hasn't for the DA or the mayor."

"Not professionally, but personally their lives are a wreck."

"And what about your dad? If he lived so virtuously, why did he go out the way he did? Can you answer me that?"

Dag bit his lip. "You know, Tommy, at least he died with honor. He died with integrity. He died knowing he'd done the best he could and didn't screw other people in the process."

Tommy stood up and put his empty bottle down on the table, while pulling another from the pack for the road.

"Thanks for the talk, Dag," he said, heading out the door.

"Did I change your mind?" Dag asked.

Tommy shook his head. "Nope, but that's not why I came in here."

"Then why did you come?"

Dag's partner laughed. "I thought you needed a beer," he said. "See ya' around."

*****

CH 68 – Cases of Robbery

2020

Dag had bits and pieces of evidence implicating the Belzikovs and exonerating Sara, but not enough to make a solid case. Without something more, he felt Morrie would have no chance going up against a determined DA and a powerful mayor. They were not going to back down easily from their efforts against Sara. Admitting a mistake this late in the election process would be suicidal, and neither man was going to do that.

If he brought Patti in for questioning, she would deny it, he thought, *as would Marvin.* It would also cripple his ability to do anything in the department ever again. The police chief would buckle to the DA's demands to have his head. Dag was also sure Marvin had already cut a deal with the DA. He certainly wasn't going to screw that up by talking to Dag. So, Dag spent the next few days searching for more clues but found himself at a dead end. He was frustrated, and there was no one there to give him any help.

To Dag's surprise, Tommy stopped in one day. He was in a good mood, believing the trial against Sara was going well and that within a few days they would send the jury off to deliberate. He was cock-sure he would get his conviction and a nice salary bump.

"Hey, Dag. Just thought I'd come to see you. What are you working on these days now that you're semi-retired?"

"You didn't bring beer this time?" Dag answered.

"No, I'm on duty. Can't do that. Gotta follow the rules, ya' know."

Dag rolled his eyes. "I'm doin' the same stuff. Can't say more than that."

"Yeah, I figure you're still working the McLaughlin case even though you're not supposed to. But Dag, it's futile. The DA and mayor have this one in the bag. The jury will be sent to deliberate soon, and I'm sure they'll come back with a guilty verdict. Then, we'll nail Marvin on some counts too."

"That way he won't be able to talk to anyone about the deal you guys cut with him, right?"

"Dag, Dag. You know the way this works. I'm not going to talk out of school with you. It is what it is as we've said before. Some things you can't change."

"You can change anything, Tommy. It's just a matter of how important it is to you and how hard you want to work for it."

"Okay, fine. Listen, I just came to drop these off. Here you go. Don't say I never gave you anything."

"What's this?" Dag asked, picking up the files and glancing through them. Quickly, he realized what Tommy had given him. "Why give me these now?" he asked.

"Why not? I thought you could use some help."

"No, I get it." Dag waggled his finger at his former partner. "You feel guilty, so you thought you'd appease your guilty conscience by giving me these. But you already know it's too late for these to do me any good. Clever, Tommy—too clever by half. The thing is, I can be clever too."

Tommy looked annoyed. "Dag, you're a pain in the ass. I was just trying to help you out, and this is what you do for me? You're a piece of work."

"What do you want me to say—thanks?"

"Yeah, that would be nice."

"Okay, thanks—asshole," Dag answered. "If it makes you feel better, then I've at least given you that. Don't say I never gave *you* anything either."

Dag took the rest of the day to look through the files Tommy had given him. They weren't homicides at all; rather, they were fraud cases. There was a case in 1970 about a woman and an accomplice who were going around conducting séances for a fee. There were numerous complaints filed against the couple for fraud. The allegations stated that the couple "posed as mediums to connect their victims to alleged loved ones in the afterlife." However, the complainants became skeptical after they talked with others having sessions with the same couple and found many had been robbed later that evening or shortly thereafter.

In each case, the couple was described as a woman in her late twenties or early thirties, brown hair, only about five feet tall, petite and small boned. They went on to describe her mannerisms and the way she carried herself.

That sounds like Terri Campbell, Dag said to himself, matching the description to what he imagined Terri looked like at the age of thirty in 1970. However, the couple had used aliases and false addresses, making it extremely difficult to track them down.

The other files were from the 1990s—1995 to be exact. Again, they were replete with charges of fraud made by individuals acting as psychics to help clients. Although in most cases, the victims stated they were able to reach their loved ones, they also claimed their homes were later burglarized as well. These linked back to the same neighborhoods Dag had found in the murder files—in Roxbury, Dorchester and Dudley Square in Boston. The description of the young, white woman involved in these cases matched someone else he had spoken to before—Patti Campbell. Some also mentioned a black man who was short, stocky, and clean-shaven. *Who was this?* Patti had been married and divorced although Mitzie had been born prior to that time.

If the past were repeated, then he should find fraud cases during or around 2020 that were similar. Those should involve burglaries following sessions with another ersatz psychic—those that hadn't also ended in a murder.

Dag began to look, and with the efficient cataloging of cases then in place and the powerful search engines available, he quickly he found something. Dag read through the case. It was a complaint against an older woman—someone in her middle or late fifties, together with a younger man, who was labeled as a possible accomplice. The description of the woman was the same as the ones in 1995, except aged a couple decades. *Patti again?* Dag thought. *Not Mitzie this time?*

The accomplice was again described as a short, stocky man, but estimated to be some twenty years younger than she. They hadn't found the culprits yet; both had used aliases and prepaid phones to make the arrangements for their sessions. Neither sources of evidence had been traceable to anyone yet.

Was it Patti who was continuing her ways of 1995? thought Dag. He was confused. *Why hadn't she passed this trade on to her daughter, Mitzie? If this were a family business, that would only make sense, wouldn't it? And why only after twenty-five years? Why every year during the intervening period?*

But the more Dag dug, the more he found. Witnesses told of seeing a young, petite woman and a black man around the buildings the evening of the burglaries. They weren't from the buildings or the neighborhood as far as these people recalled. *Was this Mitzie then?* Dag asked himself.

Dag next went to the police database and typed in the name Frank Wilkins, Patti's ex-husband to see if he were there with some sort of burglary record. He also wanted to see if his description matched that of the accomplice. Frank was there, but he didn't have much of a record—only a few misdemeanors and none had anything to do with robbery or burglary. The mugshot showed a white man with light brown hair and a full beard. He was far from short and stocky—instead, over six feet three inches, thin and angular. But if the man wasn't her husband, then who could it have been?

Dag searched for Marvin Fletcher in the database. He was there too. He did have some arrests for breaking and entering and burglary, but those were old convictions. However, the latest entry was only few weeks earlier when he was arrested and brought in suspected of aiding Sara in her alleged violent crime spree.

The headshot photo in the system wasn't much to go on. Marvin appeared to be stocky, and he was listed as being only five foot, nine inches tall. *But Marvin would have been only about five years old when those crimes were committed in 1995,* Dag thought. *It would not have been possible for him to have been involved.*

Then, he recalled Sara mentioning that Marvin's father, Dwayne, had been the driver for her mother. *But both were drivers for Sara and her family—not the Belzikovs. It didn't' make any sense,* he thought.

Dag typed in queries to find out the names of any other relatives of the Belzikovs, Prodescus or Fletchers who might have been involved in some sort of burglary racket. Initially, he found nothing, but then he spotted a hit for 1970. It was a man named Moseby Wright. He had been arrested for burglaries in the Boston area. His wife was Tamra Wright, but her maiden name was: Fletcher. *This is complicated,* thought Dag. *The whole thing seems to be a web of darkness.*

Dag took the file and went through it again. Indeed, it referred to an accomplice—a friend who was a white woman. However, it gave no

369

more details about her. Then, he looked at the officer on the case—Jag Gallagher. Closing the folder, he opened the others that had occurred in 1995. *Who was the detective?* Zag Gallagher.

To his left was a large, framed poster on the wall. Within its reflective glass, Dag noticed his image and shuddered. *Could his own father and grandfather have been complicit in covering up a burglar ring back in 1995 and 1970?* Bessie's words were echoing in his mind—haunting him. *Had her granddaughter known Jag? Had she also known Zag? Had they had an affair too?* he asked himself. *Is that why his grandfather hadn't pursued the cases vigorously in 1970 and his father in 1995? Is that why neither Terri nor Patti was investigated further?*

Dag felt dirty. He put on his coat. He had to get some air. He made it outside and around the corner before passing O'Leary's Pub. He glanced inside and saw only few patrons sitting at the bar having a cool one. So, he changed his mind and went in, where he promptly pulled up a stool.

"Aiden, pull me a draft, will ya'?" asked Dag, balancing himself on the wobbly seat.

"Looks like you've 'ad a hard day there, Dag," said the bartender, someone he had known for years.

"You could say that," Dag answered, taking the pint and quickly sucking down the nearly black stout.

It was to be the first of many that night.

*****

CH 69 - Daughters

2020

Morrie and his associate, Mike, started combing through the materials Sara had pulled down from the attic as well as other documents they found there. Sara had directed them to go through those and anything else they found to find something helpful to her case.

"I guess Sara was right in saying that Janice Prodescu and Bessie Belzikov were pretty close in high school," said Mike, looking up from his reading. "Everything I've read here points in that direction."

"Yes, it seems they were inseparable," Morrie answered, flipping through another journal.

"Wait a minute," said Mike suddenly. "When was Janice married? What was the date?"

"Uh, let's see. I believe it was ... no wait. She wasn't married. I don't think she ever married."

"So, she had her daughter, Cora Rae, out of wedlock."

"Yes, I think that's right," said Morrie.

"But it says here there were *two*. Two what?"

"What do you mean? Read me the passage."

"In this journal, it says quote, 'Just came home from the hospital. They weren't happy that I wasn't married. But when it came time to give them names of the babies for the birth certificates, I didn't know what to tell them.'"

"Names? You mean, more than one?" asked Morrie.

"It appears so, Morrie. It goes on to say that she wrote down the names for them, but she doesn't say what they were."

"*Two* babies?"

"Yeah. It also says there was a friend named James Winfield. It sounds like a boyfriend, but I'm not sure."

"I'm supposing he was Cora Rae's biological father," said Morrie.

"I'm not getting that from the notes here," said Mike.

"Why? What does the journal say?"

"It refers to James but only casually. There's nothing suggesting a romantic relationship or any feeling like that for him. It's almost like he's an acquaintance at best. On the other hand, there is another person mentioned, but that person is only referred to as 'he.' What's different is it's highlighted at times or followed by little hearts. The writing around him is totally different than when Janice refers to James. In this passage she says, quote:

> *I spent the afternoon with him. He's so loving and fun. He knows how fond I am of him. It's as if we were meant to be together. But I know it can never be. If only ...'*

"If only what?" Morrie asked.

"It doesn't say," said Mike. "But when she describes James, she says, quote:

> *'Saw James at Roger's party. He really likes me, but it's just not there for me. He wants to have coffee with me later this week. We'll see.'*

"Let me see that," said Morrie. He read the excerpts and returned the journal to Mike. "You're right about that. James and this other person are two different people. So, it sounds like this *other* person was the father of Cora Rae—not James Winfield, as the family always said. At least that's what Sara told me when I asked her about what she knew of her grandmother."

"Cora Rae married Todd Taylor, right?" Mike asked.

"I believe so. She was Cora Rae Prodescu Taylor. They had a daughter together."

"Yes, Abagail or Abby Knight," said Mike. "And what about her? She obviously married."

"Yeah, her husband was Chris Knight. They had Sara."

"And Sara is married to Vince and together they had LJ."

"Yes. So, our case begins with Dumitra as matriarch of the Prodescu family and currently ends with LJ. On the other side, we have the Belzikovs."

"Yeah, starting with Bessie," said Mike.

"And what do we have on that?" asked Morrie.

"Bessie had Theresa who married Ben Campbell. They had a girl they named Patricia. She married Frank Wilkins but got divorced. Still, they had a girl they named ..."

"... Maria," said Morrie, finishing the statement.

"Yes. Apparently so."

"I believe the woman goes by her nickname, however: Mitzie."

"Did she marry? Does she have children?" Mike asked.

"I don't know," Morrie answered, "but that's something you need to find out."

*****

CH 90 - Surprise Witness

2020

The trial continued into its third week with the DA calling expert witness after expert witness, each describing the dangers to the community of Sara and her obsession with talking to spirits. Other witnesses told of seeing her go into Claire's apartment earlier in the day. They said they didn't know why she had been there. In the case of Margaret Jenkins and her son Will, they claimed they saw someone resembling Sara go into the apartment late in the day, but all said the young woman was much younger. It had been dark inside the building—several light bulbs had burned out—so they hadn't been sure. Morrie found out later from LJ that she had gone to visit Will, her high school cult friend, at that time. Her parents had prohibited her from associating with any of them, but she had snuck out of the house in defiance and not told them.

The days in court were tedious. Each time a new piece of evidence was presented against her, Sara would sigh. She knew many of the words spoken were true, but they were grossly misleading or out of context. And in this case, she felt sure it was going to lead to a jury conviction. Yet, she was not prepared for what came next.

"The prosecution calls to the stand, Marvin Fletcher," said Johnson with his loud and booming voice.

Sara opened her mouth in disbelief. Marvin had been a trusted employee of hers for years. Morrie had considered calling Marvin to be a witness on her behalf until he found out he had been arrested too. The thought that he was now going to testify against her was unfathomable. Worse yet, she had hired Marvin because his father had worked for her mother, Abby, for a few years, and before that, a relative of theirs had worked for her grandmother, Cora Rae. It was based on these relationships that she had thought she could trust and rely on Marvin.

Marvin entered the courtroom and walked to the witness box. He was still under arrest for his involvement with Sara, but he wasn't wearing an orange jump suit or even handcuffs. Instead, he was wearing a dark gray sport coat, white shirt, and subdued, striped tie.

Contrasted with his black hair and goatee, he appeared quite sharp and strikingly handsome.

"Do swear to tell the truth, the whole truth and nothing but the truth?" asked the court clerk.

"I do," replied Marvin, lowering his hand before sitting down.

The DA got up and buttoned his jacket. "Mr. Fletcher, how long have you been employed by Ms. McLaughlin?"

"I've been her driver for about two years," Marvin answered.

"During those two years did Ms. McLaughlin ever ask you to do anything strange or unusual?"

"I object, Your Honor," said Morrie, not bothering to stand up. "The question calls for subjectivity as to the nature of 'strange' or 'unusual.'" He had objected so many times during the trial that he was growing weary of the exercise.

Judge Linda Madison had been on the bench for over a decade. She was a respected member of the judicial system—one who was viewed as impartial and fair. Only in her mid-forties, she was not particularly attractive. Her hair, now turning gray and pulled back in a tight bun, her double chin protruding up from her black cloak, and her half-frame, reading glasses, dangling in front, strapped around her neck by a long, silver chain, made her look like a particularly stern school marm or youthful, but harsh grandmother.

"Sustained," said the judge, not hesitating.

"Mr. Fletcher," said Johnson, starting again, "were you aware that Ms. McLaughlin was engaged in conducting paranormal séances or otherwise trying to contact the dead on behalf of her clients?"

"Yeah, of course."

"Do you personally believe in the ability of someone to contact the dead?"

"I object," said Morrie. "The question is irrelevant to the case."

"I will tie it together, Your Honor," Johnson said quickly.

"I will allow it," said the judge. "Answer the question, Mr. Fletcher."

"Of course not. It's a bunch of *bullshit*. She ..." he said, pointing at Sara, "... messes with them—her clients."

Sara sat dazed. Marvin had never expressed such thoughts to her or even intimated those beliefs.

"Messes with them?" repeated the DA. "What do you mean?"

"Yeah, she makes them think she's talkin' to their dead family members. But she brings me inside … you know … to case out the joint."

Sara's face turned red. It was an outright lie, and both she and Marvin knew it. She started to speak, but Morrie put his hand on her arm.

"Explain," prompted the DA.

"Well, she and her husband Vince had this gig goin' on where she'd go to their homes, have me case out the place, and find where all the jewels, money and stuff were. Then they'd go back and rob the place later."

"What!" Sara finally exploded. She stood up and shrieked at her former driver. "That's a lie and you know it!"

"Order!" commanded the judge, banging her gavel.

The gallery was in an uproar. Whispering and commotion ruled, sweeping through the hundred or so people who sat in the courtroom like an undulating wave at a football stadium.

"Order!" the judge barked one more time. Then, she turned to address Sara. "One more outburst, and I will find you in contempt!"

Sara sat down, trembling with anger. Even Marvin was stunned by the outburst. His face went pale as he sank into the hard-backed, wooden chair at the defense counsel's table.

"So, she made you rob her clients?"

Marvin looked at Sara who was still steaming, and suddenly, the expression on his face softened. Seeing this, the DA began to get nervous. His key witness was losing his nerve, and that was something he couldn't have.

"Mr. Fletcher," Johnson said, quickly taking back control, "you said that Ms. McLaughlin and her husband were involved in the burglaries. Is that correct?" He looked at Marvin menacingly.

"Uh …"

"That *is* correct, isn't it, Mr. Fletcher?" Johnson repeated forcefully.

"Objection!" cried Morrie.

"Sustained," answered the judge. "Do not lead the witness, Mr. Johnson."

The DA only glared at Marvin.

"Yes ... yes, that is correct," Marvin affirmed, this time more meekly.

Johnson went back to his table and glanced at some notes. Then, he asked, "Did you drive Ms. McLaughlin to the residence of Ms. Claire Horwath at 2309 High Street in Brookline on March 15, 2020?"

"Yes."

"And what was the purpose of the visit?" asked the DA.

"She had an appointment with Claire to contact her dead boyfriend. I don't remember his name."

"Was she able to contact him? Or, let me rephrase that ... was she able to *convince* the client that she had contacted him?"

"Objection, Your Honor," said Morrie.

"Overruled. You may answer the question, Mr. Fletcher," said the judge.

"I think the woman believed my boss been in touch with her dead boyfriend. Yeah."

"How long were you in Ms. Horwath's apartment?"

"Oh, I don't recall exactly, but I'd say an hour."

"So, you had plenty of time to case out the place and see where her valuables were?"

"Objection! Leading the witness."

"Sustained."

"So where did you go in the house while they were having their session?" asked Johnson.

"I went to the bedrooms and the kitchen. That's where anything of value usually is."

"Then what did you do?" asked Johnson.

"When it was time to leave, Sara called to me to come out, and we left. We went to the car, and the first thing out of her mouth was,

'Where is the jewelry and the money?' Just like that! She didn't care about anything but that," said Marvin.

Sara was seething. She couldn't believe what she was hearing.

"Then what?" asked the DA.

"Nothin' from my end. I would just tell her where everything was and that was it."

"Did you go with her and her husband later to break into the client's home and rob them?"

"No. That was them," said Marvin, pointing to Sara and referring to her now-dead husband. "It was only those two."

"So, it was Ms. McLaughlin and her husband, Vince, as you said before, who committed the crimes?"

"Objection!" said Morrie, sternly. "Clearly this is conjecture on the part of the witness. According to the witness, he never actually saw who committed the crimes."

"Do you have any evidence to show Mr. Fletcher had direct knowledge?" the judge asked the DA.

"Not at this time, Your Honor," replied the DA. But the damage had been done.

"Sustained," said the judge. Then she added, "Mr. Johnson, you're pushing the limits on this. Don't make me take action against you from the bench."

The judge admonished the jury to ignore those comments made by the witness, but the words had been said and, unfortunately, had been heard.

"I have no further questions at this time, Your Honor," said the DA.

Johnson returned to his chair. He was smiling—confident he had inflicted the desired wounds he had intended. He knew only Sara could refute those accusations as her husband was dead and could no longer speak for himself or her.

Morrie rose and approached the witness chair.

"Mr. Fletcher," he began, "you claim that you told Ms. McLaughlin about where all of the valuables were in the clients' dwellings, but you don't know for certain what she did with that information, do you?"

"Uh, well, I'm pretty sure that …"

"Mr. Fletcher, being pretty sure and being certain by seeing or hearing directly are two different things. Now, did you or did you not see the McLaughlins break into the dwellings of the victims?"

"Uh, yeah. I did," said Marvin, now stretching the truth beyond where the DA wanted him to go.

"You did? Really?" said Morrie. "So, you *were* there at the crime scene when you claim they broke in? But you just told us that you weren't at the crime scene. Which is it Mr. Fletcher?"

"No, I wasn't there. I'm sorry, I misspoke," he said, realizing his mistake.

"Which is it? Were you there or weren't you there? That's a pretty big difference!"

"I wasn't there. I was at home, watching football, like I told the police," said Marvin.

"So, if you are unsure about that, are you also sure about whether you cased out the homes of Ms. McLaughlin's clients during her sessions?"

"Yes, I'm sure."

"But your still unsure about being at the crime scene, is that right?"

"No … I … no, yes … I …"

"No or yes, what?" asked Morrie. "No that you made a mistake or no that you told Ms. McLaughlin where the valuables were?" The question was meant to confuse Marvin, and it did.

"Objection, Your Honor. Defense council is trying to confuse the witness."

"Sustained."

"Mr. Fletcher, when was it that Ms. McLaughlin instructed you to case out her clients' homes?"

"When?"

"Yes, when?"

"Uh, I don't remember," said Marvin, not having been instructed on how to answer that question.

"Are you sure you were instructed by her to do that?"

"Yes."

"Then what, exactly, did she tell you to do?"

"To case out the places."

"Those were her words—'case out the places'?" asked Morrie, now standing only a few feet from Marvin.

"Yeah."

"She never told you what you were to look for? Where you were to look? How you were to look?"

"Uh, I don't think so."

"You don't think she told you any of that or just parts of it?"

"I object, Your Honor. The questioning is vague."

"Sustained. Please be more specific," said the judge.

But Morrie had made his point and moved on.

"Mr. Fletcher, were you ever caught going through a house?"

"No."

"No?" Morrie walked back to his table and opened a file, pulling out a sheet of paper. He unfolded his reading glasses and perched them on the tip of his nose. "It says here you were arrested and convicted of breaking and entering and burglary ... let's see ... one, two, three, four times between 2001 and 2004. Is that right?"

"I ... I ... I'm not sure," he said stumbling over his words.

"Well, that's what your arrest record shows."

"I ... I guess ..." Marvin's head was spinning, and his face looked lost and hopeless. "Would you repeat the question?" he asked.

"I don't think I have any further questions, Your Honor," said Morrie. But before he sat down, he turned and added, "Oh, actually, I do have one more, Mr. Fletcher. Why would you provide information to Ms. McLaughlin about the whereabouts of the valuables?"

"What do you mean?" Marvin asked.

"What was in it for you? Obviously, asking you to scope out the residence for valuables would have alerted you to the fact that they were up to something that was probably illegal, but you did it anyway. Why?"

"Objection!" roared the DA. "The defense is putting words in the witness's mouth, presupposing that he could read the minds of the defendant and her husband as to their motives."

"Sustained," said the Judge.

Morrie smiled. He disagreed, but he knew he had to abide by the ruling and not argue the point.

"Then let me put it this way. You claim Ms. McLaughlin told you to get her information on where jewelry and money were hidden inside a stranger's home. Are you also saying that you never questioned why she would ask you to do that?"

"I ... I ... no. I didn't," answered Marvin cautiously. "It's not a crime to tell somebody something like that."

"Telling them—no; however, you were trespassing into areas of the property for which you had no authorization. Isn't that right?"

"Objection. Witness is not expected to know the law with respect to trespassing," said Johnson.

"Overruled," said the judge.

Morrie knew common sense would tell a person they shouldn't go rummaging through someone's place without permission.

"In addition, Mr. Fletcher, since providing that information was allegedly used in the commitment of a crime, you may be held responsible as an accomplice to the alleged burglaries and murders. Did you know that?"

"Objection," shouted the DA.

"Sustained!" said the judge.

"Back to my original question, Mr. Fletcher. What did you get out of this deal with the McLaughlin's? Money? A cut of the loot?" Then, Morrie asked, "Or were you supposed to kill for them too, and get a bigger part of the pie?"

"Objection!" yelled the DA.

"Mr. Blum, that is quite enough!" said the judge under her breath. "I will have to declare a mistrial if you continue with this line of questioning,

"I have no further questions, Your Honor."

Marvin stared at Morrie. It was clear he had bitten off more than he could chew and was worried. The DA had told him he wouldn't be accused of that. He thought his only risk if he implicated Sara and her husband was that he'd be charged with the crime Morrie had outlined in the beginning—unauthorized access and trespassing within a client's residence, thereby violating their right to privacy. Now he wasn't so sure.

As Morrie began packing up his briefcase to leave, Sara grabbed him by the arm and asked, "Do I have any chance?"

"Sure," he answered. "There's always a chance."

Those were not comforting words, and Morrie's forced grin didn't make her feel any better. Now, they could only wait and see.

*****

Part V

CH 71 - Coming Clean

2020

Dag sat in his office. He was wearing thin, having continued his late-night monitoring of Purgatory Park for days on end. For the past two days, he had struggled to stay awake as he clicked through different cases in the police database trying to find answers.

It was only when a knock came at his door that he momentarily snapped out of his trance. *No one knocks,* he thought. *They usually just come in.*

"Yeah," he barked, not bothering to see who it was.

"Uh, I'm sorry to interrupt, detective, but there is a Ms. Wilkins here. She says it's important that she sees you."

Dag looked up. It was one of the female officers who usually sat at the front desk to manage the office flow in and out.

"Sure," said Dag. "Show her back to my office. I'll talk to her here."

Mitzie came in, looking more humble than usual.

"Well, I certainly didn't expect you to visit?" Dag said with a surprised look on his face.

"I ... I really didn't expect to be here either," Mitzie answered.

"Please, have a seat Ms. Wilkins. I'm glad you came. Now, what is it that I can do for you?"

Mitzie started slowly, but as time went on, her story gathered momentum. Dag could tell it was more a catharsis than a confession. *She feels guilty,* he thought, *and she has to get it off her chest.*

"So, let me get this straight," said Dag, looking over his notes. "You say that your mother put you up to burglarizing Sara's clients' homes? Is that right?"

"Yes," Mitzie answered, ashamed. "I don't remember much about it. I believe Mom put a spell on me or something. She's capable of that sort of thing. I'm getting bits and pieces of it back in my memory, and what Mom would do is have Marvin pick me up late at night.

Then, we'd go over to the client's house to take the money, jewels or other valuables that he'd staked out while he was with Sara during her session. It was easy. We just broke in and knew exactly where to go to get the loot. It was the middle of the night, so usually the client was fast asleep and didn't even know we were there."

"They never heard you?"

"No, usually not. Maybe my Mom put a sleeping spell on them. I don't know. Claire Horwath was the only one who interrupted us."

"And you did this to the homes of Margaret Jenkins and her son, Will, and Claire Horwath?"

Mitzie nodded. "And others."

"But you say you didn't kill anyone? Why should I believe you?" Dag asked, still unsure whether to waste time on her story.

"How could I have committed those murders, detective? Look at me. I'm not even five feet tall and less than a hundred pounds."

"Yeah, but Marvin is pretty strong."

"Detective, we didn't do it. We didn't kill those people ... burglary, yes; murder, no."

"Why come clean now? Why implicate your mom, Marvin and yourself, when we are already prosecuting someone else for it: Sara McLaughlin? You could just walk away from this and nobody would ever know."

"I don't know. It's hard to understand, but it's like being given a poison that puts you into a coma. When you come out of it—*if* you come out—you're finally free of the toxin, and you can think clearly again. I'm being given a second chance—this time to do the right thing. Do you understand?"

"I believe I do."

"But I think my grandmother and great grandmother were in that coma too, and both managed to come out of it. It's my mother who is still under its influence though. She got a hold of the Fletcher family too, taking them with her to the dark side. Marvin and his father, Dwayne, were both threatened to help Patti with stealing from clients. They specifically targeted clients of other psychics so they could pin the break-ins on them if it came to that."

"But only every twenty-five years or so? Why is that?" asked Dag.

"Oh, it wasn't just every twenty-five years, detective. We did many jobs in between. However, it heated up this year for some reason. My mom made sure we had heists as often as we could. She never told me why."

"Is your mother involved in a cult?"

"What kind of cult?"

"A satanic cult."

"I don't know. She certainly doesn't go to church, if that's what you mean," said Mitzie. "As for me, it's almost like the eye of God is always watching me and what I do. It's like he's constantly judging me."

"Then, why did you start committing the crimes? Why did you let your mom intimidate you into doing it?" asked Dag.

"She said if I didn't help her, she would curse any child I ever had. And I know she meant it! She could do that." Mitzie's voice was wavering. "In the end, I think she just gave up and put me under her black magic spell instead."

"Is that why you never married or had children?" Dag asked, which he knew was out of line, but he thought it might help him.

Mitzie didn't answer. However, Dag was patient and didn't fill-in the silence, waiting for her to speak.

"I did," said Mitzie.

"You did what?"

"I had a child—a daughter. I gave her up for adoption because I didn't want her to be cursed by my mother."

"I'm sorry," said Dag.

"Yeah, so am I. I miss her. Her name was Beatrice," said Mitzie, almost breaking into tears.

"Bessie," said Dag, saying the common nickname.

"Yes—after my great grandmother."

"Do you know where she is now?"

"Yes, but I'm not supposed to," said Mitzie.

"I understand," said Dag. Then he asked, "What about your grandmother and great grandmother? Were they members of a satanic society?"

"I don't know that either. Neither one ever talked about it. Grandma Terri became really religious. She was always going to church and had all kinds of religious things all over the house – as if she were trying to keep the evil out, ya' know? My Grandma Bessie converted too but in her own way. She didn't go to church like Grandma Terri did."

"Yes. I know. I was at your grandmother's not long ago. Nice lady. And yes, she did have a lot of crosses all over the house. That is, until I went back several weeks ago. Then, there were a bunch of triangles, pentacles and other strange shapes on the walls."

"Triangles—pentacles? Not crosses?" asked Mitzie.

"Nope. All the crosses were gone," he answered.

"That's strange. I've never known Grandma Terri not to have crosses on her walls."

"When did you see her last?" asked Dag, jotting a note in his booklet.

"Oh, it's been a long time. I haven't been out there for, let's see, probably since last Christmas. It was the last time everyone was together. Mom said she wouldn't come, and she didn't. Even Grandma Bessie was there. She got a ride with me, and we met Grandma Terri and the others at her house for lunch. It was a good time."

"You didn't sing satanic carols then, I take it?" asked Dag grinning.

Mitzie smirked. "No! The rest of the family is actually quite religious. It's just my mom now. She's the one who's gone off the deep end."

"Was she always that way?"

"She's been that way as long as I can remember. Grandma Terri says she didn't use to be that way, though, and Grandma Bessie once said jokingly that it was just something hereditary—like it was in our genes or something. But then she told me that we grow out of it eventually. That was when the next generation got infected. I'm assuming Grandma Terri passed it on to Mom."

Mitzie stopped and looked at Dag. There was fear in her voice.

"I don't want to be infected, detective. Do you understand what I'm saying? I don't want to get it from my mother and then pass it on to Bea, my daughter. She's the only one I have now. I don't want her to contract it even if I'm not supposed to know where she is."

"She's of age now, isn't she?" asked Dag.

"Not for three more years. Then, I can reach out to her."

"Do you plan to do that?"

"Only if I'm certain I'm not infected with this thing, detective. I couldn't do that to her." Mitzie's eyes showed a depth of sincerity Dag hadn't seen in previous meetings with her.

"And you are willing to go to prison to stop it?" asked Dag.

"Yes. I don't think I have a choice."

"Okay, then. Let me get a full confession and have you sign it. Will that be all right? I will do all I can to get leniency for you. I think you deserve that much in return for what you've given me today."

"Yes, of course."

She got up, but Dag stopped her. "Mitzie, you know I shouldn't let you leave the precinct."

She looked at him. "Are you going to arrest me now?" she asked.

"Not until I get your signed confession. Let me get this typed up and read you your rights. Wait here," said Dag. "I'll be right back."

Dag got up to find someone to take her statement.

However, after he left the room, Mitzie felt a cold chill blow into the office. Her body shook as if suffering an epileptic seizure, and her eyes closed and rolled to the back of her head. Then, just as suddenly, she opened her eyes again and stood up. Her irises were no longer clear and lucid. Now there was a cloudy veil that had come over them. She was no longer Mitzie Wilkins.

When Dag returned, she was gone.

Dag got on the phone. The line rang and rang. There was no answering service to leave a message, so Dag contacted the local sheriff and asked that he stop by the old farmhouse where he had gone twice to talk to Terri and Patti.

"Dave? It's Dag Gallagher here in Boston. How are you?" Dag and Dave Sherman, sheriff of Essex County, had talked on the phone a few other times during their careers. They had even met each other during a charity fund-raising event one year. "Listen, I was wondering if you or one of your men could swing by a house near you ... No, you don't have to do it tonight, but if you're in the area sometime tomorrow, that would be great ... What am I looking for? Well, there's an older lady who lives there. I talked with her granddaughter about a case I'm working on, and I have some concerns about her wellbeing. I just wanted to have someone check on her and make sure she was all right. That's all ... Great! I appreciate it. Thanks, Dave."

***

Sheriff Sherman had told Dag he would stop by Terri Campbell's place as soon as he could. But in fact, he called Dag the next day.

"Detective Gallagher?" the sheriff began.

"You can call me Dag, sheriff. Were you able to stop by Ms. Campbell's place?"

"Yes, sir. We did that this morning. I'm afraid, Ms. Campbell is, well, she's dead sir. I think she's been dead for several weeks. She was sitting at her kitchen table when we found her. The coroner will take a look to determine the cause. I thought you should know."

In a way, the news was a surprise, but in another, it wasn't. With everything else happening, he suspected something wasn't quite right there. This only validated his feelings. He would get the coroner's report and analyze it. But it was what the sheriff hadn't said that told Dag much more than what he had. Terri's body had not been dismembered or disfigured. She had merely died at the kitchen table, apparently without a struggle or any sign of violence anyway. The sheriff mentioned bruise marks on and around her neck though and said the coroner would be looking at them.

Dag already knew there was nothing natural about this death, and he had a good idea about who might have killed her.

*****

CH 72 - DA's Anxiety

2020

After the debacle with Marvin, the DA began to get nervous about the outcome of the case. No longer was he certain he'd be able to slam home the conviction as he thought. Now, he was getting more desperate. A decision on the case would almost certainly come around the time of the election which was within the next two weeks—that was something he couldn't allow to go against them.

"You wanted to see me, sir?" said Tommy coming into the DA's opulent office.

"Yeah, Tommy, have a seat," said Johnson, motioning toward the pin-cushioned, leather couch next to his desk.

Tommy sat down and pulled out his note pad.

"You won't be needing that," said the DA, waving his hand. "Listen, we've got a bit of a problem now that Marvin stumbled up there on the witness stand. I'm not sure we have the credibility we need to get a conviction out of this. Plus, the one thing we're really missing here is the means to commit the murders. I mean, it's going to be a little hard to convince the jury that this small woman and her husband were able to do those things to those bodies. If there is some doubt now in the minds of the jurors about whether she committed the burglaries, I've got to have something more on the murder side." Then, his eyes met Tommy's. "So, what can you get for me?"

"Get for you, sir?"

"Yeah. I need some evidence to show how she might have done the murders—how she twisted their limbs and cut off their torsos or heads without leaving any blood behind. What do you have that I can go with?"

"I thought you were going to show that they strangled them and put plastic down to prevent the blood from going everywhere when they dismembered them," said Tommy.

"That's never going to fly now. We need something else."

"Like?"

"Work with Dag. You two figure out something."

"Dag? He's not going to help," said Tommy.

"You two look at what you have and come up with an angle. I don't care if you have to get the chief involved. You're asses are on the line! Whatever it is, it has to lead us back to Sara McLaughlin. Got it?"

"I'll work up something," Tommy answered.

"You do that," said Johnson. "And I don't care if you have to make it up. Bring in pots and saws from her house if you have to. Whatever it takes. Just make it work for me."

"Got it," Tommy said, getting up to leave.

On his way down the hall, the only thing he could think of was *How in the hell am I going to do this?* He knew he couldn't go to Dag, and there really wasn't anyone else he could go to. He was on his own, and that frightened him.

Tommy went home and opened the refrigerator, finding only a six pack of beer, a liter of Coke, a jar of spicy, hot salsa, and some week-old pepperoni pizza still glued to the box's top. His eyes scanned the inside shelves for anything else more appealing, but when that failed, he just grabbed a beer, went to the TV room, and collapsed into his well-worn armchair. He flipped on the flat screen, but quickly dozed off, waking in the morning to a nearly full, warm beer and the morning news show already underway.

"And the trial of Sara McLaughlin is now in its fourth week," said the broadcaster. "The district attorney is still bringing in witnesses and presenting evidence but is expected to complete his case within the next few days. It will then be the opportunity of the defense to present its case. That is anticipated to take up to another week.

"What is most striking is the defendant, Sara McLaughlin. Recently, her husband was found brutally murdered in their home in Dorchester. As of now, she has not been charged with that murder. But most in the courtroom find it difficult to imagine that this diminutive woman could have committed the atrocities with which she's been charged. However, the DA continues to remind us that we should not be deceived by a defendant's appearance. He continually reminds us of Ted Bundy, who was the handsome, charismatic serial killer in Florida.

"We will continue to follow the trial as it unfolds. This is Maggie Whitmore reporting for Channel Eleven News."

***

Tommy made it into the office. The hours ticked by, but still he had nothing to show for it. Finally, the Johnson's secretary called. She told him that the DA wanted to see him before he left for the day. He wanted the story that Tommy had come up with.

"I'm still workin' on it," he confessed to her.

"You'd better come up with something," she warned. "You know how Mr. Johnson gets when he doesn't get what he wants."

Tommy put down the phone and sighed. He knew he'd have to make a trip down the hall to see someone who didn't want to see him. But he was running out of options.

Dag put down his reading glasses and rubbed his eyes when Tommy came in.

"What do you want this time?" Dag asked, not so politely.

"I know you have every reason not to help me—especially since you think Sara is innocent."

"She *is* innocent."

"But what if she's guilty? What if she somehow did commit those murders. You wouldn't want her to go free, now would you?"

"Tommy, we've been over this. She's innocent." Dag was adamant.

"So, if she and her husband or Marvin didn't do it, who did?"

Dag shook his head. "I don't know."

"Then how do you know they *didn't* do it?" Tommy said, almost shouting at his former mentor.

"Perhaps, it *was* supernatural," said Dag, surprising Tommy.

"Really? Supernatural? You? I didn't think you believed in that crap."

Dag smiled. "I didn't use to, but none of this makes sense unless you consider it."

"*Huh?*" exclaimed Tommy. "The hard-nosed, just-the-facts-ma'am Dag Gallagher. *You*, of all people, are telling me that there is no earthly explanation for these crimes other than the supernatural?

Then, why would spirits make off with money and jewelry? What would they use that for on the other side? I didn't think you needed money once you in Heaven."

"Or Hell," Dag added. Then, he said, "Did you ever read the Edgar Alan Poe story, *Murders in the Rue Morgue?*"

"What's a rue morgue?" asked Tommy.

"No, Rue Morgue refers to a French section in Paris named *Morgue*, as in 'death,' of course," said Dag. "*Rue* means 'street' in French. It was one of the author's best works, I think. It's about two murders that happen in an inaccessible upper part of apartment building. It's an odd murder in that one victim is found with her throat cut and her daughter's body is found stuffed up a chimney. However, all the doors and windows are locked from the inside. There are no signs of forced entry anywhere inside the apartment. The scene is brutal and nothing from the inside was taken. The question, then, was *how* were the murders committed and by *whom?*"

"Someone must have been hiding inside the apartment and surprised them when they came home; that's an easy one," said Tommy.

"Then how could all of the windows and doors *still* be locked from the inside after the murders?" asked Dag. "The perpetrator didn't have a key to relock them once he left."

"It was a self-locking door, of course," answered Tommy.

"They didn't have those back in the 1800s when these murders happened."

"You didn't tell me that part of it," said Tommy, defensively.

"Okay, so how was it done?"

"I don't know. I wasn't at the scene. I didn't do the forensics," Tommy said sarcastically.

"Well, as it turns out, there were two additional clues the police missed. First was the strange hair that was found at the scene. It didn't look human. It was much coarser and longer than that of most humans. The second was the strange voices the neighbors overheard coming from the home the night of the murders. They said they sounded like foreigners, but none could agree on what nationality it was. They didn't understand any of the words."

Tommy just shrugged. "I give up," he answered.

"Don't be too hard on yourself, Tommy. The Inspector, whose name was Dupin[1], figured out it was a rogue ape—in this case an orangutan—that had escaped from the nearby zoo or someone who personally owned it. The beast had gotten into the apartment by going down the chimney before killing the older woman and then the daughter, pulling the young girl's body up the chimney as it left."

Tommy looked at Dag in disbelief. "Is that really true?" he asked.

"No, of course not. But it makes for a hell of a good story, don't you think?" said Dag. "It was pure genius, but then again, Poe was a genius, albeit a little crazy."

Tommy smirked. "Never heard of him."

"You never heard of Edgar Allen Poe?" asked Dag.

Ignoring him, Tommy said, "Come on, Dag. You're not suggesting that an orangutan killed those people in south Boston, are you?"

Dag had to smile at that one. "I've heard worse ideas," he answered.

"Really? An orang a ... whatever you said?"

"No, I'm not saying that. I'm just saying maybe it's something really unusual like what Poe described. Something we've not thought of ... something really crazy."

"It was crazy! Just look at the bodies!" said Tommy.

"But maybe there *is* something else going on ... or a combination of things that only make sense once they're all strung together."

"I still don't know where you're going with this," said Tommy, "but you did give me an idea. Thanks." He gave Dag a half wave and headed back down the hall.

I don't know what that was all about, but I think it gave myself *an idea too*, thought Dag.

*****

Tommy arrived at the DA's office at 4:30 in the afternoon, ahead of his appointment which was at 4:45. He expected to wait in the

---

[11] In the story, Dupin was actually not an Inspector but rather an amateur detective.

outside lobby for a few hours but was summoned by Johnson's assistant right away.

"What-da-ya' got?" said Johnson, putting down a paper with the latest polling numbers highlighting the mayor's gubernatorial race.

"I think I've got a good one, sir," said Tommy, proud of himself. "What if they conned the apartment supervisors into helping them? Sara, her husband and Marvin could have paid off the supes to help them murder their victims. They would have had the equipment right there on the premises and the muscle to do it. What do you think?"

Johnson shook his head. "That's a stupid idea," he said. "You'd have to convince the jury that two different building supes were involved in this scheme. It won't work. Too coincidental."

Tommy felt stupid. He'd rushed his idea without thinking it through. Johnson was right; it wouldn't fly.

"But ..." said the DA, his facing looking like it had just had an epiphany, "... what if Marvin and his son had been in on it with Vince and Sara. Marvin has a son. We already know that. He might have been involved too. That's it! Marvin and his son were both part of it. They had help from his son or even some gang members. With Sara, her husband and Marvin's guys, they might have been able to pull it off."

"All those people and no one heard them?" Tommy looked at the DA with a puzzled expression on his face.

"Gang members do this stuff all the time. They know how to burgle places and how to kill people."

"We don't even know that Marvin's son is part of a gang."

"He is now," said Johnson.

"But you told Marvin that if he went along with you and implicated Sara and her husband, that you'd cut him a deal."

Johnson laughed. "Boy, just like I thought. You'll never make it in the big leagues, son. Did we sign anything to that effect? Was anything I said recorded? No, of course not. I'm not that stupid. But Marvin, Sara and her attorney sure are."

"So, you're going to ..."

"Yeah, of course. Marvin and his son are expendable in the big scope of things. It's a means to an end. Can't you see that? So what if we have to sacrifice a few people along the way. If we get the mayor elected governor, we can do so much more good for the state. We can do the right things for the people who need it most."

"Yeah, sure," said Tommy, unconvinced. It still didn't seem right to him, but then again, he'd never played in the *big leagues* before.

"Now, you go and take care of all the details of how this will work ... you know, how we'll piece all of this together. Make sure you make up documents that show Marvin's son is part of a gang in his neighborhood. Then, get back to me tomorrow. I have to finish the mayor's campaign schedule for the rest of the week."

Johnson swung his chair around to look at his computer screen. Tommy's time was up, and the DA had no more to waste on him.

Tommy returned to the precinct to work on his assignment. *It's really shitty*, he thought. *But nobody else is going to look out for me, so I guess I have to. Who's Marvin anyway? Better that he's the fall guy in this, than me.*

Still, even for Tommy, it didn't seem right.

*****

CH 33 – Sacrificial Lamb

2020

Tommy did his job. He found out who Marvin's friends and those of his son, Jerel, were. He altered and replaced several internal documents in the database, adding Jerel to a list of known gang members in his neighborhood. He even appended a few case files, implicating Jerel in the group who had committed the crime. Then, Tommy threatened Jerel that if he didn't cooperate, his father would be found guilty in the burglaries, assault and the murders. He lied to him—just as Johnson had done to Jerel's father—by telling him that both of them could be spared the death penalty only if he pleaded guilty to helping in the murders and incriminating friends or "gang" members.

"I ain't gonna snitch on any of my friends," said Jerel. "You'll never get me to do that—never!"

"But that's the only way this is gonna work, Jerel," Tommy answered.

"I don't care. Hook me up to the chair if you have to, but I ain't bringin' my friends into this. No way!"

Tommy sighed. "Then you gotta confess to working with Sara and her husband. You gotta sign this piece of paper saying that you helped them. Otherwise, your dad gets fried. Do you understand me?"

The court reconvened and the prosecution amended its list of witnesses and gave it to the defense prior to the session. Morrie was confused by the choice. Marvin was again being called to the stand. He'd already been sworn in, so he was only reminded of that fact by the court clerk. But there was another witness added too.

Johnson got up and smiled at Marvin, as he had done the previous session. However, this time he started off with as much shock-and-awe as he could muster.

"So, Marvin. You said earlier that you were not part of the burglary – that you only provided information to Ms. McLaughlin, and she and her husband then committed the crimes. Is that right?"

"Yes, that's right," answered Marvin, unaware of what was about to happen.

Then the DA turned to the judge and said, "Your Honor, I realize that Marvin is not on trial here, but it is important that I ask the following questions to establish the foundation of our case against Ms. McLaughlin."

The judge was surprised at the request and almost considered an out-of-order response but refrained. "Proceed," she said cautiously, "but I warn you, that I will sustain an objection if it is not forthcoming."

"Mr. Fletcher," Johnson went on, "what if I told you that we have a witness that puts *you* at the crime scenes the nights of the break-ins?"

Marvin was stunned. "What? But you said ..."

Johnson held up what was presumably a list of witnesses.

"I object, Your Honor!" roared Morrie. "This is totally irrelevant to the case against my client. Mr. Fletcher is not on trial here."

The judge looked disapprovingly at the DA.

"Your Honor, as I said, I will tie this together, *please*," he begged.

"Quickly, then," she answered, looking very stern.

"What if I also told you that we found your fingerprints at the scenes."

Then Marvin shot back. "Of course my prints were there. I was inside with Sara when she held her séances. I told you that."

"You're right about that, Mr. Fletcher, but we also found your prints on the window jambs and back doors to these residences. Not the way people normally come into an apartment or house—do you think?"

"That's a lie!" Marvin shouted.

"Is it? Then why would we have those prints?"

"You're a son-of-a ..."

The gallery became unruly, as people began talking excitedly about what the DA had just done.

"Order!" yelled the judge. "I'll have order in my courtroom!"

397

"Objection!" Morrie roared again.

"Order!" the judge shouted.

The chaos was unsettling. Sara sat confused by what was going on around her. She leaned over to Morrie and asked, "What's going on?" But her attorney ignored her, concentrating on what was happening in the courtroom. He well understood what the DA was doing—linking Marvin in the plot, thus yielding more muscle by which they could have committed the horrendous atrocities. Given what Marvin initially told them after being arrested, there was no doubt in Johnson's mind that Marvin's prints were likely there ... he was just with two or more other people committing the crimes.

When things quieted, the judge began to say something, but the DA blurted out, "Yes, Marvin. We have evidence that shows that you were there with Ms. McLaughlin and her husband Vince when the burglaries were committed. But it wasn't just the *three* of you who were able to twist and contort those bodies the way they were found, killing the very clients that Ms. McLaughlin had sessions with earlier that day. No, it was *four!* Your son, Jerel, was part of your team, wasn't he?"

"Objection!" yelled Morrie.

"Order!"

"Objection, Your Honor! The prosecution is presenting evidence not shared with the defense. This is not permissible!"

Yet, things were now out of control. The DA's questions had led the jury in the direction he was hoping for. It planted the seed of doubt in their minds, and as much as the judge would tell them to ignore the line of questioning, it would still be there. He had opened some possibility that the three of them—or perhaps four—could have committed the murders as they had unfolded. Now it was a matter of what the jury believed was beyond a reasonable doubt. Better yet, he might get a mistrial which would push the decision well-past election day.

"Mr. Johnson ... one more word from you and I will declare a mistrial!" shouted the judge, furious with him.

"Judge, I now call my last witness. I ask Jerel Fletcher to please come to the stand."

The doors at the back of the courtroom opened, and in walked Jerel.

*****

CH 34 – Jerel

2020

Jerel took the stand. He raised his right hand and placed the other on a Bible. After taking the oath, he sat down.

"Mr. Fletcher, is it true that you helped your father, Marvin, Ms. Sara McLaughlin and her husband, Vince McLaughlin, commit the burglaries and crimes for which we've presented in this courtroom."

Johnson's question was vague and should have been faced with objection, but Morrie was still trying to process what was now going on and where things were headed.

"Yes," said Jerel.

"No!" shouted Marvin from across the courtroom.

The scene was bizarre, but it would only become worse.

"Order!" shouted the judge, banging her gavel.

"And were you part of the group that committed these crimes under the direction and guidance of Sara McLaughlin, the defendant?"

"Yes," said Jerel.

"No further questions, Your Honor," said Johnson, unbuttoning his jacket and sitting down—much satisfied with himself.

There was buzzing throughout the courtroom, and the judge was trying to get her head around what was happening.

"Uh, Mr. Blum, do you have a cross?"

Normally, he would have protested the last-minute presentation of Jerel as a witness with no time for him to prepare; however, he elected to push ahead, seeing a sliver of opportunity.

Morrie rose from his chair and buttoned his jacket.

"Ah, Mr. Fletcher. So, you are the son of Marvin Fletcher here, is that right?"

"Yes, sir," said Jerel.

"And you are coming on your own free will to volunteer this information, is that right?"

Jerel hesitated but then nodded, "Yes."

"Then, for the court, would you please identify Sara McLaughlin?"

Jerel hesitated, wondering if it were a trick.

"When did you last speak to Ms. McLaughlin?" Morrie asked, not waiting for the identification.

"Uh, I don't remember," said Jerel.

"Are you sure she's in the courtroom?" Morrie asked, throwing another wrench in the works.

"Uh, well, I think that's her," said Jerel, pointing to Sara sitting at the defendant's table.

"You're not sure?"

Jerel again looked at Morrie, hoping for some signal that he was right, but he got none.

"I'm pretty sure," said Jerel.

"You're only pretty sure? Yet, you are absolutely sure she told you to burglarize for her. Is that right? How can you be so sure of what she said when you don't even know who she is?"

"Objection!" shouted Johnson, infuriated by the questioning.

"Sustained! Mr. Blum, I ..."

"No further questions, Your Honor," said Morrie, taking his seat back at the defendant's table.

The judge was livid. She was about to call both attorneys to approach the bench, but it was the end of the day, and she didn't have the energy for it.

"Court is adjourned until tomorrow at nine o'clock," she said, banging her gavel. "I want to see both of you in my chambers ... *now!*"

***

Judge Madison closed the door to her chambers.

"What the hell was that?" she asked, trying to contain her anger.

"It was something that came up at the last minute, Your Honor." It was Johnson who was making things up as he went, hoping something would stick. "I thought it was vitally important that it be raised in today's session."

"This violates all standards of due process," said Morrie forcefully. "This cannot be tolerated! I won't stand for it!"

"I am tempted to declare a mistrial, Mr. Johnson. Is that what you want here?" the judge said, more rhetorically than inquiringly.

"If that's what you need to do," said the DA giving her a churlish grin.

The judge glowered at the DA. She had suffered his antics before and knew when he was up to something.

"I will think about this and let you know my decision tomorrow."

*****

CH 35 - A Jeweled Clue

2020

Frustration turned to anger when Dag heard about the stunt the DA had pulled in the courtroom, calling Jerel in at the last minute as a witness. He pounded the table and shouted a few expletives before calming himself. *That kind of trickery was quintessential Johnson at his worst or best, depending on which side you were on,* he thought.

After grabbing a soda from the vending machine, Dag sat down to re-review the list of items allegedly stolen from the Jenkins' case in Dorchester. He found that mainly jewelry had been taken, although there had been several collector-grade coins missing as well. As for Claire, Dag struggled with why she was burgled.

If he thought there was any validity to a supernatural explanation for the murders, he had to find a reasonable explanation about the missing pieces from Claire's apartment too. It was highly unlikely that a phantom would have any need or desire for such material things. Claire had given the police a detailed list of what had been stolen there. She had even provided photos which were used by the police and the insurance company to support her insurance claim.

Dag's finger skimmed the page, quickly covering the heisted items, but about three-quarters of the way down the page, it stopped. One silver necklace with a pentagram set with a deep blue rectangular sapphire and surrounded by small, square diamonds, the line read.

I've seen one like this before, he said to himself.

He picked up the phone and made a call.

"Claire, this is Detective Gallagher. You say here on your affidavit that there were quite a few pieces of jewelry missing from the burglary."

"Yes … several."

"The list includes mother-of-pearl earrings; a peridot and silver cross pendant; a Damascene, Toledo necklace; some rhinestone rings of various sorts and ages; and a few more things. I'm sure they meant quite a lot to you?"

"Why yes, detective. They were mostly my grandmother's. My mother gave them to me when she passed away about five years ago. They were heirlooms. Did you find them?"

"Unfortunately, no. But I want to ask you about another piece in particular. It was a pentagram sapphire necklace. It had diamonds in it. Do you recall that one?"

"Of course," said Claire. "That was the strangest of them all, but I loved it. As I think about it now, I wonder if that was what lured the phantom into my apartment in the first place."

"How so?"

"The pentagram, of course. It's sometimes considered a symbol of evil, I think. At least that's what I've been told. When I got it, I thought that too. But my boyfriend told me that was an old wives' tale, and it wasn't true."

"Your boyfriend. He's the one who died, right? That's what the report said. You asked Ms. McLaughlin to do a session with you so you could talk to him."

"Yes, that's right," said Claire.

"That item seems pretty valuable. Were you with your boyfriend when he bought it?"

Claire was quiet.

"Ms. Horwath?"

"No, I wasn't. He just surprised me. Why?"

"Do you know where he got it?"

Again, Claire was quiet for a moment. "I ... I really don't know, detective. Is that all the questions you had?" she asked.

"Uh, yes. Well, thanks for your time, and, oh, Ms. Horwath, I may contact you again if I need more information or we recover some of your missing pieces."

"Thanks, detective. Your so kind and thoughtful—it must run in your family. You're a lot like your dad."

Dag hung up the phone. *Odd*, he thought, after the fact. *How did she know Dad?*

Yet, his attention now was on following leads. He knew where to go next to try to track down that valuable piece of jewelry: Patti Campbell.

*****

CH 96 - Wedding Time

1945

Bessie and Janice had been best friends since high school. They had been there for each other, even when others had found them strange and unapproachable. Yet, there were four other girls from the school whom they were able to attract into their gravitational sphere. All were there that fateful night when they decided to have a séance and contact the dead.

The séance that was held their senior year had revealed Janice's deep and powerful psychic talents, including the ability to see, hear and feel the presence of spirits from beyond. During that same night, Bessie had acquired powers too—those even greater but of a darker and more sinister nature.

Since that time in 1939, Janice and Bessie had been in constant contact with each other as they both got odd jobs after graduation and still lived in and around the Boston area. But by early 1944, Janice stopped getting messages from Bessie. When her calls failed to go through, Janice visited Bessie's apartment to see if she were all right. She called on her several times, leaving calling cards, but still got no reply. She found that unusual, as they had not had a fallout of any sort. After nearly a year, Janice received a post in a fancy envelope.

The Pleasure of Your Company
Is Requested at the Marriage of
Miss Beatrice D. Belzikov
And
Mr. Rosco A. Turner

The wedding was to be held at the Cathedral of the Holy Cross—a magnificent church built in Boston during the nineteenth century. Janice was happy for her friend but crushed to see that she was marrying Rosco. She had no idea they were dating, let alone engaged to be married.

Feeling betrayed and slighted, Janice put on a disingenuous mask of gratulation and reached out to contact her old friend.

"Bessie, how have you been? It's been a long time," said Janice, forcing an upbeat, friendly tone.

"Yes, too long," Bessie answered. "I'm sorry I haven't kept up with you lately—with work and everything. It's just been too much."

"Yes, and planning the wedding ... I'm sure it's taken a lot of time," said Janice hoping part of the sarcasm would sink in.

"Yes, the wedding! It has been a lot—trying to get everything just perfect."

"I'm so happy for you!" said Janice. "Congratulations!"

"Rosco and I have been dating for months, but I never thought he'd ask me this soon. It's all happening so fast. I'm sure you understand."

"Well, I think it's great," said Janice. "I couldn't be happier!"

***

The wedding was originally planned for the large cathedral, but that changed for some unexpected reason, and instead was held at a small, local church near Bessie's hometown. The wedding was quaint, but perfect—just as Bessie had hoped. The sun was bright in the April sky and the reception was a drunken laugh-fest. Everyone had a great time. Janice had come with her new boyfriend, James Winfield, and by all accounts they seemed to have a good time.

During the reception, Bessie and Janice talked at length, but before Janice left, she whispered in her friend's ear. "Bessie, may I call you in a few weeks? There's something on my mind that I need to tell you."

"Of course," Bessie answered. "We need more time to catch up anyway."

After the honeymoon, Janice called Bessie and they met for lunch at a café in Roxbury, not far from Janice's brownstone. It wasn't long before Bessie pressed Janice for more.

"So, what is it that you wanted to talk to me about?" Bessie asked.

"It's James and me. I just don't think it's going to work," said Janice. "He's never around. He's always at work ... working late into the night. Sometimes he doesn't call me for weeks. He says the client load is killing him, but I don't know. Maybe he's seeing someone else or just isn't interested."

"What does he do again?"

"He's an architect," said Janice. "He said that his firm has staff to do the work but that he has to supervise it. Sometimes clients ask for things, and they need them 'first thing' in the morning. He stays late and, at times, into the early morning hours to finish the drafts."

"That makes sense," said Bessie. "So, it sounds like you're just lonely?"

"Yeah, I guess," said Janice.

"Well, why don't you come over for supper tonight. I'm fixing a roast. Rosco and I won't be able to eat it all anyway, and he hates leftovers. I'll expect you at six. Is that okay?"

Janice showed up at six o'clock. Holding a bottle of Burgundy in her hand, she rang the doorbell. Rosco answered. He was taller than she remembered. But he let her in, and they had a nice conversation about the old high school days until Bessie came down to join them.

"Supper will be ready in a few minutes," she said, greeting her guest.

"Can I help?" asked Janice.

"Sure. That would be lovely," Bessie answered.

Janice followed Bessie into the kitchen, put on a red apron, and rolled up her sleeves to help prepare a serving bowl of salad for them.

"Janice?" Bessie said, grinding the pepper to sprinkle on top of the roast. "There is something I wanted to tell you too. It may have seemed odd not to have the wedding in the large cathedral downtown as I had originally planned, but ..."

"No, not really. I just assumed there was a scheduling conflict or something," Janice said, stripping lettuce leaves from the bunch.

"No, that wasn't it. It was something else." Bessie placed her hand on her belly and smiled.

"You're pregnant?" said Janice, not knowing whether to be happy or afraid for her friend.

"Yeah!" said Bessie, bubbly and joyful. "That's why. We thought we shouldn't do it knowing that I was already preggers."

Janice laughed. "Well, that's wonderful. So, Rosco knows?" she laughed again.

"Of course, he does, silly!" said Bessie. "And if it's a girl, I'm naming her Janice."

"No! Don't do that!"

"No, I want to," said Bessie. "You're my best friend. You'll always be that, Janice."

The dinner went smoothly, and Janice commented on how delicious everything was. Bessie was pleased that Janice and Rosco seemed to hit it off well too. They joked and carried on, even after the dishes were cleared and desert was a delicious memory. Bessie was happy. She was afraid that not telling Janice about the baby would cause problems in their friendship, and that was something she didn't want. She was glad they were reconnecting—it was almost like old times again.

But it wasn't.

*****

CH 99 – Caught

1945

Janice was seeing more of the Turners these days. She would come over and hang out with the two of them, especially on weekends. Rosco had his own insurance business which he started during the war. He had severely fractured his arm playing football in high school, requiring pins and bracing. As a result, he was devastated when he was given a waiver and told he could not join the armed forces due to the limited range of motion in that arm. So, while his high school pals went off to Europe to fight, he had to remain home and find work.

But then Rosco's insurance business took off, and, like Janice's boyfriend, he seemed never to be around. Always having to work late and sometimes weekends, the situation was putting pressure on his marriage, especially with the rapidly approaching birth of their child.

Eventually, Bessie grew tired of her husband's promises that the hectic schedule and late-night hours would abate. They didn't. And when nothing changed, she knew she had to try something different.

One night, when Rosco called her to tell her he was working late, she decided to surprise him. She baked his favorite cherry pie and drove down to the insurance office to give him a cheering up.

"Hey, Fred. I just stopped by to see Rosco. Brought him his favorite desert," said Bessie, smiling and holding the tin in her hands.

"Smells awesome," said Rosco's business partner, Fred Whittaker.

Fred had been friends with Rosco and Bessie for a long time. He had gone to the same high school and been in many of the same classes. He had played football too and was blocking for Rosco during the play where Rosco got injured.

"Maybe he'll give you a sliver of it," said Bessie, cutting it into slices.

"If I beg hard enough," Fred answering, chuckling. "But I'm afraid he's not here at the moment. I'll be glad to save him a piece until he returns."

Bessie eyed Fred suspiciously, wondering why her husband wasn't there.

"No," Fred said before she could answer, "I promise I won't eat any before he gets back. I'll save some crumbs for him."

They both laughed as Fred covered the pie and took it to the back of the office.

Bessie turned to leave but heard a familiar voice coming from another part of the office. It was a woman's voice, and she was giggling like a little girl.

Bessie went behind the front desk, now vacated by the receptionist who had left hours earlier and walked through an open doorway to where the office staff had their desks. At that time of night, no one was there—all the desks were empty awaiting their owners' return the next morning.

But Bessie continued, following the sound of the woman's voice and finally reaching the door to her husband's office. She reached for the handle but suddenly stopped. It was ajar, and she peered inside through the narrow opening …

*****

CH 78 - Expert Witness

2020

The prosecution finally rested its case, and it was the defense's turn to begin calling witnesses. To Sara's dismay, she was forced to have her own daughter testify that she was at home the nights of the murders. It was doubly hard as LJ was a minor, so her testimony would be less than credible in the eyes of the jury. The sole reason Morrie insisted she testify was because Vince, the only other witness, was dead. No one else could provide an alibi.

It was a terrible ordeal as her daughter had to endure a blistering cross examination by the prosecution. As attorneys understand, it's all about winning the case regardless of whether there are casualties in the process. In this case, Johnson knew there would be plenty of casualties. That had never stopped him before and would not stop him now.

During one of his tirades, Johnson suggested that on the nights of the murders, LJ had gone to bed early, leaving Sara plenty of time to commit the crimes with her husband, Marvin and Jerel and then return home at daybreak when LJ would still be asleep before rising and getting ready for school.

It was true that LJ had gone to bed early those nights, but it wasn't true that she had fallen asleep. In fact, she had stayed up late watching *The Twilight Zone*. But under pressure from the cross-examination, she had become confused. She also didn't want to admit that she'd disobeyed her mother by not going straight to bed and *not* watching *The Twilight Zone*. She understood that her mother was on trial, but she was afraid it would make her mom look like a bad parent, so she said nothing. Her daughter, at fifteen years old, was easily painted as an unreliable witness by Johnson who made quick work of the witness with his brutal cross.

Finally, Morrie brought up a key, expert witness, Dr. Amyl Nehrugian, who specialized in blunt force trauma and physical violence in murder cases.

"Will you state your name for the court?" asked Morrie.

"I am Dr. Amyl Nehrugian."

"And Dr. Nehrugian, what is it that you do?"

"I'm an expert in blunt force trauma. I've been assisting the police department for years in solving crimes of physical violence, particularly when they result in the victim's death."

"I see. And you received your medical training at ...?"

"Johns Hopkins University medical school with an undergraduate degree in physics at the Massachusetts Institute of Technology in Boston."

"Ah, MIT. Yes, a very good school," commented Morrie, pacing back and forth in front of the witness box. "Now, you've reviewed the scenes of the murders and made your evaluations of the methods and means of the homicides, have you not?"

"Yes, I have."

"And what are your conclusions, Dr. Nehrugian?"

"Which case?" asked the doctor, needing more clarification.

"Oh, I'm sorry—the ..." It was an awkward moment when Morrie's mental lapse forced him to consult his notebook. "... it was the incident in Dorchester. It was in March of this year—a Ms. Margaret Jenkins and her son, William."

"Well, with regard to Ms. Jenkins, in layman's terms, her torso was twisted around on her body so that it faced backwards in bed. In technical terms, the left and right femoral heads and ischiofemoral tendons and cartilage were fractured, caused by a tremendous force ..." Dr. Nehrugian went on to give the rest of his technical description of the homicide.

"Basically, then," said Morrie, helping to clarify, "she died when her spinal cord snapped, resulting in the loss of nerve connection between her brain and the rest of her body," said Morrie.

"Yes. She also bled-out internally."

"But there was no blood found in the body."

"True."

"So, whatever killed her exerted a force so strong that it severed the bone cleanly, ripped tendons and other ligatures, ruptured arteries—all of which nearly tore the head from the rest of the body and left no blood within it. Is that right?"

413

"Yes."

"Now, in your professional opinion, how could that happen?" asked Morrie.

"Based on the damage done to the body, it would have taken a significant force to do what was done to Ms. Jenkins."

"What kind of force do you think was necessary for this?"

"I would estimate the force was in excess of four-hundred-foot pounds."

"What do you mean?" asked Morrie.

"An example would be revving a Ford truck, say an F-150 to 2000 rpm. This machine can exert a force of about 200 Newton meters or equivalent to 146-foot pounds. But the force on Ms. Jenkins was much more than that based on the severity of the damage done to the bone, cartilage and surrounding tissue. Revving the same engine to over 5000 rpm would be necessary."

The expert witness couched the discussion in terms the jury could relate to, and many were aghast.

"Is there such an engine that is mobile enough to get into an apartment and use against a person like this?"

"Objection," said the DA. "The witness is an expert with blunt force trauma, not machinery."

"He is a blunt trauma expert, Your Honor. He has some knowledge in this area."

"I will allow it," said the judge. "Objection overruled."

"Again, Dr. Nehrugian, are you aware of such a machine?"

"No ..." the doctor responded quickly, "...nothing that would be small enough to be carried in easily or quiet enough to be run and not heard by a neighbor in the middle of the night. No."

"Even if there were an engine that was that quiet, would it be possible to get it inside the home, to the victim's bedroom, kill her, and get it out without being seen or noticed?"

Dr. Nehrugian smiled. "Like I said—very, very improbable."

"So, in your opinion, could a woman in her thirties, weighing slightly more than one hundred pounds, do such a thing?"

"No. Absolutely not."

"And in the case of William, her son?"

"In this case, his body was found in bed and was badly mutilated in addition to being disfigured like his mother's."

"So, how was the body?"

"It was cut cleanly in half. However, there was no blood found in the bed or on the scene."

"How is this possible? How could there be no blood if the bodies were cut in two?" asked Morrie, already knowing there was no answer.

"It would require something extremely sharp and hot," answered Dr. Nehrugian. "The instrument had to be sharp enough to cut through bone and hard cartilage like the proverbial hot knife through butter."

"Is that what was used? A knife?"

"Unless you own an ancient Damascus steel sword, which are extremely rare, one of titanium or diamond would be just as capable separating the body parts so cleanly.

"Then when was the blood removed? Was it before or after the body was cleaved?" asked Morrie.

"Based on the markings on the body, I would say it was before," said the doctor.

How long would it take to drain a body, given the wound size?"

"At least forty minutes to an hour and a half. It would be remarkable not to have a single drop spilled anywhere during this time," said the doctor.

"And that's per body, correct?"

"Yes, so it could have taken more than two hours."

"What about the cauterization? Is there a portable machine you know of that can do that?" asked Morrie.

"Nothing I'm aware of. It would take even more time to cauterize every blood vessel that was severed during this crime."

"How long would that take?"

"A skilled surgeon would require another few hours per body," said Nehrugian. "And I say again, a *skilled* surgeon."

The doctor finished the sentence, and the room became quiet like a mausoleum. No one breathed, except for Morrie, who was already preparing for his next question. But he was interrupted by a late objection.

"So, in your expert opinion, is there any way this woman could have committed those crimes?"

"No."

"Is there any way this woman," said Morrie, again pointing to Sara, "could have perpetrated those crimes even with three other grown men who were not skilled in medical procedures?"

"No."

"I have no further questions," said Morrie, retaking his seat.

Johnson rose from his chair. He had a smug look on his face as if he had prepared himself well for this confrontation.

"Dr. Nehrugian, you are being paid by the defense to provide this expert testimony, are you not?"

"Yes."

"And you said your expertise is in the field of what?"

"Blunt force trauma," answered the doctor.

"I see. But you said yourself that this was not 'blunt force' was it?"

"Well, it is ...," began the doctor, before being cut off by the DA.

"The crime was committed using a hot, sharp weapon, you said. Correct?"

"One was. Yes."

"And you admit that you are not a weapons expert are you?"

"No, however, ..."

"Very well. Then, there could be weapons out there of which you are not aware that are capable of doing the cutting and cauterizing that you describe. Is that not so?"

"There could be, but I ..." said the doctor.

"There could be, yes, and you don't know with absolute certainty."

"Of course, not," responded the doctor defensively. "But no one could know *every* weapon ..."

"Doctor, isn't it possible that a certain laser might do the trick? Aren't there lasers that are hot enough to cut through flesh and bone and cauterize at the same time?"

"I am not aware of ..."

"Precisely, doctor. You are not aware of everything," said Johnson. "I have no further questions," added the DA.

Morrie quickly got up. "But does this explain where the blood went? Does it doctor?"

"I don't know what you mean?" asked the doctor.

"Even if a laser were used, there would still be blood in the bodies, correct?"

"Oh, most certainly," answered Dr. Nehrugian, a bit relieved that his credibility had, at least, been partially restored. "The cauterized wound would only have sealed the blood vessels—the blood would not have left the body."

"And the size of a laser needed to cut through bone and cartilage and cauterize the arteries would have to be of some significant size, I would imagine—something very large and hard to move in and out of a small apartment. Wouldn't you think?"

"Yes," said the doctor.

"Objection!" said Johnson. "The doctor is not an expert in lasers."

"Sustained," said the judge quickly.

"No further questions, Your Honor," said Morrie, sitting back in his seat.

The DA rose once more, "But the blood could still have been drained off *after* the killing, correct?"

"Well ..." said the doctor, reluctant to answer.

"The doctor will answer the question," said the Judge sternly.

"Yes, of course, but I don't believe that it was."

"No further questions," said Johnson, before sitting down.

The doctor sat emotionless. He was used to taking a beating of his reputation and his expertise in these sorts of trials, but usually he held his own. This prosecutor was relentless and found—or more accurately—created the appearance of weakness where none existed. He had played his hand well, and it would be up to the jury to determine which side it believed.

"You are dismissed," said the judge, looking over the top of her black-rimmed glasses.

The doctor stepped down awkwardly from the witness box and went back to the gallery. At the same time, the judge banged the gavel and called for a recess until the next day.

"We will reconvene tomorrow at nine o'clock," she said before leaving the bench.

"I'm doomed," Sara whispered, leaning over to her attorney.

"Not yet, Sara. Don't give up so easily."

But even Morrie was beginning to wonder what else he could bring to her defense.

*****

CH 99 - Late Night Visitor

2020

Sara lay in her cell; her eyes wide open after tossing and turning. She had given up on being able to get back to sleep. She had never been a good sleeper—waking up several times during the night on average. Below her, on the bottom bunk, was another detainee, Natalie Bowman. She was being held for manslaughter—a third-degree murder charge. Sara had not talked much to her, preferring to keep her distance. However, when Natalie found out she was a psychic, she pleaded for her to do a reading.

"Come on, Sara. Just one," begged Natalie from below her.

"Fine," Sara finally answered. She closed her eyes and let her mind drift. Soon, a young woman appeared to her. She was only eight or nine years old and had short red hair just past her ears. Her eyes were blue, she had freckles across her nose and on both cheeks.

"Your sister is here," said Sara, her eyes still closed. "She says she misses you."

Natalie began to cry. "That's my kid sister. She died when we were young. It was terrible—just terrible."

But suddenly, another woman eased Natalie's sister aside and came forward. She was not pushy or rough—only insistent.

"There is another, older woman now, who insists that she talk to me," said Sara. "She's got long, black hair down her shoulders. She's Asian, I think."

"No! Not her!" said Natalie. "I want to talk to my sister!" Natalie was becoming agitated, and when Sara didn't answer her, she barked at her again, "I said I want to talk to Amy!"

But Sara was deep in her trance, listening to the woman spirit that had come to her.

"Your sister says that she forgives you for what you did."

"Tell her I love her," said Natalie urgently.

"Now she's gone."

Natalie was crying. She didn't ask again about the other woman to whom Sara had spoken. But Sara had found out much from that connection.

It seemed that the woman was the grocery store owner in Natalie's neighborhood that her boyfriend had shot and killed during a robbery. Natalie had been with her boyfriend late that night. They had been doing hash and drinking heavily when they had decided to rob the place. After the incident, both had been arrested by police and both were awaiting their trials.

"Is that all she said, then?" Natalie asked. "My sister, that is?"

"Yes. She said she would see you again when the time is right."

Natalie bought the story. Sara regretted lying, but she didn't want to bring up the images of the murder scene which had been shown her. Even so, the Asian woman's spirit told Sara that she also forgave Natalie and her boyfriend for what they had done to her and the pain they had caused her family.

By nine o'clock, the prison was dark except for the emergency and other safety lights that were kept on throughout the night. All inmates were locked into their cells by seven o'clock and not released until five the next morning. Usually, it took a few hours for everyone to quiet down in their cells, and this night was no exception.

Sara lay motionless in her bunk, listening to the other women coughing, sneezing, farting and making other disgusting noises she didn't want to think about. Within an hour those would melt away and be replaced by both loud and soft snoring.

Sara couldn't recall exactly, but she later said that she had dozed off shortly after midnight. Yet, when she had opened her eyes, she could hear something else besides snoring. It was the sound of a mop bucket being dragged down the hallway that separated rows of cells on either side.

It's too late for someone to be mopping anything, she thought. However, the sound continued, scraping the concrete floor as it made its way toward her cell.

Scraaaaape, chuh ... Scraaaaape, chuh ...

Sara climbed out of her bunk and went to her cell bars to see what was going on. No one else appeared to be awake or disturbed by the irritating sounds.

Scraaaaape, chuh ... Scraaaaape, chuh

She peered out between the bars trying to catch a glimpse of what was moving so methodically down the hallway. But the source of the sound was still too far away and was blocked by the line of bars that held her captive. Turning, she glanced over to see if her cellmate were awake, but she was softly snoring—oblivious to the subtle commotion outside.

Scraaaaape, chuh ... Scraaaaape, chuh

Finally, the sound was only two cells down from hers, and she could see the image of a security guard in a tattered, gray uniform, pushing a bucket with a red-handled mop. It was a fuzzy image, and she wondered why he was working such a late shift.

It was then that she saw the guard's hands that protruded from his long, dirty sleeves.

"No!" she gasped. She wanted to scream. "No! Go away!"

The skeletal fingers pushed the mop and the bucket toward her cell.

"Stop!" Sara yelled, but the phantom passed right through the bars without stopping. Then, the image looked up. To her horror, the face was a dark skull. It appeared to be laughing at her as its entire being rose off the floor and glided toward her, its arms outstretched and reaching to grab her.

"Help!" she cried.

But no one could hear her. Natalie continued snoring soundly in her bunk, unaware of what was going on nearby.

"Help!" Sara cried again, but this time she fought to get out the words as her windpipe was being crushed.

*****

CH 80 – Cult Meeting

2020

Patti left the house and drove down the street, speeding past an unmarked, gray sedan which pulled out right behind her. It was late at night—after two in the morning—and Patti zoomed south along the toll way, exiting a few miles beyond the I-95 perimeter after twenty minutes. The rural setting was a significant departure from the hustle and bustle of downtown Boston. It was a place where thick groves of trees offered a bucolic setting for urban-weary weekenders but also excellent cover for more nefarious activities.

Turning left and then right and then left again, Patti's movements seemed erratic and evasive, but after another twenty minutes, she pulled off the road and through a broken, wooden gate marked only by a lone, tin mailbox that was made to look like a red barn. The dirt road was bumpy and rutted, yet it had a green, weedy strip down the middle that was illuminated in her headlights. Seldom used, the way grew increasingly rugged as she headed uphill a short distance before disappearing down the other side and into the woods. The trees moved past her slowly as she maneuvered the small car like a slalom skier navigating the flags on a snowy mountainside run. Finally, popping out of the trees, the car continued along an open wheat field and up to a farmhouse compound.

The house was simple—a double-story home lighted by two bright streetlights attached to tall, wooden poles on either side. It was white with clapboard siding and mossy, green shudders. On one side was a large red barn that matched the mailbox out by the main road. On the other side was a tiny white hut that looked like a large outhouse or second barn for equipment or tools.

Parked near the red barn and a muddy pen where pigs would have been kept were several expensive, late-model cars. Yet, there seemed to be no one around. The house was dark; the barn quiet; and the pen empty.

Patti left her car and walked briskly to the small white hut, opening the door and disappearing inside. But rather than finding a commode or tools inside, she descended a single, circular flight of stone stairs into the depths below the adjacent barn. She scurried down the staircase, sometimes taking two steps at a time until she reached the bottom where she found a small cove surrounded by five stone pillars. The columns were only about eight feet high—just enough to reach from the floor to the grotto's rocky ceiling. All looked solid and were partially carved into the rockface itself. However, Patti pushed on the one farthest to her left, and suddenly, the entire wall opened, allowing her to pass beneath a stone archway with the inscription overhead which read: *Hello Plottar.*

"Welcome, Patricia. We've been waiting for you," said a woman standing before an altar covered in black cloth and holding five garnet-red candles. She was draped in a scintillating gold cloak, and around her neck was a triangular, red medallion etched with a goat's head inside a pentagram. Gathered nearby were some thirty or forty others—all wearing black cloaks with the same medallion around their necks.

The room itself was round—cut from the hard rock underground. More like a cavern than a meeting hall, the rough, stone walls extended high above them, vaulting into an arched ceiling like an abandoned, Gothic cathedral.

Patti took her place next to the woman in gold, donning her red robe and pulling out two necklaces—one, a triangular medallion like the woman in gold leading the group, and another, a diamond, pentagon necklace with a dark, blue sapphire pendant at the bottom.

"My sisters," said the woman in gold, "we have come on this night to celebrate the end of our Silver Ritual. It is right that we come to worship our master, Lord Satan. He is the supreme power in the universe—a power that cannot be defeated. Evil always triumphs over good, and it is, as it shall be, a world of torment, pain, and angst for all who do not bow down to him."

The leader stood before an altar behind which rested a statue of a golden beast-with the head and legs of a goat but with arms and the chest of a man. In brilliant gold and reflecting the light from the lanterns dangling from the ceiling, the creature sat on a stone throne and held a long scepter topped with precious jewels. The other hand of the beast rested on the arm of the chair and dangled the head of a human in its grasp.

The woman in gold picked up a silver chalice encrusted with rubies and emeralds and raised it high over her head saying, "This ritual is to give sacrifice to our Dark Lord—that he may bring us power, knowledge, and dominance over all other living creatures of the planet. May they be enslaved—forced into bondage and the service of our master." She then lowered the chalice onto the altar. "May this sacrifice be satisfactory to your desires and demands, oh Dark One."

There was a rattling of chains just outside the chamber, and a set of black, steel doors creaked open. Dragged into the center of the room and inside a stone circle on the floor were two figures—that of a middle-aged man, and that of a young girl. Both wore chains around their ankles and their wrists; both were frightened beyond description.

The middle-aged man was haggard and dirty. He wore a camouflage pattern jacket and baggy, slate-gray pants, neither of which had ever been washed. He wore a full, burly beard and had a mop of black hair that curled down over his ears and shoulders. His eyes were crystal blue and seemed frozen, unblinking and terrified. He was gagged with a white cloth—unable to speak and barely able to breathe.

Like the man, the little girl was scared. She too was manacled and gagged. Only eight or nine years old, she was deathly thin and gaunt. Unlike the man, her hair was golden blonde and hung to her waist. She was dressed in a clean, white gown with lace around the collar, cuffs and hem. Sobbing inconsolably, she hid her face in her cupped and dirty hands, the tears streaming down her face and neck and soaking her pristine dress.

The woman in gold raised the chalice once more. "We shall fill this chalice with the blood of our guests. May their sacrifice to our Lord also run through our veins and strengthen us in our hegemonic cause."

It was then that one of the cloaked figures in the group brought forth a wooden chest with brass clasps. She opened it and presented the shallow case to the woman in gold, bowing before her. The leader of the group reached inside and lifted a long, curved scimitar over her head. The two prisoners in the center of the circle gasped as they looked upon the blade glistening in the light of the lanterns.

"Bring them to the altar," said the golden woman.

Patti left the high priestess and grabbed the man by his hair, pulling him up the two, short stone stairs to the altar. He seemed partially drugged and unable to fight back against what was about to happen to him. However, his mind was fully alert and aware of what was coming.

Patti pushed the man's head down on a low ledge that was attached to the black altar. There, she fastened a chain around his neck so he couldn't move and stood back.

The scene was horrific, but from those in the group there erupted a chant and the beat of drums. They chanted and danced around the stone circle, raising their arms and hands into the air and calling out the name of their master: Beelzebub, Belial, Lucifer.

Without hesitation, the woman in gold lifted the sabre and let it come down swiftly, severing the man's neck with one blow. As the blood ran across the stone ledge and dripped onto the rocky floor, Patti took the silver chalice and placed it at the end of a shallow, but wide groove in the stone, catching much of the blood as it flowed. When it was full, she took the cup and handed it to the woman who had presented the sword. Each of the sorcerers took from the cup, and when they were finished, they removed the man's head and body from the altar.

"It is the will of the Dark Lord that only the powerful and mighty shall rein over the earth. As we know from evolution, everlasting life is awarded only to those who rise to the top of their species. We are they; all others are inferior and must serve us. We are the ones destined to inherit the earth and all its riches."

The high priestess turned and entered a smaller, stone postea-room where she approached a set of ancient, wooden doors. Each was only a foot wide and three feet tall. With her hand, she drew a pentagram in the air, and then turned the skeleton key to open the cabinet.

From inside she withdrew a thick, weathered book that was encrusted with even more gold and jewels. It was heavy, and she labored to bring it out of its shrine. Carrying the book to the altar, she laid it down gently, cracking the cover and opening it to a pre-marked page.

"And Satan said, 'there shall be no greater power than that of the Dark Lord. Evil shall always conquer goodness. It is the nature of all things. It has always been and shall always be. And so it has been since the beginning of time. Wild animals kill without remorse or thought; they kill to survive. Mankind too kills to survive, as men and women are only an evolved form of the same. It is the natural

425

law of all things—laws that require us to kill or be killed. He who kills cannot be killed. He who inflicts pain shall not receive pain. He who makes others suffer shall not suffer himself. So, is the law of mankind."

After that, there was a loud chant.

Oooooooma!

All made the sound and then bowed.

"Now, let us give to the almighty Satan on this, the last day of the Silver Ritual." Then, she added, "As you know, this celebration comes only once every twenty-five years. It is a generational ritual. And, as such, your gifts must be of great value. Satan will only accept our presentments of our wealth as payment for all that he has done to strengthen and protect us. He asks that we give all that we have and obey his laws and rules. Anyone believing in another god or His prophets shall be stricken dead. Likewise, anyone giving of something less than what it appears, shall also be stricken. We cannot fool our Lord Satan."

Each member of the congregation stepped forward and placed a large jewel or precious metal, such as gold, silver or platinum, inside a chest that rested in the base of the cabinet. There were diamonds, rubies, emeralds, sapphires, and other exquisite pieces already there, awaiting another layer to be placed on top.

Patti approached the wooden chest and pulled the diamond and sapphire necklace from her neck, placing it inside the wooden chest. The sapphire gleamed brilliantly in the light given off by the lanterns and the hundreds of black candles ringing the perimeter of the room. She made a quick movement across her chest which at first looked like the sign of the cross; however, it had five movements—not four. After making the sign of a pentagram, she walked away from the chest to let others have their turn to make their offerings.

But the lady in gold stopped Patti, putting out her hand and saying, "It is time, Patricia." Patti looked at her nervously. "It is time you transfer your power to your daughter. That was your oath when your mother transferred her powers to you. It is time you did the same. The Silver Ritual is when we move on—each of us must do our part and then step aside. You knew that twenty-five years ago."

"No. My daughter is not ready."

"It is not for you to decide," said the woman in gold. "It is the Dark One who has told us that this is the way of things, and it shall be as he commands it."

Patti turned away and went back to her place next to the altar.

"Let us give thanks to almighty Satan," said the high priestess in gold, "and may he be satisfied with the souls each of you have harvested for him during this past year. For those who did not make sacrifices acceptable to Satan, he will let you know, and soon."

Then, she turned her eyes toward the little girl who was shivering uncontrollably in the center of the circle. She shook her head violently and closed her eyes, hoping the nightmare would go away.

"It is time to make our premier sacrifice to Satan. She is a virgin, and her blood will be screened for the drug we crave most. The elixir of life—of immortal life. We shall all share in it; we shall all drink of it; we shall all revel in it."

Patti walked out to the circle center to retrieve the girl—the final sacrifice of the evening. The sabre was ready, the altar ledge cleaned of the previous victim, and the sorcerers' chants beginning in earnest, growing louder as they started dancing again around their diabolical circle.

But just as the high priestess raised the blade to finish the macabre ritual, a loud, booming voice interrupted, coming from the bottom of the stairs just outside the room.

"Nobody move!" shouted Dag, pointing his gun at the group. "Boston police. Stand where you are."

But move they did. All rushed toward the back of the "chapel" pushing on another, secret pillar. Opening quickly was an exit made to look like an enormous boulder. There were too many of them to get through the small opening at once, and Dag and three other officers ran to stop them from escaping. Dag spotted Patti in the group and pushed his way toward her.

"Stop!" he shouted at her, clawing his way to get to her before she got out of the subterranean lair. He didn't want to lose her a second time.

Patti was almost to the opening when Dag grabbed the sleeve of her red robe, pulling it back. She turned and glared at him—an evil darkness embedded deeply within her eyes. Reaching for her robe, she tore the sleeve, letting the piece the detective held fall away. Dag was now holding nothing but a piece of red cloth.

Patti squeezed through the opening with Dag only a few seconds behind her. He pushed on his shoulder radio.

"All units on top. Suspect is coming up through another exit. All participants coming up. Please confirm." However, there was nothing but static on the other end of the radio. They were too deep inside the rocky cavern, and his orders never reached the surface.

Forcing his way up a much narrower, circular staircase, Dag pushed aside others in black robes trying to reach Patti. After several flights, he reached the surface, emerging from the second entry and exit point. This was a rusted steel hatch that was buried just below a layer of thin moss and leaves farther out in the woods and was virtually impossible to see when closed. However, now it was sprung open.

When Dag climbed out of the hole, he had lost sight of Patti. On the ground next to the exit was the rest of her torn red robe which she had discarded to make it harder to identify her. He hurried behind a small group running back toward the barn where their cars were parked. It was near there that Dag spotted someone who looked like Patti just ahead.

"Stop!" he yelled.

But the suspect kept running, jumping over fallen logs and stumps, and pushing back branches of trees, letting them whip back in place.

"I said stop!" Dag shouted again.

Yet, she kept running.

"Freeze or I'll have to shoot!" said Dag drawing his gun.

He was taught to only shoot when his life was at risk. But he was growing tired and out-of-breath. Very soon, he would have to stop, and she would get away.

"Stop!" he yelled once more. But, when the subject didn't halt, he fired his gun into the air.

The person with short dark hair and distinctive highlights suddenly froze. Out of breath, Dag held his gun as he walked up to the woman.

"Put your hands behind your back," he ordered, pulling out his handcuffs.

He clipped the cuffs around her wrists and swung her around.

It wasn't Patti. Instead, it was another satanic worshiper, her gold chains dangling from her chest.

"You can't arrest me," she said. "You can't arrest any of us. We haven't broken the law."

Dag began pushing her in the direction of the barn.

"You don't think so, *eh*?" he answered her, angered at having arrested the wrong person. "What about murder?"

"Since when is it murder to butcher a boar?" she said, defiantly.

"Butchering a boar—no. Butchering a person—yes. You need to come with me, miss."

Dag brought her to the red barn where a few of the others had been arrested and were now guarded by officers who had them cuffed. However, many others had escaped, having parked elsewhere on the grounds. The police spent the next several hours searching the woods and the surrounding buildings but found no sign of Patti or the high priestess in gold. Patti's car was gone.

Finding the small shed again, Dag went back into the cavern to see what evidence the other officers had found. He walked over to the cabinet where the book and chest had been kept. Peering inside, he found a pile of jewels worth millions, but what was worth even more was the diamond, pentagram necklace with the deep blue sapphire. He put on some Latex gloves and pulled it out of the chest.

"Did you find what you were looking for detective?" asked one officer standing next to Dag.

"No, not quite. I got half of what I was looking for. The other half is still at large," Dag answered.

*****

CH 81 - Revenge

1945

"Oh, Rosco, don't ... don't ..."

"*Shhhh!* Someone will hear you."

Bessie stepped back from the door and sat down, staring blankly at the scuffed, oak floor but still listening to what was happening in her husband's office. In shock, she didn't know what to do. She could only bury her head and begin to sob quietly. She cried as she listened to the pair having sex. Then, she covered her ears, but it still wouldn't go away. Finally, she had taken enough, and she began to get angry—very angry.

She went to find Fred.

"How could you?" she shouted, furious at him. "You knew! You knew!"

Fred was flabbergasted. He hadn't seen her go into the office.

"I ... I ..."

"You son-of-a-bitch! I thought you were a friend! You cock-sucking ..."

"Bessie, Bessie ..."

Bessie stormed back to her husband's office and flung open the door. Inside were her husband with his pants down around his knees, and her best friend, Janice, straddling him while sitting on the steel desktop. Both looked up surprised as the door opened.

"You bastard!" Bessie screamed at him.

Rosco's face became white and ashen.

"Bessie, no. It's not what ..."

Bessie ran from the office and got into her car. She drove straight home and began collecting her things. She had loved this man since high school and now he had betrayed her.

Throwing her clothes into the suitcase, she felt a pain in her abdomen. It was sharp and stabbing. She knelt beside the bed to catch her breath, but the pain turned to spasms and her head reeled from the combination. Quickly, she became light-headed and all went dark.

***

"Bessie? Bessie?"

She could hear the words, but the image was foggy and distorted.

"*Whaaat?*" she mumbled

"Bessie, it's me, Rosco. You're all right. You're in the hospital. They're taking good care of you."

Bessie finally woke. At the side of her bed were Rosco, Janice, Fred and a nurse who was taking her pulse.

"What ... what happened?" Bessie said.

"You fell, dear," said Rosco. "You had a little mishap, that's all. But you're all right now. The doctors and nurses here have everything under control. You just need to rest."

Bessie tried to sit up in bed, but she was too weak and lay back into her pillow.

"You lost a lot of blood, Bessie," said Janice, giving her a feeble smile. "It might take you a few days to feel back to normal."

Bessie grimaced. The pain in her belly was extreme, and she put her hand on it as if that would make it feel better.

"The baby. How's the baby?" she muttered, still not fully aware.

"You need to get some sleep," said Rosco. "The doctor will tell you all about that when he returns."

Bessie dozed off. She was asleep for several hours before the doctor came in with the nurse to look over her chart and take a blood sample. By then, visiting hours were over, and Rosco and Janice had left for the day.

"Your husband told us to tell you he would be back to see you in the morning," said the nurse as she finished filling a tube for the laboratory.

"Doctor? How's my baby?" asked Bessie, now more awake.

The doctor put down her chart and came over beside her. "Mrs. Turner, you've been through a stressful time. You took a nasty fall. It's a wonder that you were not more seriously hurt."

"My baby! What about my baby?"

The doctor shook his head. "I'm afraid we couldn't save your baby, Mrs. Turner. I'm very sorry."

Bessie lay in shock. Now she could feel there was nothing inside her kicking and making a fuss. She was empty. Her soul seemed empty too.

"And I must tell you something else. We had to do some surgery on you to save your life. I'm afraid you won't be able to have any children now. I'm sorry about that too." The doctor took her hand. "It's a lot to take in, I know. I will send a counselor down to talk to you and help you process all of this. It is a difficult time. You'll need help, and our staff is here to give you all the help you need."

*****

CH 82 - Terror in the Cell

2020

Sara woke up in her cell. Her heart was beating fast, and she was trembling. It had been more than a bad dream; it had been real. She had passed out when the phantom had grabbed her neck and begun strangling her.

How could that happen? How could a demon be conjured in here to find me and try to kill me? she thought.

All she remembered was the skeleton floating through the iron bars of her cell. She had been terrified of its presence and overwhelming black energy.

"What do you want?" she had asked as it gripped her throat.

"You are to die," it had grumbled.

"Why? Why me?"

"You are a Prodescu. I am the silver curse whose purpose is to kill the next of the progeny within your family line."

"No! No!"

The demon put its black claws around her neck and squeezed, and she could feel her esophagus being crushed. It was then that she blacked out.

The next thing she knew she was awakened by the sound of the prison bell going off, calling everyone to get up and get ready to assemble for breakfast.

"Natalie? Are you there?" Sara asked, rolling over and looking at the bunk below her.

"Of course, silly. Where else would I be?"

"I dunno. I just had the strangest dream."

"Yeah? What was it?" Natalie asked.

Sara told Natalie about the dream and how real it seemed.

"What do you think it was?" Sara asked her cellmate.

Natalie shook her head on her pillow. "No idea. But then again, I had a strange dream last night too."

"What was that?" asked Sara.

"I dreamed that I was in a deep, dark cave with only one candle. It was burning, but it kept going out. I relit it over and over with my lighter, but I knew I didn't have much fuel left in it."

"What happened then?"

"I heard someone yelling for help deeper in the cave. I only had this white candle to use to find out where the sound was coming from. When I got there, I saw a huge room, and in the center were two people—one was dark and hooded. The other was a young woman. In fact, she was a lot like you. The hooded figure was holding the woman, shaking her by the neck."

"What did you do?" asked Sara.

"It was really weird. Suddenly, my candle flared up like, you know, in a big spray of light. It lit up the entire cave. I could see everything clearly. The woman looked at me. She was terrified—shaking, in fact. But what was more terrifying was the other figure—the hooded one."

"What was that?"

"It turned toward me. It was Death. I swear it as sure as the spirit of my dead sister, it was. It was a skeleton covered with a black robe. It had no eyes, no flesh, no blood. It was a skeleton, I tell you. When it saw me, I wanted to run away. But Death didn't move. I think it was afraid of the white candle I was holding. Once it saw that, it let go of the woman and just dissolved into thin air. I don't understand any of it. But it was all really creepy."

Sara lay on her bed in disbelief. "Thank you," she finally said.

"Thanks for what?" asked Natalie.

"Thanks for saving my life."

*****

CH 83 - Outcome

2020

The trial resumed the next day with the judge coming in and all in the gallery rising in respect. She sat down and picked up her case folder to review it quickly. Then, setting it down, she ordered both counselors to the bench.

"It is my understanding that there has been a change in this case overnight. Is that correct?" he asked both attorneys.

"Yes, Your Honor," said Morrie, "We are petitioning the dropping of all charges against my client and dismissal of the case against her."

"Not so fast," said the DA. "Just because the police recovered the stolen jewelry from one of the victims, doesn't mean that the defendant didn't commit the murders."

The judge picked up her folder again.

"Well, it says here that a large body of evidence was recovered from the scene of the cult farmhouse too. That jewelry and other articles claimed as stolen from other residences during the murders were also recovered. The new suspect involved is a Patricia Campbell, is that right?" the judge asked the DA.

"Uh, yes, Your Honor, but ..."

"So, the police believe that Ms. Campbell was the one involved in the thefts and has evidence to prove this. Correct?"

"Yes, Your Honor, but ..."

"What evidence do you have linking Ms. Campbell to Ms. McLaughlin?"

"None directly, Your Honor, but ..."

"And what evidence do you have linking Mr. Marvin Fletcher to Ms. Campbell?"

Morrie interrupted. "I understand they have Ms. Campbell's cell phone records that show numerous calls to Mr. Fletcher just prior to and during the times of the crimes."

The DA stood flat-footed, not knowing what to say next, even though he was aware the judge had approved obtaining the records.

"And what evidence does the DA have to link Ms. McLaughlin to either of them other than she employed one and was at the scenes earlier during the day conducting business?"

"They have none, Your Honor," said Morrie, jumping in. "That's why I'm petitioning for my client to be released immediately."

"Well, Mr. Johnson? Do you have *any* substantive case that puts Ms. McLaughlin at the scenes of the crimes *when* they may have occurred?" asked the judge. "Based on the testimony of Mr. Fletcher and his son, I am dubious of the veracity of their statements. Do you have *any* evidence to show how she could have killed the victims in the way they were found?"

"No, Your Honor."

It was clear Johnson had resigned himself to the inevitable—that Sara McLaughlin would go free.

"Then, I hereby dismiss this case with prejudice against Ms. McLaughlin. She is free to go," said the judge, irritated at the flimsy case that the DA had attempted to hoist on the defendant and her family.

The judge repeated the dismissal, this time loudly enough for all in the gallery to hear. Sara looked shocked. *What had happened?* she thought. Only hours earlier, she imagined she would be sitting in the electric chair waiting for the switch to be thrown and current to run rampant through wires attached to her brain.

Morrie walked back to the defense table as she stood up. He hugged her, and she him. Still in shock, she whispered to him, "What just happened? Is this some kind of joke?"

"No, my dear. You are free. Now, go home to your daughter."

The bailiff unlocked the steel bracelets that clung to her wrists, and Morrie led her out of the court room. Her daughter was waiting just outside the building having been called earlier by Morrie who was confident the judge would see it fit to let her mother go.

Tears welled up in Sara's face as she saw her LJ holding a pink umbrella in the drizzling rain. The day was dark and gloomy, yet there was light and joy that neither had seen in a long time. Sara ran to her daughter and threw her arms around her, clutching her so

436

tightly that she hoped the moment would never end. She loved LJ. Her daughter was the only family she had left. Nothing else really mattered.

"Let's go home," Sara said with a smile.

"I'd like that," answered her daughter.

Together, they walked down the granite steps of the courthouse to a car that Morrie had waiting for them. Closing the door behind them, Morrie only hoped that both could find some respite from the trauma they had endured for so long.

*****

CH 84 - The Grand Grimoire

1945

Bessie refused to see Rosco or Janice while she was in the hospital, and when she was released, she had her sister pick her up and take her home.

"Are you going to be all right?" her sister asked, helping her with her things.

"I'll be fine," said Bessie.

"I'll stay the night. You shouldn't be alone during a time like this."

"No, I will be fine. You need to be home with your husband and kids. Don't worry about me."

"But I do worry about you, sis'."

"No, I will be fine. You're going home. I have some things I need to do. I'll call you in the morning. I promise."

Her sister left, and Bessie went to the bedroom and retrieved a thatched trunk from under her bed. It was where she kept her personal things and memorabilia from better and worse times. Then, she opened the trunk and rummaged for something in particular—something she hadn't used in many years. When she found it, she pulled it out and put it on the bed. It was an ancient book: *The Grand Grimoire*.

It was a rare copy of a book on conjuring and spells dating to 1522 as compiled by Antonio Venitiana del Rabina, who allegedly took excerpts from spells originally written at the time of King Solomon. She had gotten it as a gift from her cult sponsor after her first satanic meeting.

She had never been sure of its authenticity, but she figured it was as good as anything else she'd seen—*at least it looked authentic*, she thought. She'd kept it "just in case" she ever needed something like that.

The book had a musty, putrid smell of originality—something that got worse after she cracked open the cover. It was then that a rotten apple odor overpowered her. Turning pages, she finally found something of interest and stopped to read the passage. It was in Old English, and although she didn't understand every word, there was enough there to tell her the purpose of the spell.

Cursen be se Cneoris

(Curse of the Generations)

Bessie read the spell and cast her eternal curse:

"Máius the Hearm Wealdengod manshehe ānhepig cnēoris o' se cnósls n frēonds o' min fiend dat maius forrotedon cung steorfa peumaa se gecyndlum.

(May the Dark One kill each generation of the families and friends of mine enemy that they may rot like dead animal flesh from their first day in the womb.)"

What Bessie didn't understand was the lasting impact her conjuring would have on this and future generations. Hers was a curse—not only on Rosco, Janice and their families—but ultimately on her own as well.

*****

Part VI

CH 85 – On the Run

2020

Dag would have gone straight to Mitzie's place and arrested her after she left the precinct. He had been busy processing her confession, and when he had returned she was gone. He had felt betrayed. Yet, with the incident at the park and Patti still at large, Dag fought his urge to put her in cuffs immediately. Instead, he decided to stake-out the house, watching and waiting for any signs of her mother.

Dag sat in his sedan just outside Mitzie's apartment building, monitoring everyone coming and going. He'd gone through two hot dogs, three cups of lousy, black coffee and four pieces of winter mint chewing gum. It was late in the afternoon, and his eyes were getting drowsy. He fought to stay awake. *Stakeouts were so boring,* he thought

The next thing he knew, it was dark outside. He'd fallen asleep—the one thing he knew was a huge *faux pau* on a stakeout. *"Shit!"* he said to himself. *How could I have been so stupid?*

Then, there was a rapping noise coming from his car window. He pushed the button on the driver's side door and lowered the glass on the passenger's side.

"Tommy?" Dag asked. "What are you doing here?"

Tommy stuck his head inside the window with his usual, casual aplomb. "Thought you might want some company," he answered.

"You can get in if you brought me some good, hot coffee," Dag answered.

Tommy laughed, producing two white cups, complete with cardboard cozies and sipping lids.

"This is the first time in a while you haven't let me down," said Dag, grinning. "Hop in."

Tommy got in the car and handed one cup to Dag. To his, he added a splash of creamer before replacing the lid and taking a slurp.

"So, what have you been up to?" Tommy asked.

"Nothin'. Nothin' at all," Dag answered. "Just attending the usual satanic cult meeting out in the middle of nowhere. You know how it is."

"Anything going on here?" Tommy asked, already familiar with the news of the event that had blown through the precinct like a category five hurricane.

"Unfortunately, not. I haven't spotted Patti at all."

"Do you think we should go up there and see for ourselves? Have you talked to Mitzie?"

"Let's just sit tight. I have a feeling her mom will show," said Dag.

"What about Mitzie? Can you trust her?"

"Don't know that either."

There was a moment of awkward silence.

"Dag."

"Yeah, Tommy."

"I just wanted to apologize for what I did. It wasn't right. I know that now. Hell, I knew that when I was doing it, but I thought it was the best way ... you know."

"Is it?" asked Dag.

"Is it what?"

"Is it still the best way?" said Dag, taking another sip of his coffee.

"For some, maybe," Tommy answered. "But I don't think it will work for me in the long run."

"Why's that?"

"Well, it doesn't seem to be helping the DA or the mayor right now. The mayor is down in the polls. It looks like he won't win."

A recent poll had showed the mayor trailing his challenger by five points going into the final week of the campaign. The mayor had held a lead until the case against Sara McLaughlin was dismissed. It was then when reporters had vilified him and the DA for the flimsy case they had brought against her. It was chum in the water for the media sharks, and they were relentless in their attacks.

"So, I take it that you're not going to vote for them?" asked Dag.

"What do you think?" Tommy replied.

***

Meanwhile, Mitzie lay motionless on her bed—her eyes open and her body outstretched like it had been prepared for its own wake. She was there, somewhere inside that body, but she was trapped—ensnared more completely than Sara had ever been in her wretched jail cell. However, even within her mental dungeon, Mitzie could sense the malevolent force that was controlling her. It was powerful—much too powerful for her to fight. It was her prison warden, and it was telling her what she could and couldn't do. She never saw the face of the phantom, but she could only imagine that it looked very much like that of her mother.

The hours passed, and daytime turned into night. Mitzie was only vaguely aware of the slow, methodical movements of the hour and minute hands on her bedroom clock as they circumnavigated its face. Instead, she lay on her mattress waiting, but for what she did not know.

Then, she heard an urgent knock on her back door. Awaking from her trance, she made it through the kitchen to the door leading out to the rear porch.

"Who is it?" Mitzie asked quietly, listening for an answer.

"It's your mom. Let me in!"

Mitzie peered through the eyehole. On the other side was a woman she hardy recognized. Usually well-dressed and made-up, she saw one who was just fifty-nine, but who now looked over eighty.

"Let me in!" Patti insisted, beating on the door.

Mitzie opened it, and her mother quickly pushed past her.

"You look awful," said Mitzie.

"Thanks," answered Patti, sarcastically.

"What happened to you?"

"Nothing," Patti said, lying. "I was just out and stopped by. That's all."

"It's nearly 10 PM!" said Mitzie. "You never come over this late."

"Oh, it's still early, dear. Do you have anything in the frig?"

442

"Help yourself," said Mitzie, motioning toward the refrigerator. She spotted her cellphone on the counter. She knew she should make a call right away to Dag, but she held back. The prison warden was in her mind again—this time threatening her not to do something she would regret.

Patti grabbed some strawberries and a banana and put the plate down on the coffee table in the center of the main room. The apartment was small—only a two-bedroom—which, in addition to the bedrooms, had a kitchen, main living area, and a single bathroom. It did have several closets, which is why Mitzie had liked the place from the start.

"Really, Mom. Why are you here?"

"I told you," Patti answered, munching on a strawberry. "I was just in the neighborhood." She paused and then added, "And I brought you this."

"What is it?"

Patti had come in carrying a large paper bag and took from it a cardboard box. She crumpled up the paper bag before pushing the box toward her daughter without explanation.

"Just open it," said her mother, brusquely.

Mitzie carefully pulled back the lids. Inside was an old jewelry box.

"Your jewelry box," said Mitzie, taking it out. Mitzie was delighted but puzzled. "Why?"

"I don't want it anymore. Anyway, it's time I hand it down to you. I guess I was supposed to do that a long time ago, but ... Well, it doesn't matter. Take it, and best of luck."

Mitzie put the box down gingerly on the table next to her. She started to open it, but hesitated.

"You can open it. Go ahead."

Mitzie opened the fancy, carved lid. "Oh my!" she exclaimed as she was struck by a strong scent of apples wafting out. But inside, there was something more. It was filled to the top with red, Zippo lighters.

"Why are there lighters and no jewels?" Mitzie asked. "You know I don't smoke very often anymore."

"Perhaps you don't remember, but these lighters contain the Dark One's spirit. They're cursed," said Patti. "When the flame burns, it frees a black demon to do Satan's bidding."

Mitzie shuddered. "So that's how it was done."

Mitzie recalled little-to-nothing about the things she had done for her mother while under the priestess's dark spell. The prison warden inside her had made sure of her obedience while at the same time erased all memory of her debauchery and criminal acts.

"Yes," Patti answered, "but there are times when I have to project its awful power into another place or someone else's body. For that, I need my book of spells."

"Book of spells?"

"It's an ancient book that's been passed down through our generations too, like the jewelry box."

"Where is that, then?" Mitzie asked.

"Oh, Mitzie, you're not ready for that. It takes years of training and talent, and I'm afraid you don't have either."

There was silence between the two for several uncomfortable moments before Mitzie spoke again.

"Did you know Sara McLaughlin was freed today?" Mitzie asked, breaking the silence."

"No! How did that happen?"

"I heard there was an incident the other night," said Mitzie. "The police busted some cult on the south side of town. They found evidence that exonerated her. Were you involved in any of that?"

"No! Of course not. It was not an Order of Satan; I can assure you. He always protects those who are true believers in his tribes. No, the cult, as you say, that they broke up was not on the south side of town; it was out in the country."

"How do you know that?"

"I just do," her mother snipped. She paused to grab another strawberry. "Of course, now that you have the jewelry box, I need to give you one of our necklaces and pendants so you can attend one of *our* meetings with me." Patti slid a silver necklace and pentacle pendant across the table to her daughter. "Here. This goes with the box."

"What am I supposed to do with them?"

"Use the jewelry box as the place where you keep the medallion we use at the rituals and the lighters. It keeps them 'charged'—if you know what I'm saying. Black magic is very powerful, and this charmed box concentrates that energy so it will have its maximum effect."

Mitzie hesitated, not knowing whether to take the medallion or not.

"Go ahead. Take it," her mother insisted.

Mitzie took the necklace expecting it to burn her hand. But when it didn't, she picked it up and looked at. She could feel the dark energy radiating from the pentagram, like ripples flowing outward from a drop in a still pond.

"Charged? You mean, like a cell phone?" Mitzie asked, fondling the medallion.

"Something like that."

But Mitzie's face suddenly turned dour.

"I did enough for you Mom. I'm not doing this for you too. I'm not joining your cult." Mitzie pushed the medallion back across the table toward her mother.

"It's not a *cult*, and you don't have any choice in the matter."

"What do you mean?" asked Mitzie.

"I mean that it's the curse we have. It's part of our family. It's our heritage. Satan will not allow you out of the covenant your great grandmother made with him. It's impossible."

"I didn't make the covenant, and I'm not keeping it!" But a powerful voice inside her began threatening her once more. *You will obey*, it said. *You will kneel to the Dark Lord and bend to his will. He owns you. You are his servant and slave.*

"No!" Mitzie shouted.

"You *must*, Mitzie. It's the curse that started with your Great grandma Bessie. It was all part of the pact she made that night at the séance. Since then, each of us has lied, robbed and killed to satisfy the Dark One. I had no choice, and neither do you. I brought you into this as my apprentice many years ago so you could see how things worked. Each of us is required to do that with one of our daughters. However, you didn't take to it very well. You were stubborn and fought me. That's why I had to use other measures on you, my dear child."

"What measures?"

"Mind control, of course," said Patti, taking out a cigarette and lighting it. "I use a demon to control your mind when I want you to do something for me. You don't remember, of course, but it is very convenient and has allowed me to do what I've had to do."

"To keep the curse going," said Mitzie.

"Yes."

"Okay, then explain it to me. What is the *curse*?"

"As you already know, your Great grandmother Bessie and Janice Prodescu, Sara's great grandmother, were best friends in high school. Back then, Janice had the natural ability for communicating with the dead—something she got from her mother, but something your great grandma didn't have and wanted desperately. Like I said, Grandma Bessie struck a deal with the Devil the night of their little high school séance, asking for the same powers as what Janice had. Those powers were granted, but they weren't the same. They were dark and more powerful."

"That's the haunting picture of the Devil's face right behind Grandma Bessie in that picture," Mitzie murmured to herself. "It's the one Sara showed me at the restaurant."

"Most likely," answered Patti, lowering her cigarette and tapping the long ash into the tray beside her. "Both Bessie and Janice went on to do readings for people for the next few years or so, staying in touch and getting together from time to time. However, as part of Bessie's pact with the Dark One, she joined the satanic order that I belong to now. Every year we must give offerings of valuables to the Dark One, but then, every twenty-five years, there is a Silver Ritual. By that time, each member must have collected at least one soul and made other offerings of great value to Satan. The more souls and value of the pieces, the more power you get from him.

"Since Bessie didn't have a nickel to her name coming out of high school, she arranged to steal from other mediums' clients. She'd find out their clients' names or hire whoever was working with them.

446

She'd pay them to case the place during those sessions, make them help her with the break-in later, and give them a percentage of haul. Usually, someone would be killed only on those years when there was a Silver Ritual. The Dark Lord required at least one soul from each devotee, but the more people they killed, the higher they rose in the Order."

"So, we're in a period of the Silver Ritual now?" asked Mitzie.

"Your great grandma Bessie was part of it in 1945, but by 1960 she had transferred her power to your grandma Terri. She took over at that point."

"And in 1995, she gave you the power."

"Yes. Your grandma Terri gave it to me."

"So why haven't you given it to me this year? It's 2020," asked Mitzie. "It sounds like I'm next in line."

"You weren't ready," said Patti. "You're still not ready."

"Then why did you give me the jewelry box?"

"I am in violation of the Order's laws. Whether you are ready or not, I must transfer it to you," said Patti, reluctantly. "Yet, there is one more soul I must retrieve before it is done."

"One more? So, you *did* kill those people this year."

"I didn't kill anyone."

"Then who did?" asked Mitzie.

"The Dark Lord, of course."

"Why was Aunt Janice murdered back in 1945? Why did that happen to begin with? It seems like that kicked off this whole thing."

"I don't know why it all started with her."

"But wasn't Grandma Bessie over at Aunt Janice's the day of the murder?" asked Mitzie.

"Yeah, but believe me, she didn't kill her ... at least not directly," said Patti.

"Then by what? Black magic?"

Patti only smiled, blowing out a long stream of blue smoke.

"And what about Great grandma Bessie and Grandma Terri? Why did they give up the Order? Why did they convert to religion? Did they do that voluntarily?"

"They say they did, but I don't think so. They were supposed to continue in the Order even though they'd transferred their powers to their daughters. Usually, the Dark Lord sends assassins to kill those who leave his family."

"But he didn't with them."

"No. I think he believed they would be useful to him later. I think he was right," said Patti.

"So he could use them to manipulate that detective—Tommy Walcott."

"Yes, so young and naïve. Those are the ones most vulnerable to his powers."

"How did you get the power from Grandma Terri?"

"We did it on the final night of the Silver Ritual. It was part of it, where mothers would bring their daughters. We have this rite of passage, you see. After our sacrifices to the Dark Lord, we go through a specific ceremony to open a portal to Hell and contact Satan directly. After he transfers the powers, a token with the power is handed to the next in line."

"But not always?"

"No. I haven't—not yet, anyway."

"So, the last night of the ritual has come and gone?" asked Mitzie.

"Yes and no," said Patti. "It was started, but it wasn't finished. We must still do that."

"But you didn't' take me."

"No. Like I said, you aren't ready. But I may take you to watch the conclusion of the Silver Ritual when we hold our next meeting in a few weeks," said Patti. "Perhaps your daughter Bea will be the next in line for the powers. She's almost of age right now, in fact."

"No, mother!" said Mitzie. "I will not allow that!"

Patti laughed. "Again, my dear daughter, you have no choice in the matter. If Satan wants me to transfer my powers to her, then that is what shall be done."

Mitzie fumed. She wanted to lash out, but the prison warden kept her in check.

"So nothing happened to you at that ritual when you didn't bring me along to transfer your powers?" Mitzie asked.

Patti paused. "I was told it was something I was negligent in not dong. Let me put it that way."

"Well, I'm still not doing it, mother. I don't care what you do to me."

But at that moment, Mitzie felt a stabbing pain in her head. She put her hands to her temples and winced in agony.

"Like I said, dear, you don't have a choice," said her mother dispassionately, still smoking her cigarette. "You *will* come along if I ask you. You *will* join the Order. You *will* become one of us. Now, I'm going to bed. I'm tired," said Patti, stretching out on the sofa. "Hopefully, tomorrow will be an even darker day than today."

"You're staying the night?" Mitzie asked, trying to recover from the severe headache that suddenly struck her. "I thought you were just stopping by for a short visit?"

"I was, but now I've changed my mine. I'm going to be here a little longer than I expected."

Mitzie nursed her headache as she got out a few blankets and a pillow and put them on the bed in the guest bedroom for her mother. She loved her mom but hated what she had done and the group of which she was a part.

Then, instead of going to her own bedroom, Mitzie went to the coat closet and put on her jacket.

"Where are you going?" Patti asked.

"Out," said Mitzie. She left through the front door, letting it lock shut behind her.

Mitzie took the elevator down and got off on the first floor. She exited the building and spotted Dag's car across the street. His lights were off, but she could see the reflection of his wristwatch from the streetlight overhead. Walking across the street, she came up to the driver's side, and Dag rolled down the window.

"What's going on?" he asked her.

She was nervous, looking over her shoulder and back toward the apartment building.

"I ..." she began, but then she spotted Tommy sitting next to Dag in the car. "Uh ... nothing right now," she added, changing her mind.

"You haven't even heard from your mom, have you?" asked Dag.

"No. I haven't," she answered. "Why?"

Tommy started to jump out of the car, but Dag put his hand on his arm to stop him. Then, he said casually to Mitzie, "Well, let us know if you get a call or anything, okay?"

"Is she in trouble?"

"Just want to talk to her. That's all," said Dag.

"Okay, sure," Mitzie said curtly before walking off in the opposite direction.

"What was that all about?" Tommy shouted at his partner.

"Just let her go, Tommy. She's not going anywhere we can't find her."

But Tommy rolled down his window anyway and yelled at her, "Hey, where are you going?"

She turned back toward him and shouted while still walking, "I'm just going down to the store to get a pack of gum. Do you want some?"

Tommy looked at Dag.

"She'll be all right," said Dag. "Like I said, she's not going anywhere." Tommy looked uncomfortable. "You can tail her if you want," said Dag, looking unconcerned as he finished his coffee.

"Yeah, I think I will," said Tommy, letting her walk down the block before getting out of the car.

Dag sighed. He was alone again. He just hoped this time he wouldn't fall asleep.

*****

CH 86 - Final Vengeance

1945

Even though Janice had repeatedly tried to contact Bessie after everything that had happened, she had gotten no response. Janice felt terrible about the affair and the miscarriage and wanted to do something—anything—to correct it. But once the genie was out of the bottle, Janice knew deep down that it would be almost impossible to put it back.

Months passed, and Janice, who had been pregnant at the time of the incident, gave birth to her own. Bessie was in the process of getting a divorce from Rosco, and Janice had not seen either of them during that time.

It was not socially acceptable to have children out of wedlock in those days, and Janice found it particularly hard. Many of her friends abandoned her; Rosco was nowhere to be found; and the church pastor had banned her from communion and even attending mass.

However, out of the blue, Janice received a call one day from Bessie. "Janice, how are you?"

"Oh, Bessie," said Janice, "I ... I don't know what to say. I've sent you letters telling you how awful I feel and how sorry I am. I don't blame you for hating me."

"Janice, dear. It's true that I was upset over what happened. But I don't blame you. It was Rosco who instigated it all—not you. I'm sure of it."

"Oh, Bessie. I'm so sorry. I really am. Can you ever forgive me?"

"Well, I'd like to meet with you and patch things up, Janice. We've been friends for a long time, and I really hate to see our friendship end like this. I'm attending a new church, and I feel compelled to follow its teachings of reconciliation and forgiveness. Would you meet me for lunch at Field's Deli tomorrow at, say, 12:30?"

"Bessie. I will most certainly be there ... and thanks for giving me another chance."

***

Janice waited at a tiny, black table which was only large enough for two armless, wooden chairs. It was 12:40, and Bessie still hadn't arrived. It was unlike her to be late, but given the circumstances, Janice was not going to complain. Customers came and went during that time, going to the counter and ordering a shaved turkey with swiss, or a pastrami on rye, or some other delicious sandwich from a list of many.

It was 12:45 when Bessie finally arrived. She was dressed in a bright yellow, summer dress with a matching purse and red pumps.

"Hello, Janice," chirped Bessie coming in. She smiled, but it was strained and tense. Under her arm she carried a package wrapped in red, Christmas-like paper but without a bow.

"Hi, Bessie," answered Janice doing everything but genuflecting as a sign of submissiveness. "I'm so glad you asked to see me. As I said, I am sorry for what happened. I don't know what came over me. It was wrong. I know that now ... I knew it then too. Will you forgive me?"

"Of course," said Bessie, sitting and putting the package on the floor next to her chair. "I came to tell you that my divorce from Rosco is now final. You can continue to see him if you wish. It really won't bother me." She pulled out a cigarette and lit it, taking a puff and tapping it gently over a glass ashtray on the table.

"We're not seeing each other," said Janice. "We haven't since ... since that day."

"Well, if he hadn't had the affair with you, he would have been with someone else, I'm sure. He was that way in high school too, you remember. Rosco was the flirtatious one. I should have realized that before I married him."

"Let me get lunch," said Janice, starting to get up.

"No, I don't think I'm that hungry, really. I got you something—you know, for old times' sake. I remembered that you quite fancied this when we were in O'Keefe & Jellson's many years ago. I was in there recently, and they had two just like the one you saw. I thought I would get this one for you."

"Bessie, you shouldn't have! I'm the one who should have gotten something for *you*."

"It's all right. Let's just consider it a friendship gift. That's what friends do, right?"

Bessie gave Janice the package which Janice quickly unwrapped.

"Wow. This is very nice. Bessie, I can't accept it. I really can't."

"I insist," said Bessie. "It would really make me feel a lot better if I knew you had it and enjoyed it."

Inside the package was a jewelry box.

Janice started to open the box, but Bessie interrupted her. "Now, Janice, don't open it right now. You have plenty of time to do that later. I wanted to talk to you about how your mother is doing. I heard she is not well."

"Oh, Mother is fine. She just complains a lot."

"She's, what, fifty. Right?"

"Yes. She just turned fifty, actually. She went in to see the doctor last week complaining about headaches."

"She was always gifted, wasn't she?" asked Bessie.

"She always had the gifts, yes. She was clairvoyant, clairaudient and clairsentient. I was lucky to get all three too. I guess it's rare."

"Yes, those talents are so precious," said Bessie. She stared off into space as if distracted by something, but there was only the two of them in the sandwich shop besides the owner behind the counter and three people standing in front trying to decide which sandwiches to order. Then, her attention snapped back to Janice. "Well, I really must be going," she said getting up to leave. "Maybe we can get together again sometime."

"Leaving already?" asked Janice, surprised. "You just got here. We haven't had time to chat."

"Yes, I'm afraid I have a church meeting to go to. The high priest is very strict on punctuality, so I must be on my way. You understand, I'm sure."

Bessie got up and smiled but without enthusiasm. "Take care, Janice."

Janice stood watching as her friend left through the front door. She wondered what to make of the strange meeting but just figured Bessie was still working through things. She glanced down at the

453

beautiful jewelry box. I was nice that her friend had gotten it for her. Indeed, it made her feel more guilty for the pain she had caused all of them.

Janice would never see Bessie again.

The next morning, Janice's body would be found in her apartment, horribly disfigured. The jewelry box would be on her dresser—open but empty. Next to it would be a pack of Chesterfields and a red, Zippo lighter. Bessie's curse had been allowed to escape and had attach itself to Janice and, through her soul, to the rest of her lineage.

***

Bessie had heard about Janice giving birth only a month earlier and assumed Rosco had been the father. She sought her vengeance not only against Janice, but against Rosco and Dumitra, Janice's mother. It was a trifecta of souls, and her Order rewarded her proudly by promoting her to high priestess. She was told too that Satan was very pleased with the gifts she had presented him.

But Satan didn't get everything he wanted. It was only Fate that the Evil that killed Janice didn't murder the next generation that same night. By happenstance, Janice had arranged for her aunt to babysit that night. Neither of her twin daughters, Cora Rae nor Theresa Maye, were subjected to the unspeakable black spirit let loose against their mother. And it would be a later fateful event that would spare one but condemn the other and all her progeny.

*****

CH 89 - Twilight Zone Nightmare

2020

Patti couldn't sleep so she went to Mitzie's bedroom and turned on the TV. She watched the channels fly by as she pushed the tiny buttons on the black remote. Quickly getting bored with the Cooking Channel, the History Channel and a movie channel that only had westerns, she moved to others until her remote landed on the Sci-Fi Channel. There she saw the black and white image of Rod Serling.

"Good evening," came the deep voice over the network station. *"This is Rod Serling. This highway leads to the shadowy tip of reality; you're on a through route to the land of the different, the bizarre, the unexplainable ... Go as far as you like on this road. Its limits are only those of the mind itself. Ladies and Gentlemen, you're entering the wondrous dimension of imagination.*

The next stop -- The Twilight Zone."

This might be a welcome distraction, Patti thought. She lay back into the pillows and put down her remote—safe and secure in her daughter's bed.

"Tonight, we join a typical family living in a typical home in a typical town in suburbia. Each day, Vince goes to work at a computer company, writing code for computer programs that were ordered by customers. He works in the spirits lab, concocting new and frightful images of monsters and demons to be used in the latest online games. He comes home to his wife, Sara, and his daughter, LJ. But it will not be a typical day for this otherwise typical family—as all will find themselves drawn into the deep and dark vortex of ... The Twilight Zone."

Patti yawned—half asleep already and not really paying much attention. She punched her pillow a few times to fluff it up and put her head down for the next fifty minutes while the show lasted. The TV droned on as she stared at the screen, too tired to realize there were no computers or computer games when the series was made in the 1960s.

Pulling out her cigarette case, she took out a Vogue stick, and found a lighter on the dresser which she grabbed mechanically and ignited. Taking a few puffs, she settled back into the pillow. The next thing she knew her eyelids were fluttering, wanting to close. So, she put out the cigarette using the top of an empty soda can nearby.

On the television was an unusual pattern of concentric circles with a dotted circle in the center. From that were bands radiating out to the four corners of the screen. The audio was a flat, unwavering tone that was the only thing disrupting the night's stillness. Those kinds of "test patterns" were used on late-night TV after the broadcasts had concluded for the day and were a product of early television broadcasts—the 1940s through the 1960s—before color TV became popular.

Patti flipped off the tube and went back to sleep. But her eyes shot open when she heard the TV go on by itself. Again, she saw the test pattern on the screen—the very one she had shut off moments earlier. She looked at the clock which sat stoically on the nightstand next to the bed. This time its green, glowing diodes showed 2:13 AM, so she again reached for the remote and pushed the button to turn off the TV. However, this time, it didn't go off. She punched the button a few more times, but still the TV remained stubbornly on and glowing.

"*Damn it!*" she said.

Patti tried two more times, but the third time—instead of going off—the screen switched to a black-and-white newscast. It was fuzzy and the image of the broadcaster jumped about erratically on the screen, as if an old-fashioned rooftop antenna were out of alignment.

"Tonight, we have breaking news here on WEVL, Channel Four," said the newscaster, who was dressed in a plaid suit that dated to the 1970s. "The police have just discovered the scene of a gruesome murder down on the south side. We are on the phone with Dan Pittman, our Boston crime reporter. Dan what are you seeing down there in Medford?"

The reporter was also dressed as if he'd been teleported back to 1970. His brown plaid suit had ultra-wide, peaked lapels and a matching vest. His hair was long over his ears, and he wore a thick, dark mustache that wrapped around the corners of his mouth.

"Ross, I'm standing several hundred feet away from this apartment building as the police have their cars pulled up to the front. It also looks like the ambulance just arrived. I'm being told that the body of a middle-aged woman was found in an upstairs apartment at about three this morning. The police officer with whom I spoke said it was a grotesque scene that he didn't want to describe to me but added, quote, it was the worst thing I'd seen in the twenty years I've been on the force, unquote. He was visibly shaken and, honestly, white as a sheet. We don't know what went on upstairs, but I will stay with you through the broadcast in case we get something more. Ross, it's back to you."

The reporting of a field correspondent via telephone was very odd indeed. Only a still picture of the reporter was shown on the screen as he talked. Patti was used to satellite reporting and on-the-scene video streaming of what was happening—instantly. The building in the background looked familiar too, but it was too grainy for her to tell for sure.

Still in a sleep-induced fog, she pushed the button on the remote once more. Lighting another cigarette, she lay back in bed to sleep. But rather than turning off, the TV channel changed on its own back to the *Twilight Zone*.

In the middle of the screen was a little girl who had been playing in her room with her doll house. She didn't have anyone else with her, but Patti could tell it was probably late at night and past her bedtime. She was dressed in white, footy pajamas and couldn't have been more than about eight years old. Then the girl went to her closet and opened the door, reaching in. Patti couldn't see inside the closet, but it was a white, louvered accordion door that swung easily to the side. The next shot showed the inside of the closet, and on the shelf was a jewelry box. The little girl opened the box, and a grayish mist billowed up from it, filling the closet and clouding everything else within it. The scene shifted once again, showing the outside of the louvered door and the closet with the little girl staring inside.

"Now, Mr. Peoples," said the little girl, her shoulder-length brown hair tied up in a ponytail that hung down her back, "you can come out just for a little while, but I can't let you play very long. My parents would be very mad if they knew I was still up,"

The little girl pulled on something that she held in her hand. It was a coarse, hemp rope. To Patti's surprise, attached to it was a small human form with a goat's head and legs, and a man's upper body. The goat's head had horns too—long and straight—and a dark, sinister look in its black eyes. The scene was surreal, as the creature was much too large to have fit inside the closet.

"Oh, Mr. Peoples, why don't you sit right here. I'll get you some tea," said the little girl, unafraid.

The little girl went back to the closet and reached inside, her hand and arm vanishing completely, as if they had become invisible.

But out of thin air, the girl pulled out a pitcher, tray, and glass cups—all part of a red and gold tea set. It looked very expensive, particularly for the lifestyle of the family and the small home they lived in.

"Thanks, Mr. Peoples. I've always wanted a tea set like this," said the little girl, putting it on the white, fluffy comforter on her bed.

The goat-man came over and sniffed the tea set before walking back toward the open closet.

"Don't go!" said the girl. "We've only just started the party."

But the black, horned creature shook its head from side to side. It pulled out a red candle and lit it with a red lighter, handing the waxy stick to the little girl.

"What's this for?" she asked. As the little girl looked down at it, she noticed that the goat's rope had wrapped itself loosely around her ankle. She reached down to untie the knot when ...

"No! Don't run!" shouted the little girl. But it was too late.

The creature ran back into the closet and disappeared into the smoky mist. Screaming, the girl fell to the floor, dropping her candle as she was dragged mercilessly by her ankles across the room and into the bedroom closet, where she, too, disappeared. The closet door slammed closed at the same time, the ornamental, red and gold tea set crashed to the floor, shattering into hundreds of pieces. Then, all was quiet.

The episode ended with a picture of a tea cup, still in one piece, lying on its side—chipped but empty—and the red candle still burning with its hot wax dripping on the floor.

Patti started to get up, but the TV switched back to the previous news channel. However, this broadcast was in color with a satellite truck in the background.

"Yes, we have breaking news this morning. Lenny Pittman is at the scene in Medford. Lenny, what do you have?"

This time the reporter's suit was modern, as if he were standing right outside their doorstep. The apartment building in the background was clear this time. It was Mitzie's apartment building. It was mid-morning, and the news station's logo appeared in the lower right corner of the screen.

"Danny, I'm here in front of this apartment building in Medford Apparently, there was a homicide here earlier this morning. Police tell me it occurred at about 3 AM. The scene is horrific inside, as an officer told me. One of the worst he's seen in his twenty years on the force."

Patti looked at the date and time on the screen—it was that day's date, but the time was 9:00 AM. The clock on the nightstand read 2:55 AM.

What is going on? she wondered. "Mitzie?" she called out. "Are you back?" But there was no answer.

The TV clicked off on its own, revealing an eerie green afterglow that permeated the room, and as soon as she lay back against the pillow, she heard something.

Scratch, scratch, scratch ...

The first noise was subtle, but the next two were louder. It sounded like something was inside the closet.

Patti's heart began racing. She was actually frightened—an emotion she hadn't experienced in a very long time. Believing she was protected by Satan, she found her "faith" now flagging. *What if he's angry at me?* she thought. Yet, that only terrified her more. She didn't want to think about those possibilities. *No,* she thought, *it's just the radiator or something.*

Scratch, scratch ...

There it was again, but this time it sounded like ... hooves, pawing on a wooden floor.

Patti started to scream, but her throat clenched, and nothing came out. She jumped out of bed and ran to the bedroom door. Reaching for the knob, the heavy door instantly slammed shut—so hard that it cracked down the middle, splintering the white paint. She struggled with the handle, but the door wouldn't budge. Panicked, she pulled and pulled, yanking and twisting, but nothing happened.

"And we're back with Lenny Pittman again on the scene. Lenny, what's going on?"

The TV had come back on. This time, the background behind the reporter had changed drastically.

"Yes, Danny, as you can see the entire building is now engulfed in flames. We don't know how the fire started, but it erupted suddenly while we were here reporting. It's the strangest thing I've ever seen. Inside lies the body of a murder victim, but now police can't continue to process the site for evidence because of this new development. Firefighters have been called and should arrive here within the next few minutes. I will keep you informed as this story unfolds. Danny."

The pawing sound from the closet was getting louder.

Scratch, scratch ...

"Satan! I'm a believer! I'm an apostle! Don't! Don't!" Patti cried out.

She turned around and saw the closet door rattling and buckling. It was shaking so violently that the hinges on both sides of the louvered front were pulling off the frame.

"No!" she shouted, as tears of terror rolled down her face. "I've done nothing! I've followed you faithfully all my life! How have I offended you?"

Patti collapsed by the bedroom door, unable to look behind her to see what was emerging from the closet and moving toward her; yet she could hear it, and it was coming for her.

The jewelry box on the dresser creaked opened on its own. And the red lighter she had used to ignite her cigarette earlier was now standing upright, and its flame was burning high into the air.

"No. My lord! My lord! No!" Patti called out—not to God but to the Dark One.

A gray mist slowly oozed from the closet and out onto the floor. It was an amorphous fog that drew closer and closer, but even as she tried to kick it away, it kept coming. Then, she saw the imprint of goat hooves on the floor where the mist had settled, as if something were marching toward her through a dusting of snow—one print after another and each one closer.

Seeing the double-hung window nearby, Patti ran to it. Feverishly she tried to unlock it and force it open, willing to jump from twenty-three floors to escape what she knew was coming for her. The window started to go up but then stuck, frozen into its tracks and unwilling to move. Patti pounded on the window.

"Open! Damn it! Open!"

But it wouldn't yield another inch. She shrieked in terror, hoping someone next door would hear her, but her pleas went nowhere. No one was coming.

Quickly, the gray fog moved over her, starting at her feet and moving higher toward her head. Out of its center an image formed. Patti squinted to see what it was. The mist swirled and frothed, becoming more and more violent, until an image fully appeared.

Before her was a long face—grotesque and distorted, with deathly-black eyes and teeth like that of a moray eel, long and pointed. Black matted hair covered most of its rough, scaly skin, and mucous filled with small, squirming maggots dripped from its snake-like mouth. On top of its head were long, goat horns that slanted back and away from its forehead, growing out from bloody, scabby wounds like they had ripped apart skin and bone to find daylight.

Patti's hands trembled as she put them up to her face in a futile attempt to defend herself.

"Your time has come," the horrible face said slowly, coldly, impassively.

"No!" she screamed, finding her voice. "It has *not*! It can't be! I've done all you asked! I've been your obedient servant!" Patti's defiance was futile.

The black demon laughed. "You are a fool! You have *not* been obedient to my will. You have violated the pact of your Order and for that you can never be forgiven. I *never* forgive, nor do I ever forget."

"No! You can't ..."

In an instant, she fell back toward the window, her legs pulled out from under her. Clawing at the rug on the floor, she tried desperately to keep from being dragged. She screamed as the beast pulled her toward the open closet door.

"Stop! No!"

"You will be sacrificed to me, and you and your daughter's soul will be mine forever."

Patti frantically grabbed for the edge of the closet door, and she clung to it as the last hope to save herself. But violently, the monster yanked her through the opening and the closet door slammed shut. The only part of her body that didn't make it through in time was her hand, which was left still clinging to the outside of the doorframe.

The fingernails were embedded in the wood of the door, but all the blood from the hand was sucked out by the retreating fog and the wound seared closed by the intense heat. Then, the disembodied hand fell to the floor of the bedroom, unable to hang on. It started to crawl back toward the closet but then stopped and never moved again.*****

CH 88 - Fire and Brimstone

2020

After getting some gum at the corner store, Mitzie decided to go to the midnight movie and then to one of the bars before heading back to the apartment. It was late or rather early in the morning when she returned home. Tommy had long since given up waiting for her—tailing her to the cinema before making sure she was inside and watching the show. It was well after midnight by the time the show ended, the bars closed and Mitzie returned to her apartment.

As soon as Mitzie got home, she headed directly for her bedroom assuming Patti was in the guest bedroom fast asleep. There on her dresser sat her mother's open jewelry box and the lighter which was still burning brightly. She closed both and took off her clothes to ready herself for bed.

But as she approached her bedroom closet, she saw it.

Ahhh! she screamed.

Lying on the floor was her mother's severed hand, her bloodied fingernails broken and fingers blue and gray.

Oh, my God! she thought, not knowing what to do. She raced for the door but as she did the red, Zippo lighter on her dresser exploded, sending up a towering column of fire. The flame roared up to the ceiling and spread quickly across the room engulfing bedsheets, curtains, and everything else in its path.

Mitzie stumbled as she ran out into her living room. There, hanging on the inside of the apartment door was the blood-drained body of her mother, staring malevolently at her just as she'd left the body of Sara's husband.

But her mother's body began to move even though suspended by the coat hook on the door. Its face mouthed the words, *"Hello Plottar! Hello Plottar! Hello Plottar!"* Then it exploded in a demonic laugh the likes Mitzie had never heard.

"No! *No!"* shouted Mitzie, now blocked from the exit.

Behind her the fire in the bedroom was spreading fast, burning through the walls and smoke pouring into the rest of the apartment. Mitzie began coughing, choking on the fumes.

"Hello Plottar! Hello Plottar!" Her dead mother kept saying to her, still mocking her—laughing at her with her wicked, soulless eyes.

"What? What is it? What do you want?" Mitzie cried out.

"Your portal to hell, my daughter," said the body, now letting the door swing open.

Mitzie hesitated, not sure whether to run through the doorway or not, but as the flames began igniting the walls, carpeting and furniture of the living room, she ran.

*****

CH 89 - One More Soul

2020

Sara arrived home after picking up LJ from school. Things had not yet returned to normal only a day after being released from prison. However, it was a start. Sara had decided to sell the house and move with her daughter far away from Boston. They would start over, start anew, and try to put their lives back together.

That night, LJ wanted to sleep with her mother in her queen-sized bed. Neither wanted to be in the house where their loved one had perished; neither wanted to be alone after going through such an ordeal; and both desperately needed the security and comfort of the other.

However, the peace was broken at 4 o'clock in the morning when Sara heard a banging on the front door.

"Mitzie?" she exclaimed, opening it to see who was calling at such an early hour.

"I need to talk to you," said Mitzie urgently, pushing her way inside.

"What's wrong?"

Mitzie's face was darkened with black soot, and her hair tangled and hanging down into her face. A look of terror was still etched deeply in her eyes and the creases of her forehead.

"Do you still have stuff from your great grandmother Janice?"

"Yes. All that is up in the attic," said Sara. "What's this about? Why are you asking me that at this time of the morning?"

"I don't have time to explain," Mitzie answered. "My mother is dead, and we may be the next victims. You have to get rid of everything you have of theirs and the occult. You have to do it *now!*"

Sara and Mitzie went up to the attic and brought down a lot of the things Sara had stored that belonged to her great grandmother, grandmother and mother. Anything that had pentagrams or other cult symbols on them or referenced in the pages were put in a refuse pile. Then, Sara went to the garage and returned carrying an armful of newspapers. She crumpled them into light, fluffy balls and placed them under the wood in the fireplace. After stacking a few pieces of dry oak on top, she reached for a lighter; it was a red Zippo.

"Don't!" shouted Mitzie, seeing what she had grabbed. "You have to burn everything, including *that!*"

The fire roared. Hot orange and red flames danced, devouring the feast of paper and other things they were being fed. As the two tossed books, journals, and pictures on the pyre, Sara said, "Mitzie, I'm sorry about your mother."

"Don't be," came the harsh reply. "The world is a better place."

Sara didn't ask anything more. But as they neared the bottom of their stack, they heard a voice coming from the stairs.

"Mom? What are you doing?" It was LJ.

"Nothing, dear. Go back to bed."

But LJ didn't. Instead, she came over to the fireplace and looked at the two women and what they were doing.

"So, you must be LJ," said Mitzie, smiling. "I have a daughter about your age too. Her name is Bea."

Sara looked at Mitzie with surprise.

"You never said anything about having a daughter," said Sara. "Where is she now? Does she live with you?"

"Oh, no. She lives with my sister. I haven't seen her in years. It's really terrible, I know. But looking back on it, I think it turned out for the best. She's better off with Rachel than she ever would have been with me."

Finally, the last thing at the bottom of the stack was the antique jewelry box. But Sara hesitated; she wasn't sure about destroying the one piece that had connected all the women in her family throughout the years.

"I don't think I can do it," Sara said, holding the box in her hands. "It's been passed down for generations. It's part of our family."

"Sara, you must. That box is cursed. It was cursed by my great grandmother Bessie. It is the one thing that *must* be destroyed."

"I'll take it if you don't want it," said LJ standing next to her.

LJ grabbed the box from her mother, and before they could wrestle it back from her, she had opened the lid.

A frigid gust of wind blew out from the box, and a black, cloudy mist billowed from it, wrapping itself around Sara's daughter.

"Mom!" LJ cried out.

"Stop!" shouted Mitzie. "Don't you dare lay a hand on her!"

From the cloud erupted the same horrible face that had terrorized Patti earlier that evening. It laughed sinisterly as it eyed the young girl in front of it.

"My dark lord will be most pleased by this offering—a sacrifice of a beautiful, young virgin like you," it said in a deep, gravelly voice.

Then, the cloud began to materialize into earthly form, taking on the shape of the hideous beast. But before it finished, Mitzie ripped the box from LJ's hands. LJ screamed as the beast began to grab her and pull her back into the box with it. Mitzie pushed the lid closed, cutting the beast off from his prey. It screamed, howling from the lost opportunity to seize its prize.

"Go back to Hell!" Mitzie screamed. Then, she flung the jewelry box into the fireplace.

LJ stood trembling as they all watched in amazement. The box would not burn. It lay on top of the fire, defying the flames and their attempt to expunge it from the world.

Mitzie reached into her pocket and pulled out the medallion her mother had given her. That she threw into the flames too, but as it took flight toward the fireplace, the jewelry box lid opened once more. It caught the medallion before it could find another landing spot and banged shut.

Hello Plottar! Hello Plottar!
Portal to Hell! Portal to Hell!

Those words screamed out of the box, filling the room with a deafening roar.

Sara, Mitzie and LJ covered their ears as the sounds grew louder.

Portal to Hell! Portal to ...

A great whirlwind began circling inside the fireplace. Ash, embers, flames, all started swirling upward into a great, black hole that was developing higher in the chimney, pulling everything and anything it could grasp with it. As if a window had blown out in an airplane, the three braced themselves against the fury of the winds. They could hear the clawing and scratching of demons high up in the chimney—all being returned to their maker.

"Stop! Stop!" shouted Mitzie, hanging onto the leg of a heavy table to keep from being sucked into the vortex.

"Mitzie, no!" yelled Sara.

But Mitzie looked over at Sara and shook her head and sighed. She let go. Quickly, Mitzie's body was sucked into the fireplace and up the chimney with everything else. And with that, everything stopped.

Sara rushed to the fireplace, but there was nothing inside it—not even the antique jewelry box. Everything had been incinerated and pulled into the portal. Mitzie was gone.

*****

CH 90 – Final Report

2020

"Well, I guess we'll never know who kidnapped or killed her mom," said Tommy, submitting the final police reports on Patti Campbell's and Mitzie Wilkin's disappearances and presumed deaths.

Dag shook his head. "I think we already know, Tommy."

"Who did it, then?"

"It's not a who … it's a what."

"Why do you say that?" asked Tommy.

"I reviewed the evidence," said Dag.

"Yeah, and there's nothing in any of it that suggests it was some demon or evil spirit, Dag. I don't buy it."

"All right. Then *what* did all this? How do you explain it?"

Tommy shrugged.

"Exactly. We can't," said Dag.

"Well, it's over now," said Tommy. "We can go back to our lonely and boring lives, I guess. But then again, don't you think Sara McLaughlin had something to do with it?"

"Do I think she is evil and possessed somehow?" asked Dag.

"No, that she had a hand in Patti's and Mitzie's disappearances."

"No, I don't—not any more than I think you had a direct hand in suddenly turning to the dark side with the DA and the mayor. I'd like to think *you* were just temporarily possessed or something. Maybe it was temporary insanity?"

"Insanity or a demon?"

"Take your pick. What do you think?" Dag asked.

"Perhaps you're right," said Tommy. "It was a strange thing that came over me."

"It happens to most of us from time to time, Tommy. The Gallaghers were also tempted by demons but in a different form. They got seduced, quite literally. It corrupted some of what they did and what they stood for. It's something I hope I never give in to."

"I think you're safe, Dag. You've got a strong constitution. I don't think Satan himself could pull you from the straight and narrow path." Tommy paused, before adding, "So, what do we do now?"

Dag sat back and threw his feet up on his desk.

"Why don't you go get us a six-pack. I could use a beer."

*****

CH 91 – Cases Closed

2020

"I read your report," said the new district attorney, Lance Tricot, "but it doesn't make much sense. You say that the murder of your father was caused by recently released prisoners who had a grudge against Zag for putting them behind bars."

"Yes."

"And that this ... Robert Ludlow ... and a fellow cellmate ... let's see ..." said the DA looking back at the report, "... Patrick Frey, went looking for your father and ambushed him in the alleyway. Is that right?"

"Yep."

"But I don't see how the evidence points to those two. I see that they were both convicted killers who cut plea deals with the previous DA's office and probably shouldn't have been released back onto the streets, but I ..."

"Mr. Tricot, if I may," said Dag. "These two men were found shot to death by a rival gang a few months back. Isn't that right?"

"Yes, that's my understanding."

"Then the case is closed."

"But ..."

"Okay, do you want the *real* explanation for my father's death?" asked Dag.

The DA put out his hands. "Give it to me."

"There was a woman in the 1940s who was upset that her best friend and husband were having an affair. As a result, she lost her baby and wasn't able to conceive again. She put a curse on her friend's family, releasing a demon to attack them and all who followed. She also put a curse on my family because it was my great, great uncle who had cheated on her. That demon was responsible for the horrible killings in Boston that have occurred every twenty-five years and killing my father this year too. Does that work for you?"

Tricot smiled and then laughed. "Okay, then. So, we're back to the gang members, are we?"

"I think so, sir."

"And what about Mitzie Wilkins and Patricia Campbell? Are they at large or do you believe they are dead and buried someplace?"

"I don't know, sir. All I can tell you is my hunch."

"... which is?"

"It would be a waste of police time and resources to pursue those cases."

"And Claire Horwath?" asked the DA.

"We got her jewelry back to her, sir, but she didn't want it. She gave it as a donation to Policeman's Retirement Fund."

"You mentioned to me earlier that you believe she and Zag were romantically involved."

"As much as it pains me to say it sir, yes."

"And your mother does not know."

"No, sir, she doesn't, and I want to keep it that way," said Dag.

"Did the same two parolees attack Claire?"

"Yes, sir. Let's just say they were out for revenge against my dad and anyone he was involved with. In this case, it was his mistress."

"Well, I guess we've solved the murders then. I will issue a press release that it's all wrapped up in a nice, neat bow. The new mayor will be very happy with that. We've done our job."

"I guess we have sir," said Dag sarcastically. "And by the way sir, here is something else for you."

Dag handed the DA a copy of the letter he had given his police chief earlier that morning. It read:

> *Dear Sir or Sirs:*
>
> *Please find my request hereto to retire from the Boston Police Department. The retirement will be effective ... immediately.*
>
> *Detective Douglas Arthur Gallagher*

The DA read the short note and folded it up.

"We can't get you to stay on?"

"No, I think it's a practice that we Gallaghers retire shortly after murders like this happen. I don't want to break that tradition."

Tricot got up from his chair. "Thanks for your service Dag. The force will miss you," he said.

"Yes, it will, sir."

Dag left the office, never to return.

*****

CH 92 – Dinner for Three

2020

Dag passed the mashed potatoes to LJ, who politely thanked him and took a big scoop. Sara had just come back from the kitchen with warmed-up dinner rolls—an afterthought, she had insisted. She swore she had prepared them earlier for the meal and just forgotten to bring them out. She wasn't used to the temporary apartment's small kitchen, but she had pressed Dag to come over anyway, insisting that she and LJ would make something he'd like.

Sara brought out the rolls and placed them in the center of the round table next to her guest.

"Sorry about that," she said. "I thought I'd put those in the oven earlier."

"Relax, Mom," said LJ. "It's only dinner."

Dag smiled. "I like your necklace," he said, eyeing her pendant and taking a hot roll from the platter.

"Thanks," Sara answered. "It was something I got while I was in prison. I love it. I never go anywhere without it, in fact."

Around Sara's neck was a plain, black cord. Attached to it was a simple, but rough crucifix made of wood. It was what Claire had given her in the white box when she had come to visit. It was what Claire had seen in the dream she had described to Sara at the time.

As they sat down to supper, Sara made the sign of the cross as did LJ. After the prayer, Sara looked up and smiled. "I'm just glad it's over," she said. "But I do feel terrible about Mitzie. She was the one who was pressured into the family business. She was reluctant but did it anyway—for her mother."

"Yeah, but there were some in the family who bucked the trend," said Dag. "Bessie was the first to repent."

"Yeah, Mitzie said she went back on her pact with the Devil. She took up with the church and wanted nothing more to do with the dark side of the spirit world. Her daughter, Terri did the same some years later, after the death of Cora Rae."

"But not Patti," said Dag. "She never wavered."

"No, but I think Mitzie was always unsure about things," Sara said, "and we understand now she finally went to a priest to ask for help. But her mother held firm. Her ties to Satan were the strongest for some reason. She stuck with it and was faithful to her dark lord to the end – until he had no need for her."

"You do know about Cora Rae," said Dag, putting butter on his slice of bread.

"I know now that she had a twin sister, Terri Belzikov," said Sara. "How mixed up is all that? I just don't understand how all that happened."

"Tommy and I did some digging and found that your great grandmother Janice Prodescu had twin girls—fraternal, not identical. When Janice died, her aunt agreed to take one of them but said she couldn't afford both. Since Bessie couldn't have children after her miscarriage, she eagerly asked to adopt the other one—Theresa."

"And Rosco Turner was the father," said Sara.

"Yes. My uncle Rosco was responsible too."

"Wow, so our three families really *are* intertwined after all."

"Yeah, it seems the curse really did affect everyone from all our families," said Dag.

"So, I'm curious," asked Sara. "What did you ultimately say in your police report about all this?"

Dag smiled. "It said that demons and evil spirits were behind it all!" He said it with the most evil voice he could muster. Then he looked at LJ, raised an eyebrow and laughed.

"No, you didn't," said LJ.

"No, I didn't. But the story I told him, he bought. I think he just wanted to move on from it all. I don't blame him."

"What about Marvin?" asked Sara. "What are they going to do with him?"

"They have the evidence that links him to Mitzie, and they recovered other items of some of the victims from his apartment. I don't know what the new DA will do with him."

Sara took a deep sip from her wine glass. As she put it down, she asked Dag, "Do you think Bessie really killed my great grandmother back in 1945?"

"Not that we'd ever be able to prove," Dag answered. "It seems there is—or was—something about that jewelry box that was handed down from generation to generation within your family and the red lighter you all seemed to have. Did Bessie curse them before she gave them to Janice?"

Sara shrugged even though she knew the answer. "I think that will be a mystery we'll never be able to solve," she answered.

"Families can be hard sometimes," said Dag. Then he looked down at his plate and pushed around his green peas with his fork.

"What's wrong?" asked Sara, noticing his mood change. "Was everything okay?"

"Oh, no. It was delicious. I just have a lot on my mind, that's all."

"Anything I can help you with?" Sara asked.

"No," he began, but then said, "it's just ... well ... nothing."

"Tommy mentioned to me that you have a son. Is that true?" asked Sara.

"Yes, and a daughter. They both live with my ex."

"I'm sorry," Sara said, "I didn't mean to bring up something you were uncomfortable talking about."

"Oh, no. It's not that. It's just that I haven't spoken to either of them for two years now. Their mother remarried and moved to San Francisco, so seeing them has gotten difficult."

"How old are they?" LJ asked, again interested in the conversation.

"My son is nineteen and my daughter twenty-three," said Dag. "We're estranged right now—something I'd like to fix."

"Well, then fix it," said LJ, talking like a mother.

"LJ!" said Sara, chastising her.

"No, she's right," said Dag. "She's absolutely right. I need to fix it." He smiled at both of them.

Sara went back into the kitchen and returned again—this time with desert. "I made apple pie," she announced, putting it down. "I was told you like apple pie, Dag. That's true, I hope."

"My favorite," said the retired detective. "Then you know that my family owns an apple orchard. It's been in the family since the late nineteenth century. My great, great, great grandfather Arthur Gallagher," Dag said, counting the *greats* on his fingers, "planted the first apple seedlings on our farm in western Massachusetts back in 1888. We've owned the orchard ever since."

"That's it," said Sara snapping her fingers.

"What?" asked Dag, cutting a nice-sized slice of the pie with his knife.

"That's why we always smelled apples coming from the jewelry box when it was opened. It was the connection to the Gallagher family. It was a way to bring you and your family in under the curse too."

Dag nodded. "Could be, I guess. All I know is I like apple pie, and this is wonderful!"

They finished their dessert when Dag's cell phone rang.

"Excuse me. Sorry, I have to take this," said Dag, reaching for his phone.

Dag got up and left the table as Sara and LJ started to clear the dishes. Then, Sara looked at her watch. "Ooooh, yeah. It's late, young lady. It's time you got to bed. You've got classes tomorrow."

"But Mom!"

"And no Twilight Zone! Do you hear me!"

Dag was in the living room, talking in a quiet voice, and when he came back into the dining room, he had a disturbed look on his face. He began helping clear the dishes, when Sara asked him, "What's wrong now?"

"That was the police chief. They're closing the cases on Patti and Mitzie. They never found their bodies, of course. They also got the autopsy results back on Bessie and Terri. Bessie was suffocated; Terri strangled. I presume it was Patti, but, again, we'll never know for sure."

"Who called you about it?"

"The chief. He asked that I come in to talk it over," said Dag.

Sara understood. She was just happy he had come over for dinner.

"I understand," she said. "Go ahead and go."

He smiled. "Nope. I told him that I was retired. I'm staying here for a while, if that's all right with you."

"Absolutely," said Sara beaming. "Stay as long as you like."

He took her hand and squeezed it gently.

It hadn't been that long since her husband's death, but she felt a closeness to this man—something she hadn't felt for a long time. She felt guilty, but at the same time, there was an attraction there that she couldn't resist.

"Okay, then. Is there any more wine?" he asked.

*****

Epilogue

2045

"Where is she?" It was the nurse on duty at the mental hospital where the woman was being kept under locked doors. The woman had experienced several relapses over the years—the most recent having been the most severe.

"She must be here someplace," said another nurse, checking the hallway and adjacent rooms.

The two checked every room on the floor before notifying security. After an extensive search of the entire building, they found no sign of her. She had simply vanished.

***

The priest sat at his desk, preparing for the next day's homily. He prided himself on giving good sermons, and, as an older priest, he really didn't need notes to help him in his delivery. It just came naturally. But he was interrupted when the door opened, and a cool breeze flowed in from the outside. It was a scene he'd witnessed countless times before during the many years of his priesthood.

"Hello, may I help you?" asked the priest. "Are you new to the parish?"

The woman smiled. "Yes, father. You might say that. I've been through a lot recently, and I was wondering if you could help me with something."

"Oh, of course. You are a child of God, and I am here to serve. Have you come to confess your sins?"

The woman ignored the question and instead asked, "How strong is your faith, Father?"

The priest grinned. "I have been a servant of the church for nearly fifty years. I know my faith is constantly tested, but I have tried to keep it strong and in His good favor."

"Then what would your god say to this."

The woman raised her hand, and the priest's body was thrown ten yards against the church wall. Stunned, he started to get up, pulling out his crucifix.

"You won't be needing that," said Mitzie's daughter, the demons inside her ablaze with fury. Her eyes stared at him; she was in a deep trance, possessed by something unspeakable.

The cross flew out of his hand, impaling itself into the wall on the other side of the room. Then, as she wiggled her hand in the air, it loosened itself from the wall and shot back at the priest, burying itself into his throat.

"That should keep your sermons brief," said Bea, cackling fiendishly.

***

Upstairs at LJ's apartment, she tossed and turned in bed. She rolled over and looked at the dark television in the room across the hall. She had never given up her liking for late-night television, and this night was no different. However, at the age of forty, LJ had the night to herself; her only daughter having been invited over to Sara's, her mother, for a sleepover.

LJ called out to the 3D holographic projector mounted above the bed. "TV on," she commanded.

The projector turned on, and the images filled the center of the room as if she were in the middle of the action. As the program began, she pulled the covers up under her nose to get comfortable.

This program, however, was old and produced in black and white. It had been especially modified for projection as a holographic film. The first scene was that of a middle-aged man dressed in a neat suit, white shirt and dark, skinny tie. The image stood in front of her talking as if she were the only one in his audience.

> *"Good evening,"* came the deep voice over the network station. *"This is Rod Serling. This highway leads to the shadowy tip of reality; you're on a through route to the land of the different, the bizarre, the unexplainable ... Go as far as you like on this road. Its limits are only those of the mind itself. Ladies and Gentlemen, you're entering the wondrous dimension of imagination."*

But after the television transitioned to the show, it was interrupted.

"LJ, I can see you." The screen was black and there were no more images projected into her room, but a voice was still coming from the set.

LJ's eyes grew wide, and her teeth began to chatter.

"Who is it? Who's there?" she mumbled, pulling the covers up tighter around her head.

"It's your time, child. It's the time of the Silver Ritual, and we've come for your soul."

Instantly, Patti's devilish face popped onto the middle of the room. Her eyes were on fire, and a yellow pus was oozing from her mouth. A swirling circle of pale green smoke materialized—slowly taking shape in a physical form.

LJ screamed.

But there was nothing she could do. Out from the mist crawled the black and hideous body of Patti Campbell. On top of her head were two stunted horns and her mouth opened abnormally wide, showing razor-sharp, pointed teeth.

LJ looked back at the television. The figure of Rod Serling was now replaced with that of the Devil. Its hideous face was distorted but laughing madly.

"Yes, my child. Are you finally ready? For your next stop is:

My Twilight Zone."

*****

Appendix A

List of characters by era. Key characters in bold.

Character	Family	Relationship	Reference Era	Notes
Michael Arthur Gallagher	Gallagher	Great-great grandfather	1920	Detective
Taggert Arthur Gallagher "TAG"	Gallagher	Great-grandfather	1945	Detective
John Arthur Gallagher "JAG"	Gallagher	Grandfather	1970	Detective
Zeller Arthur Gallagher "ZAG"	Gallagher	Father	1995	Detective
Douglas Arthur Gallagher "DAG"	Gallagher	Character-himself	2020	Detective
Tommy Walcott		Dag's partner	2020	Young detective
Dumitra Prodescu	Prodescu	Great-great grandmother	1920	Medium
Janice Prodescu	Prodescu	Great-grandmother	1945	Medium
Cora Rae Taylor	Prodescu	Grandmother	1970	Medium
Abagail T. Knight	Prodescu	Mother	1995	Medium
Sara Knight McLaughlin	Prodescu	Character-herself	2020	Medium
Lucy Jean (LJ)	Prodescu	Daughter	2020 & 2045	

Character	Family	Relationship	Reference Era	Notes
McLaughlin				
Vince McLaughlin	Prodescu	Sara's Husband	2020	
Bessie Belzikov Turner	Belzikov	Great grandmother	1945	Cult member
Terry Turner Campbell	Belzikov	Grandmother	1970	Cult member
Patty Campbell Wilkins	Belzikov	Mother	1995	Cult member
Mitzie Wilkins	Belzikov	Character-herself	2020	
Bea Wilkins	Belzikov	Daughter	2020 & 2045	
Rosco Arthur			1945	High school friend
Danny Pittman	Pittman	Character-self	1970	Reporter
Lenny Pittman	Pittman	Son of Danny Pittman	1995	
Virginia (Jenny) Carter/Jake Carter		Mother-Son	1970	Associated with Tag
Father Jose Mercato		Abby Knight's priest	1970	Priest
Dick Johnson			2020	District Attorney
Marvin Fletcher	Fletcher	Sara's driver	2020	Bodyguard-driver for Sara
Jerel Fletcher	Fletcher	Marvin's son	2020	
Dwayne Fletcher	Fletcher		1995	Bodyguard-driver for Abby

Character	Family	Relationship	Reference Era	Notes
				Knight
Moseby Wright	Fletcher	Uncle of Dwayne Fletcher	1970	Bodyguard-driver for Cora Rae
Leroy Ritter	Ritter	Father of Nathan	1970	Records
Nathan Ritter	Ritter	Character-himself	1995/2020	Records

About the Author:

Drake Grayson is a pen name used by the author for the horror and mystical books he writes. Mr. Grayson lives with his family in Chicago. He has authored other stories, including *The Doors Have Eyes* and several short, horror stories.

www.ingramcontent.com/pod-product-compliance
Lightning Source LLC
Chambersburg PA
CBHW051937020726
47501CB00001B/168